HEART OF FIRE TIME OF ICE

A TIME EQUATION NOVEL

E. S. MARTELL

Heart of Fire Time of Ice

Fourth Edition

Copyright © 2016 by Eric S. Martell

Second Initiative Press

Visit the author's website at www.ericmartellauthor.com

Printed in the USA
ISBN: 978-0-9989805-1-5

Vox audita perit littera scripta manet.

This is a work of fiction. All the characters and events portrayed in this book are fictional, and any resemblance to real people or incidents is purely coincidental.

A Time Equation Novel

Life has hurt Kathleen so severely that she hardly dares to live. Now, people want to kill her for her time equation, and she's trapped herself in the ice age with no way back. She needs help, but she's afraid to trust a fur-clad hunter.

He's lost everyone he cared about and was waiting for death. Finding her has given him a reason for living, but his existence depends on convincing her to trust him with her heart even as he protects her from savage men and beasts.

Will the icy wilderness sweep them together before the time equation tears them apart forever?

Acknowledgments

Several things contributed to this story: My interest in time-travel, which began a long time ago, maybe even in a previous life. The fact that science is now beginning to understand that quantum physics may require time-travel. My interest in psychology, which has led me to spend considerable time studying the human mind, including extraordinary experiences such as lucid dreaming. Then add the fact that I usually write science fiction with at least a modicum of hard science.

As I was starting to plan this story, I happened to have a conversation about writing with my sister, Robin Searle. She writes historical romance stories, so we spent some time talking about the romance story genre. As a result of the conversation, it occurred to me to blend all of these diverse elements. Who doesn't like a little romantic entanglement mixed in with their adventure? I enjoyed writing the story. I hope that you'll enjoy reading it.

My grateful thanks to Aleksandra Klepacka for the original cover art and most of the illustrations. She came up with the concept and delivered a high-quality, finished product quickly.

Kelley York of Sleepy Fox Studios deserves great credit for the cover typography.

Thanks to Adriana D'Apolito and 3P Editing for her many invaluable suggestions. Her careful work greatly increased the readability of the manuscript.

Dedication

This book is dedicated to Fred Alan Wolf. His books on quantum physics are a joy to read. His ideas on extraordinary time-travel and kind emails encouraged me in writing this story.

I also want to thank my wife, Sally, for her indispensable contribution – everything I know about romance, I learned from her.

Contents

Chapter One

Kathleen: A Chilly Morning

Kathleen was awake but trying desperately to pretend she wasn't. Her dream world was always so much better than reality that she hated mornings. In her dreams, she could imagine that she was confident, loved, and perfect. Reality always insisted otherwise.

Kathleen

Her sense of duty finally made her so anxious that she opened her eyes, sighed tiredly, and kicked off the covers. The weather had changed during the night, but she hadn't wakened. Now the room was cold, making her shiver.

There was no help for it. The radiators were still turned off. Her landlord didn't believe in firing up the boiler until everyone in the building had complained at least three times.

Cold or not, she had to get up. Her desire to please Professor Mackleroy wouldn't allow her to sleep in. She had to finish her research before it was too late.

She felt stiff, the scar tissue around her waist, hip, and thighs were inflexible in the Minnesota cold. It forced her to limp as she moved to the cheap mirror screwed to the back of the bedroom door. She rubbed the sleep out of her eyes and scanned her reflection, just as she did every day.

Still the same. She saw a young woman with intense dark eyes looking back at her. Her face was, even if she did think it herself, beautiful, save for the streak of small scars along her right jawline. Her upper body was muffled in a shapeless flannel nightgown that was too short. Her legs stuck out, pale and white, with just the tip of the scarring showing on her right inner thigh.

She sighed again, then stretched as much as she could against the pulling flesh and pulled the nightgown over her head. It was cold in the room and she gasped, regretting getting up. She continued to scan her body. Not bad, except for the scarring. There had been a time when she had expected it to get better on its own, but it hadn't. The only improvement she had seen came from hours of painful stretching. She'd found that yoga helped a little. She hadn't missed an opportunity to take classes since that discovery.

⸺⸻◆⸻⸺

Pulling her mind back to the present, she inspected the scarring around her thighs. It was no better. She'd hoped that two years of yoga would have had some effect by now.

I shouldn't even wish for better, she thought. I'm lucky to be alive. If my mother hadn't gone into labor and delivered me almost immediately after receiving the saline, the scarring would have been much worse.

She knew that she had been lucky in more than one way. The attending nurse had hustled her out of the room instantly and had been moved to care for her, an act that had gotten her fired. The quick delivery and post-natal care had allowed her to survive, despite her mother's intentions. She had also been lucky that her birth mother abandoned her as soon as she learned the abortion had produced a viable if severely scarred, premature baby.

That opened the way for her adoption by the older couple she knew as her parents. They'd overlooked her physical deformities and inability to walk without pain and had provided her with as much as they could. They hadn't been well-off, though, and things had always been difficult for them and for her.

Now they were gone, and she was alone except for Professor Mackleroy, whom she counted as both a mentor and friend. Her scars, both physical and mental, had always seemed too large a barrier to overcome, and she instinctively shied away from developing friendships with anyone near her own age. It had been too painful during her childhood. The other children had rejected her harshly, and the memories still hurt.

She sighed and turned to get ready. Would she ever outgrow her problems? She looked over her shoulder and spoke aloud to the mirror. "You idiot. You're twenty-four years old. How long are you going to carry it around, anyway?"

Her reflection only returned an enigmatic gaze out of a tired-looking face.

⸺◆⸺

LAST night had been a late one. She'd stayed in the lab working on her research project. Professor Mackleroy had left his office at about seven clutching his old briar pipe in his hand. He had stopped smoking it months ago but somehow couldn't give up the pipe. As a result, he carried it everywhere, unconsciously turning it over and over in his hand.

Sometimes, he'd inadvertently raise it as if to insert it into his mouth, but then he'd realize what he was doing and self-consciously try to use the stem as if he'd intended to punctuate something he was saying. This resulted in him making a series of ineffectual stabbing motions with the pipe during his conversation. She'd been alarmed by this when she was introduced to him, but now found his mannerism to be a charming eccentricity.

Kathleen was driven in her research. Professor Mackleroy had gone out on a limb for her and used all of his influence to find a small amount of funding for her work. She was terrified that she'd lose the grant and even more afraid that she'd let him down. The professor was sick and getting sicker by the day. She wanted to give him the satisfaction of knowing he was correct in supporting her before it was too late.

At most, he had eight months. He'd smoked his pipe until he'd gotten a cough that wouldn't go away. An x-ray showed a black mass that was entwined with part of his pulmonary artery. By the time they'd discovered the thing, it had metastasized, leaving him with little choice but to wind up his affairs.

She didn't think she could stand the thought of disappointing the only living person who'd shown that he cared for her, and she was determined to finish while he was able to enjoy publishing the discovery.

She'd remained at her computer until about one-thirty in the morning. She'd been too tired to ride her bike home, so she'd called a cab. Now she didn't even remember getting out of it outside her apartment.

As for her own inclinations, she found research fascinating and that it gave her a perfect excuse to avoid other people. As a third year doctoral student, she had stumbled onto an interesting phenomenon having to do with sub-atomic particles that seemed to violate the normal time sequence.

Using a variant of the classic double-slit experiment paired with modern technology, some researchers had shown that a particle could decide whether to present itself as a wave or a particle after it had passed through the screen holding the two slits.

In order to do this, the particle seemingly received information from the future. This contradiction got her thinking about time-travel in general.

With the professor's help, she'd carefully written up a proposal for a small amount of funding that would allow her the leisure to acquire and analyze data produced by the large hadron collider at CERN. Unfortunately, the funding had proven to be inadequate, and she was constantly worrying about running out. She wasn't at all confident that the sponsoring corporation would advance more without some positive results as encouragement, and so far, positive results had been slow in coming.

Her professor was worried about her line of inquiry, and she knew he had reservations about it. Even so, he encouraged her and insulated her from the skeptics in the Physics department. They would never have allowed her to work on the topic if he hadn't been her mentor. She suspected that the other members of the group, both professors and students, thought she was crazy and that her research was an embarrassment for them.

Mackleroy had used a corporate connection to secure funding for her research. The only requirement was that she prepare periodic reports on her progress to be forwarded to interested parties. They'd mostly left her alone beyond that, although she'd recently received an inquiry relating to her theory of time travel from them.

She'd worked diligently and now thought she'd have enough of the CERN data analyzed within the next week or so to commence writing her dissertation. The only thing giving her trouble was trying to find a pathway forward with her math. There was plenty of speculative work already in place, most notably that of Cramer, but she had encountered some sticky problems that were seemingly irreconcilable. She knew she was a good mathematician, but the answers refused to fall into place without a great deal of work.

This morning she had her first-year physics class to teach. It was something she usually enjoyed, but the students were so slow and knew so little. She really wanted to get back to her own research. She felt that a little more analysis would somehow allow her to finalize the formula she was developing in her mind.

She was sure that, if she could just pin down a couple of more variables, the formula would resolve into an explanation of everything she was observing. She quickly shoved that thought out of her mind as too ambitious. She was usually more cautious and careful with her life.

———◦———

She paused as she started to get dressed. The cold room faded into the back of her mind as she concentrated again on her scars in the mirror. She didn't want to look closely, but, as always, she couldn't resist. She reached down and stroked her index finger across her thigh and abdomen. Who knew saline would burn and scar a baby so badly? That thought led directly to the next. Her diaphragm caught and convulsed as she thought, *How could my Mothe* — She interrupted herself in the middle of the sob and substituted the words, *How could any mother do that to her child?* It didn't work. Her eyes teared up as they always did. She gasped for breath, trying to maintain control, but the usual, self-pitying question intruded into her mind despite her efforts: What did I do to deserve this?

There was no answer. There never was. It had just happened, and she didn't know why. She took several deep breaths, gradually calming herself. *That was close,* she thought. *The last time, I cried for an hour.* After another breath, *I guess I'll never understand. I wish I could just forgive and forget.*

She was suddenly stricken with an intense feeling of deja vu. It was as if she'd had that same thought before in this exact same circumstance. Her mind wandered, blurring out the image in the mirror. She paused to blink away the tears that had formed, then shook her head in denial, gasped for breath for a painful moment, and continued dressing.

She jerked her long, dirty-blonde hair back into a loose ponytail, ignoring the pain. The scarring along her jaw would show, but maybe it was time to accept who she was and quit pretending that she wasn't flawed. She pulled on some baggy pants and finished with a gray hooded sweatshirt.

Shortly, she was out the door and descending the steps into the morning chill. At least the sun was shining. That was one nice thing about Minneapolis. It was often sunny, even if it was cold.

The cold seemed to make her scars even less flexible, and she couldn't muster the energy to walk quickly. She limped a couple of blocks south and back to the west to a small cafe that offered a decent breakfast at a low price. The wind was chill and blowing from the northwest, cutting in under the edge of her hoodie.

She hurried through breakfast and then called a cab while she was waiting for the check. She hoped that her bicycle was still chained to the rack outside of the old Tate lab. There had been a rash of bike thefts lately, but she didn't worry much about hers. It was so old, rusty, and unattractive that no one would realize it was tuned perfectly and rode like a much more expensive bicycle.

She shared her office with another grad student, Drew Smith. He was sitting at his desk when she reached their shared office. Holding her breath so as not to breathe in too much of his over-powering cologne, she tried to slip by quietly, but he turned his placid, bovine face towards her and immediately started in with his usual routine.

"Kath! Late again! You'd better hurry or your class will be out of control. I'll bet you stayed in the lab almost all night..."

He ran his eyes up and down her body, not bothering to conceal the fact that they lingered on her breasts, then continued, "You did, right?"

Without pausing for her to answer, he morphed into the overly familiar and slightly condescending mode that she most despised. "You look a little tired. Did you sleep well? Are your scars bothering you?"

She regretted ever trying to wear a skirt. He'd noticed her leg when she incautiously leaned back at her desk one day. Now he wouldn't let her forget the fact that she was damaged goods. She'd never told him what caused the scars. She'd refused to talk about them at all.

He knew she was dedicated to her research and took no interest in social events, but he acted as if he wanted to save her from her fate. It wasn't going to work. She had no romantic interest in him, no matter how often he tried to become more familiar.

He started to ask her out again, "Hey, how about you and me, uhh, you know, maybe go out for a beer or pasta? We could hit Loring or Suzie's, your choice— "

She interrupted, "Too busy in the lab, Smith. I'm going to get a sandwich from the machine. Now I've got to go teach my class." She opened her desk drawer and placed her cell phone inside. She'd made a rule that her students were not supposed to bring cell phones to class, not that they obeyed it with any consistency. She'd taken to leaving hers in the desk, trying to set an example. It hadn't seemed to work but she kept at it.

Would he never get the message? It might be a little more acceptable if he didn't always act as if he were doing her a favor. But only a little. She would never accept. She just didn't want to be bothered. Besides, she knew from her past experience that people, in general, couldn't be trusted. She had been rejected too many times to feel at ease with a dating situation.

As she walked out the door, he called, "By the way, Professor M won't be in until late this afternoon. He's got some meeting with a possible grant donor."

She snorted in response. Smith had transferred in with a master's degree about the time she had gotten her first research grant for her Ph.D. program. He was focused on his own research involving cosmic rays and didn't understand or even seem to respect her ideas. She'd tried to explain her theory to him once, but he'd shrugged it off, stating that he really thought the Copenhagen interpretation was adequate and that weird ideas like time-travel and multiple universes were just a diversion.

She'd angrily retorted that the phrase 'and then a miracle happens' just wasn't quite descriptive enough for her. Niels Bohr's postulate that the quantum wave function simply collapses when observed by consciousness didn't meet her personal requirements for an adequate explanation.

She was more partial to the De Broglie/Bohm interpretation since it involved a pilot wave that apparently traveled into the future and back. That seemed to best fit her developing theory, and she'd oriented her math towards that idea.

If asked, Kathleen would explain that her work held great potential for improving people's lives. If someone had a presently incurable illness, considering the current rate of medical advances, there would be a high probability that a cure would exist in the near future. Kathleen could imagine saving terminally ill children by importing future medical knowledge into the present. She had convinced herself that this was the humanitarian reason behind her research. Her unspoken belief was that she could somehow justify her existence by discovering a way to travel in time.

This aspiration, combined with the urgency she felt regarding finishing her research for Professor Mackleroy, kept her working, even when she was exhausted.

— ◆ —

Walking down the hall to her class, she reflected on her reaction to Drew. It wasn't that she wasn't interested in men, at least in a remote fashion. She'd seen plenty of guys that she found attractive. It was just that she couldn't bear the thought of rejection. Even the relatively small scars along her jaw were a source of embarrassment that she tried to hide by keeping her hair long.

— ◆ —

Additionally, she couldn't afford the time to try to develop a relationship. Her research was too important. Besides, she felt comfortable in the laboratory. There she could forget her physical problems and relax in the realm of intellectual activity.

Drew was an over-grown idiot. He knew she didn't like the nickname, 'Kath,' but he had insisted on using it to the point that she sometimes derisively thought of herself as 'Kath.'

Then she remembered Drew's last remark about a possible grant donor. That was interesting. Perhaps the professor could arrange for some of it to be diverted to her project. It would be nice not to have to constantly wonder if she'd complete her work before she ran out of funds.

Kathleen paused in the hall before going into the already full room. She was a couple of minutes late, something she hated. As she gathered herself, preparing to enter, she overheard one of the male students say, "I wish Ms. Gimp would let us go early today. I've got a date tonight."

She'd heard them before, but even so, the words were like a slap in the face. She'd become inured to insults in elementary school, but most adults on campus were usually careful to avoid insulting remarks. She shrugged them off and squared her shoulders, telling herself it really didn't matter what they thought of her.

Her class was about what she expected from a room full of hormonally challenged young adults who were more interested in the fact that it was Friday than the concept of angular momentum. They acted so bored that she broke her lesson plan to try and keep them entertained by talking about her own research.

They were moderately interested when she mentioned the idea of time-travel, "So, particles seem to reach out into the future to query where they will be. When the answer comes back from their future selves, if circumstances are right, they will move to that location, not because they're being pushed or made to move, but because they are drawn to remain consistent."

In an attempt to be clever, one of the male students asked, "You mean the cue ball doesn't make the eight ball roll into the corner pocket. It rolls in because that's where it's going to be in the future? How does it know?"

The others snickered for a moment, but became silent as she responded, "Yes, that's just about right, but we're so ingrained into the idea of cause and effect, it seems silly from our viewpoint."

He continued, "What did you mean by 'if the circumstances are right'?"

This allowed her to begin explaining the idea of possibility waves. She drew eight carefully placed dots on the board and asked the class, "What do you see?"

Uniformly, they answered a variant of "eight dots."

She then connected the dots in such a way as to create two squares and then connected the corners to form a two-dimensional representation of a cube. "This is an open box," she said. "Is the opening up or down?"

The class was split about evenly over the direction.

She then challenged them to try and see the box as opening the other way. Most were successful.

"When you saw the dots, they were just a pattern on the board; a possibility. When I connected the corners, they almost immediately formed a cube in your mind. The cube could be viewed as opening one of two possible ways. The probability of your seeing it one or the other way was roughly equal, but didn't actually count until your mind made the decision on how to see it. When you forced yourself to see it in the other orientation, you might have noticed that it didn't flip instantly. Instead, it blurred back into its two-dimensional form and then flipped. It became a possibility again until your mind operated on it and caused you to see it flip."

Her thoughts wandered for an instant, and then she had another moment of deja vu. She'd explained this to them before. When was it? She shook her head and continued, "This is similar to how consciousness acts on particles. There are multiple possibilities represented by possibility waves. Consciousness takes the future possibility wave and reconciles it with the present possibility wave to create a probability wave that relates to the actual, real-world event. In a sense, we create our own reality in this way."

A female student asked, "What about time travel? You mentioned time travel. How's that work?"

Kathleen glanced at the wall clock. Nearly time for the bell. She answered, "Briefly, if the present sends out waves into the future and receives a response, then right now our present is sending responses to match query waves from our past. Right?"

All she got were blank looks, but then the bell rang. Belatedly, she gave them the assignment for the next class, "Exercises one through five at the end of the next chapter for Monday."

The students stampeded out in a cacophony of clatter and talking, leaving her wondering if they'd even heard her.

She gathered up her materials and headed across campus to her yoga class.

———————◄O►———————

Early on, her adoptive parents had taken her to a number of surgeons, but the possible benefit of surgery on her scars seemed to be limited. They hadn't had the ability to travel to any of the more advanced clinics in the country. In addition, any surgery always promised to be far more expensive than they could afford. Given her financial situation, she couldn't foresee affording any additional medical expenses anytime soon.

Sometimes, she thought she'd stretch and stretch until something tore. Maybe then, she'd heal with a better range of motion. The pain had always stopped her.

Her yoga teacher was good and always spent some time discussing esoteric philosophy during some of the period. Today was no exception. Kathleen began to slowly stretch as the older woman spoke:

"We believe all human experiences are rooted in the physical world. There is no proof to back up this conclusion. Your awareness of being in the body at this moment implies that there is more than just your body."

"This topic may seem esoteric, but I assure you that it's worthy of attention. Please suspend any disbelief for the moment and listen to me without judgment."

She paused to change position and check the class, then continued: "I'm not a physicist, but, if you'll permit me to use some of its language, I'll try to explain what I mean more fully."

She looked around as if waiting for an objection, but everyone was concentrating on moving into the new position. She continued, "Science, quantum physics in particular, tells us repeatedly that the basis of the idea of a real physical world is flawed. There is something that exists before space, time, and matter. Let's call this thing 'the void.' Think of it as an infinitely dimensional space that provides ample space for necessary quantum processes and whatnot. Strangely, consciousness appears to play a fundamental role in this space. Consciousness seems to exist at the level of even atoms and subatomic particles. I find that amazing."

Kathleen found herself getting interested. This discussion touched directly on her area of expertise and on her research.

Ms. Jayne continued, "The void is the home of infinite possibility. Possibility is different from the probability that statisticians calculate. Let's say that possibility waves exist in the void and probability curves mark time and bind our minds to our physical existence. Clear?"

It was not, but no one objected.

She said, "Possibility waves form our personal consciousness and free our minds from time. When we direct our attention to some physical item, it is first a blur, then it comes into focus. When we move on to the next item, the first one becomes a blur again, but it's a smaller blur since we now know more about it. It's just that we are just not focusing on it at the moment. This is similar to learning a yoga position. It is a large blur at first and you have to concentrate on every aspect of your body to reach the position correctly. Then when you've mastered it, it comes into sharp focus. You know how to do it and you can move into it easily. When you move to the next position, the first one blurs again. This is the rule in the progression: first things are a large blur, then sharply focused, then a small blur. Once we reach the point of mastery, the initial blur and the second blur become the same size. This is what we call 'habit' or 'muscle-memory.' That's the goal of our practice: developing a habit.

———— ◆ ————

The teacher went on, but Kathleen's mind was racing ahead and lost to the rest of her words. The discussion linked to Cramer's theory of quantum processes in a general way; something that Kathleen was currently working on. Her math was rather elegant, but there were a number of difficult problems that seemed to imply something was missing in the formulation.

The idea of an imaginal realm was equivalent to possibility curves for quantum bits. The possibility curve couldn't be resolved into a real probability form, since it could take on a negative value. You couldn't have a probability of less than zero in the real world.

Cramer proposed that the possible negative value could be dealt with by having the present situation send an 'offer' wave into the future and the future respond with a 'return' wave. These waves of possibility could then be multiplied, which would convert the negative numbers into positive ones that could represent a real world probability.

According to Ms. Jayne's discussion, this happened in the mind. Nevertheless, once a probability curve could be assigned, the chances of something happening could be calculated mathematically.

Kathleen paused to concentrate on changing position and beginning a new stretch. The interesting thing for her research was that, if a wave went from the present into the future and was answered, it must also, necessarily, go from the present into the past.

She tried to think what that would mean in practical terms. It seemed as if the past probability could be changed by modifying the present's 'return' wave. *That would allow for,* she thought with excitement, *a form of time travel!* She'd have to wait until she could put some scribbles down on paper, but the idea continued bouncing around in her mind as she worked out.

She continued to follow the teacher's instructions but didn't even notice the progression of moves until everyone began rolling up their mats. After changing in a toilet stall—couldn't let the other students see her scars—she hurried back to Tate, anxious to get started.

Chapter Two

Success in the Lab

K athleen's lab space was a small, poorly lit corner of the basement. She'd chosen it as a place unlikely to be disturbed by the other students, and it also had the added benefit of being relatively free from various types of interference. Something about the combination of being underground and the old pipes in the building insulated it from radio signals. Her cell phone was always totally dead when she was in there.

Physics Lab

She settled into the old desk chair she used and started her computer. While it was firing up, she pulled some notes out from under her microscope.

The microscope was a gift from her adoptive father. Not being highly informed about physics, he'd purchased the antique at a garage sale and presented it to her with the vague hope that she could use it to see some atoms or something. She had grown attached to the instrument, which was medical quality and quite heavy. She had no use for it but kept it near her in the lab as sort of a talisman to remind her that two people had loved her, at least. It also made a great paperweight, so, she reflected, it was of some practical use to her.

It took a little time for her computer to start since she habitually encrypted the entire storage with a 1,024-bit encryption routine. This wasn't state of the art, but it would be difficult enough to break the key that she felt her data was fairly secure. It would probably take a few months of expensive computing time to crack.

She was deep in a meta-analysis of extremely complex data that originated largely from the CERN Large Hadron Collider. The LHC's twenty-seven-kilometer circular tunnel and thousands of magnets generated massive amounts of data from seven different experiments.

Kathleen had never been closer to CERN than New York City, but she had access to the data through a secondary source: a specialized computing grid that allowed for distributed processing handled the main analysis.

Kathleen's single computer couldn't begin to compare to the raw power the multiple labs could bring to bear on the data, but she was more interested in analyzing it in a totally different way. Her fledgling theory relied on some complex math that paradoxically didn't require more computing power than was at her disposal. This was partially because she was, in her own introverted way, somewhat of a math genius and had created her own form of analysis. The other students didn't understand it, and even her beloved Professor Mackleroy could only follow part of the logic.

After downloading a terabyte of data, she paused to fix a cup of tea. Cup safely in hand, she filtered the data, ran a transform on it, and integrated it with the other downloads. She'd previously created a routine to massage the numbers automatically. A little quiver of her lips betrayed her underlying tension as she started the program in its processing. This was going to take some time. She might as well get comfortable. It was going to be a long night.

A little while later, she noted that the routine was approximately a tenth of the way through the massive amount of data. She'd been thinking about the various possible outcomes in a kind of fugue as she waited. Her mind drifted back to the subject.

One result was that the analysis would show nothing. If that happened, she'd have to go back to square one and start over. It would spell disaster for her doctoral program, probably setting her back years. She sincerely hoped that wouldn't be the outcome.

Her desire, of course, was that her theory would be confirmed. That was a potentially earth-shaking result that would move quantum mechanics towards more fully accepting the ideas of John Cramer and would have implications that might allow some form of time-travel.

Her mind blurred for a second, and she jerked awake, reaching for her teacup. In yet another moment of deja vu, she knew that it was cold. *I'm probably too tired for this,* she thought. She stretched and sat upright in her chair to check the computer's progress. It was still cranking on the problem. She lapsed back into her reverie.

If she could show time-travel was possible, then she'd contribute to saving innumerable terminally ill children. Future medical advances would surely hold the key to curing all sorts of cancers and genetic diseases. Perhaps travel into the past could alleviate children's illnesses before they became a problem. It might allow the rescue of unwanted babies before their mother –

She flinched. Her motivation was partially selfish, and that now brought it home to her. She stubbornly completed the thought. *If I could go back and convince my mother not to go through with the abortion or maybe even keep her from being involved with the man who used and dumped her, I could just be happy.*

She ignored the paradox that stopping her mother from becoming pregnant would mean that she wouldn't exist and hence, wouldn't be able to discover her theory. She'd made a decision early on not to worry about actual implementation issues. If there were potential paradoxes, she'd let others deal with them. All she wanted was to prove her own worth by discovering something that would benefit others.

She had jumped mentally to a whole line of research based on the idea of time-travel. She had never dared to vocalize her ideas, but she cherished the thought that complex energy wave systems, on the human level, might be able to move in time. To her, this would require a mental shift. She thought it might be like awakening from a lucid dream, only to find the dream state had somehow manifested into reality, and the pre-dream reality had become the dream state.

Her yoga classes and meditation training also provided her with mental support for the idea. She knew from her own experience that she could move into a theta brain state and engage in what she termed 'virtual travel' to other places.

Sometimes the places were physical locations, and other times they were not to be found in the normal universe. She'd had numerous out-of-body experiences and felt that this was a beginning step towards actual traveling in space and time.

Her mind snapped back to the here-and-now as she reflexively took a sip from her cup. It was ice cold. She'd been in an almost dream state as she waited. *Probably too tired,* she thought. She stretched and sat upright in her chair to check the computer's progress again. It was done.

She opened the results file, her hands visibly shaking. She had to read the results twice, and then she printed it out and crosschecked her understanding. Her analysis showed that, under certain circumstances, certain types of particles behaved in exactly the way she'd predicted.

She quickly shut down her machine, grabbed a file folder, and left the lab. An hour later, she'd collected her bike and ridden home. Halfway there, she remembered that she'd left her cell phone in her desk. She shrugged. No one ever called her anyway.

⸺◈⸺

Now she was sitting on the edge of her bed in the dark, thinking. How would she go about announcing her results? Tell Professor Mackleroy first, of course. But then what? She crawled under the covers, shivering until the sheets warmed up. After what seemed an eternity of worried thoughts, she drifted into an uneasy sleep.

⸺◈⸺

IN the middle of the night, she woke with a gasp. Something had happened somewhere. Someone had been injured or was in great danger. She sat up, trembling, but the information faded and seemed to elude her as dreams often do. After a while, she lay back down and tried to sleep, gradually relaxing.

⸺◈⸺

It was nearly morning. She woke, stretched, and curled up again. She didn't have to be anywhere until later, so she felt safe in sleeping in for a bit. Besides, it's not often that one has a chance to savor the feeling of a great discovery. After some time, she fell back asleep and dreamed.

She was walking in a forest. The trees were mostly evergreens, and it was cold, even colder than normal. There was danger somewhere nearby, and she was hurrying to find a refuge. From what she didn't know, but she sensed urgency. There was a sensation of large forms moving through the trees, but they were indistinct, and she couldn't make them out. They were dangerous but not 'the danger.' She kept walking. Then she saw a figure approaching. It was male, and she was strongly attracted. As the emotion washed over her, some voice in the back of her mind warned her that men were dangerous, and she was scarred and unattractive. The danger following her was nearer, and she found herself rushing towards the male figure despite the warning. She envisioned the figure as a handsome and strong man...

With a start, she sat up in bed. She was breathing heavily, partly from fear and partly from arousal. "I wonder what that was all about," she whispered, her hand at her throat. "I've never had a dream like that before."

She tried to remember the male figure but only came up with a vague image, now fading. Frustrated, she got out of bed and prepared for the exciting news she would deliver to Professor Mackleroy.

Chapter Three

Joy and Grief

The weather was a little warmer this morning, but then it was nearly midday. Kathleen had to take her jacket off and stuff it in her backpack midway to the campus. Riding her bike was good exercise and burned a lot of calories, but it also heated her up. She coasted up to the physics building and racked her bicycle.

She started to go in, but her tendency to over-think and to worry took over. Instead, she walked slowly down the sidewalk, trying to think of all of the things that might have gone wrong with her calculations. She was anxious to present her results to the professor, but she also wanted to ensure that she wasn't misleading him. She wasn't going to burst in, get him excited, and then have him find an error. Her fragile sense of self-esteem couldn't deal with that. She lost herself in thought as she walked with no particular destination in mind.

It was two in the afternoon when she finally got up the courage to approach the door of Professor Mackleroy's office. He was the one person she felt at ease with, but that meant that she would do anything rather than disappoint him.

He was in. She paused on the threshold, gathering herself and trying to think of how to break the news.

"Kathleen! It's good to see you. I thought I'd call you later to check on your progress. How is the analysis going?" he asked, stabbing wildly with his battered pipe.

She stepped over the threshold of the office and stopped. She was suddenly shaking with nervousness. Mackleroy gazed at her, and a sudden look of concern came over his face.

"Are you feeling alright? You look a little pale. Are you sick?" he asked.

She gathered herself and answered, "No. I...I..." She choked up and stopped.

"You what? Are you sure you're okay?" he asked with even more concern.

"I...the analysis..." She gathered herself again and blurted, "It supports my hypothesis."

"What? That's great! You're sure about that, of course?" He didn't wait for her to answer. He jumped up and walked around the desk, rubbing his hands together gleefully. He stopped in front of her and placed his hands gently on her shoulders.

"Kathleen, you're going to be famous. We're going to publish this immediately. Getting your Ph.D. awarded is going to be a minor event." He paused and then continued, "I'm going to have to ask for more grant money. You should be free to concentrate on writing this up, not teaching. I'll call your grant sponsor right away. I've got a cell number for the corporate decision-maker and, and..." He trailed off.

"Professor, I'm frightened. What if my analysis is completely wrong? What if my math...if I made a mistake somewhere? Maybe I should redo the entire thing. I don't know what to do," she said quietly. She was still shaking, and he wrapped his arms protectively around her. She sighed and relaxed in the warmth of his fatherly embrace.

"Don't worry about that, Kathleen. I'll check your work and help you with the writing. Knowing you, I'm sure you haven't made a mistake. This is really great news," he was getting more and more excited. He released her and started walking around the office, speculating on what the finding would mean, waving his pipe in the air. In the middle of his discourse, Drew walked in.

"What's going on?" he asked.

Mackleroy answered for her, "Kathleen has made a breakthrough. She's finished her analysis, and it supports her theory of time-travel."

Drew started to laugh, obviously thinking it was a joke, but then noticed the two of them looked quite serious.

"You mean she isn't off her nut?" he started.

The professor interrupted. "Far from it. She may have made the most significant advance in our understanding of the universe since the advent of quantum theory."

Drew was disbelieving. "Ah. That seems unlikely to me. She's told me her ideas, but I don't think they fit into mainstream physics very well. It's more like she's some kind of New Age spiritualist or something."

Kathleen took offense. Her eyes sparked, but before she could open her mouth, the professor laughed, making it something of a joke.

"Drew, Drew. When will you ever realize that physics isn't some stone tablet handed down from above? It's always in a state of change. I realize that there are a lot of academics who would prefer to see nothing change. They've got their positions and written their books, and they don't want to have to face anything new that would upset their apple cart. However, that is exactly the way science works. Change comes along, and science advances, regardless of everyone's preferences."

They continued the discussion for some time, gradually winning Drew over to a guarded acceptance that she might have something new, although he tempered it with a dose of incredulity.

It was getting late in the afternoon when their discussion turned to more mundane topics, and before Kathleen quite understood what was happening, she'd agreed to have a celebratory dinner with the two men.

⸺◆⸺

She marveled as they entered the restaurant. She never engaged in social activities, and she'd never even considered eating in this restaurant before. It was too prominent, held too many diners, and was too expensive for her limited budget.

Dinner was exciting. She caught herself thinking that it was almost like going on a date, but she felt secure with Professor Mackleroy along. Drew was his normal boring and overly solicitous self, but even his stilted mannerisms weren't so obnoxious now.

Professor Mackleroy was charming and entertaining. He had placed a call to his contact with her corporate sponsor and asked for some additional money. He was hopeful that the sponsor would see fit to provide them with enough to allow for a second analysis and also to acquire more data. Drew seemed to be a little jealous but agreed that, if the results were what he understood them to be, she had a good chance of getting more funding. Then he ordered a beer for her, claiming that they needed a toast.

Greatly daring, she agreed to try some of the beer, the first alcohol she'd ever had. It was...interesting, she decided. Over dessert, a chocolate mousse that she found entrancing, Drew questioned her on her data and the analysis. He seemed surprised to hear that the data and all of the results were on her computer in her lab. Shortly after that, he ordered another beer for her. She started to drink it, but after a couple of swallows, she felt a little tipsy. That was interesting, also. She'd never felt that way, and it was a little strange and exhilarating.

They discussed her results in more detail. The professor was excited and felt that her sponsor would most likely be supportive. Drew was a little more reserved but pointed out that if she was correct and there was some way to place her discovery into a practical application, it would have all sorts of effects. He said, "It would change the world."

"What do you mean?" she asked.

Drew frowned and then slowly said, "It could have all sorts of applications for both espionage and the military. It seems to me that any kind of time-travel could give a country a big advantage. Just think. They'd know in advance what their enemies were going to do."

Professor Mackleroy shook his head deprecatingly, pointing at him with the pipe stem, "Drew, Drew, I don't think the military uses are as exciting as the study uses. Besides, once she publishes, it will be common knowledge available to everyone. There will be no advantage for any group."

The valley opened to the north showing a view of a large lake surrounded by thick groves of spruce and various hardwoods. There were a couple of sloughs filled with cattails that almost certainly provided shelter for elfra. It looked like a place where he'd be able to hunt and replenish his dwindling supply of dried jerky.

The view showed neither man nor beast; nevertheless, he remained still. Another hunter would be just as careful, neither moving nor giving up on scanning the landscape. He drowsed for a while, feeling safe in the watery warmth of the midday sun, his thoughts moving into a memory that he'd replayed repeatedly.

He was alone, and as a single human without backup, he was more than likely to fall prey to any of the numerous predators in the region. His best defense was fire. He was less confident in his weapons. Without the many spears of a group of hunters, the larger predators were hard to bring down. Killing one would rely on dead-certain accuracy and a considerable amount of luck. If he were injured while killing one, he was far more likely to fall to the next one he encountered.

He wasn't used to being completely alone. He'd always had a tribe, his friends and relatives, surrounding him. In their numbers lay strength. It was suicide to attempt to live alone. If the numerous predators didn't kill a single hunter, he could easily fall to an accident or be injured or killed in the hunt.

His father had named him when he was five. His people had child names, but they grew out of them quickly. Two older boys had thought to bully him, thinking that a smaller child looked like easy sport. It had been a hard fight, but he won, beating both until they ran away. His father had insisted on giving him his adult name that evening.

'Cadeyrin' meant 'master-of-battle' in the old language. That speech was rarely used now, but elements of it had been handed down for generations. Most of the people were named after their animal spirit guides or some unusual event. Only a few had special names. He was proud that his father had given him such a strong one.

Cadeyrin missed his father and, to a lesser extent, his friends. There were no living blood relatives, and his mother had died giving birth to him.

Kathleen gathered her courage and tried to explain her most cherished dream. "I think that it would offer great hope for the entire world. Look, medical science has advanced really quickly, and it will probably continue getting better in the future. If we could access future knowledge, think of all of the terminally ill children we could save."

Drew immediately made a loud scoffing noise. She looked at him, shocked.

Before the professor could say anything, Drew continued, "That's hopelessly naive. Saving ill children. What a stupid goal. They die because they need to die. They're not genetically qualified to survive. You'd stop the evolution of humanity, and it would never reach its destiny. No. Military applications are the most important."

Professor Mackleroy frowned and then said, "I don't think she is naive. Saving children is an admirable and worthy goal. In my opinion, military use doesn't rise to that level. Drew, don't criticize her on that basis."

Admonished, Drew clamped his mouth shut for a moment, and the conversation ceased, embarrassing Kathleen.

As an afterthought, the professor added, "On the other hand, there may be some paradoxical limitation on using knowledge that hasn't been discovered yet."

That set Drew off again on the dangers of time-travel.

They went on this way for over an hour, sometimes arguing, sometimes speculating wildly. Kathleen lost herself in the discussion. It was fascinating and exciting to have her ideas taken seriously enough to argue about.

Eventually, the dinner broke up. Professor Mackleroy had an early class and needed to leave. Drew tried to talk her into staying, but she refused, claiming that she was tired. She rode her bicycle for a few hundred feet, decided that she was wobbling a little too much, and then climbed off and pushed it the rest of the way home.

⸺◦⸺

By the time she hit her bedroom, she was headachy. She felt so poorly; she even omitted her nightly session with the full-length mirror. She undressed, discarding her clothes in a pile, and approached the bed.

She had felt like things were changing for her. The implications of her discovery were earth-shaking. All she had to do was verify her findings with more research, but that could come after she'd received her degree. She would be able to find a position, maybe even get tenure, and then she could follow through on her research. It would be the basis for a lifelong career.

Unbidden, a thought that had been hidden in the corners of her mind slowly formed. *My life would be wonderful. Maybe I could even find someone to share it with.* The incongruity of that response stopped her. She glanced at the mirror with a feeling of shock. She'd been so giddy that she'd even forgotten her physical deformities.

The feeling of excitement and happiness that she'd felt earlier vanished. She turned away from the mirror and threw herself on the bed. The old box springs, long past due to be replaced, cracked, and the left side of the mattress sagged in response. She sat up, staring at the crooked mattress in disbelief. It was somehow representative of her – broken and unlovely.

Then it hit her. She had done this before. It was an incredible sense of deja vu. Had the bed been broken when she came home? She shook her head, causing it to throb. Then she deliberately dismissed the problem, saying, "I've just got to concentrate on my work. I can't worry about something I'll never find."

After a moment, she added, "And I think I'm going crazy."

Moving as if her neck was made of glass, she carefully turned out the light and climbed under the covers. After a while, she sighed, rolled onto her side, and slept.

———◆———

Someone was pounding on her door. She sat up, wiping her hand over her partly closed eyes. It was too early. The sun was just starting to illuminate the window blinds, and her alarm hadn't gone off. She staggered to the closet and pulled a sweatshirt over the top of her pajamas.

"Just a minute, I'm coming," she shouted in response to a new burst of pounding.

There were two policemen in the hall when she opened the door.

She drew back in surprise and alarm, "Wha – What is it?" She was filled with dread. This had to be something serious.

"I didn't – I mean, I locked my bike in the rack downstairs. Has someone stolen it?"

She paused, thinking that she probably sounded like a mental case.

"Kathleen Whitby?" asked the older cop.

"That's right. Th – that's m – me," she stammered.

The younger one apparently took pity on her and said, "Calm down. Take a deep breath." When she did, he added, "That's better. Are you the Kathleen Whitby that is a student at the university?"

She hesitated, thinking. Had she become so inebriated that she'd done something illegal? She reassured herself, one beer wouldn't have such an effect. She hesitated, thinking it over, and then realized that she wanted to cooperate. "Yes. I'm studying for my doctorate in physics."

"I'm Officer Reilly, and this is Officer Cooper," he said, motioning towards the older man.

She looked from one to the other. The older man cleared his throat, but the younger one continued speaking.

"Your adviser is Professor Mackleroy? Correct?" he asked.

"Yes. He's sponsoring my research. Why?" she asked. Then something awful occurred to her. "Is he alright? Has anything happened to him?"

The two men looked at each other, then Officer Cooper said in a harsh, scratchy voice, "Professor Mackleroy was murdered last night."

It was like a splash of icy cold water on her face. She blanched, started to reach for a chair, but faltered. The next thing she knew, the two policemen were bracing her in the chair, and the younger one was rubbing her hands.

"Take it easy. We just need to ask you some questions. We have to interview everyone associated with the professor. This will only take a few minutes.

We'll need you to account for everything you did last night."

He paused, expectantly.

She looked away, putting her hand on her forehead and clamping her left hand under her right arm. This was horrible. Who could have done this to the professor? As far as she knew, everyone liked him.

The older man said, "Tell us where you were last night."

She gathered herself, took a deep breath, turned back to the two, and said, "I went out to dinner with the professor and another grad student. Then I brought my bicycle directly home. I've been in bed since."

The younger officer smiled at her and said, "It looks like you didn't get enough sleep. When did you go to bed?"

Placing her hand on her cheek while wondering how bad she actually looked, she answered, "It must have been about nine-thirty or so. Maybe closer to ten. Why are you asking? It can't mean – you don't suspect me, do you?"

The older officer interrupted her, "You got anyone who can confirm that?"

She flinched at the thought. "No. No one lives with me. Maybe one of the other renters heard me come in, but I don't know..." She trailed off.

The older officer was looking past her at the pile of clothes she'd left on the floor. "Are those the clothes you were wearing?"

She turned, flushing with the idea that they must think she was a complete slob. She normally put things in a hamper in the closet.

"Yes. I had a headache and just dropped them," she answered.

The two cops looked at each other, then the younger one asked, "Can we look at them?"

By now, Kathleen was completely intimidated. Wordlessly, she nodded.

They donned clear plastic gloves, sidestepped past her, and picked through her clothes, looking carefully at her sweatshirt and pants. Then they looked at each other, and Cooper shrugged.

"Better take them to the lab," he said.

Officer Reilly pulled a plastic bag from somewhere on his person and bagged her clothes.

He glanced at her and said, "We'll need these for a few tests, but you'll be able to get them back."

She nodded again as if she understood what was going on.

The younger man seemed to take pity on her. He was definitely the more friendly of the two.

"We don't think you're responsible. You don't seem strong enough and there are no obvious blood stains on your clothing. Whoever killed the professor was strong. We think the killer would have been covered in blood. The murder scene was messy," he said.

She started to cry. "The – the professor was my only friend. Nobody disliked him. Who could have done it? Who could – " She paused and then made an effort to gain control of herself. Drawing a shaky breath, she repeated, "He was my only friend. Without him, I don't know what I'll do about my research or my dissertation. I... "

She broke down completely, burying her face in her hands, sobbing. With an effort, she got her breath and added, "I wanted to finish my research before he died. He so wanted to see it published."

"What do you mean 'before he died'?" Reilly asked.

She managed to gasp out, "He had terminal lung cancer. He had only a few months left."

"We'd like you to come down to the crime scene and explain what was happening. He was found in your lab. We'd like to know if anything is missing or out of the ordinary," said the older man in a kinder voice.

She jerked her head up. "My lab? Oh, no! What would he be doing in my lab? I had a breakthrough yesterday in my data analysis. There would be nothing to steal and nothing there to kill over. Just my..." she paused in a combination of speculation and horror. "Just my computer," she whispered. "The data is all there. If it's gone, I've lost weeks of work. I've got a USB backup, but I haven't updated it for days."

Shaking, she stood up and gathered some clean clothes from the closet. She looked pointedly at them, "If you'll step out for a moment, I'll get dressed, and we can go."

The two cops looked at each other again. "We'll be outside your door, waiting," the older one said.

While she was dressing, she began to shake more violently and was barely able to adjust her clothing. When she turned towards the door, her face was wet with tears.

⸺ ◆ ⸺

The ride in the cruiser was over quickly. She was embarrassed at being seen riding in the backseat like any common criminal. She ducked her head, letting her hair obscure her face until it was time to get out.

There was an ambulance, a fire truck, and several other police cars near the entrance to the building. A large crowd of onlookers stood nearby, their speculation a dim background noise as she strode quickly to the door and entered.

⸺ ◆ ⸺

Yellow crime scene tape was strung across the door to her lab. Inside, the detective in charge close by her side, she took a quick look around. Her computer was gone, as were several binders that she'd used for notes and working out formulas. The sweep was complete. Whoever it was had taken everything except for the two sheets of paper she'd printed to show the professor when she met with him yesterday.

She started forward, and the detective grabbed her arm, "You don't want to look over there, Miss." He pulled her back, but not before she had a glimpse of a large pool of blood and splatters over the back and side of her desk and the bookshelves.

She gasped, "Oh, no. Was that where...?"

He answered bluntly, "His body was partly behind your desk. He'd been struck on the head repeatedly with a heavy object. It was odd-shaped, and we don't know what it was exactly. He must have put up a fight, though, since there's blood everywhere."

She had a moment of insight and looked around. Her microscope was missing.

"It must have been my medical microscope. It's gone. It was quite heavy. I kept it on my desk most of the time. It was a gift from my parents," she said numbly.

The detective took out a notebook and scribbled a bit, "How big was it?"

She stopped and thought and then answered, "It was an antique medical instrument about average in size, but it must have weighed ten pounds or so." Her eye was drawn to a black object under the edge of her desk. "Look! That's one of the eyepieces."

He used a plastic bag to pick it up, bagging it and sticking it into his pocket. At her inquiring glance, he responded, "May have a print or partial on it. We'll have it checked. It's evidence."

Something else caught her eye. There were some splintered debris by the leg of the desk. She bent to inspect it and saw it was the remains of the professor's pipe. It had been smashed during the struggle. She started to reach for it, but the detective said, "Don't touch that!"

She stopped and watched miserably as he bagged the broken pipe.

She was led out and then spent an interminable hour in the hall going over everything she knew. It seemed like she was forced to tell the same story about her actions leading up to the time she went to bed to at least five people. After an interminable time standing around, she was allowed to leave. The two policemen who'd brought her there were gone, and there weren't any familiar faces outside the building.

Sadly, she threaded her way through the now sparse crowd of onlookers and started towards home. It was a long walk, and it gave her a chance to try and sort out her emotions. She walked slowly, working out what she should do. It seemed like the death of her mentor had also killed her prospects. Offhand, she didn't know of anyone else in the physics department who would take her on with her admittedly unusual line of research.

The loss of the professor was something she'd expected, but she'd thought it would be in the future and that he'd die in a hospital. It was hard for her to adjust to the fact that he was no longer there. She'd never see him jab his pipe again.

About halfway home, she abruptly turned around and headed back. She'd made up her mind to see the head of the department to discuss her future. Perhaps Professor Schmidt could help. Maybe she wouldn't have to drop her research completely if she could only find someone open-minded enough to sponsor her. It would probably mean some changes in her approach or at least in the write-up of her research.

Professor Mackleroy had been near the end of his career, and as he'd said, "I don't mind shaking things up a bit. However, you do realize, Kathleen, that upsetting apple carts is not always received well in academia. You may find that your theory makes it difficult to find employment."

She'd assured him that she didn't care. She was just interested in following wherever the data led. If it supported her ideas and no one wanted to hire her, so be it. She'd told herself in that case; she'd just write a book. Maybe that would get the attention her theory needed and make her a little money on the side.

<hr />

Professor Schmidt was in her office. She was on the phone, but when she saw Kathleen, she motioned for her to enter and sit. She quickly finished the conversation, saying, "Ve need to keep a lid on this. The department and the University don't need the negative publicity. I certainly agree vith you that additional security vould be a good step for a few veeks. It will reassure the alumni that ve're doing everything ve can to protect the students. Okay. Bye."

She hung up and looked at Kathleen. "That vas the University President. He's very upset over the potential for negative publicity," she said somewhat accusingly.

That wasn't fair as far as Kathleen was concerned. Her beloved professor had been brutally killed, and all the President was concerned with was keeping the funding flowing from the alumni. She started to say what she thought, but then closed her mouth quickly. It wouldn't do to raise a stink right when she desperately needed help.

Schmidt was not what Kathleen thought of as a dedicated scientist. She'd been a physicist once, years ago, but had wormed her way into the position of department chairman and had largely dropped all research since. With any luck, she'd sit there, doing little, until she retired. She had a heavy German accent and short, spiked gray hair.

Schmidt rearranged some papers on her desk and then looked up at Kathleen. "I can see that the professor's death has hit you hard. Perhaps you have come to see me about taking a quarter off to recover?"

She seemed hopeful. Kathleen suddenly realized that she was part of Schmidt's problem. If she weren't around, it would be easier to sweep the whole thing under the carpet. She shook her head negatively and explained, "No, I came to see you about finding another professor who will sponsor my research. I'm basically through with the data analysis and ready to begin writing my dissertation. I think I can get it done in another two or three months. Then I could sit for my exams and hopefully graduate at the end of the summer session."

Schmidt raised her eyebrows, "You pose an interesting problem. There are no other professors here that vould be villing to sponsor your research. I don't know much about it, but from vat Mackleroy told me, I understand that it is likely to cause a firestorm of criticism and reaction. Ve don't need that here, especially now. I vas always going to speak to Mackleroy about that, but now it's too late. I think it vould be better if you took a sabbatical for a quarter or two. Perhaps you vould find something else to do that you liked more."

Kathleen knew her position was tenuous. It wouldn't take much for Schmidt to decide that she wasn't the sort of student they needed. She played her hole card. "But what about my corporate sponsor? They've given me a considerable amount of money, and Professor Mackleroy was going to ask them for more. Don't they deserve some consideration for their investment?"

Schmidt nodded, "Vell, there is that. Mackleroy called me yesterday. He vas excited and told me you'd made some kind of breakthrough. He'd already called the corporate representative, and he told me he vas sure they vere going to give you additional funding."

Kathleen said, "Oh! That's great news."

Schmidt held up her hand to stop Kathleen. "Ja, but that funding von't be available if you don't have a faculty sponsor, and I can't think of anyone who vould take you on. Your research vould give them a black eye. It's just not mainstream physics, my dear, and there isn't much place for odd-ball, esoteric theories these days."

Kathleen started to protest, but Schmidt said, "Here's vat ve'll do. You take a veek off and think about vat you vant. You can talk to the other professors and see vat they think. Maybe you'll be able to convince one of them to take you on. If not, vell, you can teach the rest of the quarter, but after that, perhaps you'd better see about finding another department, somewhere else."

Kathleen stood up, turned, and walked out, blindly bumping into the doorjamb as she exited.

Schmidt called out the door, "You'll see. It's for the best."

Kathleen didn't respond. She blundered down the hall and turned into the first restroom she could find. There she locked the stall and sat down, holding her head in her hands. This was even worse than she'd thought it would be. Her friend and mentor had been murdered, and the department wasn't even concerned enough to try and help her. All they wanted was to cover the whole thing up, and she was a disposable reminder of the crime.

After a while, she decided that she was, amazingly enough, hungry. It was past noon, and she hadn't had any breakfast. She exited the restroom and found her way into the student union.

She was sitting there, numbly eating a tuna sandwich that she'd purchased. The bread was dry, but she wasn't in a condition to care. Just as she finished, Officer Reilly sat down opposite her.

"Kathleen, I'm lucky to find you here. I'd like you to come with me. We've found your microscope, or at least I assume that it's yours. I need you to identify it." He looked at her critically. "The only fingerprints on it are yours."

She nearly choked on the remains of the sandwich. "Mine? Of course, my fingerprints would be on the microscope. It was mine, and I sometimes used it. Oh, not for physics, of course, but to look at things that I was curious about."

She could feel her face flushing. It sounded like she was trying to cover up something.

He didn't say anything but just cocked his eyebrow in an inquisitive way.

She stuttered and then said, "I mean that I'm not only interested in physics. Last summer, for instance, I used the microscope to look at a sample that I got from the river. There were a lot of microbes in the water, and I found it relaxing to try and identify them."

"How do you know anything about microbes?" he asked.

She flushed again. "Well, I really don't, but I checked out a book from the library and was able to figure out what a few of them were."

"Would the record of that book being checked out still be available?" he asked.

She was shaking again. She looked down and said, "You don't believe me, do you?"

He smiled and answered, "It's not that. It's just that I have to check out everything involved. A murder is a serious crime, and someone has to be found guilty."

She shook her head slowly. At the moment, she didn't trust herself to speak.

———◦○◦———

The microscope was hers. They had found it in a garbage can, and they hadn't even taken the time to clean the professor's remains off of it. There was some flesh and clotted blood mixed with hair still sticking to one side of the heavy base. She tentatively reached towards the bagged instrument, but when she saw the hair and realized it was Mackleroy's, she flinched back.

She looked at the detective. He'd taken over when she was escorted back to the mobile crime lab in the nearby parking lot. His expression was serious as he said, "Do you recognize the microscope?"

"Yes. It is mine," she shuddered. "That looks like the professor's hair on the base. Are you sure that my fingerprints are the only ones on it?"

"Yes, just yours," he answered.

She was thinking about the few mysteries she'd read. The genre didn't appeal to her much. She tentatively asked, "Could someone have worn gloves or wrapped it in a cloth to handle it?"

He shrugged and said, "That's what I've been wondering. Some of your prints are blurred as if they'd been disturbed by wiping. I'd say it was a possibility."

Kathleen was biting her lip. Suddenly it was all too much. She managed to ask, "Can I leave?"

The detective frowned and then said, "Sure, but don't leave town. We may need to talk to you again."

Chapter Four

Terror and Flight

S he left the trailer and walked directly to the library. After wandering around aimlessly, she found a study carrel in the stacks and sat, just staring numbly at the wall. She might have dozed off for a while because when she became aware again, the light from the nearby window was fading. She was tired, and she really wanted a shower. She left the library and headed for home.

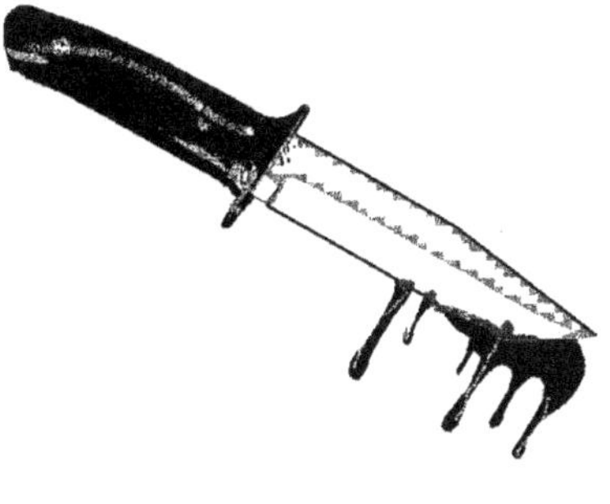

As she descended the steps, still in a sort of mental fog, she had a moment of vertigo and grabbed at the rail to steady herself. She was overcome by a dark sense of foreboding. Something bad was going to happen. She tried to think but couldn't exactly conceptualize her premonition. It was as if she knew what was going to happen but had just forgotten it momentarily. She wondered how it could be worse than what had happened earlier.

Another two steps towards the sidewalk, and she staggered again. The sense of premonition was even greater. Something bad—no, something truly evil – was imminent.

Shaken, she carefully descended the remaining steps and headed home, moving slowly, as if she had suddenly aged decades. A passing student gave her a funny look, but no one else seemed to notice.

On the long walk, she continued to mull things over in her head. Mackleroy had called the corporate sponsor. Then someone had killed him in her lab.

That someone had presumably taken her computer and data. Perhaps the professor caught them and was killed trying to keep them from taking her research. It sounded like some kind of TV plot, but maybe it had some truth to it, also.

She'd long suspected that her corporate sponsor had some kind of government or military ties. They'd been quite interested in the idea of time-travel. Off the top of her head, she could think of several potential uses for time-travel that would lend themselves to espionage or warfare, as Drew had suggested.

Would those possibilities be enough to justify theft and murder? She thought about it and then dismissed the concept. It was just too much for her at the moment. She almost walked out in front of a truck as she started to cross against a red light. Stopping, she thought to herself: *I have to have some time to adjust. Maybe Schmidt is right. Maybe I should take time off.*

That thought led to the next. Schmidt was almost sure to tell her that her presence wasn't desired around the department. Not in so many words, of course. Her funding would be pulled. Maybe her lab would be reassigned to someone else. She'd be told that no one would sponsor her research. They'd find someone else to teach her classes. She shook her head, thinking, No, I've just got to try my best to hang on here. I'd never be able to find another university.

She suddenly thought that anyone watching would think she was deranged. Her actions probably bore close similarity to some of the more dysfunctional individuals that hung around the campus area.

⚬

As she walked up the front steps to her apartment, a car braked to a screeching halt behind her. She turned, and there was the older policeman climbing out of a cruiser that had swerved into a vacant parking space. He waved for her to wait and then hurried up the steps, zipping his jacket against the nighttime cold as he came.

She greeted him, "Officer Cooper. What now?"

"Hi, Kathleen. I've been watching for you. I tried your apartment earlier, but you weren't home. Where have you been?" he asked.

"Oh. Nowhere in particular. I sat in the library for a long time. I – I don't know what to do or maybe even what to think," she said listlessly.

He smiled a little, the first smile she'd seen from him. It had a startling effect, making him seem younger and friendlier. "Well, that's going to be a normal reaction to what's happened. You'll need some time to get over the shock." Then without pausing, he continued, "I got the idea that whoever did this isn't through. You told us you'd encrypted your computer. How hard would that be to break?"

She shrugged, "I don't know. Maybe if the right equipment was available, it could be broken in a few weeks, but otherwise, I think it might take a long time." She blushed, "I was a little paranoid and probably spent more than I should on the encryption routine. It's close to state of the art."

He opened the foyer door for her and followed her inside. "You might be in some danger, then. They could come looking for a way to break the encryption. Is it something that you have stored somewhere that they could find?"

They walked down the hall as she answered, "No, it's just in my memory. I used a personal key that I'm not going to forget. I guess that means they'd be likely to try to force it out of me, but they're not going to find it anyplace else."

His eyes darkened. "Give me the door key, then stay back while I check the place."

She handed it to him and then gasped slightly. Another sense of deja vu. Whatever was coming – the evil thing – was close. She stepped back as he turned the key in the lock.

Cooper stepped in as she looked over his shoulder. Her apartment had been thoroughly ransacked. All her clothes were on the floor, the bed was turned upside down, and the mattress had been sliced open. Her books were tossed in a pile by the window, and some had been ripped in half. The place was a total ruin.

Officer Cooper pushed her back, and motioned for her to wait outside, then drew his pistol. He moved forward into the dim room. Kathleen ignored the implied instruction to remain outside. Her room was a mess. She drifted forward, almost unconsciously. As Cooper headed towards the bathroom, she started to call out a warning. She knew without a shadow of a doubt that someone was hiding in the closed closet. Speech failed her, but she made a strangled noise. He turned to look at her.

The turn placed his back to the closet at exactly the instant a ski-masked figure lunged out, something silver in its right hand. Before he could turn back, the assailant shoved the knife into the side of his throat.

Blood gushed from the wound, and Cooper staggered back, grabbing at his neck, his mouth making gasping motions. He stumbled over the mattress and fell partially on it, rolling onto the floor, still trying to hold his neck.

The metallic odor of blood filled the air. Kathleen inhaled, then shuddered as the scent overwhelmed her senses. She opened her mouth but couldn't scream. Her eyes flicked towards the still-open door. She started for it, but the attacker was too fast for her. A fist crashed home on her temple, and she lost consciousness before she struck the floor.

⸺◆⸺

She was aware that the overhead light was shining through her eyelids. It was bright, and she wondered why she'd gone to bed with it still on. Her head hurt. There was a small noise, and she suddenly understood that she was lying at an angle. Her feet were apparently off the edge of the bed.

She opened her eyes and then remembered. Wildly, she started to get up, but a strong hand roughly shoved her back down.

"Good, you're awake. You've got something I need. If you give it to me, you'll be okay. If not, well, I've got nothing better to do than to beat it out of you. Your choice," he said.

She shook her head to clear it. The masked man was squatting beside the mattress, and something about him looked familiar. She blinked, and then it was clear.

"Drew? Is that you? You killed the policeman," she said, then she realized that he'd also murdered the professor. "And Professor Mackleroy," she said, her voice rising.

He casually reached out and slapped her, his hand making a 'Crack' as it impacted her cheek. Her head snapped back against the mattress, and she groaned.

"Just you keep your mouth shut unless I tell you to talk," he said. "It's been a long haul. I'm tired of pretending to be a student, just so I can watch you. It wouldn't have been so bad if you'd been friendlier. Maybe you could have agreed to go out with me. It might have been fun, but, no, you were Miss Standoffish," he shook his head angrily.

"You were always too smart for your own good. Now you've recognized me. Too bad." He paused and then pulled off the ski mask.

He continued, "My employer needs that encryption key. Your computer is locked securely enough that it will take a lot of time and money to break into it. More time and money than you're worth, I think. Now, where is it?"

She tightened her lips unconsciously and shook her head in denial, then opened her mouth to scream. His palm cracked across her jaw and lips before she started. The impact slammed her mouth shut. She blinked tears out of her eyes and watched him but made no additional effort to call for help.

Drew abruptly stood up. "That's"you're not going to get you out of this. I'm not going to let you make enough noise to alert your neighbors, and I'm going to make you tell me."

He pulled off his jacket, throwing it on the overturned chair. Then he stretched and allowed his eyes to travel up and down her defenseless body. He slowly said, "I always thought you were attractive. Scarred and damaged, but kind of attractive. I'll bet you've never had a boyfriend. Right?"

She shook her head mutely.

His thoughts were ahead of her. "Well, we'll rectify that right now. Maybe you'll like it so much, you'll tell me where the key is, and I won't have to get violent." He laughed.

Kathleen was terrified. If she told him the key, he'd just kill her. She knew he'd killed two people, and he couldn't let her live. If she didn't tell him, he was going to rape her right now and then kill her later. Her mind filled with fear, dimming her normal thought processes.

He knelt beside her and pulled at the front of her pants. The zipper opened partly, and he stuck his hand inside. When it encountered the scarring, he yanked back in revulsion.

She had a momentary flash of hope. Maybe he'd give up.

"You're really scarred down there," he said. Then he shrugged, "I guess I'll just have to try and ignore it. It won't be too hard."

He snickered, "I mean, it won't be difficult." He stuck his hand back into her pants, shoving it downwards as he slid his other hand up under her sweatshirt towards her breasts. "Just you relax and have fun."

Her body reacted to the stress, and she was gasping for breath as her mind blanked in shock. This was happening.

Abruptly, she thought of her equations and Cramer's many-worlds theory. She retreated into herself, into her mind. Somehow there must be safety there. The room light flickered, and she sensed that reality was as she perceived it.

For a brief instant, she thought she saw herself standing behind Drew. *She was nude, her hair a mess, and blood was running from a cut across the top of her chest. She had an angry look on her face and held something in her hand.* The image disappeared, flickering out. Then she somehow changed her perception. She slipped into a sort of waking dream. There was an odd sense of deja vu as the room faded.

Now, she was walking in a forest. The trees were mostly evergreens, and it was cold, even colder than normal. There was danger somewhere nearby, and she was hurrying to find a refuge. From what she didn't know, but she sensed urgency. There was a sensation of large forms moving through the trees, but they were indistinct, and she couldn't make them out. They were dangerous, but not 'the danger. She kept walking. Then she saw a figure approaching. It was male, and she was strongly attracted. Some voice in the back of her mind warned her that men were dangerous and she was scarred and unattractive, but she was still attracted. The danger following her was nearer, and she found herself rushing towards the male figure. She envisioned it as a handsome and strong man, and he represented safety. Safety...Safety...

She was focused solely on her internal world. There were no physical sensations. Her time-travel equations suddenly came clear in her mind and stood out as if they were written in molten gold on a black velvet screen.

Possibility wave matched possibility wave from the past to the future. They combined to form a probability of +1 that her existence was present else-when. There was no transition period. She focused on being somewhere else, and it seemed in her dream-like state that she was.

Her consciousness was focused on her equations, so she did not immediately notice when her body's quantum energy wave snapped to another When, leaving no trace of her in her previous When. Her quantum wave function had instantly spread over the entire universe, and then the wave function popped with her perception that she was somewhere or 'somewhen' else.

When the quantum wave function popped, it instantly denied its existence to all other points in the universe, save where she was. She'd been everywhere and nowhere for an instant, but now she was somewhere again.

Her breathing slowed. What had happened? She hadn't noticed the room was so cold. It was dark. Had Drew turned off the light? Somewhere she had gathered the impression that sex acts were always in the dark, but no, he would have left the light on. Her eyes opened again. The mattress felt rough, and there was a light wind. The sky was clear, and she could see stars shining through the trees.

She exclaimed aloud, startled. She was somewhere else. Out in some woods somewhere. Had Drew raped and killed her, dumping her body where it was unlikely to be found? Had she survived his attempt to kill her? Had it all been a dream? Was she dead, and this was what the afterlife was like?

She felt her throat, her face – it was sore where she had been struck – and then her hands dropped to her pants. They were unzipped but still mostly in place. She lay back, exhausted. It was as if she'd been transported elsewhere right in the middle of his attack.

The stars were pretty. They'd watch over her. Maybe she was dead. If so, she was safe, and all of her problems were solved. Her mind drifted. Gradually, she fell asleep.

Chapter Five

Other When

There were some birds, maybe crows, making a lot of noise in a nearby tree. Kathleen moved a little. She was still half asleep. The crows continued, and then the events of the last night came crashing through into her consciousness. She sat bolt upright and looked around.

It was still cold, but the sun was overhead, and the long rays slanting through the trees warmed her enough so that she wasn't actually suffering. After all, I do live in Minnesota, and I'm used to cold, she thought.

She looked carefully towards the sun. From its position, it looked like springtime. It was certainly a lot farther north than it had been for the past several months.

The birds were bigger than crows. She saw one that had a patch of white on its breast and guessed that they were ravens. They were apparently excited about a hawk or owl that they'd found in a larger tree a few hundred yards away.

Whatever it was that was agitating them, they were having a regular party over it. She didn't like the continuous noise, so she pushed herself to her feet. Her scars were stiff from the cold and not sleeping in her own bed, and it took some effort to stand. She stretched as much as she felt she could and then started off towards the south, away from the racket.

The sun was shortening the shadows, and she thought it should be nearly noon. She was hungry, and there was nothing but woods. Mostly pines and spruces intermixed with some deciduous trees. She was struggling up a hill where the evergreens had thinned out, possibly due to an old fire or maybe the soil didn't have as many nutrients. It was rocky, and the footing was uneven. The process was made even more difficult by the thick bushes and alders that grew in patches. The brush was arranged in such a way that she could often walk around, but sometimes she had to push her way through.

She was hung up in one such patch, threading her way between the thickly growing alders, when she heard the howling of wolves. An icy bolt of fear tingled down her back. Wolves! She knew there were a few that were repopulating Minnesota, but they shouldn't be so far south and certainly nowhere near Minneapolis.

When she thought about the city, she became even more alarmed. Since she'd been walking, she'd heard no sounds that could be associated with humanity. There were no airplanes in the sky, and she heard no traffic noises. She'd assumed that she was in a park somewhere around the metro area, but now she was having doubts about that.

What if she'd been moved to the boundary waters area? Somewhere in the deep woods? Then there would be a definite chance of wolves and other animals, maybe even bears. She huddled down under an alder clump and wrapped her arms around her legs, resting her forehead on her knees. This was horrible. First, the professor was murdered, then she was a suspect who was likely to be kicked out of the department, then Drew wasn't a student at all. He was some kind of spy, and he'd been going to – Her thoughts failed her at the concept. She was unwilling to think about what might have happened.

She raised her head and looked around. *At least I'm alive and more or less unhurt,* she thought. Her cheek still was sore and probably had a bruise, but otherwise, she seemed to be okay. *Now, what am I going to do?*

She'd mostly been engaged in studying, but she had taken some time off to watch a few reality shows. She knew that she needed water and food and some kind of shelter. Also, some kind of weapon in case the wolves get close, she told herself. She started moving again, working her way quietly out of the alder thicket.

She was relieved to see that she'd reached the crest of the hill. There was a large boulder surrounded by alders, and she worked her way to the stone, scrambling up the low side so that she had an unobstructed view from the top.

It wasn't reassuring. There was no human sign anywhere. To the north, there was an indistinct gray line, many miles away. It looked kind of like mountains or cliffs, but she couldn't see it well enough to tell. To the east, she could see the Mississippi River or what she thought was the Mississippi. If it was, then she couldn't be in the boundary waters area. She had to be near Minneapolis somewhere.

She turned back towards the west. There was a large lake in the distance. She couldn't see it clearly, though – too many trees in the way. Finally, she looked to the south. There were more trees, although the valley at the base of the hill was open. There was mostly tall grass in the valley, and she looked hard, trying to reconcile what she saw with her knowledge of the world. She couldn't quite make herself believe that she was seeing what she thought was down there. She rubbed her eyes and looked again. They were still there. She was sure that she was looking at a group of ten or eleven large, hairy elephants. They had long, upwardly curving tusks that looked like those of mammoths. As she watched, they moved off towards the east. Their hindquarters were lower than their shoulders, and they were, she tentatively admitted, really mammoths. She was having trouble believing her eyes. She blinked a few times, but they were still there.

No sooner than she'd decided that's what they were than they confirmed the supposition. The lead cow raised her trunk and trumpeted. There was no mistaking the fact that these were close relatives of elephants. The trumpeting cow was giving a warning. A pack of large, wolf-like canines came trotting into the valley from the opposite side.

Kathleen froze in fear. They could easily get at her on the boulder. It wasn't steep enough to keep them from climbing up. She slowly squatted down and then lay flat with just enough of her head up to look down at the amazing scene.

The wolves were simply huge. They looked as large as motorcycles to Kathleen. They studiously ignored the mammoths and trotted on by the herd, heading towards the western end of the valley.

Kathleen wondered if they might be dire wolves. They certainly looked larger than the gray timber wolf she'd seen at the zoo. She shelved that question. It really made no difference. Either a dire wolf or a timber wolf could easily kill her. She needed a place of security and some kind of weapon fast.

As the dire wolves headed for the end of the valley, a small group of what looked like llamas or camels came out of a hidden depression and started off at high speed. The wolves instantly gave chase.

It was obvious that the camels weren't fast enough to avoid the predators for long. The little herd split up, and the members headed in different directions. The strategy worked for most of them, but the wolves pulled one down just as it was reaching the edge of the forest.

Kathleen watched in horror as the struggling beast was quickly gutted and almost instantly devoured. She wouldn't have a chance against those beasts. She buried her head in her arms so she wouldn't have to watch the end of the drama.

When she lifted it again, the wolves were gone, as were the mammoths. The sun was shining through the cool air, and birds were singing nearby.

She groaned and asked herself, What am I going to do? Where is this, or maybe when is this?

An image of Drew bending over her with his hand in her pants flashed across her mind, followed by the equations she'd been working on. Understanding dawned. She'd moved her quantum wave function and had re-materialized some time in the past. She looked at the Mississippi River for confirmation. The bends she could see weren't the same, but the huge lake over to the west might be Lake Minnetonka. Of course, there were many other lakes in the area. She could see three others from her hilltop, but that one was huge. She tentatively decided that's how she would identify it.

If she was between the river and the lake, buildings should surround her. None were visible; hence, she was either in the distant past or in some other, alternate universe. Her equations had largely ignored the many-worlds interpretation, but it could be right. After some thought about it, she decided to go with her own math. She was in the past, and it looked like what she'd read about the last ice age. The Pleistocene, she thought. So she wasn't too far back.

Of course, anything over a human life span would be remote. If she was right, she might be back eleven or twelve thousand years. If that was so, the gray shadow she saw to the north must be the last wall of glacier ice. It would definitely get cold in the winter, maybe far colder than she was used to.

She thought: *I'll need a house or a cabin. I think the Indians made bark shelters. I wonder how hard it could be. If I had a safe place, I would have time to work out a way to get back.*

She racked her brain, trying to regain the exact vision she had when she escaped Drew's murderous attack. It was right there on the edge of her consciousness, but she couldn't quite visualize it. Discomfort put an end to her efforts. Her rear hurt from the rock, disrupting her train of thought. She was far more likely to provide supper for some beast than to survive until it got colder.

Shuddering, she gathered her courage and climbed down from the rock. She'd head for the lake. It was more likely to provide resources such as waterfowl and fish. She thought she might be able to eat fish if she could figure out how to make a fire.

Fire! That was it. It would provide warmth and a degree of security. Wild animals wouldn't come near it.

As she walked, she tried to remember everything she knew about the period. On the south side of the hill, she stumbled upon a bed of wild strawberries. They were tiny and tart, but she avidly gathered as many as she could, stuffing them in her mouth until she had eased the edge of hunger. Then she picked more and stored them in her pockets for later.

———— ◦◦◦ ————

It was near dark, and she was wandering with no direction. She'd walked for what seemed like forever. She was exhausted and hungry again, having eaten all of her strawberries during the afternoon. Now she was walking along the edge of a clearing in the forest. She thought she might be nearing the big lake but wasn't sure.

A small group of deer started up before her, dashing along the verge of the grassland, just outside of the trees. They stopped and turned back to stare at her. They weren't even slightly alarmed at the sight of a human. *Probably aren't any humans around,* she thought.

There was a snarl, and the deer jumped wildly through the tall grass. She could see something chasing them, and then there was a bleat and a struggle as one was pulled down. There was an ambush set by two scimitar-toothed cats. One had started the deer, and the other had lain in hiding. Now the cats were snarling at each other over the carcass.

She stepped back, intending to move deeper into the trees, but her movement was sighted. Instantly, the smaller cat turned and came trotting her way. She jumped to the nearest tree, a medium birch, and began to climb. It was agony. Her muscles were sore, and she was exhausted from the walk. Her body almost refused her efforts to lift her legs from branch to branch.

The cat growled as it approached, and she increased her efforts, reaching a precarious perch high up in the slender branches. She wedged herself into a crotch and looked downward. The cat was spotted and had sloping hindquarters that made it look somewhat like an overly muscled hyena. The curved teeth were smaller than she'd expected but still significant. The creature would definitely be deadly if she met it on the ground.

The frustrated cat paced around the tree, looking up at her. Finally, it reared up on the trunk and scrambled up a few feet. Its claws weren't up to the job, and it slipped back down again. This seemed to increase its frustration because it roared. Another cat quickly echoed the sound. She looked again and saw that there were more than two of the creatures. There were now five huddled around the deer carcass, and three more were headed her way.

Each of the cats had to try its luck at climbing. One made it nearly twenty feet up but then crashed back down. It landed on its haunches, evidently hurting itself. It limped off towards the deer, leaving her to the attentions of the less successful climbers. They finally lay down near the tree as if they were prepared to wait until she fell out from starvation.

She rearranged her clothing and pulled up her hood. The predators watched her motions carefully but made no moves.

She was hungry and thirsty. Her rear hurt from her position in the crotch of the branches, and she didn't know if she could hang on in the tree all night.

The wind rose, making it colder as the sun fell. The tree swayed in the gusts, and she held on tightly. Finally, she pulled her arms out of the sleeves of her hoodie and tied the sleeves around the trunk. This provided some degree of stability.

She watched the stars rotate for a time and then dozed sporadically, jerking awake to check her position. It was a long night, and she felt nearly frozen by the time the sun showed signs of rising.

She couldn't see the cats, but then they may have moved into hiding, just waiting for her to come down. She waited until the sun was high enough so that she could see well. The cats had moved on during the night, apparently not having the patience to try and wait her out.

Why wait, she thought. *This land is full of game. They could probably find other prey easily and more quickly.*

⸎

Descending was another problem. She was stiff from cold and cramped from sitting on the narrow branches. It was a bad combination. She fell the last ten feet, landing in an awkward position that caused an intense ripping sensation from her scarred hips and legs. She caught a scream in her throat, biting her lip until it bled. The pain was incredible.

Carefully, she pulled down her pants to inspect the injury. The scarred tissue along the inside of her right thigh was torn and bleeding, though not copiously. There was already a large bruise forming across the scars and the undamaged skin near them. The left side was better, but not by much.

She leaned against the tree, seeking solace. There was none, so she gritted her teeth and started limping slowly towards the lake.

She moved cautiously, keeping to cover. She wasn't sure she could climb another tree, and it wouldn't do to be found by wolves or the long-toothed cats. She paused often and listened.

The bird songs reassured her, and she relaxed a little when she heard them. When they were silent, she retreated under spruce trees, ready to give climbing her best shot. In this way, she progressed mile after slow mile.

She had reached a more open spot in the woods. It wasn't a meadow. There were just fewer large trees there. A huge deciduous tree had fallen during the winter storms, leaving the smaller trees enough sunlight to thrive.

As Kathleen threaded her way through the smaller trees, she stumbled on a spot where there had been a fight-to-the-death. There were bloodstains on the ground and tufts of gray hair scattered around. She slowed and walked cautiously until she found the remains of two wolves. Both had been largely eaten, though what had killed them, she couldn't tell. There were tracks, but they were so blurred that she couldn't make out what kind of creature they'd come from, only that it was most probably huge in size.

She picked up a splintered thighbone. It was nearly as thick as a human femur, and the end was broken and sharp. She had begun talking to herself aloud and now said, "I can use this as a dagger. I can stab with the pointed end, and the joint makes a good handle." She paused, then shook her head. She marveled that her own voice made her feel more in control. She hadn't allowed herself to realize how frightened she actually was. Now that she was conscious of her fear, her hands trembled as she examined the bone.

The remaining joint was slippery and still covered with flesh, but she thought she could pick the flesh off and end up with a possible weapon. She turned and prepared to go but froze as she saw a pair of eyes watching her through a bush.

Kathleen gasped and pointed the broken bone at the creature. It disappeared momentarily and then reappeared under the other edge of the leaves. Its eyes were low to the ground, implying that it was not likely to be a major threat.

She knelt painfully and peered under the greenery. Obscured by the foliage was a partially hidden gray form that her mind gradually recognized as a wolf pup. The two dead wolves must have been its parents, and it was now on its own. She started to rise, intending to go on, but then it whined.

The sound was so pathetic that it pulled at her heartstrings. She held out her hand and made what she hoped were reassuring noises. The small creature, little more than a clumsy baby, whined again and backed away. Then hunger and the desire for companionship took over. It cautiously approached her.

By the next morning, the two were fully at ease with each other. They'd cuddled together under the roots of the fallen tree during the night-cold, and Kathleen had thoroughly enjoyed the shared body heat.

The warmth of the puppy seemed to help her stiffness, making her feel more flexible than usual. The fall had pulled the scars, tearing them. She hoped they would heal with more flexibility. Although motion was painful, she could walk without the pulling and sense of constriction for the first time that she could remember.

She spent some time in the early morning playing with the wolf pup. He was funny, bounding around clumsily, and she found herself unexpectedly laughing at his antics. The only problem was that both of them were hungry. At least she was. By extension, she suspected that he was starving, also.

They got lucky at a small stream. It was shallow and formed ice-covered pools with only a little free water. She found a bend in the stream where the water was a little deeper, forming a small hole. The ice was clear there, and she could see fish, which looked as though they were swimming under glass.

A stone was enough to smash the ice covering the pool. Then she used a spear-like stick she'd found to poke at the fish until one accidentally ended up on the jagged point.

Kathleen held the stick against the bottom and carefully reached into the frigid water. The fish was large and fat. She didn't know what kind it was, but it was food.

Cutting it up was difficult and messy since all she had was a jagged piece of stone, but it sufficed. After a brief hesitation, while she rationalized: People eat sashimi all the time; this is just the same and gagged down a few bites. Then hunger took over, and she found herself practically gobbling the rest of the fish.

The wolf puppy whined, and she guiltily dropped the fish carcass. He didn't seem to mind that it was mostly devoured. He jumped on it and finished it off, bones and all, in just a few bites.

This experience heartened her, and she worked until she caught three more fish, though none was so large as the first. She ate one, and the pup ate the other two. Then, bellies bulging, they found a sunny hillside and took a nap.

It was nearly dark when they awoke, and she was instantly desperate to find shelter. After casting about, the two found a large hollow tree. The hole in the trunk was so small that she had to worm her way inside, but once she did, there was enough room for the two of them to curl up.

There was another hole about twenty feet over her head. Looking up in the gathering darkness, she could see the outraged glare of an owl that probably regarded the tree as his exclusive property. The large bird quickly became convinced that they weren't leaving and flew off without a sound, gliding on muffled wings over the forest.

The two cuddled up and fell asleep. Before she nodded off, Kathleen reflected that things weren't so bad. She had shelter, a friend, and she'd managed to get some desperately needed protein. Maybe survival was possible after all.

Chapter Six

Smilodon

The wolf puppy was an early riser. He was content to sleep, curled up with her until the air smelled of morning, but then he felt that the day was wasting. He stretched and cautiously poked his nose out of the hole. Naturally housebroken, he slipped through the opening.

Kathleen could hear him snuffling around the tree, and then there was a trickling sound, followed by scratching as he kicked dirt over the spot. She smiled quietly. She felt a strong attachment to the young creature. She hadn't known what a difference having a companion could make in her attitude.

The pup came back inside and sniffed at her face, then momentarily closed his jaws on her hand. In return, she gently grasped his face in both hands and ruffled his ears with her fingers. He sighed, then made a 'chuffing' sound, pushing closer to her.

The drawstrings of her hoodie brushed against him, and he mock-attacked them, jumping up and snapping at the strings. He caught one and pulled, shaking his head. She laughed and caught at his leg. He jumped back and then danced forward, burying his small teeth in her sleeve. This wasn't a good idea, as she had no replacement clothing, so she caught him and pulled him close. He wiggled and tried to get free but then grabbed her drawstring again when it brushed his face.

When the sun was above the trees, the two were well away from their resting place, headed towards the big lake. Kathleen was fairly sure she knew where it was, even though she was deep in the spruce forest. They walked quickly, and she was pleased to find that her walking was limp-free. The torn scars still hurt, but not as much as she'd thought they would.

They were passing a cluster of large boulders when a great, tawny cat with long, curved fangs sighted them. It was some distance away when she saw it. She instantly recognized it as a saber-toothed tiger. She even knew the Latin name: Smilodon.

She gasped as it snarled and headed directly towards the two of them. It was in no hurry to reach her, and it seemed sure that she was trapped.

She looked at the boulders. They were too low to be of much help. There were some holes under them where they rested on each other, but none big enough to save her. Fortunately, there was a convenient spruce tree. She broke all records climbing its not-very-welcoming boughs.

Seeing her receding out of reach, the Smilodon snarled with a sound like a sheet of steel being ripped in half, then trotted forward. It was distracted by the wolf puppy before it reached the tree.

Accepting Kathleen as its pack, the puppy was fully prepared to give its life defending her. During the time they'd been together, its coordination had improved, and it now charged at the great cat, stopping when it got close with a growl. The tiger pounced at the puppy, but he dashed to the side before it could reach him. As the cat pounced, Kathleen saw that it was stiff on the left side. It had been injured and apparently was not the threat it might have been.

The puppy continued its darting attacks, even going so far as to nip at the tiger's haunch in an unguarded moment. It roared horribly in response and intensified its efforts to capture its small tormentor. Kathleen was sure that the pup would be killed. It was gradually being forced towards the boulder pile, and she was afraid that the cat would pin her friend against the stones where his motion would be restricted so that he could not evade its charge.

At the last minute, the wolf pup, obviously figuring that discretion was the better part of valor, ducked into a deep hole between two massive stones.

The tiger snarled and scrabbled as far as it could reach into the hole, but the pup was safe. The cat continued to dig for a few moments and then suddenly remembered Kathleen.

The next few minutes were terrifying. She clung to the swaying tree as the tiger attempted to reach her. Due to its injury, it couldn't climb well enough to get her, but the tree wasn't large, and she was only a couple of feet over its best jump. She was sure that it would eventually manage to jump high enough to reach her.

It paced back and forth, snarling and then pausing to rear against the boughs. Finally, it leaped up onto some of the lower branches. She bit off a scream as it did, thinking her time had come, but the spruce boughs bent, and the cat slid back to the ground.

At that moment, she caught sight of a buckskin-clad man approaching. He was carefully keeping a screen of trees between himself and the tiger while he readied some form of spear.

She watched as he raised his face to hers. Their eyes met, and she felt almost an electric shock. He was blond-headed with a short blond beard, and she thought he was quite handsome in a primitive fashion.

His eyes widened as he took in her face. Then the next minute, he was moving forward again, all concentration and totally focused on the saber-tooth.

Kathleen clung to the tree and helplessly watched the life and death action develop, her heart beating so hard that it seemed it would come through the wall of her chest.

Chapter Seven

Cadeyrin: Travel Alone

He expected himself to be completely self-reliant and unemotional. He was successful in the first. As for unemotional, he was still working at that.

He knew almost all of the elements of his world, all of the animals, all of the hunting techniques, how to survive in the cold wilderness. But this place south of the ice was a different land he'd come to. There were possibilities that he might not know about. Things that he might not know how to fight. There were certainly enemies who wouldn't hesitate to try to kill him.

He paused just below the crest of the hill he'd been climbing. He carefully lowered himself and gradually worked his way through the dried grasses. The chill wind from the north passed over the crest of the hill, causing repeated waves in the grass and carrying scents from below to his sensitive nostrils. Cadeyrin didn't have as good a sense of smell as the animals he hunted, but he was able to detect scents that a modern human would have missed entirely.

There was a rock at the crest, and he slowly moved near it until he could survey the far hillside and valley without allowing his profile to be easily seen. Other humans in this wilderness would be more likely to be enemies than friendly.

Three warm seasons ago, he'd briefly had a mate, a girl from one of the few other tribes of his people that they had met. She hadn't survived long. A saber-tooth took her within two months of their union. They had barely begun to know one another when she died, but he still dreamed about her. He was always sad afterward. Now there was no one that he was close to.

On the other hand, he had been training with the tribe's Shaman and believed in fate. He had half a mind that his present isolation was a gift from the All-Spirit. The tribe sometimes engaged in vision quests, and that led Cadeyrin to hope that he would find some form of spiritual enlightenment in his travels.

Cadeyrin knew he couldn't hope to hold out against his worst enemy: other men. As a result, he'd become scrupulously careful in his daily life: only hunting smaller game, traveling carefully and circumspectly, and taking the extra time to fully assure himself that he was truly alone before moving.

The sun was warm, and what little breeze there was served to bring scents to him. He relaxed, stretching out on the ground. His mind drifted again. He'd moved many miles westward since the day he'd lost his tribe. His thoughts were tinged with guilt and regret as he followed the memory path.

———◆———

It had been months ago, during the early days of the previous spring. The weather had been cold, and the tribe's hunters hadn't brought in any fresh meat for several days. The game seemingly had vanished from the prairie.

The only thing they'd seen had been a few flights of ducks heading northward towards the great ice wall. The normal herds of large animals weren't to be found. Neither ulfalda (camels) nor viosana (bison) were feeding, although the snows had begun to melt off, and the grass was starting to grow again. The only blessing was that, with the absence of large game, there were few predators other than the smaller cats that tended to stay close to their territory. They were no threat, preferring to hunt small game rather than men.

The tribe had approached a deep glacial cut that was filled with dense conifers. They'd seen it from some miles away and had been steadily walking towards the arm of the spruce forest that extended from the end of the valley.

Once they reached the shelter of the trees, they'd scouted along the margins of the woods, looking for game signs. They'd been in luck. There was a game track.

Cadeyrin knew what it was as soon as he saw it. It had been made by a solitary norsii (mastodon). These large beasts were not like the more common mammoths. They did not travel in herds but were more likely to be found in small groups or alone.

This was a large bull from the size of the track. The bulls had a way of moving from one feeding ground to another in a cyclical pattern, only coming together with others of their kind during musth, their breeding season. Then they became violent and dangerous to hunt. The musth-ridden male would even attack females of its own kind if frustrated by not finding one ready to mate.

Directly down the trail, an innocent spruce tree was shattered, the white wood of the trunk splintered and trampled into the soft ground. The scent of musth blended with the aromatic spruce aroma. The hunters paused and glanced at each other. It would be dangerous to proceed. After a moment, Cadeyrin's father nodded his head, his gray-streaked, reddish-brown beard bobbing in the shadows.

That was it, then. The tribe needed meat, and the bull, dangerous though it may be, was meat. They'd try to get it. They would be cautious as they approached. With luck, they might be able to find a safe ambush location.

The hunters returned to the main body of the tribe, and the group separated into two. The women and children remained near the edge of the forest, setting up a temporary camp as the hunters trailed the bull. Two men remained behind to watch over the weaker members of the tribe. One was the fire-starter, and the other was the old Shaman. Neither was young enough to hunt, though they could still fight to defend the women and children.

Cadeyrin followed his father into the dense trees. The mastodon wasn't close, but they could tell by its scent on the ground and the dung heaps they found that it wasn't too far ahead. With luck, they'd find it near a water hole with limited access. If it couldn't get away easily, it might be possible to ambush.

After trailing the beast for an hour, the men were able to hear the sounds of its stomach rumbling. Like modern elephants, the mastodon wasn't silent. It was so large that predators would stay clear. Man was the only threat, and man wasn't common in this primal wilderness just south of the giant glacial walls.

Like shadows, the hunters slipped into the surrounding trees, moving cautiously to surround the bull. It wasn't visible until they got close. The wind had died, and scent wasn't working for or against them. The heavy spruce masked their human odor, and the bull didn't take alarm prematurely.

The black bulk of the animal loomed suddenly through the smaller trees. It was located in a small clearing fronting a pond. The trees were broken and damaged from its feeding, but now it was approaching the pond to drink. The hunters watched as the huge bull, well over twelve thousand pounds in weight, waded into the water. The pond bottom was soft, and the animal's legs sank deeply into the muck as it sucked up water with its trunk, its red, piggish eyes alertly glancing around.

This was about as good as it was going to get. The mastodon was facing into the water and might be slow getting free of the deep mud. Cadeyrin's father raised his hand slowly. When he dropped it, a flurry of spears, launched from the atl-atls of the hunters, shot through the trees and buried themselves in the mastodon. The shafts dropped free, leaving the fore-shaft with its bound-on, fluted point sticking in the animal.

The bull shrieked and bellowed as it plunged forward and then turned towards the bank. The muck didn't slow it much, and it was out on the shore almost immediately, trunk questing the air and reaching to feel the short fore-shafts where they stuck out of its hide.

It looked as if two or three of the shafts were in vital spots. One, in particular, was in the throat, and a gush of blood was pouring out of the wound. That would be fatal, eventually. The bull charged straight forward through the trees, mowing them down as if they were blades of grass.

His path led him directly towards Cadeyrin's father, who ducked to one side but not quickly enough. The bull's red eye focused on the hunter, and the trunk swept in a lightning-fast blow, sending the man flying. Another few steps and one of the younger hunters jumped and ran from behind a small spruce. By now, the bull had decided that the men were to blame for its pain, and it altered its course as quickly as a cat to run the boy down, pausing to crush him into the ground with its head. He screamed once and then was still.

The other hunters had retreated quickly as the bull moved, and they now began to gather by the water. They would trail the animal until it stopped moving and then circle in for the kill. It would be weak from blood loss by that point and largely unable to fight. This part was routine. They'd done it many times before.

Cadeyrin knelt down by his father. The trunk had struck hard. He lifted his father's body, holding it close. A trickle of blood ran from the mouth, but that was all. The older man had died almost immediately.

Despite being used to deaths, for the tribe lost many men to such hunting accidents, Cadeyrin was in shock. His father had always been there and was the mainstay of his life. He looked over his shoulder at the others and said, "We must inter him in a tree; otherwise, his spirit might be trapped here by the water."

Bear-Son answered, "We'll need to go back and get the Shaman for the rite. We'll also inter Cricket; the bull crushed him into the ground."

Cadeyrin nodded numbly. He carefully closed his father's eyes and took most of the spear points out of the older man's shoulder pouch. They'd leave one in the pouch for his father's journey to the celestial hunting grounds, but the points were valuable and could be reused. They shouldn't be wasted. Belief was one thing, but the practical requirements of survival were another.

Some of the men set off to follow the bull. It could still be heard crashing through the trees towards the west. The others set off to return to the tribe and bring them back for the rite before moving on to the kill site.

Cadeyrin sat back on his haunches and waited. He'd guard the bodies until the tribe returned.

He sat there, thinking about his father. Without realizing it, he began chanting softly, first wordlessly and then adding words requesting the All Spirit's guidance for his father's journey. He chanted for a time but then suddenly stopped. He'd heard something. It was muffled by the thick spruce, but it had come from the area where they left the women and children.

He stood to listen better and then heard Bear-Son's war cry. There was something attacking the tribe. He glanced once at his father's body and then dashed down the track, readying his spear for battle. He reached into his pouch as he ran and came up with a second fore-shaft with an attached point. The blade and shaft made a serviceable and very sharp knife.

When he got close to the edge of the trees, he could hear the sound of fighting, but it was dying down. He veered off the trail to the right and sneaked through a heavy copse of trees until he could see.

The tribe had been attacked by a group of the enemy. These were darker-complected men with long black hair and scraggly beards. He knew these people; they had fought before over hunting grounds as his tribe migrated from the drylands to the east.

They used more primitive weapons than Cadeyrin's carefully shaped flint points. Their spears were tipped with bone lined with tiny blades of sharp obsidian or chert. The weapons were ones that Cadeyrin looked down on, but they were effective enough. These men were fierce fighters with no mercy. He could see that they were systematically killing the male children while the women were wailing as they were being led off towards the south.

The small group of hunters had run into an overwhelming force, and all were dead. Cadeyrin paused, not sure what he could do. His father had been his only surviving relative, and he had no other direct blood ties. If he had, he would have attacked regardless of the odds.

He thought about trying to free the women and girls, but there were at least fifty men dragging them away. Too many to handle. Then he thought about the other hunters who were following the bull. He retreated into the thick copse and headed back parallel to the trail. He checked the bull's trail periodically and quickly saw that it was dying and wouldn't travel too far before it gave out.

Finally, he got close enough to the dead bull's location to be able to hear sporadic talking. A little closer and he was able to tell that it was not his language. He sneaked off to the north and cut back through a particularly thick area of forest until he could see that there was a group of the enemy cutting up the dead mastodon. There was no sign of his friends. He didn't know if they had been ambushed and killed or had detected the enemy and had skulked off in another direction.

As he watched, a sudden gust of wind stirred the trees and blew his scent towards the kill site. One of the warriors stood up and made an exclamation. The others grabbed their weapons and spread out, facing his location. He'd been detected.

Cadeyrin instantly retreated. He was silent as he moved quickly through the trees. After several hundred yards, he found a stream and waded down it to break his trail. There was a large deciduous tree with a vine hanging from it that he used to climb out of the water and onto some rocks. From there, he ran westward, ever deeper into the spruce forest. He was sure the enemy would trail him, but if he kept moving, they probably wouldn't catch up. The necessity of puzzling out his trail would slow them enough so that he could continue to increase his lead.

⸺ ❧ ⸺

He'd never seen any of the hunters of his tribe again, and now it was many moons later. He'd lost the enemy trackers. They'd given up after following him for a few days. He no longer worried about them. It seemed unlikely that they would follow so far or so long for only one man.

Now he was in a new territory, one where the glaciers were nearby, a land of many lakes and streams bounded on the north by a massive wall of ice. He'd crossed one mighty river, full of ice melt. It was wide and cold, too cold to swim. He'd been forced to make a small log raft for the crossing. Once he'd crossed, he traveled slowly for a couple of days, arriving at his present location just this morning.

⸺ ❧ ⸺

He jerked his head slightly and peered around the hilltop. There was nothing there. He'd been completely asleep, something that he rarely did, but the sun's warmth and the relative safety had relaxed him. He ran his hand over his face in an effort to clear his mind. As he did, he noticed that his beard was getting too long again.

In the interest of cleanliness, he kept it trimmed short. It was less likely to carry food odors, and trimming it also made it harder for various parasites to bother him. He glanced around again. Still nothing. His hand dug in his pouch and pulled out a leather-wrapped object. He carefully pulled the leather open and folded it back to expose a sharp obsidian blade. It took a while, but by carefully holding sections of his beard tight and slicing through the hair with the blade, he completed the job. He was meticulous with the task and ended up with a neatly trimmed beard. Finishing, he re-wrapped the blade and stowed it away.

Now it was time to move down to the sloughs and hunt. He needed meat. He'd eaten his last jerky two days ago, and his stomach was letting him know that it didn't appreciate the lack of food. As he moved down the hillside, he gathered some seeds and chewed on them. They were dry, but anything was welcome at this point.

Two days later, he'd scouted the area thoroughly and was settling in for a lengthy stay. There was plenty of deer in the brakes and sloughs, rabbits galore, and other small game. He'd only found the tracks of a lone panther, and it seemed to be ranging more to the west. It would eat a deer every other day or so, but as long as it kept out of his area, the local deer would feel more secure. He'd move off to the east to hunt and leave the animals in the immediate vicinity alone until he really needed them.

There was a nice campsite near the large lake. The lake was a wonder of finger-like coves interspersed with broad stretches of open water. It was full of fish and also offered him the chance at waterfowl. Best of all, there was no sign of other humans, and he was minded to stay through the last part of the winter. More snows might yet come, if they came at all.

The climate south of the glacial wall was cold but extremely dry. Most of the water was bound up in the glaciers, and it didn't snow much during the winter. In contrast, the land that he'd come from had been subject to deep winter snows until recently. Then it had become much colder and drier.

He remembered that when he was a child, there had been a bright flash in the night sky. Days later, word had come from a tribe to the north that there had been a huge flood. A river had suddenly flooded and now over-flowed with icy cold water. It emptied into the sea and had driven all of the fish and waterfowl away. The massive influx of cold water seemed to have impacted the weather. There were huge dust storms that killed vegetation and drove off the game. The bad weather extended into his tribe's lands, and they were forced to travel west following the game animals.

It had been difficult to survive. The weather was much colder, and the game was sparse as a result. Some of his tribe had died, smothered in the intermittent dust storms. They had finally reached the forested land where the fatal mastodon hunt had occurred. That was an unfortunate location, and reaching it had doomed his tribe.

It seemed that the bad weather had followed him as he traveled westward to escape the enemy. The climate had changed, and even the summers were chill with little rain. The dryness impacted the grass. Once prolific, it was sparse and slow-growing. This meant that the large herds of bison and camels had gone elsewhere. It was rare to see the land covered with large grazing beasts. Even the mammoths were less prevalent.

On the other hand, twig and acorn eaters like deer were fairly plentiful. That suited him perfectly. Fewer herds meant fewer predators like dire wolves and saber-tooth tigers to watch out for. Of course, there were still smaller cats, gray wolves, and possibly short-faced bears. Those latter were to be avoided at all costs. They were huge and would attack anything they encountered if they were hungry, and they always seemed to be hungry.

Cadeyrin settled into his campsite and daily routine. There were no other humans around, and he felt safe lighting a fire at night. It provided warmth and protection from any wandering predators. The fire allowed him to cook and to dry jerky. The only worry was that there was no suitable rock nearby to work into spear points. He'd carried a couple of cores in his pouch, but the necessity of knapping points had reduced them to unusable pieces of stone. However, he still had sixteen good points plus the two that he kept bound to the tapered fore-shafts.

There was a slough full of slim saplings that were acceptable as spear shafts, and he had carefully fabricated two additional shafts as back-ups. These were as long as his outspread arms, with a slight indentation on the butt that fitted the hooked end of his atl-atl. The other end had a socket that accepted the tapered butt of the fore-shaft that carried the partially fluted flint point, carefully bound on with sinew. He knew and trusted this weapon system. It could bring down almost any beast if the hunter's skill was adequate.

The day had been overcast and warmer, but the clouds were blowing off in a chill wind, leaving a few stars peeking out far above. He sat drowsing beside the fire, his mind far away. In the distance, a wolf howled, but he didn't move. It was only letting the remainder of its pack know where it was. Thirst eventually caused him to stir. He stood and stretched, gathering his atl-atl and spear. A drink would be good.

Chapter Eight

A Spiritual Journey

Cadeyrin paused at the edge of the firelight, searching the breeze for any sign of life. There was nothing there. He felt confident that he could walk down to the lake, drink, and return safely. Pausing a moment longer to make sure, he inhaled deeply of the night. The wind was cool, verging on cold, and it blew through his unconstrained, blondish hair, ruffling across his head like a lover's caress as he set off to the distant inlet.

Returning from the water, he struck on an idea. He needed spiritual guidance. The tribe's Shaman had selected him as the one who was most likely to become his successor, and he'd had some training in the ways of the spirits. However, he had mostly found it boring and secretly had determined that he would not step forward when it came time to take over. Still, the thought of gaining spiritual insight was attractive to him. The loneliness was wearing at him, and he felt that a helpful spirit would be more than welcome.

The chill wind was blowing from the north. The stars were burning brightly in the sky, but the moon was not visible. As he walked, he became aware of some presence in the wind and grass surrounding him. At first, he thought it might be an animal, but then he knew that it was spiritual energy he sensed.

He diverted from his path, searching for an appropriate stone. When he found it, he placed all of his problems underneath, carefully laying the stone down to trap them in place and hold them until later.

Next, he opened a sacred space by facing the four cardinal points and softly calling for help from the spirits of each direction. "Help me. Give me guidance, oh swift Arna, fearsome Piskata, mighty Norsa, and fierce Esbern."

Once he was sure that the space was free of unwanted spirits that might interfere with his quest, he asked for guidance from his personal animal spirit: the ulfa. He was sure that it was favorably disposed towards him and had the power and expertise to ensure that he received valuable advice. He paused and looked around. He was standing in a bare space covered with short grass and packed earth. The grasses around the area had not yet started growing in the cold spring weather, and there was no place for any carnivore to conceal itself.

He felt connected to the spirit world through the north wind at the moment and didn't want to move, but he knew he couldn't stay where he was. It wasn't safe. He needed to return to the fire.

Cadeyrin tentatively started off towards the flickering light along an old bison path worn in the prairie grass. After a few steps, he became aware that a friendly animal spirit was leading him.

Wolves suddenly howled in the near distance. The eerie sound led him to recognize his guide as his personal wolf spirit.

Together he and the spirit walked through the grass until they came to a rise, which they ascended. On the other side was the open space with his fire in the middle. It had burned down in his absence and was guttering, sending out flickers of flame as the wind ignited gasses rising from the coals. As he stepped into the open space, he sensed other spiritual entities around the area, but none intruded on his immediate consciousness.

The wolves came closer as he built up the fire, but he felt no threat from them. It was as if they were just curious about his presence and waiting to see what would happen. The flames grew high, and his spirit guide took on a feeling of wildness mixed with joy. He followed it as it led him on a triple circuit around the fire. The flames shot out sparks, and a larger burst of flame ascended. At that moment, his companion shifted into a huge wolf-like figure. Together they raised their heads and howled upwards, and then he was following the spirit guide, traveling through the sky, far away from the fire circle.

His sense of being accompanied faded, and he ended up in a high location, as if on the peak of an immense mountain. As he looked down, he could see through both time and space. He could see his childhood: his father teaching him to hunt, one of the old women teaching him about medicinal plants, and the tribe's path across the plains as they came from the east. He could see their excitement as they encountered herds of bison, and he felt the fullness and satiety after a successful hunt. He could see the attackers as they killed his people while he watched, hidden. He saw his path to this current place. He saw himself by his fire and then he could see his path winding into the future. He traveled towards a forest, then back, then a figure appeared, but it was unclear and hazy. He followed it, and it receded into the future. He paused, and it came back. He felt that somehow it gave him a sense of completeness and he yearned for more of that feeling.

Now the sky was glowing, and he sensed the Earth's spirit as a whole. All of the life on the planet and the planet itself were vibrating, making a chorus of musical notes reminding him of an immense flock of singing birds. The figure came close, seemingly drawn by the music, and he felt happy that it was near.

He saw that the figure was aware of his observation. He prayed to it, chanting "Please forgive me for my errors. Guide me to a place where I can find someone to help me. Thank you."

He chanted the prayer repeatedly. After a few repetitions, he received a sense of acceptance in return that made the prayer seem holy and meaningful.

Then the world around him faded out, and he somehow moved higher, instantly receding to a distance where he was able to sense the entire range of sounds played by the Sun. The Sun was radiating a huge band of energy in a harmonic of hundreds of sounds covering all of the land and all of its life. He repeated his prayer to the Sun and received a sense of acceptance and belonging. His body seemed to be shaking with a rapid vibration, and as he prayed, the vibrations increased smoothly.

He was hovering in space, and he became aware that he had expanded in size. Now he was immense, covering all of the stars. He repeated his prayer-chant and saw a vision of a vast, immense consciousness rolling like a gently moving sea underlying everything he was seeing. It was aware of every single musical note that was being sung by everything simultaneously. All of the information that existed everywhere was instantly available to it, but the flow of information was too vast for him to comprehend. He became aware all that he had previously known was on the Earth, but that was just one tiny section of the entire chorus.

He bowed his head and humbly asked for assistance and understanding. The knowledge came to him then, that, although he was just one tiny portion of the music, his notes were important to the entire tapestry of sound. Again he chanted his prayer and received acceptance. He felt that the spirit he'd seen was approaching, and he was glad.

It gradually dawned on him that it was time to move back down to his camp. He slowly began the return as the vision faded. He was suddenly at the level of the flames of his fire.

The spirit figure was absent, but his guiding wolf spirit bounded up with a joyful greeting. It led him around the flames in a counter direction for three circuits, and then disappeared, leaving him alone on the prairie, standing by his fire and facing east.

Cadeyrin passed his hand over his face in amazement and then cautiously checked the wind. There had been wolves nearby. He was sure of it and could smell their presence, but it was fading now. They'd gone, and he was alone.

He sat facing the flames and wondered at what he'd experienced. He remembered the holy one of his tribe, the Shaman, explaining about the spirit world and how it might be visited.

After contemplating the experience, he concluded that his life had been pointing to this event. He was becoming a Shaman in his own right. It seemed good, but it was a hard path. If only it wasn't so painful. He'd lost everyone he loved, and he was alone. The loneliness hurt more than any physical injury.

For a moment, he wasn't sure being a Shaman was worth the pain and trouble, but then he remembered the spirit figure he'd met. He was sure it was coming to him. He resolved to begin his search for it as soon as the sun had returned to the sky. Meanwhile, it was still, with no predators around. The wind had dropped to a gentle breeze, and he relaxed, drowsing in front of the guttering fire.

The night had fled, and the dew was on the grass. Cadeyrin kicked the fire to life and heated a small cut of deer back-strap from the previous day's kill. The meat was tender and lacked only salt for it to be a true feast. He ate, distractedly, wondering which way he should go. The guidance he'd received had been clear. The signs indicated that someone or something was coming towards him. He needed to meet them to ensure the best outcome.

He'd puzzled over the meaning of the vision for most of the night and had finally come to the conclusion that the current campsite would have to be abandoned in the interest of fulfilling the oncoming event. He hoped that the person who was heading his way would be friendly. The vision had been overwhelmingly positive, and he assumed that the person would mean well and have a good impact on his life. Even so, he would be cautious. Meetings with strangers in his experience were fraught with hazard.

He covered the fire, and after some false starts, decided that heading back towards the east felt the best. He believed thoroughly in the idea that spirit visions told the truth, but he also knew that his actions could impact the way the vision played out. For this reason, he tried stepping out in each of the four directions and then waiting to see which felt the best. East was it.

Chapter Nine

An Expected Meeting

Cadeyrin walked carefully along the edge of the spruce forest just inside the verge. He'd picked his position carefully with the intent of concealing his presence from any potential observer hidden in the prairie grass to the south.

It was nearly midday; the sun was as close to the zenith as it was going to get. He checked his environment. There was nothing that he could sense. After looking around a second time, just to make sure, he sat under the shade of a spruce and ate some jerky.

There was no sense in killing himself on this journey. He had no definite location that he was heading for and no definite time that he had to be there. He was simply sure that he was heading in the right direction, and in the fullness of time, he'd meet whomever he was supposed to meet. From that point, the vision had been indistinct, except that he was left with the impression that his situation would change radically. He hoped that it would be for the better. This single life had been fine – for a while. He'd long ago reached the point where he wanted companionship.

After he ate, he headed east again. A short time later, he paused. A growling sound could be heard in the near distance. As he listened, it came again, and this time he was able to identify it as a saber-tooth cat. It sounded frustrated and angry.

He readied his spears and proceeded, moving from tree to tree, keeping in cover and near the trunks. The big cats were heavily muscled and stocky. They could run short distances but wore out over the long haul. Their claws were made for grasping their prey, but their muscles weren't arranged well for tree climbing. Cadeyrin hoped that if worst came to worst, he could avoid the cat by climbing a tree.

The saber-tooths were deadly and difficult to kill. Even if attacked by a group of hunters, one or more men were more than likely to be injured or killed before the predator was vanquished. Their coats were highly valued among his people as a result, despite not being very durable.

The cat continued to growl, and then he heard a human cry. He broke into a full-out run, still keeping close to the trees. There was a low rise in the land, and as he crested the top, he could see a lone spruce tree that was located several yards out into the prairie standing by itself. There was a woman clinging to the trunk a little over halfway up. He halted.

The tree was swaying violently, and the woman screamed again, closely followed by the tiger's growl. As he watched, the cat dropped off the lower limbs on the far side. It had been trying unsuccessfully to climb high enough to reach its intended prey. He caught momentary glimpses of its dappled brown and yellow coat as it moved around, trying to figure out how to reach the woman.

He glanced up at her. She was mostly hidden in the thick spruce boughs, but he saw her face, her eyes wide with fear. She was looking directly at him and shaking her head back and forth. He recognized the gesture. It was the same his people used, and it meant, "No." He grimaced as he understood that she was trying to protect him from the cat.

Cadeyrin readied his atl-atl and spear. The cat was staring fixedly at the woman, sitting a few feet back from the far side of the tree. It stood and paced around the trunk. As it presented its side to him, he stepped forward and cast his spear with all his force.

The shaft flew true and struck the cat in the ribs, though it was a little too far back to be instantly fatal. The tiger reared on its hind legs and clawed the air, falling over sideways and snapping at the spear shaft, which had fallen to the ground. The fore-shaft was embedded in the cat's ribs with only the last inch or so sticking out.

The cat bit through the detached main spear shaft with a snap, and then the enraged animal turned its head and tried to reach the fore-shaft. It was unsuccessful, not having the flexibility in its stocky body. Failing that, it roared at the woman as if she were its attacker.

Cadeyrin had reloaded his atl-atl with his second and last spear shaft, having left the back-ups at his old camp in the interest of traveling quickly. He had retreated behind the edge of the spruce tree after he launched his first spear, and the tiger hadn't seen him as yet. The cat reared again and roared, echoed by the woman's cry of fright.

As it reared up, he threw the second spear directly at the spot between its shoulder blades. The spear struck slightly to one side, bypassing the spinal cord and driving deep into the chest cavity. The cat spun, slashing with its claws at whatever had attacked it from behind. It suddenly saw Cadeyrin and instantly sprinted in his direction.

He drew his last fore-shaft, holding it as a man would hold a knife to stab downward. The atl-atl, though light and flexible, could be used to thrust into the cat's mouth as a distraction. Cadeyrin braced himself for the impact, intending to jam the atl-atl into the tiger's mouth and spin away to the left. He hoped that would give him a chance to bring the spear-point into play.

The tiger faltered as it closed in. Its front legs collapsed, and it rolled head-over-heels. As it somersaulted forward, Cadeyrin leaped in and stabbed at its throat. The point penetrated but missed the vital areas. He jumped back as the tiger swiped at him with its right paw, then circled as the cat snarled at him. It tried but was unable to regain its feet. Backing up, he waited as the fighting light faded from its eyes. It drew a ragged breath and expired.

Cadeyrin stepped forward and prodded the cat in the stomach with his spear-point. There was no reaction; it was truly dead. He noted that both of its saber-like incisors were broken. It was an older male that had most likely been driven away from its pride.

He paused to open his senses to the environment. The saber-toothed cats almost always hunted in groups. This allowed them to more easily bring down the large prey animals that were their primary targets.

He scented the wind and listened carefully. There was nothing save a faint odor of frightened woman mixed with an unusual scent that he'd never smelled before. It was coming from her vicinity, though, so he ignored it for the moment. He listened again and heard a faint whining noise. He moved towards the tree, wondering what it was, and then saw a wolf puppy tumble out of a hole under some rocks. The puppy shook itself and trotted towards the tree. He lifted his knife in preparation, but the woman said something he couldn't understand, though it sounded like an agitated warning.

He relaxed. The puppy was no threat. It was too small. Then he turned to the tree and raised his eyes to meet those of the woman. He wasn't able to see all of her, but what he could see made him pause. She was beautiful! More so than any of the tribal women he'd ever seen. Fine features and long, beautiful hair graced a slightly scarred face that regarded him with trepidation.

He stepped forward and held up his hand in greeting, "Hello. You are safe now. My name is 'Cadeyrin'."

She looked puzzled and replied in a melodious voice, speaking a series of sounds that he could barely recognize as language.

He smiled to reassure her and motioned for her to climb down. She shook her head back and forth. They might not have spoken the same language, but he recognized her refusal. He motioned again. When she still refused, he shrugged and walked over to the tiger's body.

He deliberately turned his back on her and began to skin the animal. He didn't need the meat, and it would probably be stringy and unappetizing; the beast was obviously old and far past its prime. However, the skin was still valuable. The fur was thick and would provide protection against the cold.

His first spear point pulled free easily. He inspected it for damage, but it had done its job without striking bone. The long, fluted point was intact, and the binding that held it to the short, tapered shaft was undisturbed. He wiped it carefully with some convenient grass and returned it to his pouch. The fore-shafts weren't installed in the long spear shaft until they were needed.

The second point had glanced off a rib, and the tip was broken off, leaving a jagged, sharp edge. That edge had torn through the cat's heart and ensured a quick death. He wiped it also, sighing as he did. He could re-point it when he had time. It wouldn't be as useful, though. A long blade mounted on a fore-shaft made a great knife. A short one didn't.

He had put his third blade, the one he currently favored as a knife, near the body. Tugging the cat over onto its back, he picked up the knife and slit along its inner hind leg, methodically working through the series of cuts that were needed to remove the skin.

Midway through the process, he heard the woman descending the tree. She was far from silent, but he didn't turn, choosing instead to ignore her. If she didn't want to associate with him, he could understand. In this vacant land, every stranger's motivations were suspect. She had no way of knowing that he didn't have rape and murder on his mind.

He continued working. The wolf-pup came up and sniffed at the dead cat, licking some of the blood off the uncovered meat. He smiled and cut off a large piece of its thigh, then tossed it to the puppy. It jumped in surprise and then grabbed the meat, obviously hungry.

The pup settled down nearby and chomped its way through nearly the entire piece before it sat back and burped.

The entire time, Cadeyrin had felt the woman's eyes watching his every move. He had reached the point where the carcass was nearly free of the skin. All he had to do was to pull it over so that he could free the remainder and then roll it off the skin. He tugged at the leg, a little off-balance, and his hand slipped off, precipitating him into a sitting position. There was a small snicker behind him, and the woman came up and grabbed the back leg to help pull. He smiled at her, and she smiled back. Feeding the puppy had been the correct thing to do.

He was a little puzzled about the wolf. He'd heard of tribes that lived in close proximity to wolves, but he'd never envisioned meeting a woman who took care of one. His people always treated the gray woods-runners as competitors. This was different. He started to worry about her. Was she some kind of spirit? He'd never seen anything like the way she was dressed nor smelled any scent like the strange one that came faintly from her. Still, his animal guide was a wolf, and the puppy was sitting nearby, watching him with bright eyes. He decided that it was harmless and probably meant well.

Now the woman, on the other hand, was worthy of more attention. He turned to her and carefully looked her up and down. She blushed and hung her head so that her hair concealed the scarring along her jawline. Then she raised her eyes to stare at him defiantly.

His initial impression had been right. She was beautiful; even the scars couldn't damage her looks. They only served to enhance them, making her look somewhat mysterious and strong. He liked that.

Her clothes were a mystery. He looked at her, asking mutely for permission, and reached slowly out to touch the sleeve of her shirt. It was of an unknown material and was as soft or even softer than his own well-tanned buckskin shirt. She allowed him to touch her for an instant but then pulled back as if she were afraid that he'd do more.

He smiled, and she smiled back tentatively. She pointed to the wolf pup, then opened her mouth and pointed to it. He laughed. She was hungry, too. She was smart and quick with her mind. She'd just told him, you fed him, now feed me.

He reached into his pouch and removed a deerskin-wrapped package of dried fish. She carefully chose a small piece and began to chew at it. It wasn't long before she took another piece, looking to see if he objected.

While she ate, he removed some sinew from the cat's back-strap and used it to tie the bundled hide. Fresh sinew wasn't really good for such a purpose, but it would hold the heavy hide in a manageable package so that he could easily carry it. Standing, he hefted the hide and motioned towards his last campsite. That was the closest, really good place he could think of.

She stood and followed him as he led the way.

It took until after midday to get there. He had plenty of time to wonder exactly what he'd gotten into, taking her on. Would she be a burden? Would she leave quickly? What if she stayed? His heart beat a little faster at the thought, but then he remembered his deceased mate, and a sense of depression settled in, accentuated by the feeling that he was somehow betraying her memory.

He rationalized that his mate was gone, so there really could be no betrayal. Two things continued to bother him, though. Would he be able to protect this mysterious woman? And, what if he became too attached to her? Would she feel the same way about him?

Chapter Ten

A Primitive Existence

Kathleen followed the man. He was obviously a primitive hunter. Probably with a whole tribe waiting for him and probably with a wife or maybe even a whole harem. She was worried about how he'd treat her. Would she be a slave, or would he want to bed her? The thought made her feel funny inside. He was probably ignorant and most likely of low intelligence, but he was certainly handsome. He gave off a confident male aura that was almost intoxicating. Still, she might be walking into a situation that would be more than she could handle.

Yet, his smile was charming and open. He wasn't dirty or grubby. His face was clean, and his beard was cut short. He obviously took care of himself. Even his leather clothes were clean—worn, but clean. Maybe he wasn't stupid. She had the opinion that stupid people didn't take good care of themselves, hypocritically ignoring the fact that she often wore the same dirty clothes for days.

Aside from his looks, the primary advantage that she could see was that he knew how to survive. He'd killed that huge cat with just two spears, and he hadn't hesitated in facing it either. He must be very brave. She thought that it would take a lot of courage to stand in front of such a cat, even if one were armed with a modern rifle.

Now that's a funny thing, she told herself. There are no modern rifles in this time. Any rifle would be a thing of the future. That led her to start thinking about his spears and the curved handle that he used to hurl them. Why doesn't he have a bow and arrow? She wondered.

After due consideration, she concluded that maybe the bow hadn't been invented yet, or, if it had, he didn't know about it. Maybe some people somewhere on the globe currently used that technology, but he didn't know about it. That could be something she could show him that would help demonstrate her value.

Try as she would, she could think of nothing else that she knew would be useful. She couldn't show him how to make a bicycle, for instance. That led to another thought. Perhaps she could teach him about metal. He was using funny-shaped flint points that seemed more primitive than the few arrowheads she'd seen in her past. She mentally shrugged. She didn't know much about primitive weapons.

<hr>

Eventually, they reached an open area that showed some use. There had been a fire here; even Kathleen could see that. Her guide threw the saber-tooth skin down, stretched, and then turned to her. He indicated that she should stay there, so she settled down on the grass with her wolf pup.

He laid his weapons down and then walked off, returning shortly, dragging some dead branches. He piled these by the fire. Then he repeated the action, bringing both dead and green wood. After about ten trips, he was apparently satisfied.

She watched as he prepared a small fire with dry wood and then uncovered some still-burning coals from the previously buried fire. He bent over and blew on them, simultaneously doing something with some dried grass, but she couldn't tell what, exactly. Shortly he had a small fire going. He built that up until it was a fair size. Kathleen had to move back a little. The heat was surprising, demonstrating how used she'd become to the chill air.

She hadn't noticed that evening had approached. The sun was on the verge of setting, the fire was hot, and she felt warm for the first time in days. The hunter got up and walked over to a nearby tree to retrieve a hanging bag. She was happy to find that it was packed with dried meat of some sort. This wasn't fish, but some kind of lean meat. She wondered if it was venison, but she didn't know and couldn't identify it by taste.

The combination of the meat's aroma and her hunger made it delicious. It was chewy and required a considerable effort to eat, but she diligently continued until she felt like she was starting to lose the edge of her hunger. Then she looked around for something to drink.

The hunter had been eating at the same time, occasionally pausing to toss a scrap to her puppy. He'd been watching her eat with a sort of half-smile on his face as if he recognized the extent of her hunger. When she looked around, he laughed and mimicked someone drinking from a cupped palm. She smiled and nodded.

He took that as an affirmative and got up. He led her over the nearby hill to the edge of a large lake. Lake Minnetonka, she thought to herself. She'd finally reached it. If she could just return to the future, she could be home in less than an hour.

She looked around at the wilderness and then watched him hopelessly. She just had to remember how she'd translated in time. She needed to get back. She couldn't live here. Her research demanded her presence. She could change people's lives for the better. Deep within her mind, she cherished the hope that she could somehow rescue injured children. She wouldn't admit that aspiration was a cry for help from her own childhood. Children's lives depended on her.

He squatted on a rock and dipped up several palms of water, drinking. Then he carefully splashed water on his face, rinsing any bits of food out of his beard. She watched and then emulated him. She thought about possible water-borne disease organisms, wondering whether she'd be better off boiling the water first. She'd been content to drink from streams the previous days, and she told herself that she'd better get used to drinking directly from lakes. She might possibly have to spend the rest of her life here.

That last thought set her off. 'Here' wasn't somewhere she really wanted to be. She'd wanted to flee from Drew's attack and, in that, she'd been successful. But what a price! She was trapped in a primitive existence and most likely would never be able to return to her normal time. So much rode on her returning and finishing her research. Humanity needed to know that time-travel was possible. She briefly thought again of the many lives that could be saved.

She still wasn't sure how she'd managed to work her equations to get here. She guessed that somehow she'd changed her possibility wave function and then popped the quantum function while randomly viewing herself in the past. Perhaps if she meditated on the situation, she could figure out how to reverse her actions. She focused on the flickering firelight and went into a waking dream.

Her thoughts flowed over her equations, but somehow there wasn't any force behind them. She couldn't make herself move into the future. She was concluding that she wasn't motivated enough, despite her fear of the wild, when a growl from the darkness outside the firelight interrupted her reverie. She flinched and looked around.

There was a brief reflection from glowing eyes out there in the dark. She glanced at her hunter. He was still seated, but he had his spear device assembled and was watching the darkness intently. There was a chorus of growls, and he stood up, alert. The wolf puppy pressed closely against her side, a baby growl in his throat.

She got to her feet, also. After a moment, she thought that perhaps she should be armed. She'd dropped her sharp wolf bone when she'd climbed the tree to escape the saber-tooth, so she searched through the pile of wood for a likely-looking club. Finding one she believed would work, she picked it up and moved over beside him. He glanced at her and smiled encouragingly.

Pointing at the darkness, he said, "Makkata."

She tried to copy him, and he corrected her pronunciation. She repeated, and he grinned engagingly. Then she smiled in return. It must be his name for whatever kind of animal was out there.

The fire flickered brighter for a moment, exposing the head and shoulders of one of the smaller, long-fanged cats. This was one of the ones she'd seen pull down a deer when she'd first arrived in the past. She pointed at it and said, "Cat!"

He glanced at her, nodded, and then repeated her word perfectly. Then he repeated, "Makkat."

She memorized his word for the beast. That seemed a good place to start. While they watched the prowling cats, she pointed at herself and said, "Kathleen."

He grinned again and repeated it with some difficulty. She corrected him. He silently mouthed "Kathleen" and then said it nearly perfectly. This time his smile was radiant. It practically took her breath away.

He laughed aloud and said "Kathleen" again. Without pausing, he indicated himself with a gesture towards his chest and said, "Cadeyrin."

That must be his name, she thought. It took her a couple of tries to begin to approximate it. He finally spaced it out, slowly, "Ca—dey—rin." This time, she got it right, and he smiled approvingly.

They watched the darkness quietly until it became apparent that the predators had departed. She hadn't noticed them going until he relaxed and put his hand on her shoulder, turning her towards the fire. The wolf pup abruptly sat down and scratched his ear calmly. The danger was gone.

They sat and continued the language lesson. Kathleen learned Cadeyrin's words for fire, wolf, or puppy – she wasn't sure about that one – dried meat, and, after some gesturing, the words for man and woman.

Working on communicating was exhausting, or maybe it was just the release of the tension she'd felt for the past several days. She lay on her back looking at the moon, which had just peeped over the hill.

He said something that sounded reassuring, and she glanced at him. He was sitting in a way that seemed to imply he'd keep watch, so she relaxed. The wolf puppy came over and curled up beside her, and, for the first time in days, she fell asleep feeling secure and unthreatened.

⚬

She slept intermittently. After midnight, the wind picked up and chilled her back. She rolled around a little and changed her position. When she woke again, Cadeyrin had covered her with the bloody tiger skin, fur side against her. It didn't smell good, but it kept the wind off. She raised her head in time to see him throw another piece of wood on the fire.

He glanced at her and smiled. She smiled back and tried to go back to sleep. When she awoke again, it was getting towards morning. Dawn's fingers were just moving into the sky.

It was frosty. The wind had dropped, and the cold had fallen down from space. The lank grass and the nearby trees were covered with frost crystals. She shivered and pulled her hoodie closer to her face.

Cadeyrin was still awake. When he saw that she was stirring, he gave her some more dried meat and pantomimed sleeping. She nodded, and he stretched out to grab a little rest while she ate.

She finished eating and decided to let him sleep while the sun gradually came up. The sunrise was spectacular. There was dust or something in the air to the east, and it made the sun's rays extremely colorful. It was the most beautiful sunrise she'd ever seen. It faded as the sun showed over the nearby trees.

Birds were singing, and somehow she felt happy. She petted the puppy and thought about her situation.

She'd escaped Drew. He would have undoubtedly killed her when she eventually gave in and gave him the encryption key. She had no doubts about her lack of ability to resist torture. The thought of him forcing himself on her made her shaky. She'd have given him the encryption key immediately in order to avoid that, but she knew it wouldn't have stopped him.

Her fear had forced her mind to momentarily jump from a theoretical grasp of her equations to a full, working understanding. She figured she had to thank Drew for that. His attack had pushed her over the hump. The only problem she now had was that her understanding seemed to have faded. Even the saber-tooth tiger attack had not brought it back. Somehow she had to find a solution. She had to return with her knowledge.

Now that she'd found a friend – She paused. Was he really a friend? How could she know? He was a stone-age hunter. Who knew how his mind worked? His idea of a good life most certainly wasn't the same as hers, and his idea of how to treat a woman surely wasn't the same either.

Kathleen grinned wryly. Even she didn't know how she wanted to be treated. She'd never thought about having anything but the most superficial relationship with a man. Now she found herself in a position of needing this caveman. She hated the idea. She didn't want to feel like she was in a weak position, owing him anything. She didn't know what she had to offer, other than her passing idea about bows and arrows. Maybe he already knew about such things and refused to use them for some reason that was beyond her experience. No, she just had to return. Then he could do as he pleased.

The wolf puppy shoved his head under her arm at this point, demanding attention. She affectionately ruffled his ears, and he took her hand in his mouth, putting just a little too much pressure on her skin with his sharp teeth. She flinched, and the movement tore the skin on the back of her hand. He immediately released her hand and wagged apologetically.

She looked at the scratch. It was bleeding a little. The puppy didn't understand how thin her skin was. She held her hand out to him, and he licked at the scratch. Then she thought that maybe she was just teaching him that she tasted good, something that she might regret later. She pulled her hand back but then observed that he still looked contrite. It was obvious he knew he'd done something he should be ashamed of.

Birds were singing a little in the trees down by the lake, but everything was quiet. In the stillness, she gradually became aware of a sound that was increasing in volume. It was a low rumbling noise that was coming from over the hill to the south. She stood up in alarm to look but could see nothing. As the noise gained in intensity, she was able to determine the distant thunder was the sound of running hooves.

A tall shadow loomed in the margin of her vision, and she jumped in fright, letting out a little squeak. It was the hunter. He stepped up beside her and took her upper arm in his hand, gently laying two fingers over her lips to indicate silence. She quivered but remained still while he listened.

⚬

Cadeyrin recognized the sound. A herd of viosana was running in the nearby valley. They'd undoubtedly been spooked by a predator. If an attack was in progress, they'd probably continue for a couple of miles. Once the predator had dragged one down, the herd would rapidly calm and go back to grazing, knowing the danger was past for the moment. The urge to graze was too important to them to ignore for long.

If they slowed and spread out in a mile or so, they might be in striking range for him. There would be danger from other predators, but he was nearly out of meat, and now that the woman had joined him, they would need more food.

He still wondered what she was doing with the wolf-pup, but she obviously wanted to keep it. He thought giving it food might be wasteful, but he had no objection as long as there was plenty to eat. In the end, they might run short, and then, if things got desperate, they could always eat the puppy. He'd eaten wolf numerous times before. It wasn't bad, although he'd rather have deer or bison.

With that thought, he started to head towards where he anticipated the bison would be when they began to graze again. He took two quick steps and then decided that he couldn't leave Kathleen. She could stay by the fire, but he was sure that she couldn't defend herself. She had no weapons, and he guessed that she'd survived so far simply by luck.

She couldn't have come far with the poor woods-craft that she'd demonstrated. It was a puzzle to him. He wondered where her people were or what had happened to them. Still, he thought, I can't leave her. I'll have to take her with me. She might be a liability, but she has to come.

He motioned to her to come and set off again, not waiting to see if she was following. As he reached the crest of the hill, he glanced back. She was right behind him while the wolf pup ranged a little out to their right side.

They continued over the hill. There was a dust cloud farther along to the left in the valley, but the dust in front of them was already settling. The bison were well down the valley on their side of the river.

They hurried along the hillside, below the crest of the hill. He didn't want to expose their silhouette against the skyline, making them visible to any hostile eyes.

After several steps, Kathleen came up beside him and touched his arm. He stopped. She pointed ahead at the valley. The dust there was settling, also. She looked puzzled. He knew then that she'd never been on a hunt before. He didn't know how to tell her that the bison had slowed and were stopping to graze.

The wind suddenly picked up and thinned the remains of the dust cloud as it gusted up the valley. She drew in her breath as she saw the herd for the first time. He nodded and pointed towards them. She looked doubtful but followed as he started moving again.

This was ideal. The bison had keen noses and could scent a man at a long distance. With the wind coming towards him, they could not smell him, and their eyesight was far from sharp. He could see a ravine descending from a low spot between the hills ahead. The bison were heading in that general direction. The herd had spread out, not too far as yet, but by the time they would reach the ravine, they would be absorbed in grazing. Their constant need for food meant that they put danger out of their minds quickly.

He stopped and pulled Kathleen close. Her reactions were odd. She first smiled and moved hesitantly towards him but then shivered and pulled away a little. He ignored that and pointed out a possible approach for them.

The terrain was rolling, and there were two small knolls that would hide their approach until they could reach the shoulder of the hill above the ravine. Then it became a little chancy. If the grass was deep on the hillside, they could worm their way down and into the ravine. If not, they might have to climb higher, over the crest of the hill, hoping to reach a point where they could intersect the ravine without being seen.

She followed his pointing and nodded. Together, they set off along the planned route, the pup trailing along behind.

⸺◆⸺

Before long, they'd reached the ravine. They'd had to climb the hill; the grass on the hillside was sparse and offered no concealment. The wolf pup was alert and intent on following them. Somehow he'd deduced that they were after the bison. His instincts had taken over, and he was cooperating fully to the best of his limited experience, acting as if they were his pack.

They'd crept down the ravine until they'd almost reached the river. Here, the dry grass hung lushly over the edge of the ravine. The bison were moving their way alone and in small groups, grazing as they came.

Cadeyrin paused and assembled his spear shaft, making sure the fore-shaft was tightly fitted into the main spear. He hooked the atl-atl into the socket of the main shaft, holding the entire apparatus in his right hand.

Kathleen watched him carefully. He looked at her and decided that she'd be best waiting right where she was. She looked so clueless about what he intended. He caught her arm with his left hand and moved her against the bank of the ravine. Letting go, he motioned for her to stay. She nodded.

He moved down the dry ravine to a point where the walls were lower. Here he cautiously slipped out and into the tall grass. Something touched his leg, and he slowly looked around. It was the wolf-pup. It looked inquisitively at him.

He didn't know what to do. The pup was likely to attract the bison's attention and cause them to run again. He thought about tying it to a bush but feared that it would make a noise and alarm the herd. Perhaps it was best to just ignore the friendly animal and pretend it wasn't there.

The bison were getting closer. He peered through the grass and decided on a yearling bull calf. It was ahead of the main group and looked likely to pass within spear-cast of his location. He slowly scanned to his sides and back. The wolf-pup was gone. He hadn't heard it leave; it was certainly quiet enough. Maybe it understood what he was doing.

He waited, breathing as quietly as possible. He could hear the sound of the bison. There were sounds of grazing mixed with some quiet lowing as the animals called to each other. He risked another look. The bull calf had turned and would pass out of range. He started to move forward, but then he saw it come to attention, looking at something off to its left. It lowed in alarm and trotted towards him.

Looking past it, he could see the wolf-pup briefly lift its head over the grass. It was herding the calf directly into the ambush. He felt a flash of gratitude. This was something he hadn't thought of – the pup could help him hunt. Kathleen must have known this. How, he didn't know. He suddenly thought that there must be other things she knew that he didn't, things he could find useful.

He readied himself. The calf was close. At the perfect moment, guided by his years of hunting experience, he stood and made a smooth, strong throw. The spear left the atl-atl with all the velocity his muscles could impart, arced over the grass, and struck the calf exactly where he'd aimed. The fluted point slammed into the base of the calf's neck and slid directly into its heart. The calf bawled and leaped forward, unsure of what had happened. It ran past Cadeyrin and crashed over the edge of the ravine. He dashed back, following. It was lying on its side, moaning as it breathed its last. Blood poured out around the fore-shaft. It wasn't going anywhere. It made one last effort to lift its head and then died.

Cadeyrin turned and retraced his steps to retrieve the main spear shaft. It was lying in the grass, having come free, just as it was designed to do. He picked it up and checked on the rest of the herd. They were bunched now and heading up the hill away from the river, staying away from the ravine as they went. They weren't panicked but were making good time, led by a couple of wise cows and followed up by the bulls.

By the time he returned to the ravine, Kathleen was standing near the calf, her hands covering her mouth, an expression of distaste on her face. He looked down from the bank at her. Who was this woman? A woman of his tribe would already be butchering the animal. Kathleen looked as if she'd never seen a dead bison.

Kathleen was shocked. She'd eaten the dried meat and found it good, but she hadn't prepared herself mentally for the actual procuring of such meat. She knew intellectually that the hunter had to kill game, but it had seemed remote and somewhat romantic. Now, staring at the dead calf, it was horrid and messy. The bison's tongue was hanging out, and blood still flowed out around the protruding shaft. She had nearly cried out in surprise when she discovered the body. She didn't know how she could stand to eat any more meat, knowing that some animal had died to provide it and that the death was brutal.

The wolf pup jumped down beside her and ran over to the dead bison. It stopped and licked at the pool of blood. She was disgusted, but common sense told her that the puppy had to eat. It was a wolf, after all.

Cadeyrin slid down and strode over to the calf. He glanced at her with puzzlement. She was surprised at that but then concluded that he was used to killing and didn't understand that it was abhorrent to her. He knelt and began to strip the animal, grunting as he rolled the heavy carcass so that he could remove the entrails.

Kathleen watched. It was obvious that he knew what he was doing. He slit the belly, turned the body to one side, and pulled out the intestines and other abdominal organs. Then he reached in, cutting through the diaphragm. Once that was done, he cut the throat, freeing the windpipe. Then he reached deep inside the chest cavity and tugged on the windpipe.

With a grunt, he pulled out the heart and lungs, still attached to the windpipe, blood smearing his arm. This emptied the entire body.

Kathleen thought that she would faint, watching the process. It had only taken him a few minutes, and the body was completely gutted. He had already started skinning it. She drew a deep breath, trying to ignore the heavy scent of blood. She knew how to help with the skinning. She'd helped him skin the saber-tooth, at least a little. If she was going to spend any more time here, she had better learn to help. She steeled herself, trying to quell her heaving stomach. She stooped and grasped the skin where he was cutting it loose. He looked at her and nodded. She tugged, pulling it loose.

⚬

It was a long process, and she was exhausted by the time the skin had been removed and the body had been cut into pieces that could be carried. Cadeyrin stood and looked appraisingly at her, then helped her lift the heavy skin. He loaded himself with prime cuts of meat and led her back towards their original camp.

She thought that she'd pass out before they reached the fire. It had died down but was still burning. He built it back up and spread the skin, laying the meat on it. Then he turned and headed back towards the kill-site. She put her hands on her hips, trying to get her breath. When he looked at her, she made a face and said, "Really?"

He understood somehow. He nodded in the affirmative and started off, plainly giving her the option of remaining by the fire or coming. She watched him for a moment and then sighed deeply. When he looked back at her, she followed.

Chapter Eleven

Kathleen: The Lake Camp

It had taken several trips to get the bison meat back to camp. Kathleen had worn out after two passes. It wasn't so bad walking the mile and a half to the kill site, but carrying the heavy meat back was exhausting.

Cadeyrin continued until he'd brought back everything he'd cut free from the carcass. She sat by the fire and kept it going as he worked. His last trip was completed in the twilight, and then he had to go and gather more wood. Kathleen had no idea how he'd driven himself to complete the day.

They'd paused a couple of times to finish off the dried meat from his pouch, but she was worn out, practically starved, and well on the way to working up a good case of outrage.

He was some kind of crazy slave-driver who didn't understand that her scars hurt. She couldn't walk well due to the pain, and one of the torn places had broken open again. She was bleeding a little. She examined the spot and dabbed at it with the cleanest part of her hoodie. She pessimistically thought that she'd still probably get an infection and die as a result.

Cadeyrin came up behind her unannounced as she was looking at her leg. She'd thought he was on the way out to gather more wood, but here he was. Her pants were unzipped and pulled down, showing her undergarment. She'd never been one for the idea of a thong, always choosing comfort over style, so her panties didn't reveal much, thankfully.

The first thing she knew about his presence was a thump as he dropped the branch he was carrying. Then he stepped closer, his eyes narrowing as he looked at her scars.

Her resentment flared, and she started to say something, but then fear took over as she thought, *Uh-oh, here it comes. He's either going to dump me because I'm deformed, or he's going to want to have sex right here. What should I do?*

She felt intensely vulnerable and helpless.

He squatted so that he could get a closer look. She prepared to try and fend him off, but then he surprised her.

He focused closely on her torn scar, and when he looked up at her, his eyes were wide with concern. He pointed, mutely asking her permission, and for some reason, she nodded, even though her mind screamed at her to pull up her pants.

He gently reached out and felt her thigh, running his fingertips over the corded scarring, leaving her feeling a strange tingling sensation in the pit of her stomach. Abruptly he stood and walked quickly into the trees.

What was that all about? Kathleen asked herself. He's probably gone for good.

Common sense told her that she was being silly. His spears and the stick he used for throwing them were lying nearby, as was the rest of his kit. He'd unloaded most of it to lighten his load as he brought in the remains of the bison. She shook her head, remembering the tingling sensation. It had not been unpleasant, unlike the medical doctor's touch on her scars. Her doctor had been the only other man to ever touch her in such an intimate place. The scarring was worse where he'd touched her on the inside of her upper right thigh.

She pulled up her pants, hoping that the opened wound would be all right, and then turned to the meat. By the time Cadeyrin had returned, carrying some roots and some willow branches, she'd arranged the bison parts on the hide. She didn't know what to do with the cuts of meat beyond placing the similar parts together.

He smiled at her as he put his load carefully on an unoccupied corner of the hide. Then he grabbed a long, heavy piece of meat that he'd removed from the back of the bison; there were two of them, one from each side of the spine. Kathleen didn't know what to call the cut, but as he roasted slices over the fire on a couple of green spits, the smell that arose was heavenly. The pup sat alertly and watched. Cadeyrin cut some smaller chunks of meat off a haunch and fed him.

They ate, and she decided that if he was a slave-driver, he more than made up for it by being an amazing cook. She'd never gone in for flame-broiled meat before, and maybe it was just the setting and her hunger, but it tasted wonderful.

After they'd filled themselves with broiled meat, he busied himself with the roots and bark. She watched as he used two stones to grind the materials into a sort of sticky paste. He mixed in some bison fat and that made the texture smoother and more salve-like. Then he turned to her and made a circular motion.

She didn't understand until he grasped her pants and pulled downward lightly. She blushed. She'd somehow let him touch her before, but this was too much.

Reading her face, Cadeyrin laughed softly. When she looked up at him, her face flaring red, he took a little of the salve and rubbed it on his hand, then sighed and said, "Ahhhh," in mock relief. He handed the salve to her, watching.

Kathleen understood that he expected her to apply it to her scars and was waiting to see if she did. She started to turn her back but then defiantly pulled her pants partway down facing him. He nodded approvingly.

Her hoodie was long enough to cover her hips. She carefully smeared the salve onto the injured parts of her thighs. It felt greasy, but one of the ingredients almost immediately worked to remove the pain from the torn scars. Even the widespread bruising felt better after she covered the spots with the salve. She found herself sighing in relief, then looked at him and laughingly repeated, "Ahhhh."

He pointed at the eastern sky and held up one finger, then pointed at the zenith and held up a second, then at the remains of the sunset and held up a third. She'd just been given a prescription: apply three times a day on afflicted areas.

—◦—

The stuff really worked. By morning, the stiffness and pain had lessened, and she felt that she could walk again, though she resolved to take it as easy as she could.

Cadeyrin had slept intermittently, stirring at dawn to cook breakfast. He was sitting quietly, examining a broken spear point that he'd removed from his pouch.

As she watched, he pulled a smooth piece of bone and a pointed rock out of the pouch and set to work, painstakingly chipping off tiny pieces of chert near the broken tip. He worked carefully and methodically, often pausing to hold the piece up to the sky to better examine it.

She sat down nearby and composed herself. He glanced at her and then continued the language lesson as he worked. By the time he'd finished re-pointing the spear-tip, she'd learned the words for spear, his spear-thrower, and the point itself. He'd picked up the English words more easily than she'd learned his. His language was full of odd sounds and was difficult for her.

Kathleen was no linguist. She'd taken German as an undergrad but hadn't done anything with it. Besides, Cadeyrin's language didn't sound like German. It was like nothing she'd ever heard, except it had sounds that seemed familiar but weren't combined in the way she expected.

After he'd finished with the point, Cadeyrin went immediately to work on the bison and tiger skins. He worked them, dragging the flesh-side over a nearby boulder time after time. The boulder had a rough edge, and the skins gradually grew more flexible as he scraped the fibers against the stone.

At dusk, he paused and cooked more meat, then used some of the bison's brains to treat the rubbed skins. Kathleen felt drowsy watching him rubbing the material into the tiger skin, and she stretched out by the fire. Before she was fully asleep, he'd finished and gently placed the skin over her, fur-side against her body. It still smelt, but it was noticeably softer.

She fell asleep with the wolf-pup by her side, comfortable and warmed by the skin and the fire. Cadeyrin worked on, tanning the bison hide.

It was days later. Kathleen had lost track of the exact number. They were still living near the big lake, but now she was far more comfortable with her circumstances and almost content, with the sole exception of dwelling on how she could return to the future on what seemed to be an hourly basis.

Cadeyrin had put her to shame with his linguistic ability. They were now conversing; maybe on a basic level, but he could communicate just about everything he needed her to understand.

She wondered if he were capable of thinking more deeply. All his life seemed to require was dealing with immediate needs and pressing circumstances. Theoretical thinking was something she enjoyed, and she missed talking to Professor Mackleroy and her classwork and books. She doubted whether she'd ever be able to discuss scientific concepts with the hunter. The thought was bleak and depressing. How could she resign herself to such a primitive life with a non-intellectual, Paleolithic hunter?

On the practical side, however, he was gradually teaching her a whole body of knowledge required for survival. The cold no longer bothered her as much. They kept warm with the skins and the fire and often spent hours sleeping during the day, relaxing on a grassy hillside with a southern exposure. The wolf puppy had lost much of his puppy-like shape and was now a gangling youngster, well able to help in the hunt.

Cadeyrin had proven to be a more than able provider. He hadn't brought in any more bison, but there had been deer and some animals that were similar to pronghorns, along with what she thought was a camel.

She hadn't liked the camel meat much, but it was food, and fueling one's body took precedence. Living outside in the cold weather burned a tremendous amount of calories, and she ate like a lumberjack, putting away more at one meal than she'd previously eaten in an entire day.

There were other things to eat, also. They'd found herbs, roots, berries, nuts, seeds, and some mushrooms. She was cautious about the mushrooms, but it was clear that Cadeyrin knew exactly what he was gathering and wouldn't accidentally poison them.

He had taught her to fish using an ingenious fish trap he constructed by pushing sharpened sticks into the shallow river bottom to construct a fence that guided the fish through a funnel-shaped narrow part into a pen. The silly things didn't seem to be able to figure out how to escape once they'd gotten inside. The two of them checked the trap daily, and Cadeyrin showed her how to dry the excess catch so it could be saved for later.

She was even more surprised when he showed her another fishing method. He had made a long length of thinly braided sinew and tied it to the middle of a short, double-pointed stick. Then he embedded the stick in a piece of meat. This improvised hook was thrown into the water, and when a fish swallowed it, and the sinew became taught, the double points would wedge in the fish's throat. They'd caught several big, toothy fish that way. She hadn't known that fish could be caught without a metal hook.

Kathleen was amazed at herself. She found that not only could she do the work, she was actually proud of her growing ability. She was grateful to Cadeyrin for the knowledge, and as a result, she was developing a certain degree of trust in him, despite her habitual misgivings.

She'd always been cautious and prone to extensive self-analysis. Thinking about her feelings was ingrained into her nature. She was attracted to him, but she rationalized that it was simply due to her dependence on his knowledge.

He might not be educated in the way she was, but he was knowledgeable in the ways of survival, and it couldn't be denied that he was quite handsome.

His good looks caused her to evaluate her flaws critically. She thought to herself: it's without a shadow of a doubt that he wouldn't even look at me twice if we had met on campus. He'd have his choice of all of the best-looking women. They wouldn't care what kind of a student he was. He could be flunking out, and women would flock to him. I wouldn't have a chance. Besides, what am I fantasizing about, anyway? I've just got to get back to share my theory with the world. I can't think about him or myself when so many would benefit from my formula.

As a result of her self-criticism, she made a conscious effort to be more restrained around him. Possibly she carried it a little far at times, for she saw him looking at her with a slight crease between his eyes when he thought she wasn't watching. She refused to try to put a name to whatever it was he was feeling.

There was a large herd of bison moving along the river valley. The day was the coldest she'd experienced since she'd come into the past. Both Kathleen and Cadeyrin were wearing double layers of clothing. During the past several days, he'd created two rough coats of the tiger skin. The heavy fur provided enough insulation to keep her warm, although her legs were cold.

They huddled close together in a clump of brush strategically situated along the route that the bison would likely travel as they moved between the steep riverbank and an encroaching hill. Kathleen was shivering, partly from the cold and partly from excitement and anticipation.

They needed meat again. Cadeyrin's constant hunting had driven off the smaller prey animals in the area. Deer, once plentiful, were nowhere to be found. He'd told her that they'd have to move their camp soon if a migrating herd did not come by soon. Luckily, one had.

The bison were grazing about a half-mile down the river valley, coming their way slowly. All looked good for their ambush, but now the bison were starting to show signs of nervousness. The herd bulls were lowing and tossing their heads, and the lead cows had stopped grazing and were moving faster.

Her wolf pup suddenly poked his nose through the bushes, then wormed through a narrow gap and came up to them, looking at the bison over his shoulder. His tail was down, and he seemed alarmed.

Cadeyrin whispered to her, "Big-teeth hunt them."

His English had progressed greatly, and he was able to make her understand all but the most complex concepts. *Of course,* she thought somewhat disparagingly to herself: *maybe he doesn't think in complex terms.*

She was convinced that, as capable as he was, his intellectual prowess was not up to her standards. If questioned, though, she would have been hard-pressed to recall an instance where he had been less than capable. She now relied on him for everything. The few days that she'd spent on her own seemed foggy in her memory, like a bad dream after waking.

She leaned close to reply, unavoidably inhaling his scent, a mixture of wood smoke, animal hide, and just plain man. She reflexively took a deeper breath, and his scent made her feel as if butterflies were in her stomach. The involuntary response startled her, and she drew back, whispering more loudly than she'd intended, "What is it?"

Cadeyrin held up his hand, motioning her to be silent while his eyes searched the grass and bushes down the valley. Abruptly, he gathered his weapons and turned. He grasped her arm and led her deeper into the bushes.

"We go now. Too dangerous here. Many big-teeth hunt viosana. We move farther away. Wait for them to stampede," he said, using his own word for the bison herd. He tended to revert back to his language when distracted.

She understood perfectly. The saber-tooth tigers hunted in groups, similar to lion prides. It was far easier for the strong but relatively slow cats to drive their prey into an ambush. That strategy greatly increased their rate of successful hunts. A single tiger, hunting alone, would almost certainly starve to death.

If the tigers were hunting in a large group, it would mean that she and Cadeyrin were likely to encounter at least one. If Cadeyrin killed a bison this close to their ambush, the tigers would know about it. Then the predators would drive them off or kill them both in an effort to steal their kill.

He led her back through the bushes, skirting around the hill, moving upstream and up the hill at the same time. When they got to the edge of the brush, he paused and then motioned her down into the tall grass. She looked at him, and he pointed silently down towards the river.

She risked a quick look, raising her head to see over the stems. He pulled her back down, but not before she'd seen three of the huge cats trotting directly towards the ambush position that they'd occupied just moments before.

The position was a natural bottleneck, and the tigers were as adept at picking out hiding locations as was Cadeyrin. They were coming from up the river, so they'd probably circled around far behind the hill in order to cut the bison off.

Cadeyrin and Kathleen began to move quickly uphill. The saber-tooth's sense of smell wasn't as keen as that of a wolf, but there was no doubt that the three cats would know that the two humans had been hiding in the bushes. They might decide to investigate.

Kathleen hoped that the lure of a bison kill would keep the cats focused on the main hunt. She followed Cadeyrin as he crawled quickly upwards, keeping her back below the tops of the dried weeds and grass. The wolf trailed along nearby, staying close as if he was fully aware of the danger.

The wind blew harder as they reached the top of the hill, making large waves that glided across the stems with a rushing noise. The sound and motion made it more difficult to detect the approach of a predator. They crested the top and then began to run along the far side of the ridge, hidden from the bison.

Kathleen now had no difficulty keeping up. Her scars were far more flexible since the bruising had faded. The salve that he'd made for her had worked wonders. She didn't know what Cadeyrin had put in it, other than a rather disgusting mixture of roots, stems, and animal fat, but it had the effect of easing both the pain and the stiffness.

When they'd reached the point where the hill connected to the main body of hills that rimmed the river valley, they turned upstream again and hurried along until they were over a mile south of the bison herd. Cadeyrin pointed towards their destination, and she saw that he was heading towards a small clump of willows. These were close to the river and might offer a useful hiding place if the bison continued up the valley near the bank.

They were still perhaps about a quarter of a mile from the willows when the sounds of the saber-tooth attack reached them. There was an initial roar, followed by the bellowing of the frightened bison. Then other noises were drowned out by the gathering rumble of hundreds of stampeding hooves carried on the dense, cold air.

The hunter began to move faster, and Kathleen had difficulty keeping up. Before they reached the willows, a mass of bison came running past their original ambush point. She could see the animals shy away from the bushes as several tigers leaped out.

Some of the bison were pushed off the riverbank in the confusion and floundered through the shallows below. There was an agonized bellowing as the tigers pulled down two of the shaggy grazers at the edge of the water. In response, the lead cows sped up, coming along the riverbank at a dead run, thundering right for the two running humans.

Cadeyrin turned and ran back to her, motioning for her to go back towards the hillside, as she was still too far away from the trees to get to them safely. There was a boulder there that had been dropped by the glacier that had cut the river valley. It wasn't very large, but it might be enough to offer them some protection should the herd come directly at them.

Panting, they stopped behind the sheltering stone as the main body of the bison herd surged past, just a few yards away. At this point, the herd was clumped into one mass of animals with a few stragglers. The tigers had their kills, and the bison were intent on escaping the vicinity.

Cadeyrin and Kathleen watched the running animals pass their shielding stone. She wondered if he was going to kill one, but he seemed content just to watch. When she looked at him, he shook his head negatively and pointed downstream towards where the tigers were now clustering around the downed animals. They were too close to risk a kill.

He led her back up the hill, and they followed the bison upstream. As they crossed the top of the second hill, they saw a lone straggler. A bison that had been driven into the river had broken its ankle, unobserved by the cats. It had run on three legs with the herd for a time, but now that the fear had faded, its injury had slowed it down, and it was limping slowly along the beaten track.

Cadeyrin said, "We run. You come fast. I kill it. Maybe tigers won't know." Then he started off at a pace that she could not hope to match.

Kathleen kept coming, making the best time she could. She ran a hundred paces and then walked twenty, alternating to catch her breath. She knew that she wasn't in nearly as good a shape as Cadeyrin. But then, she hadn't lived the hard life that he had, and her endurance wasn't equal to his.

When she panted over a slight rise, he was standing beside the dead bison, holding a spear shaft. The fore-shaft was sticking out of the bison's side, just behind its front leg. The wolf pup was sitting nearby, tongue lolling out, a pleased expression on his face.

They began to cut the back-straps out of the animal, moving quickly. Cadeyrin dissected off a hind leg, picked it up along with a tenderloin, and said, "We go. Tigers follow herd soon. They eat fast. We must be gone before they come."

Kathleen replied, "I can carry more meat. Can't we get more?"

She was resentful. She'd practically been run to death on this hunt, and she wanted more out of it. He obviously didn't have too high a regard for her carrying ability. She knew she could carry more than the large chunk of meat he'd handed her.

He looked back down the valley with a worried expression on his face, bent and cut out the animal's tongue. He handed it to her, saying, "We must go."

She looked at the slimy tongue in disgust and sighed. He was probably correct. Even if he wasn't, she knew that he'd insist on going.

Together they headed up the hill, leaving the bulk of the carcass for the tigers.

———— ◆◇◆ ————

That night they feasted on bison tongue. She hadn't known how good it would be. The meat was fatty and seemed to meet some nutritional needs that her body had discovered. It was delicious.

The smell of cooking meat drew in a pair of smaller cats, possibly cougars, that circled the fire again and again out in the darkness, occasionally growling. They were afraid of the light and the humans, but the meat smell was too attractive for them to leave.

Kathleen fell asleep watching the leaping firelight reflected off of Caderyin's face and the wolf looking out into the darkness and listening to the circling cats' growls.

———— ◆◇◆ ————

THE fire had died down and was now just a flicker. The pup was curled at her back, sleeping. She raised her head, and the movement alerted Cadeyrin. He roused himself and looked around.

"The small cats have gone. No danger now, Kathleen. You sleep while I watch," he said.

She said, "No, I'm awake now. Why don't you sleep, and I'll watch? I can wake you if anything comes near."

She stood and stretched, flinching with a momentary twinge of pain as her scars pulled a little.

He also stood and turned his back to the low fire, moving to stand nearby. She was tempted to pull back but then accepted his closeness, wondering what he had in mind.

He pointed at the dark sky. The moon was down, and he indicated a slightly orange-hued star high to the north. "That is Kekab. It marks the point all others circle."

Kathleen looked at him in amazement. Not only was that the most elaborate English sentence he'd spoken, it indicated that he knew more about astronomy than she'd thought.

He continued, "The other lights – "

She interrupted him. "The lights are called stars."

He smiled and said, "The other stars by Kekab are named 'The Cub'. Like a young bear, The Cub plays, spinning around Kekab. Once you know Kekab, you always know direction you travel."

She was intrigued, "We call it the 'Little Bear' and the other, there," she pointed, tracing the outline, "we call the 'Great Bear.'"

He laughed, making a low friendly sound, then said, "It is the 'Mother Bear,' the mother of the cub. You know the sky animals. Do you know more?"

Kathleen thoughtfully answered, "Yes, but why don't you tell me what you call them? That way, I'll learn your names for them."

What followed was rather amazing from her point of view. He gave her a detailed tour of the heavens. Far from being ignorant, he was more knowledgeable than she on the arrangement of the stars and their movements through the sky.

She knew that he spent much time awake, watching, during the night hours. The most entertaining thing he had to watch was the sky, so he could be expected to know something about it. What stunned her was that he also knew about comets and meteorites and differentiated the planets from the stars, describing the former as unblinking stars with special properties of motion.

He knew that the moon circled the earth and explained to her how the earth likewise circled the sun. This threw her completely. She'd been sure that the idea of heliocentrism was first proposed by the ancient Greeks but was more commonly attributed to Copernicus. She was forced to re-evaluate her opinion of Cadeyrin's mental abilities as a result.

As she listened to him speak, she gradually came to the conclusion that he was as intelligent as a modern human. It was just that he lacked the education that a modern human might have. On the other hand, he was knowledgeable in the ways of the wild land he inhabited. In some ways, he was far more able than a modern man. He'd learned English more quickly than she'd been able to pick up a smattering of his language. She thought that must be due to the fact that his culture had no written tradition, and they were used to remembering everything they heard.

She'd read somewhere that a man of the middle ages only encountered about as much information during his life as was contained in one daily copy of the New York Times. She, of course, had access to far more information both on the Internet and in the books she could read. Perhaps he had more available capacity to learn, or perhaps there were some subtle differences in brain structure. Children learned languages easily until they reached a certain degree of maturation. His people might not reach that point until later in life.

What bothered her was the idea that maybe humans were designed to operate more effectively with less information. Cadeyrin didn't ever seem to have difficulty making up his mind. He instantly evaluated a situation and seemingly knew exactly what to do. She knew of no one in her past life who had been so decisive. She couldn't decide if that was a good quality or not, but she liked it. It made him seem more masculine and desirable to her.

He gradually trailed off in his description of the sky and then said, "I'm tired, and dawn is near. Will you watch for a time?"

She assented, and he slept, leaving her to mull over her feelings. She was attracted to him. She felt a warmth in the pit of her stomach when she saw him approach. But her past experience had taught her that she was far safer not feeling anything but a cold dispassion towards other people, especially attractive men.

Still, the scars around her hips were better. She could move far more freely. Perhaps she wasn't as undesirable as she imagined, especially for a Paleolithic hunter? The thought made her wince mentally. Was she really ready to give up on her vision of returning to the present or future, whatever it should be called? More importantly, was she doing something she'd sworn she'd never do by starting to care about what a man thought of her?

Chapter Twelve

Cadeyrin: The Lake Camp

Three days later, they had eaten all of the bison meat. Cadeyrin had gone hunting, taking the wolf pup with him.

The puppy was no longer such a little fur-ball. He was growing quickly and, although he was obviously still young with a puppy's enthusiasm for play, he was getting lanky and becoming more able to assist in the hunt. The young animal had already demonstrated his value and, although no one he'd ever heard of hunted with a wolf, Cadeyrin was quick to see the potential.

Kathleen had started calling the puppy 'Wolfie'. Cadeyrin thought it was silly to name a wild animal, but if you were going to name one, it needed a good name. The name she'd chosen was demeaning. If the little wolf was to grow up to be a strong creature, it should have a strong name. However, he didn't want to go against her on the issue, so he had started calling the animal 'Ulfsa' since it was a small ulfa. Ulfaa were strong and good hunters, and that was exactly what the pup would grow into. He hoped that it would retain its friendly demeanor and bond to both Kathleen and him as it became adult.

The two of them, man and wolf, ranged along the forest edge to the west. Deer were likely to bed up in the edge of the trees during the main part of the day. Once dusk approached, they would move out to graze and that would be when they were most vulnerable.

Normally, Cadeyrin would hunt elfraa during the twilight hours, but with Ulfsa along, he thought that he could use the pup's powerful sense of smell to locate deer that were bedded down.

The only problem was that there were no deer to be found. He'd been hunting in the area for days, and his activity had driven most of the game animals to move to safer locations. He'd known this was going to happen. It always did. His people solved the problem by moving to a new location. To them, camps were simply a temporary place, not a long-term home. He sighed as he walked, thinking that he'd have to move their camp. It might be difficult to explain the reason to Kathleen.

His thoughts drifted to her. She was a complete puzzle to him. She was beautiful, more so than any woman he'd ever met. She could have any man she wanted, and yet he'd encountered her alone in the wilderness with no man and no tribe. She was quick-witted and picked up the things he taught her easily, but she had no more idea of how to live and survive than a baby. It was as if she'd been dropped onto the cold lands south of the ice wall from the stars themselves.

Perhaps she was some sort of spirit. His spirit guide had indicated to him that he'd meet someone, and it was obviously she. She'd appeared the very next day. Perhaps she'd been sent to test him. He was doing his best to take care of her and teach her the things he knew that she'd have to know to survive.

He found her attractive. Since she'd been with him, there had been moments where he had almost taken her into his arms. In every instance, he'd sensed that she wanted him to touch her but had some sort of reservation. She'd lean close, catch herself with a jerk and pull farther away than was necessary. He didn't know what to make of it, but he had resolved to let her make the first move.

He wouldn't force her in any way, but it was difficult to resist his desire for her. He wanted to hold her close and keep her safe for an eternity. He knew only too well that relationships were often interrupted by tragedy. The beasts of prey killed many humans, and survival was always a struggle.

That led to another mystery. Her scars. He'd treated them the best he knew. The tribe's Shaman had taught him some herbal cures, and he'd used one that was good for wounds and stiffness. He hadn't really seen how high the scars on her thighs went, but he suspected that they were more extensive than she'd shown him.

The compound included an herb he called 'Tiger's Claw' that helped stiffness and scarring, another plant he knew as 'Dove's Breast' for the bruising she'd had, and willow bark for pain relief, all mixed with animal fat. He knew the resulting salve smelled terrible, but the odor was compensated for by the fact that it worked. She'd been applying it to herself several times a day and had run out twice. He'd had to search hard each time to find the Dove's Breast plant. It didn't seem to be common in the area south of the lake.

He couldn't decide what had caused her scars. He'd seen many people who were horribly scarred, mostly by beasts and sometimes by battle. As nearly as he could figure, her scars were due to some sort of burn. The one time she'd allowed him to apply the salve to her legs, her injuries seemed superficial to the extent they hadn't deeply involved the underlying muscles. He was a self-taught expert on musculature and skin. When you cut up animals on a daily basis, the way they are put together becomes quite familiar.

Despite the lack of deep muscle involvement, the scars were still severe. He knew they made it difficult for her to move, especially when she was cold, but the underlying tissue was whole. If the salve worked as it should, the stiffness would eventually go out of the scar tissue, and it should become more flexible.

He tried to think what that would mean to him. Would she be grateful? And, if she was, would she see him in a better light? Her pulling back from him was almost like a flinch, and he'd become concerned that it was because something about him repelled her.

He kept himself clean as a matter of course since he knew it led to better health. Her pulling back had caused him to become even more scrupulous in his personal cleanliness, but it hadn't seemed to help.

His reverie was interrupted by Ulfsa's snarl. Readying his spear and thrower, he ran forward to see what the wolf had encountered. The lanky pup was standing just outside the edge of the trees with every hair on his hackles bristling. Just as Cadeyrin came up, two dire wolves appeared, walking stiff-legged with their ears flattened, obviously ready for battle.

He wasted no time in hurling his spear. The cast was good. One of the heavy beasts went down, writhing around and trying to bite the spear that had entered its side. The other ignored Ulfsa and charged directly at him.

Cadeyrin had not prepared his second dart and just had time to grasp the fore-shaft in his pouch. He swung the atl-atl and banged the chest-high beast on the end of its nose. It snapped at the spear thrower, momentarily distracted, then angrily lunged and caught his forearm, causing him to drop the thrower. Its fangs went deep, and he yelled in anger, pulling his arm back and dragging the dire wolf close enough to thrust the chert-pointed fore-shaft deep into its throat.

The creature let go of his arm and leaped up, striking his chest and knocking him to the ground. Despite the blood that was pouring from the beast's throat, it hadn't slowed, and Cadeyrin was hard put to use both arms to hold the madly snapping animal away from his neck and face. He couldn't get the fore-shaft in play while he held the dire wolf's head away.

There was a loud growl, and his attacker stumbled. Ulfsa had leaped forward and snapped at one of the dire wolf's hind legs. It turned towards the enraged pup, exposing its side to Cadeyrin. He thrust the sharp point home between its ribs and jammed it deep, reaching for the animal's heart. With a last snarl, the dire wolf staggered and then dropped dead.

Cadeyrin immediately felt in his pouch for a length of sinew, pulled it out, and tightened it around his arm to stop the bleeding. The bite was quite painful, and he was afraid that it had done a lot of damage.

The bleeding slowed to a trickle as he retrieved his spear from the other dire wolf. The two had been a mated pair, separating from the main pack to prepare a den for the spring season. He painfully butchered one, removing the haunches to carry back to camp. It wouldn't be as good as a deer, but it was meat. It would enable them to survive a little longer.

He was worried that the bite would prevent him from hunting. It was on his left forearm. He'd transferred the atl-atl as he grasped the fore-shaft with his right hand. He threw with his right hand, so he thought he could hunt as long as the wound didn't get hot and swollen. Preventing that was his foremost thought.

It was a long walk back to camp, and it was getting dark as he approached. He could tell Kathleen had been busy gathering wood. The fire was high, and there was a large pile of branches nearby. She was standing by the blaze, anxiously watching the tree line, her hands clasped together. Ulfsa had run ahead and was sitting by her, unconcerned as if killing two dire wolves was a normal event.

It took a moment for her to see him in the shadows as he approached. When she did, her face lightened with a smile, and she waved her arm in greeting. By now, he was feeling the wound's effect and was just about at the end of his endurance.

Kathleen suddenly understood that something was wrong with him. She sprinted forward, running quickly. Even feeling the pain of the bite, he was able to appreciate how much easier she moved.

"What happened?" she asked.

He held up his arm, and her eyes locked on the torn and bloody buckskin sleeve.

She gasped, concern causing tears to well up in her eyes as she asked, "Are you alright? I was so worried that you weren't back when it began to get dark. What can I do?"

Cadeyrin dropped the haunch and his weapons, saying, "Help me get this shirt off. I need to see my arm."

She started unlacing the front, and he added, "It is a daoilfa bite. Two attacked us. I killed one, and the other bit me. Ulfsa attacked it, and we killed it, also."

Kathleen pulled the shirt carefully off of his arm. With the sinew removed, the bite was bleeding again. When the wound was exposed, she inspected it in the firelight, her eyes wide and dark.

"It looks bad. What should we do?" she asked.

"I must wash it carefully. Fill the extra pouch with water. I will drop some hot stones in it to heat it. Hot water is best for this," he said.

She started off towards the nearby inlet. He gathered his spear and atl-atl and watched at a distance. He wasn't going to let her take any chances. It was nearly dark and getting to be prime time for predators.

She returned to the fire uneventfully, the pouch brimming with water. It couldn't be set down as it was soft and would collapse, so she continued to hold it. Water dripped out of the seam in a slow stream.

He used a couple of sticks and painfully picked up some smaller stones from the fire ring, heated from the coals. Once they were dropped in the pouch, the water hissed and began to boil, causing Kathleen to quickly grab up a short stick and hang the pouch on it in order to keep her hands out of the hot steam.

When the water was no longer steaming, Cadeyrin carefully washed the bite. The skin and muscle were torn. The dire wolf had shaken his head, tearing the flesh.

Cadeyrin explained to Kathleen, "It's not so bad. The bite will heal. There are no deep tooth holes. I fear those the most. They become hot with white running out. If the skin is red, and the redness spreads, the man often dies."

She told him, "That is what we call 'infected.' The white fluid is a combination of white blood cells that are there to fight off the tiny animals that are causing the wound to become hot. Hot water is a good thing to use since it removes most of the tiny animals. They are called bacteria."

Cadeyrin gave her a searching look. "How do you know so much? I know of no tiny animals. My people say it is the evil spirit of the attacking animal that tries to finish the kill. If the spirit is successful, the man dies."

Kathleen said, "We use special tools that enable us to see the tiny things in the wound. There are tiny animals everywhere that we can't see. These bacteria will attack us when we have wounds that are dirty. Do you know of any herb or plant that will fight the white fluid?"

That question reminded him of the next step, and he said, "There are some plants, but I can't find them in the night. Do you have any of the salve left? It will help, I think."

She carefully doctored the wound with salve and wrapped a clean piece of tanned hide around it, binding it so that the slight pressure stopped the bleeding.

"We will check it during the night and in the morning," he told her. "I'm sorry, but I must rest for a little. Please watch for me."

She nodded as he lay back and sighed in relief. He slept for several hours as she kept the fire going. In the middle of the night, he cried out in his sleep, and she placed her hand on his head. It wasn't hot, so she judged that he had just had a bad dream.

The fire was built up and wouldn't need wood for some time, so she lay down beside him and wrapped her arm over his body. He didn't stir, and she let the combination of his body heat and the fire gradually relax her. Ulfsa came up and lay down, leaning heavily against her back. If any creature threatened, Ulfsa's acute senses would warn them. Kathleen fell asleep, too.

<hr>

Cadeyrin's arm hurt, but he didn't want to move. He'd awakened and opened his eyes to the delightful sight of Kathleen's face resting against his shoulder. His heart leaped. The slight pain of the wound was worth it. Having her next to him was something that he'd wanted ever since he'd first seen her. Up close and sleeping, she was more beautiful than he'd realized. He lay there, his eyes fixed on her face, enjoying the warmth and soft feel of her body against his.

It was not yet dawn, but Ulfsa had risen and was out in the grass doing his morning routine. As Cadeyrin continued to take in Kathleen's face, her eyes opened and met his. She smiled for a moment, and then she sat up in alarm, "Oh! I fell asleep. I should have been watching. And your poor arm! How is it now?"

Cadeyrin did his best not to look disappointed, but it was frustrating. If it took getting bitten to get her close, he would willingly do it again. After a moment, he moved stiffly and sat up, extending his arm.

"Let me look," he requested.

When Kathleen had removed the binding, he could see the wound was clean and showed no signs of infection, as she called it. They washed his arm again with hot water and re-bandaged it with a clean piece of leather.

Kathleen cooked some pieces of dire wolf. The meat was stringy and tough, but they both ate as much as they could stand. Then, together, they went into the forest surrounding the lake.

Cadeyrin was looking for a specific plant that he knew as 'yellow root,' which had anti-infection properties. After searching through the undergrowth awhile, he stumbled upon a clump of the plants. Kathleen helped him dig up the roots. It didn't take long before they had a pouch full of them.

Returning to the camp, he used two stones to grind the roots into a paste. The motion aggravated his wound, and Kathleen took over. Once she'd prepared the paste, he asked her to smear it on the ripped flesh.

By the time she'd finished dressing his injury, it was nearly midday, and they were hungry again. Neither wanted the stringy meat, so they walked over to the river valley. Ulfsa ran down a rabbit along the way, but he ate most of it before they could get close. Shortly after that, Cadeyrin was able to throw a stone at a grouse, knocking it out of a low fir tree.

The roasted bird served as a late lunch, but then there was nothing for supper. Cadeyrin looked at Kathleen and said, "We have to go. There is no game left in this area. We must eat."

The prospect was depressing, and Kathleen's face showed it. With some bitterness, she complained, "This is the best place I've been since I got here. I feel relatively safe in this location, and the idea of leaving and possibly encountering some danger that we can't deal with is frightening. Maybe you can hunt farther out or go around an arm of the lake or something. Why do we have to leave?"

"The game has moved. I go farther, then carrying the meat back takes too long," he replied, reasonably.

She tossed her head, making her hair shine in the sunlight as she shook it in a negative gesture, "I can help you carry the meat. Why don't you give me credit for helping?"

Cadeyrin was puzzled, "I know you can carry. You carry meat often. You do not carry as much as I do, but I am happy for your help. What is this 'credit' thing you want? Tell me. I will find it and give it to you.

Kathleen looked momentarily startled, then laughingly replied, "Credit is saying you're happy for my help. I'm glad you're happy, but I still don't like the idea of moving."

He looked to see if she was making fun of him, then gazed off across the slope towards the hills, hoping that she was not. After a moment, he said, "We need to move. Maybe not far. We could go along the lake for a day, and there might be game. If we stay here, there is only bison or camels to come along. Maybe. There are not as many of them like before. We might have to wait a long time for food."

He paused and then added, "Ulfsa eats the rabbits he catches. I can snare some, but they won't last long."

Kathleen sighed, then asked, "Won't you try to snare rabbits for us? Maybe we can eat them for a while, and the game will come back, or a herd will come by."

She smiled so prettily that Cadeyrin's heart gave a double beat. He didn't want to disappoint her, but she obviously didn't know how bad the situation was. He pondered it and then replied, "I will try to catch rabbits and maybe some grouse, but if there is no game in a hand of fingers' days, we must move."

Kathleen reluctantly agreed with him. She said, "I guess if we have to. Now how do you snare rabbits? Is it something I can learn to do?"

Cadeyrin was happy to change the topic. His mind kept wandering to the moment that he'd awakened to find her lying close. He'd do anything to have that happen again. If he had to go hungry for a few days to make her happy, then so be it.

Followed closely by the young wolf, they walked to a willow thicket. There was numerous rabbit runs threading through the dense stems. The runs were full of sign indicating they were actively being used. Cadeyrin pointed out a clump of fur that had been snagged on a broken branch and some places where the bark had been gnawed.

"This is a good place. The rabbits run through these narrow paths. A snare placed there will catch them," he said.

He showed her how to use a thin willow withe bent back on itself and tied with a slip knot to make a snare. Once positioned a few inches off the ground with the loop cunningly held by the surrounding plants, the snare was ready.

Kathleen asked, "Why isn't there any trigger? The loop will just hang there, and the rabbit won't be caught, will it?"

"The rabbit jumps through the loop. It hits the side or bottom. The loop gets tight. Then we catch it. We must set many snares to catch a few rabbits. Now we move to the next location," he explained.

By the time they'd set twenty snares, it was nearly dark. He led her back to the first snare to check. They'd been working a considerable distance away around the far side of the thicket, and it took a while to walk back.

Kathleen seemed startled and gasped. There was a rabbit hanging in the snare. The loop had closed over its neck, and it was dead. She stepped forward and stroked her hand over the soft fur, then looked up at him, eyes wide.

Cadeyrin's focus was solely on her face. Her eyes were amazing, and he lost himself in them. He belatedly understood that she was upset.

"What's wrong?" he asked.

"The rabbit...it's dead. The snare seems so cruel..." she said in a quiet voice, and then she added, "...but we need to eat."

He smiled and said, "Rabbits are the prey of many animals. They don't live long, but they have many babies. There will be too many rabbits if they are not eaten. The snare kills quickly. The rabbit dies in much pain in the jaws of some beast. It is just the way of life. All things live in their time, and all things die. Only the spirit world is permanent."

He stooped and removed the rabbit, resetting the snare, as he said, "Now we have supper. We must thank the rabbit for feeding us."

Kathleen looked at him with her eyes wide. When he finished, she said, "A warm supper might be worth a few rabbits here and there."

He smiled and replied, "There are always rabbits."

Her mind jumped to a different topic. She asked, "Do you believe in the spirit world? What do you think it is?"

He wondered at her change of topic. Rabbits didn't seem to be connected to spirits. The people he had known hadn't been given to such mental jumps. Maybe that was something that her people did. He started to explain as they walked back to the smoldering fire.

"Every man in my tribe is dead. The women were taken – " he began with a slight catch in his voice but stopped as she asked a question.

She looked at him closely, "Did you – I mean, was there – was there anyone, uh, a woman that you lost to them?"

Her face flushed as she asked the question. Cadeyrin's face fell a little as he answered, "Not to that attack. I had a mate three warm seasons ago. She was killed by a piskat, a big-tooth, only two moons after we'd bonded."

Kathleen was silent, wondering if she'd gone too far.

He continued, "I will not go through that again."

He immediately saw that he had upset her. Her face fell, then she looked down as she apparently thought over what he had said. He had intended to convey that he'd always protect her. He wasn't sure what she thought he meant.

She looked at the horizon, then changed the topic back to her original query, "What about the spirit world?"

He glanced at her and wondered why she looked so sad. Perhaps she'd lost someone she cared about. It might be best if he continued with his discussion.

"I was taught by the Shaman of our tribe. He said I would become Shaman after him, but I did not want that. I'm a good hunter but not so good a

Shaman. I can heal only a little."

She nodded but didn't speak. They continued walking, watching Ulfsa as he ranged far out to their left side and then returned.

"I also visit the spirit world. Before you came, I wanted guidance. My totem spirit is the Ulfa – 'wolf' as you say. When I ask, it sometimes comes to me with knowledge. I was camped at this same camp, where we are now. The night before I killed the big-tooth, the old piskat that was after you, I visited the spirits. The Ulfa came to me. It showed me that someone was coming into my life. The next day I met you. The spirits know everything, but they do not tell us everything."

Kathleen was silent until they arrived at the fire. Cadeyrin quit talking as he pulled the skin off the rabbit, shucking it cleanly. Then he showed her how to use a flint blade to gut it. He threaded the body on a green spit and began to roast it over the coals.

As they ate, she explained to him, "I don't know exactly what you mean by the spirit world, but I have sometimes left my body behind as I was falling asleep or while I was meditating. It is as if I am not fully present in my body and can go elsewhere or see things that are elsewhere. Is that what you mean?"

He replied, "Yes, but there are spirits in that place. You ask for help, and they will guide you to knowledge."

Her face betrayed both confusion and disbelief. She said, "I've never encountered spirits as I meditated. I've only been able to – "

She abruptly stopped in realization.

"What is it?" he asked.

"That's how I got here!" she was excited. "I somehow entered a lucid dream when Drew attacked me, and I used my formula to translate in time."

It was Cadeyrin's turn to look confused.

"What do you mean?" he asked. "Who attacked you? Where is he? He will not attack you again," he said with an angry look.

She smiled, "He's not here. He's in the future. A long time in the future. and he can't reach me now."

Cadeyrin heard the words, but they didn't seem to make sense, "Do you say that your attacker is not now, but moons from now?"

Kathleen took a bite of rabbit thigh. Waving the leg in her right hand, she tried to explain, "I was studying time. Actually, I was studying travel in time. I thought that it would be possible to move from one time to another, and it turns out that I was correct. I traveled from the far future back into my past to your now. I was in danger, and I was...I had lost someone who was dear to me..."

Her face crumpled at the memory of the professor. A tear ran down her cheek. Cadeyrin scooted over beside her and wrapped his arms comfortingly around her, taking a chance that she wouldn't object.

She sighed and relaxed into his embrace, resting her head against his chest. She raised her hand and placed it against his chest, sliding it over the heavy muscle to the center where she paused, feeling his heartbeat. She raised her face to his, inquiringly, hope and trust in her eyes.

His skin was flushed, and he shivered in the cold breeze. It was as if every ounce of his blood had flowed to the skin under her hand. He lowered his face to hers, and their lips met. She sighed and pressed closer, but the next minute she pulled back, turning away from him.

He took a deep breath in consternation. What had he done to offend her? She was unreadable. One minute he thought she wanted him, and then she gave him a totally opposite signal. All he knew was that his heart was beating as quickly as if he were preparing for a battle. He held his hand out towards the fire and observed that it was shaking. Then he looked at her and saw that she was quivering, also. Perhaps she was cold. He stood and threw more wood on the fire, then looked at her.

Kathleen shakily began again, "I traveled into my past to reach this time. Now I'm stuck here. I don't know if I'll be able to return to my own time. They need my knowledge, but now I have to live in this wild land with you, and...and I don't know how."

Cadeyrin understood her. She was from what was almost surely a much better place than he was able to offer. Perhaps she had a man there, a man who could give her much more than he. He thought of her clothing. She'd been wearing the piskat skin coat he'd created for her over the top of the clothing she'd had on when he rescued her.

That clothing was a sort of a miracle to him. It was amazingly soft and stitched so finely that he couldn't comprehend how someone could make it. If that was the sort of thing she had in her time, how could she ever be content with the crude things he could create? How could she be content with him? Sadly, he turned to look out over the gathering darkness.

His voice was harsh with hurt as he said, "Perhaps you will learn how to return to your place in time. For now, I will give you what I can, though it is not much. Perhaps the one you lost is waiting for you to return."

❖

Kathleen had been looking wistfully at his profile, wondering why he seemed so sad, but at his last statement, she raised her eyebrows. He sounded angry. She didn't reply, and when he turned back, she kept her head down and gnawed at the rabbit leg.

Ulfsa stood up and growled softly. The odor of the cooking meat had attracted a homotherium, a medium-sized saber-toothed cat with long forelegs and shorter hind legs. Cadeyrin pointed it out to Kathleen as it walked, hyena-like, circling the fire at the edge of the light. "Makkat, he commented. "There were many in the past, but they no longer circle the fire as often as they once did."

Kathleen remembered that some of them had treed her on her first day in the past and that they'd circled the fire several nights. If they were rare, she was afraid to know what common would mean. She didn't like the thought that the cat was stalking around the fire, just trying to figure out how to get at her.

"Can't you do something about it?" she asked plaintively.

Cadeyrin glanced at her and said, "It harms no one. It is afraid of the fire and will not come near. Other predators will stay away if it is here. Leave it be."

That seemed like a rather cavalier dismissal of her concern. Hurt, she decided to ignore him, and, with a shudder at the thought of the cat, she lay back as if she was unconcerned.

Ulfsa decided that there was no immediate danger and walked over to lie beside her. She mulled over what had happened as she tried to sleep.

It had been both a wonderful and frustrating evening. She was now convinced that Cadeyrin would never have anything to do with her. After all, she thought, he said he would never have another woman.

Still, the memory of his kiss and the amazing feel of his chest muscles under the buckskin danced through her head. Try as she would, she could not forget the feel of his lips burning against hers.

Perhaps she shouldn't have pulled away. Perhaps she should have – the thought was simultaneously frightening and arousing. She wasn't sure how such things progressed, and she was fearful that he would be disgusted if he saw the extent of her scars. Besides, she couldn't risk it. If she became pregnant in this raw land, what hope could she have? Even if he stayed with her, scars and all, she'd probably die in childbirth or be eaten by some horrible beast.

She rolled over and buried her face in her arms in despair. It was better if she didn't get too involved with him. That way, when she was killed, as she was sure she would be, he wouldn't have to suffer. She just had to concentrate on understanding how she got here. Perhaps she could figure out how to get back. She didn't fit here. She missed her own time and felt she somehow owed it to society to publish her research.

The cold stars slowly circled the pole star as the night wore on. Long before the fire died down, the makkat grew tired and left to seek prey elsewhere. Cadeyrin sat, moodily staring into the coals. He'd been sure that she loved him. He'd been about to tell her that she meant everything to him, and then things had somehow gone horribly wrong. What was he to do now?

He thought sadly of his vow. He hadn't wanted to fall in love with another woman, ever. But that was then. Now it was too late.

He looked over at the woman's sleeping form and admitted his feelings aloud, whispering softly to himself, "I love you, Kathleen. I don't care where you came from, and I don't care if you had someone there. I only want you for myself."

How he was going to win her, he had no idea.

Moving

F ive days later, hunger forced them to leave the camp. There had been fewer rabbits than Cadeyrin had thought, and they'd been unable to snare any for the last two days. No herds had come up the valley, and even though he'd been hunting from dawn until dusk, he hadn't seen any game. The only good news was that his arm was healing without any sign of what Kathleen called 'infection.'

He had brought in one grouse, but it was barely a meal for the two of them without considering the growing wolf.

Reluctantly, they gathered up their sparse belongings, tying the bundled hides with sinew for easy carrying. Cadeyrin made up two packs consisting of the bundled hides and some improvised shoulder straps. Kathleen picked up the extra pouches while he buried the fire, and then they set off, the wolf ranging ahead once he understood which way they wanted to go.

They headed westward along the southern side of the lake. The day was cold and blustery, the wind gusting hard and then dying down intermittently. It was a long, hungry walk that put Kathleen's endurance to the test.

By late afternoon, they were approaching the western end of the lake. It seemed as if they'd passed hundreds of inlets and coves, sometimes having to detour for miles to cross the intervening water. Her scars hadn't bothered her for the first several hours, but now they were pulling a bit, and she found the sensation irritating. That irritation added to the overall feeling of discontent she had with herself. She was unable to bury the sense that she should just give in to her feelings for Cadeyrin, but that way lay danger.

She couldn't seem to reconcile her previous, intellectual life with the concept of becoming a primitive hunter's bride. Besides giving up on physics and her research, her life expectancy would undoubtedly drop radically. *Of course,* she thought to herself, *that's nothing I'm not already facing, especially if I can't figure out how to return to the future.*

One minute she'd think along these lines, and the next, she'd find her heart speeding up as she watched Cadeyrin's movements. The contrast was enough to put her temper completely on edge.

Finally, she snapped at Cadeyrin, "Haven't we gone far enough? What is it with you? Do you think we have to walk all the way to the Black Hills in one day?"

"What black hills?" he asked, puzzled and obviously a little hurt by her tone. "Do you know what lies ahead?"

She instantly regretted her attitude and tried to speak more pleasantly, "I know a little, but the Black Hills are many days away, far over a flat stretch of land. As far as this lake is concerned, this territory is new to me."

He looked around, appraising the lay of the land. A narrow cove coming from the western edge of the lake extended through the trees that covered the hillside. They were near the top, on the north side of a hill. The view was mostly obscured by forest both to the east and west.

He led her up to the crest of the hill. From that vantage, there was a good view to the southwest. They could see groves of trees interspersed with meadow and sloughs in the dimming light. The sun's rays were lengthening, and the trees cast long shadows in which predators could be hiding. Kathleen shuddered at the thought and stepped closer to his strength, despite her ill humor.

As they watched, a flight of geese flew overhead and landed with splashes and happy honks in a nearby slough. In the distance, there was a family group of mammoths browsing near a grove of deciduous trees. The lead cow raised her trunk and trumpeted, sending a brassy echo rolling up and down the rounded hills through the rapidly cooling air. Kathleen paused in wonder. It was an incredibly beautiful scene, despite the sense of wildness that it held.

Without saying anything, Cadeyrin placed his arm around her shoulders. Together the two stood side-by-side watching the sunset. As it grew darker, there was a squalling noise from a far distance. It was faint, but Cadeyrin said, "That's a piskat, a big-tooth tiger. It's angry about something. Perhaps it missed its prey."

He turned to Kathleen, placing both hands on her shoulders and looking into her eyes. For a moment, their eyes met, but then her nerve failed again, and she lowered hers, looking at the ground. He sighed, turned away, and said, "We need wood for the night. It's getting dark. Come."

They returned to the other side of the hill and busied themselves with setting up camp.

It was morning, and Kathleen was, as usual, hungry. Her stomach was rolling around as if it were thinking of going hunting on its own. When she stood and stretched, it made a loud rumble, startling Ulfsa. Cadeyrin laughed. When she shot him an angry glare, he dug in his pouch and pulled out a small, hide-wrapped package.

"Here. I've been holding this back. This is the time for it," he said as he handed it to her.

It was some small pieces of jerky. She hadn't known that he was carrying it, or she might have asked for some before. Now, her hands trembled as she hastily shoved a piece into her mouth. It was tough, but it tasted wonderful.

Ulfsa came over, wagging his tail and looking at the dirt around her feet to check for scraps that she might have dropped. She glanced at Cadeyrin for approval, and when he smiled, she dropped a piece and said, "Oops."

The wolf snapped it up almost before it touched the ground. They both laughed as he looked beseechingly at her, wanting more.

Cadeyrin twisted with a small groan and stretched his back. It had been colder last night, and it was apparent from the way he moved that he was stiff. Kathleen had a moment of pleasure, reflecting that she wasn't the only one who had suffered from their long walk. Then she felt guilty, thinking that he'd been saving the jerky for her. He was both tired and hungry, and he hadn't complained. She was just a burden to him. She sniffed a bit. Her emotions seemed to be going all directions simultaneously.

She watched him pick up his weapons. He turned to her and said, "If we're going to eat today, we'd better hunt. I'd like you to come with me. This is a new area, and it might not be as safe as our old camp."

"Let me wash my face first," she said and started towards the nearby lake. He watched for a moment and then trailed along after her. He could not sense any immediate danger.

<hr>

Kathleen disappeared behind a tree for a short time and then came out, wearing a strained expression. When she looked at him, Cadeyrin asked, "What?"

She looked around, seeking escape from the necessity of speaking. Then she drew a deep breath, gathered her courage, and said, "I'm bleeding. It's my time, and I don't have any..."

She paused, searching for words.

Cadeyrin looked puzzled for a moment. She knew he'd been alone for a long time, but he couldn't have forgotten about women. Then a look of comprehension came over his face as he figured out what she was trying to tell him.

"Oh," he said, "I hadn't thought about that."

He looked back at her inquiringly.

She tried again, "I need something to – to soak up the blood, or my clothes will become a mess."

She was horribly embarrassed. She'd always had a very light, intermittent flow, and this was the first she'd had since arriving in the past, but she didn't want to ruin her only undergarment. She'd been washing it nightly since the first few days, and it was showing signs of wear. She didn't know how long it would be before she would have to go 'totally primitive', as she put it to herself.

Cadeyrin looked a little surprised as he asked, "Can't you use rabbit skins? Those are what the women of my tribe used."

Kathleen was even more embarrassed. "Rabbit skins?" she repeated slowly. "I guess that would work. I didn't think of that."

He paused, then asked curiously, "What do women do in your time?"

She shook her head. She was embarrassed enough already. Couldn't he see that? Why did he have to be so curious?

Without waiting for her to answer, he dug around in one of the pouches and pulled out one of the three skins that he'd taken the time to cure.

She was unfamiliar with the concept and looked at it helplessly. He took it from her with a serious expression and showed her how the women had trimmed and folded the skins.

Her face was flushed and hot by the time he was finished. Somewhat tentatively, she took the folded pad from him and returned to her sheltering tree.

Ulfsa had gone on to the water, but Cadeyrin waited until she ventured out again. He smiled at her and asked, "Will that work?"

She wished he'd just forget about the topic, but she tried to answer amicably, "Yes. It feels funny to me, but it should do the job."

⊶◆⊷

Some time later, they were stalking a deer that she'd sighted. The animal was still browsing in some brush near the edge of a grove of spruce trees. Cadeyrin had directed her to wait for five hands of breaths and then continue walking towards the deer. She was keeping Ulfsa with her. Cadeyrin had moved deep into the trees and disappeared. She hoped that he would pick the right location for an ambush.

Once she'd waited, she released the lanky pup. He wasn't sure what they were hunting as yet, since the wind was quartering away from the deer, and he hadn't seen or scented it, but he was quivering with excitement. Still, he was experienced enough to move quietly beside her until he understood what was expected of him.

Presently, the deer raised its head, looking her way. She froze. It wasn't sure what it had seen. Then the wind gusted around the trees in such a way that Ulfsa caught the animal's scent.

Instantly, he was off, moving swiftly through the tall grass and staying out of sight. Kathleen watched, waiting for the drama to develop.

The doe had decided that she didn't like the area, but she wasn't alarmed enough to flee. She started moving towards the sheltering conifers, stopping to nibble twigs along the way.

As he came out of the tall grass, Ulfsa began to run. The doe leaped high and bounded towards the trees, easily clearing the tall bushes with each jump. As the deer leaped over the last part of the thicket, there was a flicker from the trees that impacted her side. She came crashing down, struggling to rise, but by then, Ulfsa was on her. Kathleen heard a bleat as he caught her throat, then everything was silent.

Cadeyrin appeared at the edge of the spruces and waved for her to come on. By the time she'd caught up, he had gutted the deer, and Ulfsa was hastily eating something disgusting from the pile of entrails.

Chapter Fourteen

New Ideas

Back at the camp, they ate until their stomachs were bulging. Kathleen thought that she'd get fat if she kept eating like this, although common sense told her that food was scarce, and she was getting far more exercise than ever before. She glanced at Cadeyrin's lean middle with a sense of appreciation. Living in the cold

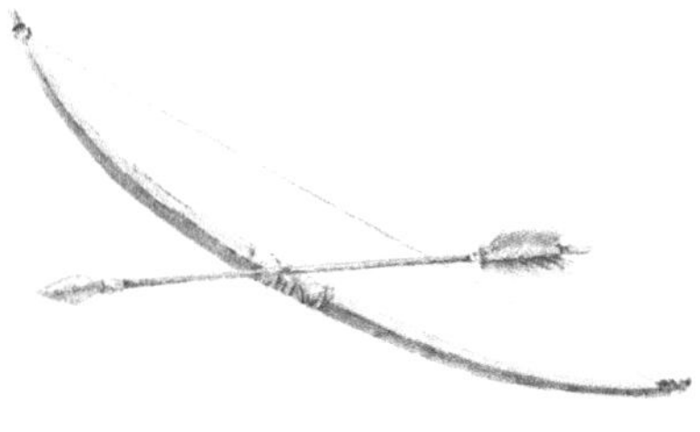

required so many calories that getting fat was the least of her worries.

He was stretched out on the skins and trying to nap, but Kathleen wasn't sleepy. She regretted getting angry with him over the relocation. It seemed that he had been correct. The game had moved. Here, in this new place, it wasn't hunted and was less alert. She wanted to do something to show him that she was sorry and that she was an asset.

Now that she thought about it, she came to the conclusion that she spent too much time feeling resentful over being so dependent on him. She was literally helpless in this land. She glanced at his relaxed, sleeping form. She'd been incredibly lucky to encounter him.

He'd rescued her and had been more solicitous and caring and less demanding than any man she'd ever heard of. She doubted that any male of her time would have treated her as well.

Her initial expectations of a Paleolithic hunter had been wrong. When she'd first seen him, she'd almost been ready to throw herself to the saber-tooth. She was sure that the hunter would force her to have sex at the first opportunity, and she'd momentarily thought that being eaten would be easier to bear.

Now that she knew him, she wished... She had a sudden insight that interrupted that train of thought. She whispered, "I haven't had any instances of deja vu since I came through time."

Her mind raced in speculation. *Perhaps the several times she'd felt that she'd done the same thing before were caused by her gradual understanding of the time-travel equations. If so, deja vu was a sign that she understood enough to make use of the equations. Perhaps the deja vu experience amounted to some sort of miniature time translation where she was sending her perception forward or backward in time. She resolved to watch for the next case. It might signal that she was ready to return to the future.*

That thought stopped her dead. *Did she want to return? Of course. Life here was too hard. But what about Cadeyrin? Could she leave him?*

These thoughts shot through her mind in an instant, followed by a rationalization. *I should go back to my own place. The primitive hunter knows how to live here. I don't. And, besides, I don't really have a commitment to him. I'm attracted to him, though. True. I can't risk becoming pregnant here with no medical care. I'd most likely die. No. I should go back.*

She shook her head. *Enough daydreaming. She had to live with him until she could go back. Right now, what could she do to show him that she was valuable and capable? Modern weapons came to mind. She had no metal and no knowledge of working it either, but maybe, just maybe, she could make a bow.*

She was in awe of how well he used his spear-thrower. It allowed him to cast the light spears farther and with more force than anyone could have thrown them by hand alone. He was also deadly accurate with the thing. He rarely missed. But a bow...

Now, with a bow, he could carry smaller arrows, and they would be lighter, so he could carry far more of them. That would increase their security by an exponential factor. Maybe she could learn to shoot arrows, also. That was an appealing thought. She'd be able to take care of herself. Encouraged, she began to look for some kind of wood to use.

She was confident that it was safe since Ulfsa wasn't stirring. Cadeyrin raised his head and looked at her when she stood. He sniffed the wind, then lay back, closing his eyes. His actions confirmed her judgment.

She searched along the edge of the trees and finally settled on a piece of dried alder. It wasn't too thick, yet it seemed strong enough while still being flexible. She bent it by placing one end against her foot and pulling the nearly straight shaft against her knee. It took an effort, but it bent, snapping back when she released it. It might do.

She returned to the fire and searched in the pouches for some sinew. None of the strips were long enough to work, so she took two and tied them together. They still didn't seem thick enough to hold up.

She took more, knotted them, and then twisted several together. This made a rough and irregular cord. It might work and, anyway, she didn't really know how to make a better string. She'd just have to try this.

She tied one end around the alder shaft. Then a problem arose. She wasn't strong enough to hold the shaft bent and simultaneously tie the other end. She thought about it and then got one of Cadeyrin's flint-tipped fore-shafts. It made an excellent knife.

Using the razor-sharp flint, she carefully cut a deep groove around the free end of the alder. Then she tied a loop in the string, making sure the string was several inches shorter than the length of wood. This time, she was able to bend the wood across her knee and shakily place the loop over the end, settling it in the groove. It held when she released the wood. She had a bow of sorts.

She experimentally pulled the string, and it made a low thrumming sound as she released it. Both Ulfsa and Cadeyrin immediately sat up, looking at her.

She held the bow out to Cadeyrin and he looked at it somewhat suspiciously.

"What is that?" he asked. "Are you stretching the sinew for some reason?"

She proudly explained, "No. It's a weapon. You can take arrows, smaller darts, and shoot them with it."

"Smaller darts." he said, wonderingly. "Will they be heavy enough to fly far? And, how can this shoot anything? It's too long to hold one end and throw with."

Kathleen somehow had convinced herself that he'd recognize the bow and automatically know how to use it. Cadeyrin was remarkably intelligent in her experience and quick to pick things up. Perhaps this was just too much of a jump. She tried to explain.

"No. You hold the middle of the wood and place the end of the dart on the sinew. Then you pull back and release it. The wood straightens and the dart flies away quickly. It doesn't have to be heavy because it goes so fast."

Cadeyrin's brow furrowed as he tried to imagine what she was describing. Then the wrinkles smoothed, and he gave a merry grin, "That is a great thing you've made! It is clear to me now. I've never seen such a thing, but I understand what you say. I will try it."

He grabbed one of his spear shafts. The spears he used were about five feet long without the fore-shaft attached. He grasped the bow clumsily and rested the spear across it. Then he pulled back and released. The spear traveled a few feet, and the sinew cord broke, one of the ends snapping across his arm and leaving a red mark. He winced.

Kathleen hastily said, "I must have made the cord wrong. It shouldn't break."

He inspected her work without comment. Then he said, "I think I can make it stronger."

She cooked some more deer while he sat cross-legged and worked with some moistened sinew. By evening, he had made and tested several other cords, finally getting one that satisfied him.

The spear shaft was obviously too heavy for the light bow. The farthest it traveled was in a looping arc of about thirty feet.

Kathleen explained to him, "You need a much smaller and lighter arrow. Maybe one that is the thickness of my little finger and about the length of your arm."

That set him to gathering willow shoots. By the time he'd finished, it was getting dark, so they ate more venison. She watched him work on smoothing the willow shoots until she drifted off to sleep.

Cadeyrin was taken with the idea of the new weapon. It seemed to him that this bow thing that Kathleen had invented could be a major advantage, if he could just get it to work the way she said it would. He spent most of the night smoothing and working over the willow shoots he'd selected. He would make small points for the arrows.

The spear points he made were usually a finger in length. They were cleverly designed to be re-usable if they broke. It was not unusual for a point to strike a bone and break in half, leaving the base attached to the fore-shaft and the tip stuck somewhere in the animal.

When this happened there were two different techniques he could use to salvage the point. If the break was close to the shaft attachment, he would re-shape the tip, mounting the fore-shaft in the flute that was a distinctive feature of all of his people's points.

If the break was near the tip, he was sometimes able to chip away until he'd created a new point on the broken part. It was shorter than the original but could still be used. He had plenty of experience doing this and thought that he could, if he were careful, make some smaller points from the spare pieces of flint that he still had in his knapping pouch.

While he smoothed the willow shafts, he studied the alder branch with the groove that Kathleen had cut. It was crude so he decided to smooth it also.

When Kathleen awoke, Cadeyrin was sleeping beside a small pile of perfectly smoothed willow arrow shafts and the newly smoothed alder bow. The bow looked almost like something that could be purchased in a sporting goods store to her untrained eyes.

She built up the fire and cooked some of the venison. They had at least another day's worth. It went quickly, since Ulfsa had put on a growth spurt and ate several pounds of meat daily. Once the odor of cooking meat had intensified, Cadeyrin woke, stretched, and sat up, rubbing his eyes.

"How late did you stay up?" she asked.

He yawned and replied, "Dawn was near when I lay down. I have the bow ready, now I need to use the cord to tie the ends of the bow together."

"It's called a bow-string," she said. She knew that much at least.

He carefully bent the alder staff and looped the cord he'd made the night before over the ends. It held, and he looked the bow over carefully, experimentally pulling and releasing the cord.

It twanged with a mellow tone. Their eyes met and she smiled at him, eliciting a smile in return.

Taking an arrow shaft, he held it against the bow with one hand and pinched the other end with two fingers. This time, when he pulled and released, the shaft shot over a hundred feet. It wobbled and ended up landing sideways on the ground.

Kathleen tried to remember what she knew about arrows. She said, "It needs feathers on the back end. They will keep it going straight. The other thing is, I think you hold the arrow on the string differently, but I'm not sure."

"How do feathers help the arrow?" he asked, curiosity shining in his eyes.

She thought about trying to explain drag, balance points, center-of-gravity, and aerodynamics, but then answered simply, "They work like a bird's tail. Birds have tails to help them fly straight, and arrows have to fly straight so you can hit what you shoot at. In addition to the tail, the weight of a point will help it fly straighter."

Cadeyrin looked closely at the end of the shaft and then said, "We have no feathers."

Kathleen knew that catching grouse or other birds was always problematic, a matter of opportunity rather than planning. She thought about the birds and their habits. Perhaps it would be best to try and find a spot where they were roosting. There might be some discarded feathers there. Then there were the geese on the lake. Those might be an option.

She shivered, thinking about that. The water was still icy cold this early in the spring. It wouldn't be a smart idea to try to catch waterfowl if it involved getting wet, but the geese or ducks might be nesting. Perhaps that would be a solution.

Just as she arrived at that conclusion, Cadeyrin stood and clicked at Ulfsa. He said, "I'm going to the lake to look for feathers."

He'd arrived at the same conclusion as she had. I must be learning, she thought with a touch of pride. She jumped up and said, "I can help with that. It should be easy."

They searched the reed beds and the undergrowth that grew close to the water. Once Ulfsa figured out that they were looking for prey in this odd area, he was more helpful.

He'd been wandering around, sniffing here and there, but not concentrating on waterfowl until Cadeyrin found a spot where a duck had been resting. There were no feathers, but the scent was strong enough to give the pup a clue as to what game was afoot. He immediately began ranging quickly along the shore, working through tangles of brush that the two humans found impenetrable.

After an hour of exercise and scrambling through thickets and reeds, they had a handful of discarded feathers. The count went up significantly when Kathleen found a spot where a mink had killed and eaten a wood duck.

After gathering the wood duck feathers, they called a halt. They had collected more than enough to attach to the arrow shafts. The problem was they weren't quite sure how to attach them.

Kathleen knew that they were supposed to be split and glued to the shaft, but she couldn't think of any adhesive to use. On the way back to the camp her mind worked overtime examining various ideas. By the time they'd arrived, she thought she had a workable idea.

Cadeyrin sat down with the feathers and picked up a shaft. He inspected it carefully, engrossed in the problem, ignoring her. He held a long feather against the end of the willow stick, moving it around to see how it might best fit. She saw that he was somewhat at a loss trying to firm up the concept.

She took another arrow and some feathers to the other side of the fire near the pouch containing some bits of sinew. She used a flint chip that had been stored in the flint-knapping pouch and carefully split the sinew into thin threads. Then she tried to shave a strip of feather off one side of a quill. Her first effort was only partially successful, but by the time she'd ruined three feathers, she discovered how to split the quill rather than shave the feather and quickly ended up with something she thought would be suitable for fletching.

Cadeyrin was still studying the problem when she cleared her throat. He glanced up and saw that she was holding up an arrow shaft that appeared to have grown its own feathers. He dropped what he was holding and moved over beside her.

"How – " he started, but then he saw what she'd done. The strips of quill were carefully tied to the shaft with sinew. She'd tied the quill strips at three points to ensure they stayed attached.

Kathleen was elated at her success. "Watch this," she said. She stood and threw the shaft like a miniature spear. It flew smoothly through the air.

He jumped up and threw his arms around her in a happy hug that she eagerly returned. He looked down at her, smiled and said, "You are wonderful. How did you know how to do that?"

Her face was flushed as she smiled back up at him. "I just thought about how best to attach the feathers and then tried it. It works well, don't you think?"

He nodded without saying anything, his eyes locked on hers. She glanced at the arrow and started to pull back as if she was going to pick it up, but he tightened his hold.

She looked up, trying to understand his intent. Then her eyes widened as he lowered his face to hers. As their lips met, she tightened her arms around his neck.

She was elated. Her heart was beating a thousand miles a minute, and she found it difficult to think. He was kissing her again. She gloried in the feel of his hot lips on hers. The sensation was something that she had never imagined in her prior life.

He lifted his head, breathing deeply for a moment, and then lowered to her mouth again. She responded eagerly, but then that awful, suspicious and fearful part of her mind kicked in.

What if he wanted more? Would she be happy with him? Would he discard her when he saw the scars on her hips?

No, she tried to reassure herself. *He's already seen my thighs when he first put the salve on the scars. He didn't look disgusted then. He only looked concerned. But her mind continued working at the idea. She thought, Maybe he would treat anyone that way. Of course. It was simple compassion for a wounded human. He wouldn't really want me if he saw all of my body.*

With that last thought, she pushed against his chest until he released her. Then she walked over and got the arrow. As she turned back to him, she gave a shaky laugh, trying to make it seem as if she'd just been caught up in the celebration and not deeply aroused.

"Now all you have to do is to put a point on this and it will be ready," she gaily said.

—◇—

Cadeyrin was trying to control his emotions. It was all he could do not to wrap his arms around her again, but it was apparent that she'd only been momentarily engaged due to his praise. It was extremely frustrating.

He wanted her with all of his heart, but she didn't seem to understand. He had no experience in how to deal with such a situation. It was normal for his people to signify their attraction to each other by a series of discreet glances. He'd tried that with her, but she didn't seem to get the idea. To him, kissing her had practically shouted that he wanted her as his mate, but now she seemed to be making light of that, also.

He sighed deeply and took the arrow with a negative shake of his head. He inspected the fletching and said, "I'll do this to the rest of the shafts. Then I will need to practice. If I point the shafts, it's likely that the points will break as I practice. I don't know how to work this thing yet and it will take experience to know what to expect."

Kathleen nodded soberly. He watched as she became more animated. An idea had grabbed her attention. She asked, "Can we make a bow for me? I'm sure I could learn to use one. I'm not strong enough to throw spears like you do, but I could use a weaker bow. If I could learn to shoot, think how much safer we'd be. With two people shooting arrows, nothing would dare to approach us."

That was a new idea. In Cadeyrin's experience, women would fight if forced, but they usually used knives and stones. He'd never heard of a woman using a spear-thrower. In fact, it seemed a little frightening to him. His people had a tradition that atl-atls were only to be touched by men. The Shaman had told him that a woman's touch would cause the atl-atl's spirit to depart, and it would never again launch spears accurately.

Then he came up with a suitable rationale. The bow was something that Kathleen had invented. It was hers in some indefinable way and as such, it wouldn't take offense if she used it. She'd even made the one he was planning on using, so it must be acceptable for her to touch it.

He nodded affirmatively to her, "I will learn what it needs by using it first, and then I can make one that will work best for you."

Unaware of his momentary reservation, Kathleen nodded in agreement.

Cadeyrin took the bow and tried pinching the butt of the arrow to hold it in place against the cord. The bow had also dried somewhat overnight and felt more difficult to pull. The cord slipped out of his pinch before he'd pulled the arrow fully back. Nevertheless, the arrow shot out over the grass and disappeared into the top of a spruce tree that was more distant than his farthest spear cast.

He shouted in amazement. Ulfsa jumped up and looked around, ready to fight whatever was attacking them, but then saw Kathleen laughing and sat back down with a sheepish expression on his lupine face.

Ignoring the two, Cadeyrin ran excitedly to the tree and began searching. He discovered the arrow lying on the far side of the spruce and returned to Kathleen.

"It went farther than I could have thrown a spear," he said, amazement on his face. "I didn't think that such a small and light shaft could go so far."

He hefted the bow in his hand and looked at it carefully, as if searching for the magic that made it so powerful. Then he looked at her, saying, "This is truly magical. Are you sure you're a woman and not a heavenly spirit?"

Kathleen blushed. "No, I'm only a woman, and not even a very good one," she said.

He frowned, "You're the best woman I've known."

He felt a twinge in his heart at the memory of his deceased mate, but then he decided he was only telling her what he truly believed.

She snorted and shook her head. "Why don't you pick out a target in the grass to shoot at?"

He saw the utility in that suggestion and pointed out a small weed that stood near a barren spot where the soil was poor. It was at about the maximum distance he could throw a spear, so he thought it would be a good test.

Remembering how the cord had slipped from his pinch, he experimentally tried hooking his forefinger around the string and pulling it back. It was easier, but hurt his finger. Kathleen stepped closer and said, "I think you should use three fingers to pull with. Hold the arrow between them."

That worked. This time, he was able to fully draw the bow and the arrow shot through the midday air and landed a few feet to one side and beyond the weed. He thought about the shot as he retrieved the arrow. He needed to adjust the trajectory. It flew in a flatter arc than his spears. As for the deviation to the side, he thought that the base of the arrow had bounced a little off the bow. He could correct that by holding it differently.

⸻◆⸻

By mid-afternoon, he'd shot the arrow so many times that the shaft had finally splintered. Kathleen had watched for a time, but then had busied herself, fletching the other shafts. She ran out of feathers before she'd finished, but he now had ten more arrows.

He practiced until the light grew dim. He'd broken two more arrows and accidentally lost one that ricocheted off the barren ground and slid into the tall grass, but he'd adjusted his technique and aim and was now able to strike within a few inches of the weed with nearly every shot.

That was quite accurate enough for hunting. Some hunters never managed that accuracy with their spears. He knew he could hit what he aimed at with the bow.

He spent the evening hours working on knapping a small point. It was about half the size of his normal spearheads, and the work was more exacting. By the time Kathleen was yawning and ready for sleep, he had one point created and was working at mounting it on an arrow shaft. This involved splitting the shaft to insert the base of the arrowhead between the halves and then binding it in place with moistened sinew. When the sinew dried, it would shrink and the head would be locked in place.

Later he would work pinesap into the sinew, coating it thoroughly. That would protect it from becoming wet and loosening.

⸺⊙⸺

Kathleen settled down to sleep, hearing the sound of a saber-tooth's roar in the far distance. She felt secure in the knowledge that Cadeyrin was there to protect her.

Her last conscious thought was the memory of how satiny-smooth his lips had felt. She sighed and drifted off, smiling.

Chapter Fifteen

Daoilfa

Cadeyrin was now on his third bow. The first one had broken when he pulled the cord back farther, trying to see how far a longer arrow could fly. The second one had been made from spruce wood and had cracked after only a few shots.

This one was made from a lone hedge apple tree that he'd found growing far to the south of the camp. It had been standing in the middle of a grassy plain as if it enjoyed the challenge of fighting the elements by itself. When he'd tried breaking off a small branch, he'd been astounded at how tough the wood was.

It took quite a while to haggle off a suitable dried branch, and he broke two spear points on the hardwood. Shaping it had been difficult, but he went slowly, using a larger piece of flint that he repeatedly sharpened.

The hedge bow was stronger and took a lot of effort to pull, but the result was that the arrows flew even straighter and faster. He had gone through a lot of them, also.

He'd made a long, narrow pouch with a shoulder strap, and it held fourteen arrows. With the bow and arrows and his atl-atl and spears – he couldn't convince himself to give them up yet – he felt armed as strongly as an entire tribe.

He'd returned to the hedge tree and cut a slimmer branch for a lighter bow. Kathleen was still practicing, but she showed promise. Her shots were almost as accurate as his, though they didn't go as far or as fast.

The biggest obstacle he'd encountered was creating the smaller points. He was now out of flint. He only had one mostly-used core stone, and it was now gone. He didn't know where he could find any suitable rock in this territory, and that was bothersome. He resolved to keep on the watch for any likely locations.

He had to hunt soon. They needed meat. The last of the venison had been gone for two days. The weather was still quite cold, but it was spring, and the grass had started growing. Because of the season, it was likely that some herds were on the move somewhere. He just had to figure out where. Perhaps a little farther to the west would be a good place to hunt.

Cadeyrin was preparing to leave early the next morning. He wanted to discuss it with Kathleen, but, after their brief moment of closeness, she'd retreated and now only spoke to him when she had to. He understood that she was upset, but he wasn't sure what he'd done to merit her displeasure. He had the momentary insight that she was afraid to open her emotions to him due to her prior experience. He could sympathize. He'd felt the same for a time, but now things were different for him.

Finally, he cleared his throat to get her attention. When she looked at him, he said, "We need meat. I leave in the early morning to hunt. Herds will be moving. The grass has started growing again. It may take more than one day. If I kill a large animal, it would be better to make camp at the kill site and not carry meat back. Ulfsa will come with me, and he will be a great help. I think you should come, also. You will be in danger here by yourself."

He could see that he'd upset her somehow. He wanted her to come. He could use her help. She was almost as good a shot with her bow as he was. He didn't want to leave her in the way of possible danger. He'd thought that he was stating the obvious, but somehow she'd taken offense.

She frowned at him and replied, "You don't think I can help? I'm not helpless. I can shoot arrows too. I might even shoot a bison myself."

He stuttered as he started to reply. The last thing he wanted was to have her be angry with him.

"N – No. I know you can help. I do not want to risk you staying alone."

Her stomach was hurting, demanding food. The hunger was wearing at her, and she wasn't minded to give him any quarter.

"So you think I can't take care of myself. I'd be lost without you. I think I'll stay here. Just go ahead and see if I care. Oh, and you can take Ulfsa too. I don't need him," she snapped.

The look on his face instantly made her regret the outburst. He looked both sad and hurt as he replied, "No. Please. I want you to come with me." He swallowed. "I need your help."

She was glad that he'd asked the way he did. She hadn't wanted to stay by herself. He was right. It was too dangerous, and she was used to relying on him for security. She'd let her emotions control her.

She tried to smile as she said, "That's good. I'll come with you. I'd miss Ulfsa too much, and, besides, you might get hurt and not be able to return. It would be better with two of us."

Cadeyrin frowned as he tried to understand what had just happened. Finally, he said, "Good. We need to sleep since we'll be leaving early."

⚬

Kathleen wanted to talk in the hopes that she could somehow make him understand that her hunger had made her speak so angrily, but he walked off out of the firelight to relieve himself, leaving her mulling over how she could have dealt with the situation better.

He returned abruptly. He'd taken a spear with him, but now he put it down and took up the bow, looping the quiver over his shoulder as he turned back towards the darkness.

Kathleen sat up, alarmed. "What is it? What's out there?" she asked, belatedly noticing that Ulfsa was also standing, the hair on his shoulders bristling and his tail held low. Whatever it was, it was something that alarmed him, and from the way he held his tail, it was a serious threat.

Cadeyrin didn't turn his head from the darkness. He addressed her in a low voice, "There are daoilfa coming. By their scent, it is a big pack. They mean to attack."

"Aren't they afraid of the fire?" she asked.

His reply wasn't reassuring. "Only a little. They can still attack us. If there are many of them, we may be killed. Get your bow and take a knife for your belt."

Then he added, "They will run right up to the fire to attack, but they might be frightened if we hold flaming sticks."

She looked at the flames. There was only one suitable piece of wood. The rest were too large or mostly burned. She took her bow in one hand, looping her own quiver strap around her neck, and grabbed the flaming branch in her other hand.

Ulfsa braced himself and began to growl, sounding like someone tearing sheet metal in half.

There was a chorus of snarls in the darkness, and then she could make out a group of glowing eyes reflecting the firelight. The dire wolves were trotting directly towards the fire. Without being told, she put the branch at her feet and shot an arrow into the middle of the pack.

It struck one, and the animal whirled madly, snapping at the arrow shaft and its nearby neighbors. Cadeyrin started shooting arrows steadily, one after another.

The arrows were taking effect. Several of the dire wolves dropped or turned and retreated, arrows sticking out of them, but the main body of the pack continued to advance.

This pack was large, composed of more than twenty members. The dire wolves were used to attacking in strength and knew they could overwhelm almost anything, even one of the giant short-faced bears. The arrows were something new, and they slowed, milling about in confusion for a moment.

Cadeyrin had exhausted his arrows. He dropped the bow and grabbed his two spears and the atl-atl. Kathleen shot her last arrow and stooped to pick up the flaming branch, taking her knife in her right hand at the same time. They'd killed or wounded more than half of the pack, but there were plenty of the big beasts left.

The pack leader snarled and began to circle the fire. Cadeyrin and Kathleen had slowed the advance, but perhaps the pack could encircle them. There were no more arrows falling among the dire wolves, and they rapidly regained their confidence. Two of them suddenly broke out of the circle and charged directly at the humans, hunger getting the better of their caution.

Cadeyrin cast one spear, striking the nearer of the two beasts in the chest. It yelped and collapsed. The other came on, barely giving him time to ready his other spear and meet it with a thrust. The creature dodged the spear thrust and snapped at his leg, trying to hamstring him.

It was interrupted by a furious charge from Ulfsa. The gray wolf pup had grown a lot since Kathleen had picked him up, but he was still far shy of his full growth. The dire wolf was fully grown and weighed as much as a large human. There could be no doubt as to the outcome if the two fought.

As the dire wolf turned to meet the pup's charge, Cadeyrin jumped forward, driving the spear into its stomach. It screamed, making a surprisingly human-like sound. Its intestines looped out of the hole as he pulled the spear back. The wounded wolf turned and snapped at the piece of intestine as if that were the enemy that had wounded it.

Catching its own guts, it yanked, pulling more of them out while spinning madly around trying to fight its strange, snake-like attacker. It broke abruptly and ran back towards the other members of the pack. They fell on it, and there was a brief melee of growls and shrieks as they tore the unfortunate creature apart. They huddled over the carcass for a moment and then glanced at the two humans, their eyes glowing green.

Cadeyrin put his fingers to his mouth and whistled shrilly. The loud whistle seemed to discommode the pack. They shrank back. He whistled again, and they retreated, looking fearfully over their shoulders. He laughed sharply and then whistled once more as the pack faded into the darkness.

Cadeyrin turned to Kathleen with a little grin and said, "I've heard of wolves being frightened by strange noises. The Shaman told me that a whistle can sometimes make them run away. I have never tried it before."

Kathleen was happy he'd remembered the idea. She motioned at the darkness, "Are they still out there?"

They both listened intently. The only sound was the susurration of the breeze and an occasional snap from the fire as an ember exploded.

"No," he answered after a moment. "They are too far for me to hear them, and I can only smell the dead ones now. They are too frightened. I think they will try to find easier prey."

"Should we retrieve our arrows?" she asked, motioning at the barely visible fallen bodies.

"I will get them. You stay here. One of the wolves might only be wounded. I will take the flaming branch and my spear."

She handed him the branch. It was still burning, although not so brightly.

He walked off, returning after a few minutes with several arrows in his quiver and dragging the nearest dead dire wolf.

"We will cook this one. They wanted to eat us, so it's only fair that we eat one of them. Besides, I'm hungry," he said, rubbing his stomach with a doleful expression.

⸻ ◆ ⸻

Kathleen was glad that he'd seemingly forgiven her. The danger was past, and she'd done well, she thought. She'd shot all of her arrows and knew that she'd killed more than one of the large predators. Her stomach was empty, too, and a chunk of roast dire wolf haunch would be welcome. She laughed at the thought.

He glanced at her, trying to see what she found amusing.

Still smiling, she said, "Before I met you, I had never even thought about eating wolf meat. Now it seems almost normal."

Cadeyrin's voice sounded defensive as he replied, "I've eaten it many times and always been glad to get it when I was hungry."

She belatedly understood that he'd taken it as some sort of criticism. He must have thought she intended to tell him that she was used to far better food. She quickly added, "I'm glad to get it, also. My stomach hurts so much it's making me upset. I'm sorry I've been hard to deal with."

There, she thought. *Now I've apologized to you, also.*

Though stringy and heavily flavored with an unpleasant, bitter taste, the dire wolf meat was filling. As their hunger pains subsided, so did their unhappy mood.

Kapel and Makkat

Morning arrived before Kathleen was ready for it. The temperature difference between air and earth had created a heavy ground fog that didn't look like it was planning on going anywhere soon. The wind was still, and the dense, gray mist lay thick among the trees and in the hollows. Overall visibility was low, although the sun was starting to burn off the fog on the hilltops.

By the time the birds began singing their morning tribute, she, Cadeyrin, and Ulfsa were far down the valley, walking along the hills that formed its north side. They stayed well up on the hillside, a little above the worst of the mist. A light breeze was blowing sporadically from the west, creating swirls and odd shapes in the top of the mist.

Kathleen was fascinated by the constant action. She kept tripping over obstacles because she was watching the fog. Finally, she fell over a bush and banged her elbow on a rock, spilling her arrows with a clatter.

Cadeyrin came back and helped her rise. He seemed unhappy that she had made so much noise, but helping her stand resulted in their close proximity, and her nearness brought a tender expression to his face.

"Kathleen, are you hurt? You must be careful. You could injure yourself, and the sound will carry," he said as he pulled her to her feet, standing much closer than absolutely necessary.

She momentarily swayed towards him as if attracted by the magnetism of his body. She replied, "I'm sorry. I was watching the mist and tripped."

She inadvertently put her hand on his chest, feeling the swelling muscles beneath his buckskin shirt. Her lips parted, and her eyes met his, but the next instant, she remembered herself and yanked her hand away.

He sighed, catching his breath, and said, "It is not important. There are no animal sounds from below. We will continue for a while and then wait until the mist goes away so we can see."

—◇—

The sun had moved higher by the time they paused. The three were resting in the shelter of a large boulder left behind by a retreating glacier and watching the remains of the mist swirl in the slight breeze down on the valley floor. Ulfsa was stretched out in the sunlight, obviously enjoying the warmth on his gray coat.

The breeze died down to just a whisper of motion through the grasses and brush. Ulfsa lifted his head, cocked an ear, and then stood up, shaking to arrange his fur. Then he looked alertly at a thick patch of mist, sniffed loudly, and glanced back at Cadeyrin.

Both of the humans stiffened to attention. There was a distant, faint thudding. Something was coming down the valley. The mist rolled thicker, preventing them from seeing the sound's source. Then it thinned, and through the wisps came a small herd of horses, moving at a slow trot.

Kathleen glanced at Cadeyrin, expecting him to give her instructions for an ambush. Instead, she saw he had an expression of amazement on his face.

She whispered, "What is it? Are we going to hunt them?"

He replied, "I am not sure. I have never seen these beasts before. They are amazing. See how they run with such pride?" He extended his arm to point.

Kathleen was amazed in turn. Had he never seen horses? She seemed to remember that they had been introduced to the Americas by the early Spanish explorers and had then spread out over the plains mostly on their own. Obviously, they existed in North America during the glacial period.

She had the proof in front of her, but why did her knowledgeable hunter not know about them?

She said, "They're horses. They are grass-eaters and can run quickly. In my time, men ride on their backs."

Cadeyrin's eyes shone with admiration as he watched the horses. He replied, "I heard tales of such animals. I have never seen them. I did not know they were real. It was said that they lived in the old land that my people came from many lives ago. The Shaman called them 'Kapel.' You call them 'horses?'"

"Yes. We could eat them – " she started to say, but he interrupted.

"No. They are spirit creatures. See how they hold themselves. They are not for us – " He was interrupted by the sound of an alarmed neigh from below.

The herd had been passing a clump of brush when a huge lion-like cat had charged out. The horses reacted instantly, bolting directly ahead down the valley. The lion gave chase, picking out one of the slower animals.

The chase came to an abrupt end. There had been a second lion, slightly smaller, lying in ambush, and the slower horse's life came to a bloody end in its jaws. The larger cat trotted up, and the two squabbled, snarling at each other before settling down to eat.

Kathleen watched the brutal scene with the detachment of someone watching a TV special on predators. She was becoming inured to life and death in the wild. Her primary emotion at the moment was jealousy. She wanted the meat for herself.

Cadeyrin climbed to his feet and started up the hill, cautiously keeping low so that the lions didn't see him. He motioned for her to follow. Ulfsa glanced inquiringly at the humans. They didn't seem inclined to hunt, and the big cats looked intimidating. He followed without a backward glance.

When they had reached the other side of the hill, Cadeyrin said, "Those are lahanaa."

Kathleen replied, "I call them 'lions', but they are large compared to lions of my time.'

Cadeyrin repeated the word to himself and then told her, "Lions or lahanaa, they are the largest cats and very dangerous. It would take a whole double-hand of men to bring even one down. Two are beyond question. Even the piskata, the big, long-tooth tigers, back down from them. I have never heard of a single hunter killing one."

He motioned towards the green of the forest, "Our game hides elsewhere. Let's go back towards the trees."

The valley had trended southwards away from the forest, and it took them some time, working their way over glacially deposited stones and boulders, to reach an esker. This was a ten-foot-high, sloping wall of stones and sand, left by a retreating glacier as it melted and dropped the stones from a freshet that had cut through the ice. The esker meandered over the terrain, paralleling the trees for a distance before turning towards the north and vanishing between the spruces.

The two climbed the steep side and found that the top was quite flat. It was heavily traveled by animals, as wolf and dire wolf tracks along with occasional cat tracks were mixed with the spoor of prey animals on the elevated path.

They walked quickly along, enjoying the respite from scrambling over the broken ground and rocks. They had nearly reached the trees when Cadeyrin stopped, squatting down. Kathleen stepped forward, trying to make out what interested him.

He turned to her, his face serious. He indicated a depression that was, in her opinion, too large to be a track.

"This is the track of an esbern. I have not seen one for many seasons. I wish not to see this one. As fierce as the lions are, the esbern is much worse. It can run more quickly and farther. Much farther and faster than anything but a wolf. It is so large that it can bring down any prey. Even the mammoths fear it," he said with a frown.

Kathleen was frightened by his seriousness but couldn't figure what kind of animal it might be. She asked, "Can you describe it to me?"

Cadeyrin stood as he answered, "It walks on all four legs and stands as tall as me at the shoulders, but it can stand like a man on its hind legs. When it does, it is more than twice as tall as a man. It hunts alone and eats meat only. There is another animal like it, but it dens in caves and eats mostly plants."

She was getting the idea. Standing on its hind legs was the key. She said, "Oh. I think you're describing what I call a 'bear'. But I never heard of one so large. Is it white?"

He smiled, "No. I have heard of white ones that my people encountered on the long voyage to this land, but I have never seen one. This one is mostly a brown color. If you know of the white ones, then you know what this animal is. It is like them. There are also smaller ones living in the forest, but they have long faces. This one has a short face."

He turned, surveying the tracks. They went straight down the middle of the esker. He commented, "It is good. These tracks are old. See how the edges are flat? That is from weather and the passage of other animals. There are no other esbern tracks here. This one might have only used this pathway once. They cover lots of area and do not have a fixed den to return to."

She said, partially to herself, "A short-faced, big bear. How bad could it be?" Then, smiling at Cadeyrin, she added, "I'll watch out for big bears, but right now, I'm hungry."

He nodded and started along the esker. Ulfsa had gone ahead of them and was now peering off to the south about a hundred yards ahead of their position. When they reached him, he glanced at them and wagged, then returned his attention to whatever it was he was sensing.

Kathleen understood from the wolf's attitude and attention, that he had detected something he thought they could hunt. Cadeyrin stood still until he apparently caught a slight scent on the breeze. She saw him stiffen as his eyes searched the heavy brush that spread to the south.

Kathleen knew enough not to disturb him. She couldn't sense anything at all. His senses were more acute or more trained than hers. Whether this was through practice or due to her senses being blunted by city dwelling, she didn't know, nor did she really care. She simply relied on him to point things out to her. Now he was sniffing and systematically searching the brush.

He slowly raised his arm to point, whispering, "There is a deer feeding somewhere in that farthest thicket. Let's climb down, and you go to the left with Ulfsa. I will go to the right. If we are careful stalking, the deer will not notice us until we are close. The wind is blowing towards us, so it will not scent us." He looked at her for confirmation, "Do you understand?"

She nodded. Together, they started down the gravel side, half sliding on the loose stone but trying to remain as quiet as possible. Ulfsa made his own way to the bottom, disturbing far less gravel.

At the bottom, Kathleen clicked her tongue at the wolf, and he obligingly followed her. When he saw the direction she was heading, he accelerated and circled far out to the side of the thicket. She suddenly saw that he understood their plan and was adding to it by circling around to the far side of the thick brush. If the deer started in his direction, he'd try to head it back towards them.

She kept low, with an arrow held beside her bow. From that position, she could quickly draw and shoot. She concentrated on keeping the noise of her passage to a minimum.

It seemed like it took an eternity to get close to the left side of the thicket. Her back was on fire from the constant effort of stooping to keep her head low. Finally, she raised her head carefully, looking through a thick patch of weeds.

She was close. She could see the deer moving towards her. It was near her side of the thicket, pausing every few steps to nibble on twigs. She placed her arrow against the string and readied her bow.

The deer raised its head suspiciously. It must have sensed something. Then it looked over its shoulder, back towards Cadeyrin's side of the thicket. It paused, searching the air for scents with its head up. She saw its tail flip upright in warning. It abruptly turned and made a high bound, heading in her general direction but starting to angle off towards the south.

She thought about running towards it. The direction it was heading would shortly place it out of her range. It leaped over a thick bush and then swerved back towards her. Ulfsa was running to intercept its flight.

It was now heading directly at her. She took a deep breath, pulled her bow, and waited, not noticing the strain as she held the arrow back. At what she felt was the exact instant, she adjusted her aim upwards slightly and loosed the arrow.

It flew straight, curving in a flat arc that intersected the deer's path as it started to leap over a bush. With an audible thunk, the arrow struck. The deer dropped to the ground, thrashing around in the brush. It leaped straight upwards, its mouth open in mute distress, fell back, and then regained its feet, turning to run away from her.

It bounded twice, and then Ulfsa was on it. The young wolf leaped at its throat, catching hold and dragging it to the ground. By the time she arrived, the deer was gasping its last as Ulfsa held tightly, doing his best to strangle it.

There was the sound of breaking brush behind her, and she turned to see Cadeyrin's excited face as he pushed through the thicket. He trotted over to her, pride showing in his expression. She thought that he'd run most of the way through the thicket in order to arrive so quickly.

"You are a good huntress," he panted. "Few women can say the same. Women of my people rarely learn to use spears."

She laughed shakily, "I didn't use a spear. I used an arrow. If I had to throw a spear with your thrower, I don't think I could hit a deer."

She felt suddenly faint and quickly sat down. Her hands were shaking.

Cadeyrin smiled at her, saying, "This is your first hunt. Everyone shakes from their first kill."

She tried to laugh and asked, "Even you?"

He answered, "I shook before I cast a spear at my first deer. I only struck its leg. I had to run close to hit it with my second spear. Then I felt sick. I am not proud of that, but it is true."

That made her feel better. She said, "Well, it really wasn't my first kill. I shot some of the daoilfa the other night, but this was more exciting, somehow."

She stood and added, "We'd better cut this one up and head back to our camp."

He looked around, checking the brush, and nodded in agreement, telling her, "I do not like this area. We cannot see well, except from the gravel trail. It is not safe. Any beast that is downwind will smell the kill and come to steal it. If the esbern is near, we will lose the deer and our lives. We must be quick."

<hr>

Together they stripped the carcass, making two packs of meat. They were done and moving towards their camp along the esker before the sun was directly overhead.

Kathleen felt so pleased with herself that she could barely keep from breaking into a song. She'd demonstrated to him conclusively that she was truly capable. She could feed herself and contribute to their defense. Somehow the kill made her feel far more desirable and capable than she'd ever felt before. Cadeyrin now knew that she was an asset.

The trail had widened, making more room. She sped up and pushed him lightly to the side. He obligingly made space for her. She bumped him with her shoulder, and he laughed.

Their gaze met, and she saw his eyes widening. Before she was fully aware of what she was doing, their arms were around each other, and she was lifting her lips to his. The kiss was wonderful, igniting a flame that ran from her heart down to her lower stomach. She felt almost as shaky as she had after the kill.

After a moment, he lifted his head for a breath. He said, "We should keep moving. It is a long way to camp."

She replied, not releasing her arms, "I know."

He dropped his face to hers, and they kissed again, deeply.

They were interrupted by Ulfsa's growl. He was looking directly down the esker at one of the smaller cats with shorter, curved fangs. Her mind flashed with sudden fear, simultaneously realizing that it wasn't a saber-tooth but one of the sloping-backed cats that had treed her when she first transited into the past.

Cadeyrin grunted, pushing her behind him as he prepared to shoot an arrow. He confirmed her identification, whispering, "Makkat."

Kathleen struggled out of the pack straps, dropping the package of meat to her feet, and then arranged an arrow against her bowstring.

The oncoming predator snarled and trotted quickly along the path towards them. Ulfsa growled again and then suddenly spun, looking back past Kathleen. She turned in surprise and saw another cat closing in quickly along the path from behind. They'd been ambushed.

She raised her bow and aimed, hearing Cadeyrin's bowstring thrum as he released it. Her shot followed close on his. The second cat shrieked at the arrow's impact and bounded at full speed towards her, seemingly not slowed at all by the shaft sticking from the hump of its shoulder. She drew another arrow but had to wait on the shot.

Ulfsa had charged forward and was in the process of dodging to the left of the injured cat. It made an effort to catch him, but the arrow slowed its reaction. He ducked under its reaching foreleg, and his jaws slashed as he passed, laying open a long, bleeding tear on its side.

The cat was enraged. Recognizing the wolf as a more familiar threat, it turned to meet his attack.

Ulfsa had spun and was trying for a disabling slash to the tendons of the cat's hind legs. He was forced to jump back quickly as it slashed a paw full of claws past his face.

Behind her, she heard Cadeyrin's bow twang again and then again. Kathleen drew back her arrow and released it. Her second shot struck the makkat in the back of the neck. The arrow passed through to the front, releasing a thick stream of blood. The cat shrieked again and spun to face her.

Ulfsa leaped forward and slashed at one of the exposed hind legs. His strike was accurate, and the cat's rear leg failed. It tried to leap at Kathleen, faltered, and then choked and fell on its side. The right forepaw clawed at the arrowhead protruding from its neck for a moment, and then it lay still.

She spun to Cadeyrin's aid but almost collided with him. They were face to face again. He'd made sure of his cat and was turning to help her at the same instant.

Seeing that her attacker was no longer a threat, he said, "Pick up your pack. We must go quickly. Makkata hunt in groups. There will be more coming. We leave these two here."

He stepped past her as she donned the heavy pack. After he'd retrieved her two shafts, he recovered the three that he'd shot. They hurried along the esker to the point where it turned towards the forest, then descended.

The land was now a little smoother, with more grass and less brush. Consequently, their progress was easier. After a mile or so, they turned towards the valley, which was now much closer to the trees.

She paused for breath and said, "Our camp must be over those hills in the distance."

He nodded, pointing. "It is between the forest and that larger hill. We have not much farther to go. We will be there before sunset."

◆

The venison tasted better than any she'd eaten before. Perhaps it was because she'd killed the deer herself, or perhaps it was due to the excitement of killing the makkat, or maybe simple hunger. In any event, her sense of happiness included Cadeyrin. He had kissed her again, and it was wonderful. In addition, she was grateful to him for rescuing her. He'd been nothing but a gentleman. She'd assumed that a stone-age hunter would be a brute of a man. His unexpected behavior would compare favorably to that of any modern man.

She warmed herself by the fire as she ate, acutely aware of his presence.

Elusive Happiness

I t was late. The fire had died down, and Kathleen was tired. The emotional strain of the hunt and the makkat attack had worn on her more than she'd thought. Ulfsa was curled up close to her, satiated with venison.

His presence led her to think about how they had come to depend on the young wolf. Cadeyrin insisted on treating him almost as if he were a human and took the wolf's preferences into consideration, especially when hunting. She doubted that a modern man would be so egalitarian. In a way, it seemed naive and just the sort of superstitious behavior that one would expect from a primitive man. In another way, she supposed, it was a wise attitude to have. Ulfsa's senses added immensely to their security.

As if spurred by her thoughts, the wolf jumped up, trotted off to the side of the fire a bit. He looked intently into the darkness, his hackles beginning to rise. Cadeyrin watched the wolf for a moment and then moved out beside him.

The man looked tense for a moment but then returned to the fire, sitting down beside Kathleen. She was conscious of his masculinity, glorying in knowing that his strength protected her. There was a sudden squalling sound from the darkness, and she jumped and grabbed his arm. Then, without quite knowing how it happened, she somehow found herself enclosed in his arms with her head resting against his chest.

He spoke quietly, the sound rumbling into her ear through his chest muscles, "It is only a smaller cat, a panther. It will not bother us. It smells the meat and wants it, but it is frightened of us and Ulfsa."

She tightened her grip on his arm, nodding as she did, saying nothing. She didn't want the moment to end. Her mind was busy, kicking out its usual doubts and self-criticism, but the sense of security she felt was enough to overwhelm her worries.

Perhaps, just perhaps, she could relax and be herself with him. He had never given any sign that her scars bothered him. He was always kind and patient with her, even when she made mistakes.

He tightened his arms slightly, and she ran her hand over his biceps. It was breathtaking. *What would it be like, living in the past with him? Well, she was already doing that, but living as his mate? Wife, she corrected herself. Would she be happy or would she miss the intellectual life of the university and her studies?*

And what about her formula? She felt momentarily guilty, then returned to her prior thoughts.

Would interacting with him be enough for her? She suddenly remembered their last kiss.

She rather timidly thought, *Maybe he could be happy with me.* He seemed to read the thought and sighed, shifting slightly. She snuggled closer, moving her head back so she could look up at him. When she did, she saw him looking back at her with a tender expression she'd never hoped to see on a man's face.

His face loomed larger in her gaze as he lowered his head. As their lips met, Ulfsa growled.

Cadeyrin quickly rose, catching up his bow and an arrow. Kathleen scrambled to her feet in alarm, searching for her weapons. She had no idea what he'd sensed, but Ulfsa had growled, and his warnings weren't usually false.

She stood beside Cadeyrin, searching the darkness. When she didn't see anything, she looked at him inquiringly. He continued looking, then turned to his left. He whispered, "It's a piskat; a big-tooth tiger. It has driven off the smaller cat. It now circles us, looking for an opportunity."

"Will it attack us here by the fire?" she asked.

"I do not think so. They fear fire as much as do the smaller cats," he said, bending to grasp a flaming brand.

He turned and threw it in a high arc into the darkness. The flaming stick left a looping trail of sparks as it flew. It landed and bounced near a large form that let out a surprised snarl and then quickly retreated. Cadeyrin laughed, "See, the piskat is not so brave after all. It leaves to seek other game."

He glanced down at her, "Do not be worried. Ulfsa will alert us if anything else comes."

He sat down, and she sat beside him. The momentary alarm had taken its toll on her system. She'd been tired before, but now that she had burned off the adrenaline, she felt exhausted. A deep wave of tiredness overwhelmed her. She leaned against him and yawned, then said, "I'm going to sleep."

He simply nodded and helped her arrange the skins for warmth.

⁕

Cadeyrin sat, watching the fire. There had been no other prowlers, and his mind was free to contemplate their situation. Kathleen was learning to hunt, and she could shoot well. They still needed a more secure camp. If an esbern hunted this territory, they would not be safe. Sooner or later, it would happen across their fresh trail, and then it would hunt them. Fire wouldn't stop it. He'd heard of the giant bears walking into camp and grabbing a hunter from his spot beside the flames.

He was determined to keep Kathleen safe. He reflected on their relationship. It was moving in the direction he most desired. Some men would have taken a more aggressive posture with her, but he also instinctively knew that she was extremely sensitive. She'd had plenty of opportunities to advance their physical relationship, but she always pulled back with a display of caution or fear. He was unsure which it was, but he suspected that she was fearful. Perhaps someone had hurt her terribly in the past. He wished that he could find some way to reassure her that he wouldn't do that.

He'd been convinced that she was rejecting him because she was from somewhere that was far better. He now knew that her world was indeed a better one than his. He felt unsure about that. How could he offer her the things she must be missing? Perhaps in her time, humans always had enough to eat and were always warm. The thought seemed hard to grasp. He gave up. His imagination would only take him so far.

Still, she didn't pull away tonight. He took that as a good sign. He wanted her with every fiber of his being, but he also wanted her to come to him on her own terms when she was ready. It would be wonderful if she would commit to him fully. Then he'd be convinced that she would be a life-long partner.

As he gazed at the fire, he gradually sank into a dream state. Ulfsa would warn if anything threatened and the fire was warm. He gazed at the coals, losing himself in the flickering light and then recognized the signs. He was ascending into the spirit world.

This time there was an abrupt transition. One minute he was sitting in front of the fire, and the next he was looking down at the scene from high overhead. *He was aware of the cold light of the stars, and it seemed as if they were each conscious, spiritual points of life. As he looked down, his vision expanded until he could see all of the land below. The locations where animals were hidden and spending the night were betrayed by a dim glow. He could see the track of the saber-tooth that had visited them earlier. It was now far down the valley. Feeding, he thought. Far to the south was a brighter light. He moved in that direction, but then quickly retreated. It was the esbern. He could sense the ferocity in its aura.*

He called on his animal spirit, the wolf. Immediately, he was aware that Ulfsa knew what was going on. The wolf pup was approaching, wagging its tail in greeting. It gently clamped its jaws on his hand as if to say 'Hello.' He grasped its muzzle in return, but then he knew it wasn't actually Ulfsa. It was his spirit guide, or perhaps the two were the same. He was confused.

The wolf spirit led him to the west, and he followed. The spirits of the stars lighted the journey, and it only took an instant, although he understood that they'd come a long distance.

The wolf spirit showed him a place of safety that lay in some rocks on the south side of a hill by a small lake. He thought to investigate it, but there was a shift, and he was suddenly hovering over the campfire again, looking at Kathleen's recumbent form. She moaned and placed her arm over her face in a motion that betrayed grief and loss.

Things blurred, and he found himself looking at the coals, back in his body. He quickly glanced at her. Her arm was over her eyes in precisely the position he'd seen. What he could see of her mouth seemed to show sadness that tugged at his heart. He wanted to comfort her but did not want to wake her.

Sitting up straighter, he made the decision. They would leave tomorrow and head west. Somewhere there was a safer place. He'd take her there, and then perhaps she would finally accept him as her protector and, he hoped, her lover and mate. Just thinking about the possibility left him breathless.

He shook his head in denial. He was a man, a hunter, and a warrior. Feeling this way about a woman, even one from the future, seemed almost a repudiation of his masculinity. Certainly, no one in his tribe had ever acted so infatuated with a woman, at least to his knowledge. He felt, in some undefined way, that his pride was at stake. He would commit fully to her, but only if she'd demonstrate her commitment to him first. He would be cursed if he forced her or rushed her in her decision.

On the other hand, he would do everything in his power to make her decision a logical one. He'd provide her with all of the care he could. He hoped that would convince her. He tried to imagine what else he could do but gave up.

He wasn't from the future, but he was intelligent enough to know that he had no hope of even beginning to imagine what her life had been like before he'd met her. He could also imagine what having her fully love him would be like, and he wanted that with all of his being.

⸺⸺◆⸺⸺

They'd been walking for what must have been hours. Kathleen was more than ready for a break. It seemed to her that Cadeyrin was being unreasonable. He'd set a fast pace from the beginning. It was as if something was driving him, or perhaps something had frightened him. That idea frightened her in turn. If something in this world frightened the man, it would certainly be far more than she could handle on her own.

She'd come to depend on his presence. It was a comforting feeling, knowing that he was nearby. She still was worried about possible rejection, but she understood that, for whatever reason, he would do his best to ensure her safety. Besides, she now had her bow, and she could shoot nearly as well as he.

The morning had dawned with a covering of mist or fog. The wind was from the south, and the warmer, moisture-bearing air condensed as it passed over the colder ground. It had been clear during the night, and what heat there was had radiated away into space. The fog covered everything with tiny droplets that soaked her leggings, increasing her misery.

She'd made the change to full buckskin garb. Cadeyrin had proven to be as good at sewing as he was at nearly everything else he did, and he'd created pants, a shirt, and a jacket that fit her quite well. She still wore her fleece sweat-pants and hoodie at night, but she didn't want to wear them out while traveling. They would only last so long, and of course, she couldn't replace them. They were the last link she had with the modern world, except for her sneakers.

Those were another thing. The sneakers were holding up well, but they'd wear out eventually, too. Kathleen had inspected Cadeyrin's footwear. He wore a type of moccasin that was boot-like. It rose high over his calf, providing protection against thorns and brush. He'd promised to make some for her when he obtained the right leather, but he hadn't done so as yet.

The fog had soaked her buckskin clothing, and now that the sun was up, the leather was uncomfortable. The inside was still soaked, but the outside was drying and getting slightly stiff. She complained to Cadeyrin, and he looked embarrassed.

"I needed to tan your leather better. I will make you another set when we reach the safe place," he said.

She had been accepting when he wanted to move camp, but now she was uncomfortable and less willing to continue blindly.

"What is this safe place?" she asked. "Have you been there before? Do you really know where we're going?"

Cadeyrin slowed until they were side-by-side. "I saw it last night in the spirit world. You were sleeping, and my guide came to me. He led me to a high place where I could see the land." He paused.

Kathleen didn't know what to think. Were they taking this long hike based on a dream? In a disbelieving tone, she said, "Go on. What did you see?"

He continued, "The stars were above me. They each have their own spirit, but they are far away. I saw where animals hid during the night. I saw the esbern. It is far away. I saw it is dangerous and fierce from the light around it. That is why we must get out of its hunting territory. We cannot fight it. My guide led me to a place far to the west. It is where rocks come together. There is a hole there where we can camp. It is safe there."

Kathleen asked herself, Am I depending on a crazy man to protect me? Maybe he was out-of-body and saw some things, or maybe not.

She didn't have any choice but to go with him, and the lack of alternatives made her unreasonably angry.

"What is this spirit guide you keep mentioning, anyway?" she demanded.

"Oh. It is the wolf spirit. It has always guided me from the time that I was a small child. I can always depend on it to give me good advice, although sometimes the advice is unclear," he answered.

"Are you sure you weren't imagining that Ulfsa was talking to you?" she asked sarcastically.

He glanced at her with a little hurt in his eyes and then answered softly, "No. I thought it was my guide. I know there is a safe place to the west. I want to take you there. It will make it easier for me to protect you."

Kathleen felt like she couldn't win with him. When she tried to argue, he refused, treating her as if he was afraid to make her angry. What was worse, she felt guilty about attacking him. She knew he was doing his best. He couldn't help it that he was a primitive man lacking knowledge.

Then she thought, *No. That isn't right. He knows his world well. He's survived only because of his knowledge. He just doesn't know any modern science. But maybe his spirit-world is similar to my meditation, like my lucid dreams. That must be what he's doing.*

They continued a while, not speaking. The only sound was the swishing of their steps through the grass. Ulfsa had gone on ahead, occasionally dropping back to check on them.

Kathleen finally couldn't take the silence. She said, "I don't think I have a spirit guide, but I may have gone to the spirit-world before. In fact, I think that's sort of how I traveled through time to get here."

Cadeyrin's expression lightened. He responded with a happier tone, "Everyone has a spirit guide. We have to call on yours. If you have gone to the spirit-world, then you understand that sometimes you can see things there you do not when you are awake. That is how I know there is a place where the rocks are stacked. It has a hole where I think we can camp. It will make it impossible for an animal to come at us from behind. We will only have to defend our front. A fire can be built there to help in defense."

After they pushed through some thick, low brush, he added, "I have been thinking. I never worried about over-hunting the game before. I always just moved to a place where the game wasn't afraid. If we hunt in one direction from our camp until the game leaves, then we can go in another direction. By the time we hunt in all directions, the game may come back to the area that we first hunted."

Kathleen elaborated on the idea. "We can divide the land into four territories and hunt each one in sequence. I think that would give the game time to recover in each area, as long as we don't hunt them too often or come back too quickly."

He nodded and then indicated a distant boulder. "We will stop there and eat some jerky. You must be tired. I don't think future people walk as much as I do."

Kathleen laughed. How right he was. She said, "No, we don't. We have other means of getting from one place to another. We walk short distances but use..."

She paused. How was she going to explain an automobile or even a bicycle to him? He didn't even know what a wheel was.

It was Cadeyrin's turn to say, "Go on. Tell me how you travel long distances."

She considered, then said, "You know how I said that men in the future rode on the backs of horses...uh, kapella?"

He nodded, "I remember. I thought you were joking. Do they really sit on the animals, and do the animals carry them without complaint?"

She gratefully took the opportunity he offered. Explaining something as obvious as a wheel would probably take all day. She answered, "Yes. The kapella can carry a man much faster than a man can run and for a long distance, also."

After a while, Cadeyrin said, "They are few, I've never seen them before, but perhaps we should try to capture some of those creatures. Do you think they would carry us?"

If they were as rare as he said, it would probably be a long time before we see horses again. I'd have time to explain what I know about riding, which, she thought critically, *isn't very much.*

She said, "We could possibly teach one to carry us. It might be difficult. I don't know too much about it. Maybe we'd just better concentrate on walking."

He smiled and said, "Not just now. We're at the rock. Let's rest."

She gratefully settled down in the shade of the granite, pulling some jerky out of her pouch. After a short time, Ulfsa stuck his head around the rock near her and sniffed loudly. She laughed. He was always there whenever anyone was eating anything.

—◆—

By nighttime, they'd come many miles. Kathleen was back to her habitual insecure and suspicious mode. She was exhausted, and with her tiredness had come the suspicion that her life was going to be far more difficult than she was prepared for. She could try to be a good Paleolithic wife, but would she be capable? She didn't have any confidence that she'd measure up to Cadeyrin's standards. He'd be better off dumping her and finding a woman of his people.

She was so tired that she almost kept walking past him when he stopped to set up camp for the night. He called her back and made her sit and rest while he gathered wood.

She watched numbly, while he built a fire. She hadn't questioned how he did that without matches before. He lit tinder so quickly that she had previously taken it for granted. He made a pile of thin pieces of birch bark and then struck a spark using two stones. One must have been flint and the other some metallic element, she thought.

The spark caused the tinder to smolder, and then he brought it to a full flame by blowing gently. From that point, it was a simple matter of adding larger pieces of fuel. She thought that she could probably learn the task with a little experimentation.

They had a small amount of venison left that he'd carried along with the pack of cured skins. It wasn't long before he'd cooked it, and they ate. It was a little strong, but Kathleen thought that she'd eaten worse. Without realizing it, her digestion had become more robust. She might once have been sick from the slightly high meat, but now it was just food.

She was so tired that she didn't sit with him after eating. She rolled up in the saber-tooth hide and went directly to sleep, Ulfsa by her side.

—•—

Cadeyrin reclined on another skin and watched the fire and Kathleen. She'd held up well under the stress of the long walk. She initially had given him the impression she was weak and vulnerable. Now he was revising that thought. She was simply unused to living the kind of life he lived. She had learned to hunt. She could walk as far as he could. He shook his head in approbation. He was probably as tired as she.

He also liked the fact that she seemed to take an interest in everything he had tried to teach her. She was learning what it took to survive.

He thought about it. He had been in love with her from almost the instant he'd seen her. Now he knew that she was far more capable than she seemed and that only served to make him appreciate her more. He wondered again, what would it take to earn her love?

He rested, depending on the wolf's senses for warning. The night was quiet. They'd walked a long way onto a grassy plain, and there was no game nearby. He doubted that there were any predators around that were more dangerous than a coyote. Certainly, they were out of the immediate territory of the esbern, and it was unlikely that piskata would come this far away from the broken lands they preferred. They could not run down their prey, depending instead on ambush. The tall grass-covered plain would not be a good hunting ground for them.

The night wore on. When the moon rose, there was a distant chorus of howls from a coyote pack. The small, clever wolves sang to the moon in yelps and yodels for many minutes before they went silent. Cadeyrin smiled to himself. They were a good sign. They wouldn't be so noisy if there were larger predators in the area.

Chapter Eighteen

The Lake Cave

They started out the next day before the sun had peeked over the horizon. When morning dawned, they were miles along their way. The meat had all been eaten, and they were both alert for possible game, although Cadeyrin wasn't hopeful. The grassy plain seemed to extend into the distance with no sign of a break. There wouldn't be anything to hunt here unless a migrating herd came by.

The land was deceptive. It looked flat, but there were shallow sloughs and occasional streams meandering through the grass, hidden in deep arroyos. There were muskrats in the sloughs, and he thought about killing some of them, but that would be a last resort. Their meat was unpleasant and strongly flavored. He doubted that Kathleen could be persuaded to eat one.

They came over a small rise and there, in the distance, was a herd of deer-like animals. He was able to see straight horns with forked tips on their heads. They looked like deer to a certain extent, but he could tell they weren't. They were something else, something he'd never seen before. He pointed them out to Kathleen.

She looked long and hard at the distant figures. Finally, she said, "They must be some kind of pronghorns, at least, that's what I think they are."

Cadeyrin again wondered at the extent of her knowledge. She seemed to know animals that he'd never before seen. He tentatively asked, "Are they good to eat?"

Kathleen replied that she thought so, but she didn't know how good they were. She explained that she'd never heard of anyone eating one, but that didn't mean they were bad, just uncommon.

They were sitting in the tall grass on the crest of the low hill. Apparently, the pronghorns were as curious about them as they were about the pronghorns. The beasts moved towards their location in spurts, sometimes trotting their way and other times displaying a complete indifference, stopping and grazing.

In this way, the pronghorn herd approached to nearly within bowshot. Then there was a problem. The herd seemed content to stay at that distance. They were grazing, and though occasionally one or another would stick its head up and study the humans and Ulfsa carefully, they didn't approach any closer.

Cadeyrin was wondering if he could use Ulfsa and crawl through the grass to get within arrow range when there was a sudden commotion in the herd. The pronghorns went on the alert for an instant and then burst into a full-out run. A long and lanky cat creature had somehow sneaked up close, and now it was pursuing one of the small pronghorns at an amazing pace.

The small prey animal tried dodging and turning, but the cat was its equal. The chase came to an abrupt end when the pursuing cat somehow tripped the pronghorn, sending it rolling head-over-heels. In an instant, the cat had hold of the smaller animal's throat. Still holding the throat, the cat lay down, its chest heaving.

Cadeyrin looked at Kathleen. Perhaps she knew what the cat was, also. She didn't disappoint him. She pointed at it and whispered, "That's a cheetah. They are able to run extremely fast for short distances. Their speed enables them to catch fast prey like pronghorns. I don't think they are really fierce fighters. They aren't as strong as the larger cats, but I don't know what one is doing here."

The cheetah was starting to recover from its burst of speed. It was standing, looking around suspiciously. It immediately saw them as they stood up. It looked indecisive for a moment, then grabbed the pronghorn and started to drag it directly away from them.

Cadeyrin started towards it at a trot. Ulfsa glanced once at him and then took off like an arrow, directly towards the tired cat.

Seeing the wolf coming, the cheetah dropped the pronghorn and prepared to defend its kill. It was larger than the young wolf, significantly outweighing him, and it was confident that it could fight him off.

Ulfsa cleverly dashed in and out, circling the angry cheetah, trying to nip its hindquarters. The cat sat back on its haunches and spun, trying to keep the wolf in front of it until Cadeyrin got close. Then it jumped up and deliberated charging at the man for a moment before caution won the upper hand. It turned and trotted quickly away.

Ulfsa was already working on the pronghorn when Cadeyrin reached it. The young wolf couldn't help growling a bit. He was hungry, but he also knew Cadeyrin was his pack leader, so he didn't protest when the man began to cut the pronghorn into pieces.

They had no wood, so they packed the cut-up meat and continued walking, leaving Ulfsa to satisfy his hunger on the remains of the carcass. It wasn't long before he caught up with them. He looked ridiculously satisfied, and his stomach was bulging so much that he was content to walk at their speed.

By late afternoon, they had crossed the plain and were in an area of low hills that were closer to the glacial wall. They could see the high gray line of the ice way off to the north. The air seemed colder, and Kathleen shivered until Cadeyrin wrapped a piece of buckskin around her neck and shoulders.

They climbed hill after hill in the teeth of a brisk and chill wind, finally reaching a glacier-formed lake. There were trees around the medium body of water and rocks piled high in two places along the eastern shore. Cadeyrin led them unerringly towards the more distant rocky hill.

The huge pile was composed of large boulders, some of which were three or four times as tall as a man. The rocks on the south side of the pile formed an open shape with the arms stretching out to the southeast and southwest, facing a narrow part of the lake. Directly in the center was a large crack where two huge stones leaned against each other.

The crack extended upwards higher than a man's reach, and then the rocks dovetailed together to close it. When Cadeyrin and Kathleen walked through the narrow opening, they found that the area inside extended back about ten strides, ending in a pile of rocks that formed the back wall.

There had been some kind of predator living in the hole at one time. There was a nest where it had slept, surrounded by bones of prey that had been carried in. The animal was long gone, and there was no sign of any current occupant.

The crack was mostly closed at the top, with only a small opening at the back near the wall. Cadeyrin saw Kathleen inspect it. She pointed, saying, "We can have a fire right below that. The smoke will rise and go out of the hole. It will make this a good place to stay."

He wasn't sure that the smoke would go where she said. In his experience, smoke always went where it wanted. He was also a little reluctant to give up the idea of having a fire at the front, to defend the entrance, but he didn't want to argue about it. He turned and went out to gather wood.

By the time he had returned with a load, Kathleen had unpacked their skins and other things and was busy arranging a ring of rocks around the location where she wanted the fire. He threw the wood down beside the ring and went out for more.

Several trips later, he had enough to last the night. It was just in time. The sun was shining its last rays over the trees on the other side of the lake, and the water was glinting with the light.

⸻ ◆ ⸻

The fire burned brightly in the back of the cave. The smoke did exactly as Kathleen had said it would, rising up to the hole where most of it flowed out. There was a thin pall of smoke that drifted along the top of the cave, but it didn't drop low enough to bother the two humans.

Ulfsa was sitting at the mouth of the cave. The fire didn't bother him, but he instinctively wanted to be able to keep watch, and the opening was the only place he needed to guard.

⸻ ◆ ⸻

The evening wind picked up. It had switched around and now was blowing from the northwest. The gusts were cold and carried the feel of nearby ice.

Inside the cave, the fire flickered on the walls. The wind blew intermittently down the chimney crack, but the smoke filtered out between gusts. The inside was warm and cheery. Cadeyrin and Kathleen were sitting on a bison hide, eating strips of roast pronghorn.

Ulfsa had come inside when they started eating, and his eyes glowed as he watched each bite go into their mouths. Kathleen tossed him a bone with a large chunk of meat attached, and he caught it in mid-air and retreated back to the entrance to eat.

Kathleen felt wonderful. This was almost civilized. She'd been living out-of-doors so long that the modest shelter offered by the cave seemed like an incredible luxury. No animals could sneak up on them, and she didn't have to worry about being eaten in her sleep. She could rest securely here.

Exhaustion from the long walk set in and mandated that they sleep. Ulfsa lay by the mouth of the cave, ready to set up an alarm if anything intruded, while Kathleen and Cadeyrin lay side-by-side next to the gradually dying fire.

They woke a little after dawn. It was dark in the cave until Cadeyrin built up the fire. Ulfsa had disappeared, probably outside doing his morning duty.

Kathleen and Cadeyrin exited the cave, walked to the lake, drank, and then cleaned up. Once they were back in the cave, they sat by the fire and cooked the last of the pronghorn meat.

Kathleen busied herself with the cooking while he dug in his quiver. When she surreptitiously glanced at him, he was looking at an arrow that needed some kind of adjustment.

He had been totally accurate in his statement about the cave's location. Kathleen didn't quite grasp how he had known. Something had happened to give him that knowledge, something mysterious and a little spooky. From what he had told her, his spirit guide had been a great help.

She wondered if she could find a guide, also.

"Cadeyrin?" she started.

He turned to look at her.

"Can you help me find my spirit guide?" she asked hesitantly.

Cadeyrin replied, "I can try. I will have to think on it. I have been led by my guide for so long, it is like the wolf-spirit has always been there. I think I can help you, but it must wait until tonight. We need meat, and we should go hunting today."

She had other plans. "You go without me. I want to stay here and work on the cave."

"Work on the cave?" he repeated. "What will you do?"

She was reminded that they didn't have the same backgrounds. She wanted a nice place to live, and she'd already been planning on cleaning the cave and rearranging their few possessions. She said, "Take Ulfsa. I don't need him to guard me. I'll build a fire near the entrance and keep my bow nearby."

He asked, "Are you sure?"

She suddenly thought that her desire to clean might be some kind of nesting syndrome. Her face flushed as she wondered if she was trying to prepare herself emotionally to give her future to him. Was living a cavewoman's life good enough for her? Was there actually any choice?

The feeling of being trapped frightened her, and she said bitterly, "Yes, I'm sure. I want you to go. I'll stay here."

Cadeyrin looked perplexed. He rubbed his face and said, "I will check the area completely before I travel too far. If there's any danger, I'll come back."

She nodded mutely, gazing down at her hands. She felt that she'd hurt him. It made her miserable, and she wanted to make amends. As that thought came into her mind, she considered that maybe she cared more about his feelings than she had believed.

He had gathered up his weapons and was preparing to leave. Kathleen jumped to her feet and caught at his shoulder. He turned to her, and she said, "I...I'm sorry. It's just that I want this place to be cleaner since we're going to stay here."

He transferred his weapons to his left hand and hugged her with his right arm, pulling her towards him.

She resisted for a moment and then moved close. Their bodies touched, and the next instant, she found herself kissing him. The experience left her breathless.

He broke the kiss and laughed shakily.

"The game will not wait for me. I must go now if the hunt is to be successful. I will be back as quickly as possible," he said.

She nodded, "Please be careful. And don't worry about me. I can shoot arrows almost as well as you, so I can defend the cave."

He grinned, "Your shooting is good. Just keep the fire going, and you will be safe."

⸺ ⬥ ⸺

Once he was gone, she carried firewood over to the entrance of the cave. The huge rocks were closer here, and the opening was so narrow just inside the entrance that there was barely enough space for a man's shoulders. Cadeyrin had had to turn partially sideways to pass through.

She gathered up lose stones and made a fire ring where the entrance passage started to widen. There was room enough to come inside and then step around the fire, but if it were really blazing, the flames' heat would effectively block any but the most determined invader from entering. She laid a fire and then lit it with a flaming brand from the main fire.

She stepped back and watched. There was a draft coming in through the entrance, and it carried the smoke back towards the exit hole in the back roof. More smoke built up near the roof, creating a haze that floated well over her head. After a few minutes, the fresh smoke found its way back to the chimney hole and blended itself with the smoke from the main fire on its way out of the cave.

Kathleen sighed in relief. She had thought that the smoke would go out, but there had been a little doubt in her mind. She was happy that she'd once again demonstrated her competence. She could do this. She could make the best of the situation.

She had finished picking up the debris and rocks that were scattered around. She wanted to sweep the floor, but she couldn't think what she would use as a broom. Finally, she decided to go outside and find a spruce bough. There were some trees nearby, between the rocks and the lake. She could take her knife, formerly one of Cadeyrin's spearheads, and cut off a branch. That would work nicely as a broom.

While she'd worked, the entrance fire had died down. Now it was a glowing bed of embers. She probably should have paid more attention to it, but having it cooler was convenient.

She took her bow and quiver of arrows and slid between the fire and the rock wall. The wall was radiating heat, and she was forced closer to the fire. It was slightly cooler there.

Once outside, she looked around carefully. There was nothing out of the ordinary. She reached the trees and selected a bushy, low-hanging branch. Then, stepping inside the screen of boughs, she began sawing at the branch with her knife.

She finished cutting the branch. She could step out from under the overhang and drag it free. Suddenly, she froze. There was something wrong. Some latent instinct, honed by her exposure to the wild, had warned her.

She searched the area again. There was something...There! She'd seen a movement near the far edge of the rocks. She quietly readied her bow and watched. Nothing happened for several minutes, then the face of one of the long-toothed cats gradually appeared, pushing through the undergrowth. It was looking at the cave mouth from under the edge of a bush.

This cat wasn't one of the big ones that Cadeyrin called 'Makkata' or 'Piskata'. It was a smaller cat, one that she hadn't seen previously. Its canine teeth were much smaller than those of the makkat's, protruding about two inches below its lip. Still, it was obviously dangerous. She paused, wondering what to do.

If she tried to stay hidden, the cat would inevitably sense her as it prowled around. The idea that it might leave without investigating thoroughly was ludicrous. She thought to herself, Cats are known for their curiosity.

Running for the safety of the cave wasn't possible, either. She was a little too far from the entrance. Her running speed was better than it had ever been, but she had no doubt that the cat could catch her.

No, the only thing to do was to get clear of the bushes and face the danger. She'd shoot if it charged. If it didn't, she'd walk slowly backward to the cave entrance. Then she remembered Cadeyrin. When he returned, he might not detect the cat if it were still hanging around. She had to keep him safe. The only reasonable action was to kill the beast.

Taking a deep breath, she ducked out from under the dense boughs and quickly retreated until she was several yards from the trees. The cat had disappeared the instant she showed herself. It was undoubtedly sneaking through the trees, trying to find an advantageous location from which to launch an attack.

Kathleen stepped cautiously back towards the cave, keeping a close watch as she scanned the dense evergreens. A branch moved slightly, and she tensed, raising her bow. The cat burst out of the boughs, snarling. She didn't wait but launched her arrow instantly, drawing and nocking another arrow almost before the first struck.

The attacking cat screamed as the arrow struck above its neck, embedding itself in its shoulder muscle. It hesitated and then started forward again. Her second arrow struck its foreleg and the cat snapped at the shaft, biting it in half.

It looked at her once again, and she drew herself up and stepped towards it. It hesitated and then quickly retreated. She let it go, hoping that it would go off somewhere to lick its wounds. With any luck, it would be afraid to come round again.

———◦○◦———

Once back in the cave, she spent time sweeping and cleaning until the place was about as clean as she could reasonably expect. There was a hail from outside as she prepared to build up the door fire. She dropped the wood she was carrying and went out.

Cadeyrin was standing back from the trees, carrying a deer slung over his shoulder. He had an arrow mounted as his eyes scanned the nearby undergrowth.

"Hi," shouted Kathleen, waving. She suddenly pictured herself as the little housewife greeting her husband as he came home from work. The image and the contrast with her present situation caused her to laugh.

Cadeyrin called back, "I smell blood here. Did anything attack? What happened?"

She motioned for him to come ahead, "There was a smaller Makkat. I shot it, and it ran away."

He glanced at her, and his expression betrayed mixed surprise and admiration. He started towards her, still keeping his arrow mounted and his attention on the trees.

She glimpsed movement at the other end of the trees. Ulfsa came trotting through an opening with his tail in the air, wagging gaily as if he hadn't a care in the world. If the cat had been hanging around, he would have detected it as he circled the grove. He'd come up between the trees and the lake, smelled the blood, and been satisfied that there was no danger.

He ran up to her, and she stooped to pat his head. She didn't have to stoop nearly as far as she had just a short time before. The pup was growing up quickly. He'd be fully grown before the summer was over.

The deer was butchered, and she recounted how she stood off the cat to Cadeyrin. He interrupted her several times to ask questions.

When she finished, he was quiet for a moment and then said, "It was good that you saw the cat before it could ambush you. If it survives the wounds, it won't ever come here again."

He smiled at her and then enveloped her in his heavily muscled arms.

"I am proud of you. You could not defend yourself when you first arrived here, but now you can. You could survive, even without me," he said.

That alarmed her. Was he planning on leaving her? Had he only been staying out of pity, and now he felt that he could get away? She tried to draw back, but he tightened his arms.

She leaned back to look into his eyes. What she saw there needed no words. His gaze held inexpressible tenderness. He said, "I am not leaving you, but sometimes people are killed by beasts. I want you to be safe."

She thought it over, suddenly realizing how badly he'd been hurt when the saber-tooth killed his mate. The thought brought a wave of sympathy, and she caressed his cheek with her hand. Her other hand slipped behind his neck, and she pulled him down to meet her lips.

Kathleen felt suddenly warm. Her stomach quivered, and her heart raced. Then, as the blood flow increased in her skin, she started to shiver. The cave was actually rather chill, and the cool air drew heat away from her feverish skin at a high rate.

Cadeyrin was shivering himself, but he didn't stop kissing her. His lips seemed drawn to her face like a magnet.

Kathleen was wholly involved in the kiss and the accompanying sensations, but then her fear kicked in. A portion of her mind drew back and observed her rapidly increasing arousal. She was breathing deeply. It felt as if his lips were on fire as they moved from her mouth to her cheek, then down to the scars on her jawline. That was too much for her to bear. His loving actions jerked her fears of intimacy to the front of her mind. She pulled back, and this time he let her go.

Cadeyrin wanted her with his entire body. He couldn't remember feeling so much in love and so aroused. He was so attuned to her that he instantly felt her doubt when it arose. He reluctantly released her. The time was not yet right. She was giving him every sign that she accepted him, but then something always caused her to pull back.

He mentally cursed whoever had caused her so much pain. It was obvious that she wanted him. He believed that she wanted to let go of her past and trust him, but she couldn't release her fears. He took a deep, shaky breath and said, "Let's store the venison. By then, it will be getting dark. I thought of a way to help you contact your spirit guide, and we can work at that. It should be safe here for both of us to enter the spirit-world."

Kathleen saw that he was shaking, and she mentally reprimanded herself. I shouldn't get so close to him, no matter how much I want to. Sooner or later, he'll – no, we'll – lose control, and I could end up pregnant, living in a cave. What would I do?

She asked, "What do you think of the fire that I laid by the door?"

He was silent a moment, and then he said, "If it were built up, it would keep any creature from entering. It would be too hot to get by. I think that it was a good idea. I think you are very clever."

She flushed at the simple compliment and turned, taking up some of the venison.

"How do you want to store this?" she asked.

"It will not last long in the heat of this cave. We need to dry it. My tribe sometimes dried fish by splitting them and hanging them in the sunlight. We could hang it outside to dry," he replied.

Kathleen had an idea. She put the meat down and searched through the firewood. She grunted as a stick poked her hand but then came up with a slim branch that had a forked place near the thick end.

"Look. We can cut this branch so that it makes a hook. Then, if we tie a piece of meat to it, we can hang it from those small ledges near the top of the cave," she explained, pointing upwards at the protruding rocks that she'd noticed earlier in the day.

He took the branch to examine it. A few strokes with his knife stripped the twigs off, leaving him with a nicely hooked stick. He sharpened the longer end to a sharp point, carefully cut some barbs near the tip, and then he handed it back so that she could examine it.

"If we stick the barbed end into the meat, the barbs will hold it, and then we can hang the hook over the stones," he said.

Kathleen was rather amazed at how quickly he understood her intent and improved on it. She asked, "Did your people store meat like that?"

"No, they would hang it on a drying rack, but your idea with the ledges is better in here. We won't have to worry about knocking the rack down when we move around, and no birds or small meat-eaters will steal our meat," he said.

As he'd predicted, it was fully dark by the time they'd gathered enough forked sticks, prepared them, cut up the meat, and hung it up in the smoky atmosphere near the roof of the cave. During the process, they'd cooked some of the haunch and made a meal that they ate while working.

Kathleen enjoyed the companionship, and the shared feeling of accomplishment as the two of them worked on the project. She felt quite domestic and was proud of both the clean cave and the stored meat. It seemed to bode well for their future together. That made her think of her desire for him. She felt warm all over as she remembered their kiss. If she just wasn't so worried about him deciding that her scars were too disgusting and leaving.

That thought was put out of her mind by Ulfsa jumping to his feet in alarm, followed by the nearby roar of a saber-tooth. It sounded like it was just outside the cave, roaring directly into the opening. Cadeyrin grabbed his weapons and carefully approached the entrance. The fire there had died and was now a bed of embers.

Ulfsa cautiously sneaked past the embers and looked out on one side of the entrance while Cadeyrin looked out the other side. There was a sudden renewal of the roaring followed by what she recognized as battle sounds.

Cadeyrin continued to watch without moving back. Kathleen moved over behind him and tried to peek past his shoulder. He raised his arm, blocking her as he whispered, "Two piskata are fighting near the entrance. I think they both came to claim the cave as a den, and now they are fighting over it...or to see which gets to attack us first."

Kathleen whispered, "What are we going to do?"

He answered, "Let them fight. The loser will leave, and the winner may be too injured than to be a threat to us. We watch, for now."

The battle didn't last long. While the big cats were fierce, they were also smart enough to avoid fatal encounters with each other. As soon as the smaller one realized it was losing, it retreated. They could hear its bad-humored snarling as it trotted off through the trees.

The victor watched until the loser couldn't be heard any longer, then it turned and started towards the cave. The conflict must have come on the two cats quickly before they could investigate the cave thoroughly. It took two steps forward before it sensed that they were watching it.

It stopped with a curious expression and lifted its head to better sample the scent in the area. As it exposed its breast, Cadeyrin's bow twanged, sending an arrow directly into the lower part of the animal's chest. He was a past master of animal anatomy and knew precisely where the tiger's heart lay.

The piskat jumped as the arrow struck, took two staggering steps, and collapsed.

Cadeyrin looked down at his bow and commented to Kathleen, "I could never have been so accurate or thrown a spear that deadly before. This thing you thought of makes us far safer than any weapon I had before. You have made our life much better."

She smiled. It was nice to receive a compliment, even if it wasn't really deserved.

Together they dragged the dead saber-tooth into the cave and skinned it while Ulfsa dozed by the fire. When she grew tired, Kathleen crawled into her bed of skins and relaxed, watching the profile of her stone-age hunter as he concentrated on flensing the hide. He had built the fire up so that it was brighter, and now he was scraping bits of flesh off the hide with a razor-sharp stone blade. Eventually, he stood, stretched his back, and then built up the fire at the entrance. Once that was done, he settled down near her. She belatedly remembered that he had been going to help her find a spirit guide, but it was too late. He was asleep.

Ulfsa got up, shook hard to arrange his fur, and trotted outside, returning shortly. The young wolf was naturally housebroken and had never made a mess close to their sleeping area. He curled down near the front fire. Kathleen could see the gleam of his eyes as he kept watch.

Chapter Nineteen

Esbern

During the next few days, Kathleen found herself more drawn to Cadeyrin and less frightened of physical affection. She now had no reservations about his holding and kissing her. In fact, it was quite the opposite. She found opportunities to accidentally bump into him in rather provocative ways that initiated embraces.

Despite her interest in him, she hadn't fully worked through her fears and was still anxious about deeper intimacy. This fear resulted in what she felt was a terrible argument.

Cadeyrin had always been careful to keep himself clean. Kathleen had believed that primitive people would be filthy since they were always portrayed in that fashion. He seemed to be an exception to that idea, but she didn't know if that were true of his people in general or just for him.

When she asked him why he kept his beard short and washed often, despite the cold air and icy water, he answered, "If you clean your skin, there will be fewer problems and less sickness. I've seen people die from their skin rotting or from simple wounds. Somehow, washing seems to help. I think it keeps tiny things from biting me. Cutting my beard keeps it cleaner and gives less opportunity for me to carry bits of food and grease from eating. The lack of scent helps me when I hunt. I learned some of this from our Shaman and some on my own, also what you told me about invisible animals."

Kathleen was gratified that her earlier discussion of infection had been taken to heart. He seemed to actually understand some elements of germ-based illness. Ever since that conversation, she had been even more scrupulous in her daily ablutions. The water was incredibly cold, and she wished there was some way to heat it, but after a few days, she became somewhat used to the icy experience.

The two bathed at the same time, only not together. She was careful to find a place where a screen of vegetation shielded her, although she always remained fairly close to him for security. He was more alert by habit than she and always checked the area thoroughly for any lurking danger.

•◦•

Cadeyrin had gone hunting, and Kathleen had elected to stay at the cave. With hours to kill, she decided to try and clean out a narrow crevice at the back of the space where the rocks came together. She'd ignored the tight crack for days, but then she'd discovered that there was a faint breeze moving through the opening. A quick inspection with a torch showed that the rocks leaned together tightly, but the space behind seemed to open up, creating a hidden room of unknown dimensions.

Cadeyrin apparently knew it was there but was content with their occupancy of the main cave. Kathleen's curiosity was piqued and she imagined a more secure room behind the rocks, possibly a good place to hide or store food. She pried at some of the loose stones that blocked the entrance and was able to move them a little. That settled it in her mind. She was going to get back there and see what was what.

After Cadeyrin had gone, taking Ulfsa with him, she began to work at moving the stones that constricted the entrance to the crack. It had taken a lot of effort, but she had moved most of them. There was just one large one left. It was too heavy for her to lift, and it was the one that really blocked the entrance to the crack.

Finally, she was able to tip it forward by prying it with a long branch. She kicked some gravel under the base to prop it up and moved her lever to a better position. Then, gathering herself and taking a deep breath, she leaned on the lever with all of her weight. There was a moment where the tall, heavy stone resisted, and then it toppled forward with a crash.

The narrow crack was fully exposed, and Kathleen wormed her way through, a flaming branch extended in her hand.

The room inside was smaller than she'd thought, about a meter wide. The two side walls leaned together, making the top quite narrow. The crack was deep, extending a long-distance and gradually narrowing so that she could only work her way back a little over three meters. Thereafter, the space was choked with stones that were too large for her to move. The intriguing thing was that there was a current of moist air that flowed from the back of the crack and moved between the stones.

The place was dust-filled. There had been some animal or animals that had denned there, and the floor was covered with debris and dried excrement. She'd have to clean this out, but once clean, the room could be used for storage.

By the time she'd gotten the dust and mess removed, she was covered in dirt. It was disgusting and smelled a little. The dirt was probably full of bacteria from the animal waste, and she wanted to bathe right away.

Cadeyrin was gone, but she decided that she'd be safe enough if she took her bow. She investigated the area carefully, watching for anything that was out of the ordinary. There were the usual small birds in the trees and undergrowth, and some squirrels played in the branches. She could detect nothing amiss.

Once at the lake, she moved to her usual bathing spot, a place where the trees grew thickly close to the shore. She had brought her old clothes to change into; her buckskins were too dirty and would need washing and then a long drying period by the fire, followed by a laborious working of the leather to remove the stiffness.

She quickly undressed, washed her hair, and cleaned her skin using a handful of sand to scrub the dirtier areas with the icy water. As she was dressing, Ulfsa showed up. She greeted him and hurried. Cadeyrin must be back.

She gathered her things and moved around the vegetation. Cadeyrin was standing just outside the edge of the trees, his bow at the ready. He glanced at her with a frown on his face and said, "There's some kind of cat that's been stalking you. Get to the cave, and I will follow."

Kathleen wasted no time. She trotted up to the entrance and then turned to cover him with her weapon as he followed. There was no sound from the thick spruces and no sign that anything was there, except that the birds were all gone. She could hear birdsong in the distance, but nothing nearby.

Cadeyrin looked grim and said, "You should have waited until I was back. You might have been attacked, and I wasn't here to guard you. I did not know where you were. Ulfsa tracked you down. I looked around the trees and saw you in the water. Then I tried to see what was hunting you."

He paused, and she replied defensively. After all, she was capable, and she was justified. She'd been quite dirty.

"I was too dirty to wait for you. You might have taken hours more before you returned. I didn't know – " she started. Then a thought struck her. He'd seen her in the water, naked.

"You were spying on me!" she gasped.

He shook his head negatively and responded, "I had to know where you were. I think it was one of those small, tufted cats – you called it a lynx, I think – and it could have caught you unawares. I was not spying. I was relieved to see that you were not hurt."

"But but you saw me," she said, almost in tears.

He must have seen the full extent of her scars, the horrible rough ridges on her skin that ranged from her right thigh up to her waist and inward across her stomach, thinning, but still extending down along the inside of her thighs.

"You saw my scars," she said quietly. Tears were now streaming down her cheeks.

Cadeyrin looked surprised.

He said, "I did see your scars, but I've seen far worse on other people. They don't – "

She interrupted him, "They're horrible. They make me ugly. You must be disgusted."

He again shook his head, "I am not disgusted. I was worried about you. I want you safe."

She didn't believe him. All of her previous experience had taught her that everyone pitied and rejected her when they found out about her scars. She retreated into the cave and tried to ignore his presence for the rest of the day. She'd been looking forward to showing him the hidden room, but now it was completely forgotten.

By evening, she was speaking to him a little. When he tried to discuss the incident with her again, she refused. The cave's atmosphere that night was tense, and the night itself seemed far longer than ever before.

At dawn, Cadeyrin began to gather his things. He hadn't killed any game the previous day, and they now needed food.

"I'm going hunting out to the west on the other side of the lake. I would like you to come with me. If I get a large animal, it will be better to have two people to carry than one," he said.

She nodded with a bleak expression on her face. They were low on food, and she could always help carry. Maybe that's what he kept her around for. To carry things. She sniffed experimentally, trying to work up a case of self-pity, but she wasn't quite as upset as the day before, and it didn't work.

They set out and soon were around the lake, moving along the edge of a valley that trended in a westerly direction.

—◦—

It was approaching midday. Since she'd been here, the sun had changed its track, gradually moving farther to the north in its daily path across the sky. The weather was still uneven, despite the increased solar exposure. Some days it was winter-like and other days showed some promise of warmer spring-like weather, but it never lasted.

They were on the northern side of the valley, walking just a little below the rim. Despite the warmth of the sun's rays striking the ground, the air was cold. Kathleen deviated from the trail that Cadeyrin was following and slanted up the hill until she could see over the top. The reason for the cold air was immediately apparent. They were near an arm of the ice sheet. It wasn't as thick as the main ice sheet, but its presence served to chill the air.

From what she could see, the ice began about a mile from their position and extended along a front that was several miles in length. The main ice sheet was toweringly thick, but this arm might have been a hundred yards tall at the crumbling edge.

Kathleen's position was on a sort of ridge that outlined the valley, and she could see down onto a flatter area that ended under the ice sheet. She scanned the plain, hoping to see something that they could kill.

Far in the distance, there was some kind of activity but she couldn't make it out clearly. She called Cadeyrin, and he dutifully trudged directly up to her position. When he got there, he confirmed that something was happening.

"It looks like a herd of deer have been scattered by something that attacked them. See, over there?" He pointed. "There is a cluster of animals that are regrouping. Some of the others are circling to catch up with them. If we hurry along behind the ridge, we might get close. Let's go."

He set out at a jog that was within Kathleen's ability to follow. Ulfsa had been investigating a rabbit trail down on the valley floor. When he saw them running, he came trotting back up the hillside, his tongue lolling out. He caught up to Cadeyrin, who waved his arm upwards towards the top of the ridge. Ulfsa obediently ran up the slope, looked over the edge, and instantly flattened down to minimize his profile. He glanced back at the two humans and then sped up to lead them along the valley.

It had only taken him one glance to assess the situation, and by his actions, he too thought it possible that they'd be able to make a kill.

It wasn't long before Kathleen had to slow down. She'd toughened up amazingly in the time she'd been here, but she couldn't keep the pace set by a life-long hunter.

Cadeyrin glanced back and slowed down so she could catch up to him. He pointed ahead where there was a large boulder embedded in the ground at the top of the ridge. "You stop in the shelter of that rock. Rest and get your bow ready. I will go ahead and send Ulfsa to circle behind the deer. He will drive them this way, and I will keep them from escaping into the valley too quickly. Some may run by close enough for you to shoot. Be ready."

Minutes later, they approached the rock. It towered over their heads, a huge granite sentinel, left by the ice to guard its last retreat. Cautiously, the two looked around the edge, screened by the stone and some brush.

The deer were not too far now and were heading towards a strange rock formation that stretched out for a long distance. It looked like someone had stacked human-sized piles of stones every few meters. The piles extended in a straight line for perhaps a kilometer, and there was a gap in the line of piles where the ground dropped into a depression screened by a low hill.

Kathleen felt Cadeyrin tense as he saw the stones. He whispered, "It is a deer fence. The deer mistake the piles of stones for something frightening. They will break through the open area to escape, and hunters wait in the gap to kill them."

She asked, "Are there any hunters there now?"

"It is an old trick, the stone men," he answered. "The stones may have been there for many years. There may be no hunters now. I have not seen signs of any men here. Let's watch the deer. If they break through the gap, they will go down and out of sight. Then we can run to that gap between the two low hills."

He pointed again and asked, "See it?"

She nodded, and he continued, "If the deer come along the low land, we will be above them, and they may be within arrow shot."

They watched for a time as the deer milled around. Finally, the constant urge to graze overcame the animals' wariness, and they began to browse at the short vegetation as they came.

Kathleen looked closely at the animals. They were caribou. She'd been expecting the white-tailed deer that she was used to, but these creatures were definitely larger and carried impressive racks of antlers. She pointed and whispered, "Those are caribou, not deer."

Cadeyrin glanced at her and said, "They are deer but different from the woodland deer we have been killing. These travel long distances at different seasons. There have not been any in our area, but maybe they are coming now. There should be many more of them."

He stiffened, "Look! They go through the open area between the stone men. Let's go."

As the caribou descended out of sight behind the gentle hill, he rose and started down the slope. Kathleen followed. As she made her way down, she could see a lone wolf coming across the plain a long way out. Ulfsa had circled far around and was now running hard to cut off any possible escape.

They were about half of the way to the gap when Cadeyrin abruptly stopped running. She stopped by him and listened. There was a confused melee going on over the hill. She could hear the sounds of caribou, interspersed with the shouts of men. Hunters had been stationed in the depression, and the two of them had nearly stumbled into the middle of the hunt.

Cadeyrin reached for her hand, and together they turned to retreat back to the lookout by the boulder. In a low voice, he said, "They may be friendly or not. Once you're hidden, I will go to where I can see them. If they are of my people, I will know. If they are the enemy, I will come back to you. If you do not see me standing and going to greet them, go to the other side of the valley and start back to our cave."

"Who are the enemy?" Kathleen wanted to know. This was something new. She had no idea that he viewed some people as automatic antagonists.

"They are a different people. They come from the west, and they have different colored skin than my people. They are all black-haired, also. My people are light-skinned and have lighter hair, some my light color, but some do have brown or black hair," he explained and then added, "I do not want you to be caught by the enemy. They will kill me, torture me if they can catch me, but you they will keep as a slave. You will become the property of some warrior to use as he wishes."

He paused, and then, with a long look at the far hills, he said, "They killed all of my tribe, even the children, but they took many of the young women captive. That was the last time I saw them."

She panted, regaining her breath. When she could talk again, she asked, "Couldn't you rescue them?"

He shrugged, "Too many for one man to attack. I tried to find the rest of the hunters I was with. Together we might have attacked, but when I found them, they were all – "

He stopped, listening. The sounds had changed. The men were yelling in excitement, and then there came a loud roar.

Cadeyrin jumped at the sound, "Esbern! It attacks the hunters to steal their prey. They will be busy with it. Let's run back and look. If they are my people, I must help them."

Kathleen took a deep breath and turned to follow. This time he didn't wait for her but stretched his legs out in a full run. He quickly pulled ahead.

When he neared the gap between the hills, he slowed until he could see what was happening. Kathleen saw him pause and then dash forward, holding his bow ready. She redoubled her speed and came, panting, upon a fierce scene.

⸺◦◇◦⸺

She pulled up at the exit from the gap. The low area of ground formed a narrow valley that wasn't visible from any great distance. There were a group of men bunched together, their spears pointing at an enormous bear that was trotting towards them, a spear shaft hanging from its humped shoulders. Behind the bear, two injured or dead hunters, along with six dead caribou, were spread out upon the ground.

Kathleen surmised the hunters had killed the caribou, and the bear had then attacked. It may have been watching the hunt, content to let the humans do the work before it came down to take the meat away from them.

The bear had a curiously short muzzle that vaguely reminded her of a bulldog. Despite the short jaw, it still looked dangerous, and it seemed as big as a bull. Its size amazed Kathleen. It was as tall or taller at the shoulders than any of the hunters, including Cadeyrin.

She sought out his blond hair. He was a short distance in front of her, crouching behind a large boulder and drawing his bow. She glanced at the other men. Some of them were also blond, and they were light-skinned as far as she could tell. From Cadeyrin's actions, they must be his people. She doubted that he'd help the enemy.

He was aiming carefully, and she watched as he released his arrow. It smacked into the monster bear, striking in the ribs behind its shoulder. It roared in response and charged the group of hunters.

The men scattered, but not before some of them threw their spears. She could see they used atl-atls and were accurate with them. Several of the spears struck the bear, infuriating it even more. It let out a roar that made its previous effort seem puny in comparison.

By then, Cadeyrin had reloaded, and he stood and shot, striking the bear in the abdomen. This elicited a violent response. The creature spun rapidly, trying to bite at the arrow, which was just out of its reach. Then it saw Cadeyrin as he was readying another arrow.

Ignoring the pinpricks that were bothering it, the bear headed directly for the blond man that it now took for the source of the attack.

Kathleen was standing directly behind and above Cadeyrin. He was perhaps ten meters closer to the bear than she was. She pulled an arrow, nocked it, drew and released almost at the same time. Before the arrow's flight had ended, she was nocking a second one. Her first arrow struck the animal's head, embedding in its cheek, and her second struck near the base of its neck. It roared again with a ragged overtone of extreme anger, a bone-chilling sound that made her shudder. It was looking directly at her, and the ferocity in its gaze made her knees weak.

Cadeyrin yelled to get the bear's attention. It refocused on him and started forward. He yelled loudly and raised his arms over his head, taking a posture that an attacking bear might. In response, the huge creature stood upright on its hind paws and roared.

It towered incredibly high, standing like some kind of primitive monument to fury incarnate. Cadeyrin didn't let the exposed chest go to waste. He drove an arrow feather-deep between its ribs. The bear coughed and swiped at the end of the shaft, breaking it off.

Kathleen had been momentarily stunned by the height of the creature, but then she drew her bow and sent another shaft at the bear. This one struck low on the right side in a more vital area. The bear coughed again and dropped to all fours.

It staggered a little but then came at Cadeyrin in a full run. He shot once more as it advanced, but she didn't see where the arrow struck. She was fumbling for another arrow, her eyes wide with horror as the bear charged Cadeyrin.

A gray blur shot across in front of the bear, slashing at its front legs. Ulfsa had arrived just in time to distract the bear, and it turned towards its new attacker. Cadeyrin used the chance to load and shoot. The bear spun back towards the hunter, ignoring the wolf.

Cadeyrin waited until it was almost upon him before ducking behind the boulder. He dashed around the rock as the bear was turning around it. Once he was in the clear, he shot another arrow that buried itself deep in the animal's guts. It turned, more slowly this time, coming back into the open area.

Kathleen shot an arrow that struck it in the back of the neck. The bear's muscles were so thick that the arrow did little damage beyond distracting it. It glanced behind to see who was attacking from that direction.

As it looked back, Cadeyrin ran forward, pulling his bow back as he got close. This shot went deep into the side of the bear's neck. He'd aimed at the carotid artery in a killing shot, and the blood spurted out around the arrow's shaft. The bear wasn't done yet. Despite absorbing enough punishment to kill several lesser animals, it still had fight left. It turned back to him and started forward, slowly this time. The multiple wounds were beginning to wear on its great vitality.

Cadeyrin backed towards the remaining hunters. As he did, three of them ran up and launched their spears as hard as they could. The shafts struck the bear's breast and neck. It took two more steps, stumbled, and then went down on its face, its hindquarters still standing for a moment. Gradually, the bear's hind legs failed, and it rolled onto its side.

The hunters let out exultant yells and ran forward, surrounding Cadeyrin. Kathleen prepared to shoot at them in his defense, but then she saw that they were pounding on his shoulders and back and talking at the top of their voices.

Shakily, she lowered her bow and descended to inspect the kill.

Chapter Twenty

Wrong Assumptions

I t took hours to butcher the bear. The meat had a lot of fat in it and was highly desirable for that reason. The fat could be used in cooking. Besides having a high caloric count by itself, the bear meat added flavor to venison, making it taste much better. It could also be used to make a mixture of ground meat and dried berries that could be preserved as trail food.

Aside from the meat, the bear's hide was valuable in itself. It was thick and would be used for clothing or sleeping skins.

The hunters were of Cadeyrin's people. He'd never heard of their tribe, but they spoke mostly the same language. Kathleen still hadn't mastered their speech and missed much of what they said.

Cadeyrin had taken to English as if it were his native tongue and with a speed that made her feel intellectually inferior. As a result, she hadn't concentrated on his language and now found the lack of fluency a distinct disadvantage.

The two hunters that the bear had taken down had saddened her. The first had suffered a blow to the head that had crushed his skull, but the second, a mere boy, was paralyzed with a broken neck.

He was still alive when the group surrounded him. He couldn't speak loudly, but he was still breathing and could whisper. The hunters looked at each other with grim expressions. Then one, apparently the leader, bent over the boy and said something. As he did, he covered the youth's eyes with his left hand. The boy said a few words back, and then the hunter drove his stone knife into the boy's heart.

There was no movement from the youth except for a brief exhalation. When the hunter removed his hand, the boy's eyes were closed.

Kathleen started to protest the cruel treatment, but Cadeyrin stopped her.

"The boy would die soon. He would never be able to walk. The hunters could not care for him. They would not leave him to be eaten alive by scavengers, so killing him quickly was the only thing they could do," he explained.

She didn't like it, but she saw the necessity. It was a little easier to bear when she understood that the boy hadn't even felt the blade as it stopped his heart.

The group was grateful to them for joining in the battle. Without their arrows, there would have been many more dead, and the outcome would have been in doubt. The bows were a major object of interest to the hunters, but Kathleen also noticed that many of them couldn't seem to take their eyes off of her.

I'm not that fascinating, she thought to herself. *Maybe it's because I helped in the hunt, or maybe they just don't have many women in their tribe.* She was not used to being the center of attention and did her best to remain unobtrusive. It made her feel uneasy and somewhat resentful.

Cadeyrin spoke at length with the hunt leader and finally turned to her.

"They want us to come with them to their camp. They have set up a summer camp over those hills. They come here to harvest the caribou. The main herd has not arrived yet, but when it does, they will need many hunters. With our bows, they believe we will make up for the two men who were killed," he explained.

He glanced at the leader, who was discussing the loads of bear meat that were being packed.

He said, "I think they also want us to teach them how to make their own bows. I can see no harm in it. Can you think of a reason not to help them?"

Kathleen considered and then answered, "They can see the entire bow, and that's the whole secret. Anyone who sees one can duplicate it. The only difficult thing would be to find the right wood. I don't think we can keep it from them now. We might as well help."

Cadeyrin nodded, "That is what I thought. They also are a little afraid of you. Their women do not hunt, and they are amazed that you fought. Some of them think you are a sorceress, but others want us to join their tribe. That may be good or not. We can go and see."

She said, "Maybe they have a good camp. Surely their large numbers will mean more security for us."

It seemed to her that Cadeyrin appeared dubious about that.

He looked down and said, "Maybe. Sometimes it is easier for a small group to go unnoticed by the enemy. I do not know if we will want to stay with them, but we can stay long enough to help with the deer hunt. They live off the caribou. They even call themselves 'the Deer People.' Just remember, their ways are not mine. They may not act like me. I had to tell them to leave Ulfsa alone. They never saw a wolf that hunts with a man. They wanted to kill him." He shook his head negatively. Then he looked directly at her. "Some of the men have said things about you. They have been arguing with each other. Some think you should be banned for doing something women never do, but others think you would be good for their tribe. Be careful, but do not worry. I will be there to protect you."

She nodded solemnly. It was frightening to think that she was the center of attention, especially if some of it was negative.

--------⋅◦⋅--------

Hauling the heavy packs of bear meat back to the camp of the Deer People took the rest of the day and well into the night. By the time they'd arrived, Kathleen was staggering. The pack she was carrying was much lighter than those the men carried, but it now seemed to weigh hundreds of pounds.

As they approached the camp, they halted in the darkness and called to the occupants. The entire tribe, old men, women, and children, came running out and relieved them of their loads.

Although Kathleen was tired, she took an interest in the camp. The Deer People's hunting camp was composed of nearly a hundred small, deerskin-covered huts or tents; she wasn't sure quite what to call them. The best part was that they provided some shelter from the elements and the insects that were now hatching after the long winter.

The tribe held an impromptu celebration that featured hastily cooked bear meat and involved almost every hunter standing and telling the story of how the bear was killed. They wanted both her and Cadeyrin to join in, but Cadeyrin explained that he didn't think it would be right for guests to take part in the celebration.

They assured him that the two of them were welcome in the camp and could stay as long as they liked. One of the tents had belonged to the older man that was killed, and the lead hunter offered it to Cadeyrin and 'his woman.'

Cadeyrin glanced at her and accepted for the both of them, explaining that she was a member of his tribe and his hunting companion.

Well, she thought, *it isn't as though we haven't been sharing a cave for weeks.* She assumed that the tribe believed they were mated, and the concept made her blush, though she wasn't sure why. She decided that she was still angry with him and embarrassed that he'd seen her naked in the water.

She tried to put the 'mate' idea out of her thoughts; however, her mind repeatedly turned to the subject as she watched the hunters reenact the fight. It wasn't hi-res video streaming, and there was no script, but it was an entertainingly wild scene.

When they retired, she was yawning and glad to crawl into the tent and lie on the skins. Cadeyrin lay beside her, and Ulfsa curled up by the entrance.

As she was falling asleep, he raised himself to lean over her and whispered, "Thank you for your bravery. Your arrows really helped. I might have been killed without you fighting along with me."

His lips descended to hers, and she pulled him down for a sleepy kiss, forgiving him for the moment. He lay back, and she rolled onto her side, facing him, then dropped into sleep, the memory of his lips on hers making her smile.

The two arose at dawn and ate some bear meat that had been roasted at the big fire. Cadeyrin intended to speak to the tribe's elders about helping them. He wanted to firm up their status with the tribe.

He went off, leaving Kathleen in the care of a group of young, unmated women, and walked to the tent of the lead hunter. On the way, he noticed that several of the young women were trailing him.

He smiled to himself. There were few chances for the young people of the tribe to meet any strangers. The girls assumed that he was available since Kathleen wore her hair loose rather than braided. The girls were trying to work up their courage to approach him. He ignored them as he walked up to the group of elders that were standing beside the lead hunter's tent.

The men seemed a little reserved this morning. They'd been quite welcoming the night before, but now it was as if something had quelled their enthusiasm.

Cadeyrin greeted the leader, "Good hunting. I've come to speak to you about our stay here."

The leader raised his hand in greeting and answered, "You and your witch-woman are welcome as long as she hunts no more."

That was new. Cadeyrin asked, "You saw what she can do yesterday against the esbern. Why do you call her a witch-woman, and why do you not want her help in the deer hunt to come?"

The leader looked nervously over his shoulder at an older man who was among the group of warriors.

Cadeyrin followed his eyes and thought: *Ah. The Shaman. This could be a problem.*

The leader turned back and answered, "Women should not hunt, and a woman using some strange weapon that hurls little spears is unnatural. If she comes on the deer hunt, the deer will not come. The deer spirit will abandon our tribe, and then we will starve. She may not hunt."

He looked around again and added, "I have spoken, and it is not to question."

Cadeyrin shrugged. Kathleen would be an asset on the hunt, but she wasn't absolutely needed. She would probably be safer staying in camp.

"The woman need not hunt. She can stay here. She is of my tribe, and I say she is not a witch. She is under my protection," he said, wanting to make it clear that no one was to bother her.

The leader glanced back at the Shaman again and then said, "You are welcome on the hunt. We need all the men that we have so that we can kill enough deer. Our scouts have told us that they are coming and will be here in possibly two days. As for the woman, you say she is no witch, but she does unnatural things. No woman has ever helped kill an esbern. She may stay here, but she must not do anything else that is unnatural. If she does, she'll be banished and unwelcome."

Cadeyrin decided that the leader's grudging acceptance was the most he could hope for, especially since it appeared that the leader was going against the wishes of the Shaman. He momentarily considered leaving, but he wanted to go on the deer hunt. He'd never participated in such a thing and was eager to see it.

The two spoke further about the hunt. Cadeyrin ended by agreeing to help them with it, but he didn't promise more than that.

The talking had left him thirsty, so he left to get a drink of water. The stream was located on the other side of a nearby ridge that was covered with spruce trees and boulders. His female entourage had hung around chattering animatedly among themselves while he talked to the elders, but they mysteriously stopped following him when he left the camp.

He let out a sigh of relief. It was good to get rid of them. He hated to disappoint them, but he was already committed as far as he was concerned.

He'd have to convince Kathleen to braid her hair as the married women of the tribe did. That way, the tribe would accept her as his mate. They wouldn't know that the two of them were still trying to figure out their relationship. His heart beat lightly as he imagined Kathleen with her hair braided for him. Maybe that would lead her to act the part of his mate.

Then a gloomy cloud came over him. He couldn't deceive her or trick her into accepting him. His pride wouldn't allow it. He wanted her to come to him on her own. He wanted her more than anything, but he instinctively knew that it would be meaningless unless it was her decision.

⸻ ◆ ⸻

On the way back from drinking, he heard a woman calling his name from behind some rocks a little off the trail. He went to investigate. Perhaps someone was in distress and needed help.

⸻ ◆ ⸻

The women of the Deer People wore their hair in two different ways. Kathleen observed that the young women who were unclaimed wore their hair loose, while the mated women uniformly braided their hair. While she couldn't talk to them, they were friendly, and several of the young women appointed themselves as her escorts, showing her about the camp.

She was the center of attention for everyone and soon attracted a following that seemed to consist mostly of single, young men. She wondered why for a time but finally realized that her loose hair was taken as a signal that she was available. If she'd been mated to Cadeyrin, her hair would be braided according to their custom.

She enjoyed the attention for a while but then began to feel uneasy. The girls had led her to the far side of the camp, showing her where the women's facilities were. They had a designated area for each sex to use for elimination.

The young men who had been following her waited patiently in the village until the group of girls returned, then followed along behind, not saying much. Their attention was beginning to wear on her, and she felt nervous. Some of the older women and men had given her glances that seemed somewhat hostile. She continued towards the middle of the camp, searching for Cadeyrin. He wasn't in sight, and she wondered where he was.

When she reached the central fire, a place that acted as a town square, she saw the hunt leader. Summoning what little she knew of the language, she asked him where Cadeyrin was.

He frowned at her and said several things she didn't understand, but she finally got the idea that Cadeyrin had gone to the nearby stream to drink. The hunt leader pointed, and she set off along the way.

Somewhere near the edge of the camp, her escort dropped off, seemingly unwilling to leave the camp boundaries. She found herself alone, walking down a well-beaten trail that wound through thick clusters of spruce trees on the way towards the river. As she reached a turn in the trail by a pile of large granite boulders, she heard conversation and a woman's laughter.

She backtracked and circled around the boulder pile, stopping in shock as she saw Cadeyrin facing an attractive young woman who was completely nude. She couldn't help admiring the girl. She had no visible blemishes and made Kathleen feel ugly in comparison.

As she watched, the girl giggled and stepped towards him, raising her arms to put them around his neck. He lifted his arms in response, and Kathleen suddenly couldn't stand to see any more.

She averted her gaze and spun around, walking back towards the camp with tears springing from her eyes. *What was she to do? She'd come to depend on Cadeyrin. She'd been near to the point of accepting that she had to live the rest of her life with him, and now this! He was...he was...* Her mind refused to complete the thought.

It must be her fault. He couldn't wait for her forever, and she hadn't made it clear that she wanted him. She wasn't even sure what she wanted, but she knew that her heart was breaking now. Maybe he would never have accepted her as a mate because of her scars. She didn't know.

Her emotions flew through the entire gamut of sadness to jealousy to a blinding fury and back. She'd never felt so betrayed, so alone, so lost.

Finally, she found herself facing the central fire. There were few people about, so she just sat down and stared at the embers without seeing them.

After a time, she noticed that several of the young men were watching her. They all carried bundles of one sort or another.

When she looked at them, they stirred and nudged one man forward. He shyly came up to her and laid his bundle on the ground near her. She glanced at it. It was a tanned hide that was tied with sinew. She glanced at him incuriously and then back at the fire.

When she looked up again, another man deposited his bundle by that of the first. She wasn't sure what they were doing, perhaps showing her that she was welcome to the tribe. In any event, her heart was breaking, and she wished they'd just leave her alone.

Over the course of a few minutes, each of the men had laid his bundle near her and retreated. They stood in a group, watching her expectantly. Not knowing what to do, she finally reached out and pulled a bundle towards her. A finely cured cheetah skin practically shimmered in the sun. It was attractive, and she rubbed her hands over the fur, distracted from her misery by its softness. She picked it up and felt it with her cheek.

When she picked it up to admire it, the man that had offered it made a triumphant yell, raising his arms in the sky. Startled, Kathleen dropped the skin on her lap. The other men looked disappointed but then seemed to congratulate the first. Then the entire group quickly walked off somewhere between the tents.

She took the skin and laid it down nearby, wondering what had transpired. It was beyond her.

The next moment, she was surrounded by a group of laughing women. They knelt beside her and began working on her hair. At first, she tried to push them away. She felt too miserable to be bothered, but they persisted, and after a while, it didn't seem to matter to her any longer.

They finished arranging her hair in a braid and then left her mercifully alone with her thoughts.

Her life was a mess. It had always been a mess, but now she'd had a chance to experience Cadeyrin's affection, what little affection she'd allowed him to show. The thought that he was out in the bushes, mating with some unknown girl, was simply too terrible to contemplate.

It was at that point that the cheetah skin's owner approached her and said something, then pointed at a nearby tent. She didn't understand what he wanted until he reached down and grasped her arm, pulling her to her feet. Then he pulled her towards the tent.

Kathleen resisted. She didn't want to go to any tent right now. She just wanted to sit alone in her misery, but the young man kept pulling at her. She struggled to get free and momentarily glimpsed Cadeyrin standing between two tents with a horrified look on his face. She forgot about her anger and hurt and called out to him, "Cadeyrin, help!"

He'd started to turn away, his normally proud posture slumped into a dejected slouch, but at her call, he turned and came.

He interposed his arm between the two of them when he got there. A type of tug-of-war ensued over Kathleen's arm until the man quit pulling at her and said something that sounded hostile. He then stepped back and drew his knife with an expression of outrage on his face.

Kathleen was alarmed, but before the hunter could decide to act on his implied threat, Cadeyrin asked him something. She couldn't understand the exchange, but the young man tucked away his knife, choosing to talk rather than fight the tall, muscular warrior.

The two spoke for a few moments. The younger tribesman seemed furious and spoke aggressively. His hand dropped to the hilt of his knife in the middle of the conversation, but Cadeyrin remained calm. She mentally evaluated the two. It was obvious which was dominant. She thought that the younger man was smart not to want to fight.

Cadeyrin turned to Kathleen with a hurt look.

She was puzzled, not having understood the exchange.

"What is it? What's going on?" she asked.

"Is it true?" he asked in return.

The memory of him with the nude girl passed through her mind, and she angrily asked, "Is what true?"

"That you've accepted Spotted Cheetah's gift?" he responded.

"He gave it to me. It's beautifully tanned," she said.

"Then there is no place for me here," he said, sadly turning away.

"Wait! What do you mean?" The importance of what was happening just started to penetrate her mind. "Where are you going?"

Cadeyrin answered, "You accepted his gift. That means you have agreed to stay with him. You wear the braided hair of a mated woman. I never gave you a gift. I just thought that you wanted to stay – "

She interrupted him, "I didn't agree to stay with him."

She wanted to say, "I'm going with you! I mean, we've become..." The thought lost itself in the jumble of things she wanted to tell him. Instead, she said, "I mean, you need me. I can help you. You have no tribe, and you've taught me to help."

As she started to speak, the image of him raising his arms to the naked girl again passed through her mind. Anger flashed through her, fueled by a sense of betrayal.

She snapped, "Even if I did want to stay with him, what business is it of yours? Why do you even think I want to stay with him?"

She glared at him as if daring him to speak.

He replied, "But you took his gift. To these people and mine, that means he is acceptable to you. Are you saying that you did not know he wanted you?"

She carefully replied, "I'm scarred, and no one – "

Once again, her voice failed her. After a moment, she continued, in a quavering voice, "No, I didn't know that the gift meant he wanted me. He can have it back. Just wait here, and I'll give it back to him."

Cadeyrin shook his head. "When a single woman receives such a gift, she can touch it. If she does not want the man, she shouldn't pick it up. If you return it now, it will be a deadly insult to him."

Kathleen shook her head in denial. The idea of becoming a stranger's wife, living with him, and bearing his children was more than she could fathom.

"I mean no insult. I just didn't know what was happening. I don't want him." She repeated, emphatically, "I don't want him."

Then she added bitterly, tears starting in the corners of her eyes, "Why did you mate with that girl I saw you with? I should go with that man. He wants me. Maybe he wouldn't mate with the first girl he sees."

Cadeyrin's eyes widened in surprise.

She continued, "I saw you. Just because she's prettier than me, you went off behind some rocks with her."

He shook his head in denial and then asked, "Kathleen, did you see what happened? The girl made it clear that she wanted me, but I would not commit to her. She hid behind the rocks and called when I passed by. When I went to see what was happening, she was without her clothes. She tried to hold me, but I pushed her away. I told her I was not the one that she wanted. She left. I am not sure where she is now."

By this time, she had worked up a serious case of outrage. She was furious. She heard his words, but they seemed to have no meaning. Her face was red, and her eyes glared at him as she said, "That sounds unlikely. I saw you. She was naked. You were about to – to – "

She couldn't force herself to say it. Instead, she angrily spun around and marched towards the young man's tent.

⋯⋯◄◊►⋯⋯

The young hunter sheathed his knife and stared aggressively at Cadeyrin, saying, "It is well. If she had rejected my gift now, I would have killed you."

Cadeyrin wasn't listening. He was staring at Kathleen's back as she entered the man's tent. Once she was inside, he turned dejectedly towards the tent where they'd spent the night. His mind raced over the argument. Custom dictated that the agreement was between the man and the woman. Outside intervention almost always led to fighting and death, sometimes of both men and the woman, should one of the disputant's relatives become involved. He couldn't think how he could convince her to come with him. If she truly wanted Spotted Cheetah, then he should accept that. Especially, since he was a guest of the tribe. It would be bad form and would gain him a lot of resentment from the warriors.

He gathered his things, glancing sadly at her possessions but leaving them alone. He simply could not stay and face Kathleen, happy over her marriage. It would be more than he could bear. The pain he felt was already so bad that he wanted to die. If he saw the two together, he might snap and attack the man. That would be an unforgivable action. He had to leave.

He headed away from the camp, moving in the general direction of their cave home. As he passed the last row of tents, he glanced back. The hunt leader and several men were watching him leave, unreadable expressions on their faces.

He turned and trotted into the brush. Ulfsa came out of a thicket and followed him.

Cadeyrin could only think of returning to the cave. He'd been happier there with Kathleen than he'd ever been. Maybe there, he'd be able to get over losing her.

It seemed like his eyes were blurry. There was something in them, and his throat held a knot, making it difficult to swallow. It was not manly to break down. He tried to deny his emotions, but his eyes were leaking, and the knot wouldn't go away.

He breathed raggedly and closed his eyes for a moment, opening them quickly when he stumbled over a tuft of grass. There was no joy to be seen in the surrounding forest and brush. It was lonely and quiet, the contrast reminding him of happy walks with Kathleen. The way he felt, he'd be grateful if he were attacked by something. He wondered if he'd even fight to stay alive.

Kathleen had no idea what she was doing in the tent. Once she'd entered, the seriousness of the situation struck her with full force, and her anger started to fade. She'd let her anger and feeling of betrayal force her into a choice that she didn't want. She hoped that Cadeyrin was regretting his actions. Let him suffer, she thought to herself vindictively.

The tent shook, and the young hunter entered. He said something that she didn't understand, then looked at her expectantly. When she didn't move, he repeated his statement impatiently.

She looked at him and shook her head negatively, trying to indicate that she didn't understand.

His face clouded, and he pushed her down on the bed of furs, then knelt and started tugging at her pants.

She struggled in alarm. Now she knew what he desired, and she wanted no part of it.

He held her down with one arm and pulled her pants down. He was watching her face when his hand encountered her scars. He started and jerked back, looking down.

His eyes widened when he saw the scars; then, he said something that sounded like a curse. He drew back farther with an expression of mixed fear and disgust on his face, making some kind of warding sign with his fingers.

Kathleen saw the look on his face and began to cry. Her scarring disgusted even this man who had wanted to marry her. She struggled to pull up her pants, trying to control her sobbing as she did.

When she looked up again, the young hunter had left. She was at a loss as to what she should do, but then she remembered her supposed mated status. That reminded her of her braided hair. It was the work of just a moment to undo the braid. Maybe now they'd understand that she hadn't meant to accept the man's proposal.

Fearfully, she left the tent. The young man was standing by the fire, arguing with several of the hunters. They all turned and looked at her with hostile expressions when she emerged. One of the men plucked some grass and hurled the stems at her in a sort of symbolic gesture.

She gathered her courage and approached the chief hunter who had been standing apart from the group. He maintained a carefully neutral expression on his face. She hoped that meant that he still held some respect for her due to her participation in the battle with the great bear.

She hesitantly asked, "Where Cadeyrin go?"

The chief hunter responded silently by pointing in the direction from which they had come. Cadeyrin must have decided to head back to their cave. Even if he hadn't, she wanted to go back there. It had been the happiest place she'd been since she'd come into the past. If she could get back there, she'd never leave again. If she was attacked on the way, well, at least her troubles would be over.

She walked back to their overnight tent and gathered up her equipment, sadly noticing that his was already gone. Then she walked back through the camp. The hunters by the fire studiously ignored her until the Shaman chanted something that sounded like a curse. Then they made jeering noises and warding signs towards her. The young hunter who had rejected her was not in sight.

Some of the women were watching her as she walked out of the camp. As she passed the last tent, the women shouted something that sounded derisive at her back. When she turned to see what they wanted, they threw small sticks at her.

None of the sticks struck her, but the act made it clear that she wasn't welcome to return. She sighed and headed into the brush. It was a long walk back to the cave, and it would be getting dark in a couple of hours. She needed to move fast.

She wanted to get clear of their territory. It would be better if she didn't encounter any of them again. She broke into a slow trot, trying not to think of the mess she'd made of everything. She kept looking for Cadeyrin, but he didn't appear. Finally, she quit searching and jogged along numbly.

It was nearly dark, and she had only traveled a few miles. After some searching, Kathleen found what she believed would be a secure campsite, sheltered by a great boulder. If she built a fire a little distance before the boulder, she could sit between it and the rock. Her back would be shielded so that all she had to do was watch for attacks from the front.

As she gathered some wood, she thought back on what had happened. *Cadeyrin had denied having anything to do with that girl. He'd said that he'd pushed her away. She'd heard him but hadn't believed him. Her experience had taught her that people lied. Men lied.*

Her mind would have none of that. *She'd never doubted anything he'd said before. To the best of her knowledge, he'd never lied to her or misled her in any way. He had to have been telling her the truth.* She gulped down a sob. *What a fool she was. She'd rejected the only man who had ever shown her affection. He was lost to her now. She'd be lucky to ever see him again. She wanted to die. If only she could just return to the future. People there needed her formula and technique. She had a career to build. Her research would make her famous. Maybe she could forget about Cadeyrin.*

That thought was too much, and she bent her head and sobbed softly as she dragged the last branch back.

She had hauled enough wood, so she used the technique Cadeyrin had taught her, striking two stones together to create a spark. She was glad he'd forced her to practice with the flint and metallic stone over and over. Her fingers had hurt, and she'd been resentful, but now she knew the importance of mastering fire starting.

The darkness crept over the trees and rocks as she gazed into the burning fire. She paid no attention, simply losing herself in the flickering flames.

Thinking back on Cadeyrin's actions, she knew deep in her heart that he had always wanted her. *She hadn't allowed herself to recognize that fact. His repeated kisses weren't simply an attempt to seduce her for his own pleasure. His consideration and care were too consistent for that. She'd felt comfortable with him, except for her own self-generated fears and prejudices.*

She was afraid of getting pregnant. Well, so what? How did she think humans survived to the twenty-first century? They got pregnant and had children, of course.

Her feeling that Cadeyrin wasn't her intellectual equal was a stupid prejudice. Simply because he hadn't gone through the years of formal education that she had didn't mean that he wasn't intelligent. He knew about the heavens. He knew any number of things that she didn't. What good would her degrees do her? They were just meaningless pieces of paper, anyway. They only said that she'd taken some courses, and those probably didn't even relate to the real world accurately. No, he was very intelligent in the only way that really mattered. He could do things, anything that was necessary to survive.

Her thoughts went back to how quickly he'd picked up English when she'd just barely managed to learn a few scraps of his speech. *Perhaps that was because he was willing to work at learning, and she was willing to take the easy route and let him learn her language rather than laboring at learning his, or perhaps it was due to some difference in brain maturation.*

She didn't know much about it, but she knew that at a certain age, modern humans lose the ability to learn new languages easily. She'd read that was due to changes in brain structure. What if it were also affected by information saturation? Modern man is exposed to far more information than even relatively recent humans. Maybe her brain was so full of information that she found it hard to learn a new language.

Maybe – oh, never mind that. All she wanted was for him to be with her right now. She didn't care about his education. He was perfectly adapted to life in his time, far better than she. She had been so proud of herself. She'd learned to hunt and to shoot an arrow, but it was all due to Cadeyrin's patient teaching.

Her thoughts were interrupted. Something was out there in the darkness. There was a sound of something coming through the brush. She stood, drawing an arrow and nocking it on the bowstring. She almost shot before she saw what it was. There were two glowing eyes that were approaching. She tightened the string, pulling it back farther.

The vague shape suddenly resolved into a dear and familiar wolf face with a happy, almost foolish grin upon it. Ulfsa trotted up to her fire, walked around it, and took her hand in his mouth in greeting.

She collapsed to her knees, hugging the wolf to her breast in relief.

"Where is Cadeyrin?" she asked. "Ulfsa, where is he?"

As if he could understand her, Ulfsa glanced over his shoulder. She raised her head and followed his gaze. There was a movement in the dark, and a familiar voice said, "I'm here. May I come to the fire?"

Kathleen stood, trembling. She could barely talk, but she managed to get out a shaky, "Yes."

Moments later, Cadeyrin was standing on the other side of the fire from her.

"I saw the light of your fire," he started. "I wasn't traveling very quickly. I thought – "

He stopped and looked at her. "What happened? I thought you were going to stay with that man."

Kathleen raised her hands towards him, "Cadeyrin, I'm so sorry I didn't listen to you. I was angry. I thought you'd mated with that – that woman. I wanted to hurt you. I didn't think. I didn't want that hunter. He pulled my pants off to take me, but my scars disgusted him. I think he was afraid of them or something. He let me go. I followed you. I want to go back to our cave."

He moved around the fire towards her, laying down his weapons as he did. "Kathleen, I told you the truth about that woman. I pushed her away. What she did was a poor trick, but it might have worked with another man. She did not know that I only want one woman."

Her lips moved silently, framing an unspoken question.

He moved closer, "You. I only want you."

Kathleen felt as if her heart would leap out of her chest. She said, "I was a fool. I've wanted you for a long time. From the first time I saw you, but I didn't realize it. I was sure that you wouldn't want me, but you've seen my scars, you know what I look like, you know how little I know about living in your world. Are you sure you want me?"

His eyes were wide and dark as he said, "With all my heart. I loved you from the moment I saw you in the tree."

They were holding each other tightly by now. The fire snapped, sending up a cloud of sparks just as their lips met.

Ulfsa sat by the fire and watched the darkness. Every so often he glanced over his shoulder at his two human pack members. They were holding each other closely and moving in a steady rhythm while breathing heavily. The woman gasped and cried out, and the man's low moan soon followed.

The wolf sniffed. There was a faint but definite musky odor in the air. His tongue lolled out. Evidently, spring was the time for human mating as well as for wolves.

He returned his attention to the darkness. All was well with his world tonight. Tomorrow would be another day with its own set of challenges. He'd deal with them as they occurred.

Chapter Twenty-One

Unexpected Ecstasy

Kathleen lay secure in Cadeyrin's arms. His breath was slow as he slept. She listened to him breathe and watched the rotating wheel of the stars in the night sky.

The fire had burned down but was still providing some light and heat. Ulfsa's lack of movement indicated that there was nothing dangerous nearby.

She had been amazed at the intensity of sensation and emotion she'd felt when they made love. She'd been afraid, but Cadeyrin had been gentle and caring. There had been a brief feeling of pain, but it was quickly washed away in the overwhelming sensation of pleasure. Now she felt a little sore but pleasantly warm in all of the right places.

She wondered why, exactly, *she had waited so long to yield to him. He'd made it clear that he loved her. Maybe she wasn't sophisticated like other, more socially adept people, but she was sure that her current feeling of happiness could never be matched by anyone. He loved her, and she now knew that she loved him. She'd been fighting it, afraid of commitment from the beginning, and it had taken a near disaster for her to come to her senses.*

Ulfsa interrupted her reverie by stretching and coming over to sniff at her outstretched arm. She tickled his ear a little, and he leaned into her hand, acting more dog-like than was proper for a wolf. Cadeyrin stirred, sensing her movement. Then his eyes opened.

"How can a man get any sleep with you playing with a wolf?" he teased.

She pushed her face into his neck and kissed under his ear, whispering, "You shouldn't be sleeping. You should be paying attention to me."

His arms tightened, and he moved to kiss her, his lips hushing hers. She pulled back a little and asked him a question that had been bothering her.

"Why didn't you make me do this sooner? It's so enjoyable, I would have been glad if you had made me," she said.

After a little pause, he answered, "It is not right to force a woman against her will in my culture. The entire tribe looks down on a man who cannot control himself. He is unsuitable as a warrior." He laughed a little and continued, "It is also dangerous."

She didn't understand. "What do you mean?" she asked.

"If the woman is unhappy about it, she might stab the man at the first chance. How well do you think he would sleep if he thought she might stick him with a knife?" he replied.

Kathleen could see how that might be a deterrent, but she still had a question. "Wouldn't she get in trouble with the tribe?" she asked.

He sighed as if he were too tired to answer but then said, "No. If they knew that she didn't want him, they would not judge her. Besides, I know you mean to ask about my not forcing you. I would not be able to live with myself. I want you with all my heart, but I was too proud. I wanted you to come to me because you wanted me, not because you had no choice. Now that you have, I can think of nothing else that I want."

That was what she was waiting to hear. She stirred and kissed him again, then lay back, resting her head on his shoulder. The stars continued their stately dance overhead. There was a quick flash as a meteor burned in its passage through the atmosphere, and then she closed her eyes in contented sleep.

———◆———

They were up at daybreak. They'd awakened once in the middle of the night. He'd fed the fire, and they'd made love again.

Now, Cadeyrin wanted to get started for their cave. He agreed with her that it would be best not to encounter any of the Deer People. He thought that they'd been understanding enough, but there was still the potential for them to decide the tribe had been insulted. It was also possible that the young hunter would think he had to seek revenge.

The two loaded up and set out towards the rising sun, walking shoulder to shoulder whenever the undergrowth and trees allowed it. Ulfsa ranged ahead, indulging his hunting instinct while keeping on the lookout for any dangerous beasts.

They'd traveled for several hours, only pausing for brief rests. The ice wall to the north gradually trended away from their path. They'd been close to it, but now it was just a gray mass in the distance, almost like a cloudbank. The evergreen forest had taken advantage of the temporary retreat of the ice and had sent out sorties into the glacier-scoured land. The main body of trees was to the south, but they walked through innumerable groves that extended northward.

Now that the ice was moving south again, the trees would suffer the penalty for their ill-timed advance. They'd eventually be ground under and buried.

The arm of the forest they were traversing was extremely dense, forcing Cadeyrin to take the lead. Ulfsa was somewhere far off, probably hunting. They hadn't seen him for a while.

Kathleen was having trouble keeping up and had fallen a few yards behind. She was tired, and the trees seemed to clutch at her, causing her to stumble while she continually pushed them out of her way. She was pausing to take a breath when she heard Cadeyrin grunt in pain.

She shoved through the screen of branches and saw him on his knees in a small clearing. There was a spear shaft hanging from his shoulder. Her mouth opened in alarm, but caution and her experience stifled her outcry.

Instead of running to his side, she shrugged out of her pack and readied her bow. She was deep in the trees and couldn't be seen easily, so she froze in position and waited.

There was a laugh, and then the young hunter who had rejected her moved out of the shadows on the far side of the clearing. He said something to Cadeyrin in a mocking tone. Kathleen couldn't understand the words, but she knew the tone. It was the same one that her grade-school classmates had used when they made fun of her.

Cadeyrin grunted again and pulled the spear shaft loose. He rose to his feet, swayed, and then regained his balance. His left arm hung limply at his side. There was no way he could draw an arrow. Realizing that, he reversed the light spear and prepared to defend himself.

The hunter stopped partway into the clearing at a distance that was too far for Cadeyrin to reach him with an unaided spear cast.

———— ❖ ————

THE young hunter had a triumphant expression as he said, "Now you will suffer for shaming me in front of my tribe. Then, when you're dead meat to my spear, I'll find the witch woman and kill her also. I'll even kill your wolf if I see it."

Cadeyrin replied, "To ambush a traveler from a hiding place takes no bravery. If your people were here, they'd be shamed that one of their own was such a coward. Come forth and fight me like a man. See, I only have one arm. What are you afraid of?"

The hunter shook his head in denial. "I'm not afraid of you. There's nothing you can do to me. You can't reach me, and I'm not a fool to be baited into coming closer to you. You can't duck away from a close spear-cast. My next throw will feel your heart. The witch-woman will be next. She wears the mark of a witch, and she will die. Perhaps you'll live long enough to watch me kill her."

He prepared to launch his second spear, putting on a show as he tried to elicit some sign of fear from Cadeyrin.

———— ❖ ————

Kathleen had no idea what had been communicated in the exchange, but she saw the man readying his atl-atl and spear. She drew her bow, breathed deeply, and shot as his arm was coming forward.

The arrow took him in the throat, its impact causing him to release his spear too soon. It arched upwards and fell off to one side. Before it had landed, she'd drawn and sent another arrow at him.

With one arrow in his throat and another in his chest, he bent forward and slowly collapsed with his face in the short grass. Cadeyrin wobbled forward and planted the spear he held in the middle of the hunter's back with all the force he could muster. The hunter's body didn't twitch.

Cadeyrin turned to her, his face pale, "He is dead. Come and get your arrows. We need to keep going. I hope a predator finds him before someone from his tribe. We do not want them to come after us for revenge."

He pulled the spear out and leaned on the shaft, panting. It wasn't a two-part spear of the type that he used. The Deer People only used single shafts with the spearhead mounted directly on them. They either hadn't discovered the fore-shaft or had abandoned it as too complex.

Kathleen's eyes were drawn to the bloody spearhead. It was similar in shape to those that Cadeyrin made. The tip was broken off, and she hoped that it wasn't left in his shoulder.

"Was the tip broken off before you stabbed him in the back?" she asked.

Cadeyrin looked at it and said, "I do not think it was. I did not look closely. It probably would not have gone in as easily if it had that break."

Kathleen pulled her knife resolutely and knelt beside the dead man.

"What are you doing? He is dead," exclaimed Cadeyrin.

She replied without looking up, "I know, but I'm going to make sure the broken piece is in him. I want to know that it isn't in your wound. If it's in you, I'll have to get it out somehow."

She cut the back of the hunter's shirt open and then made a transverse cut between his ribs right over the spear wound. She tried to pull the exposed ribs apart, but they resisted, so she enlarged the cut, freeing one rib. She couldn't see into his body, so she steeled herself, trying not to think of what she was doing, and forced her hand into his chest cavity.

She groped blindly and then exclaimed, pulling her hand out with a fragment of flint. "Here it is!"

Cadeyrin made a relieved noise and said, "Good. I am glad you do not want to cut on me. Let's go. I will not be able to walk as fast as before, and we need to get away from this place."

Throughout the rest of the daylight hours, they kept a slow but steady pace. He was obviously in a lot of pain, but he refused to stop, only reiterating the need to be far away.

Kathleen was worried. She thought he'd overdo it and then wouldn't be able to travel the next day. He'd lost a considerable amount of blood, but the wound hadn't involved any major vessels. It had mostly quit bleeding after they started out. He wanted to drink, and that made her worry that he might be bleeding internally.

She had no sterile bandages, so she'd opted to leave his wound open, hoping that would work. The bleeding wasn't bad. It hadn't struck his lung; he had no difficulty breathing. The main problem was that his arm was almost entirely immobile.

They had stopped at the first stream they found and cleaned the blood off. She washed the wound, taking care not to get too close to the actual opening. She didn't want to introduce any bacteria by accident.

Cadeyrin kept a lookout for the yellow-root plant, and they finally found some growing near a shagbark hickory. She'd dug the roots and grated off some fine pieces with the edge of one of her arrowheads.

They bound the mass of grated pieces held in place by some moss, making a poultice over the wound. It wasn't much, as far as she was concerned, but Cadeyrin swore that the yellow-root would help keep the wound from rotting. That process took more time, and he was impatient to continue traveling.

Ulfsa had caught up with them while they paused, preparing the yellow-root. He seemed to know something was wrong, and he quickly isolated the main problem to Cadeyrin, who now was walking very slowly. He stayed nearby for the rest of the day.

In the early evening, Kathleen asked Cadeyrin, "Why can't we make camp?"

"I want more distance. We have not come very far, and I may be sick tomorrow. I will not be able to travel as I can now," was his answer.

That was something she had also been worrying about. He had been gradually slowing down all day, and now his pace was a mere crawl. She wished he'd stop and rest, but the way he was driving himself showed her that he was greatly worried about the Deer People.

Following his instructions, she gathered some willow bark at the next stream. The salicin in the bark worked a lot like aspirin, and he chewed on some of it, letting the liquid trickle down his throat.

"I cannot use too much of this," he told her. "Too much can make a man unable to pass water, and he will usually die. It is better if it is soaked in water and you drink it, but even chewing on it helps with the pain and feeling too hot."

They camped for the night under an overhanging rock on a stream bank. It was a cold and humid camp. The leaves and litter on the ground were damp and seemed to impart a chill to their bones. Even the fire seemed smoky and without much heat.

The next morning, Cadeyrin's face was flushed, and he was running a fever. He seemed hot to the touch, and when Kathleen placed her lips on his forehead, it almost burned. Despite feeling sick, he insisted that they travel as far as they could during the day. He slowly got to his feet after allowing Kathleen to change the poultice of yellow-root.

Taking a chance, she added some ground willow bark to the mix. If it was good for fever, perhaps it would take some of the inflammation out of the wound, which was now showing some red swelling around the edges.

She privately wondered if there was anything she could do to help. Without modern antibiotics, she feared the infection that was obviously starting would kill him in a few days.

She racked her brain for a solution. *If she could only travel back to her own time, she could easily get some medication. Even one of the older antibiotics would likely work in this pre-antibiotic world. She knew that she could get some tetracycline at an aquarium store without a prescription. That would be the best source. She could just imagine what a doctor would do if she asked for a prescription to treat her lover, who was in the Pleistocene. She'd end up involuntarily committed to a mental facility.*

Eventually, common sense took over, and she quit fantasizing about modern medicine. She'd have to find some way to help him in the here and now. What worried her was his continued insistence on traveling. He was much slower and less alert. That could easily make the difference between life and death in this hostile environment.

Cadeyrin had to stop often. He was now suffering alternate chills and fever attacks. Just before sunset, he asked Kathleen to find a suitable camp. She had seen a huge, uprooted tree along their path and helped him backtrack a few hundred paces to it.

The roots had spread far and wide, so when the giant had fallen to a storm, it had pulled up a large plate-shaped oval of thick dirt mixed with rocks. One end of this mass had slumped, and there was a hole under it. The space was big enough for the three travelers, and the broken branches offered plenty of dry wood for a fire.

She gathered wood and built a fire in front of the opening on a bare patch of raw earth. The heat reflected nicely into the hole where Cadeyrin had stretched out. Kathleen searched around for another load of wood. The giant tree had pulled down others as it fell in the densely wooded area, and there were plenty of dry branches.

She picked up some broken branches and then paused by a larger tree with a hollow trunk. There was an opening at ground level shaped like an inverted 'V' and another, smaller opening farther up, perhaps four meters or so, where the falling giant had ripped a branch off. There was something that was curious about the upper hole.

She looked closer. Bees were coming and going around the small hole. There must be a hive inside the trunk. A hive meant honey. She'd read something about honey somewhere on the Internet. She had a bad habit of browsing websites and reading all sorts of miscellaneous posts when she couldn't make any progress in her research. She tried to recall what she had read.

Then it came to her. She'd read several articles on 'prepping.' The idea of living off the land had seemed ludicrous to her, but one article had been about herbs and things that could be used in place of drugs. That was what she needed.

Now that her memory was jogged, she also remembered that raw honey was a useful antibiotic. If she could get some from the hive, it might help.

She hurried back to their camp. Cadeyrin was sleeping while Ulfsa sat by the fire as if he knew he was on watch. She woke Cadeyrin.

"Wake up. Wake up," she said, shaking him gently. He moaned and then opened his eyes slightly without saying anything. That frightened her.

"I've found a beehive. How can I get some of the honey?" she asked.

He made an effort to concentrate, his eyes half-closed, then said, "Honey would be nice. It tastes good. You have to smoke the bees so they will not sting. Then you can get the honey."

After that, he collapsed back and closed his eyes.

Kathleen took a flaming brand and went back to the hollow tree. She built a small fire in the bottom hole and smothered it with damp leaves. That created a lot of smoke. Some got in her eyes and she moved away, rubbing them until the stinging quit. She dried her tears and went back to the tree.

The tree was hollow throughout its length, and the smoke was drawn in and upward, emerging from the higher hole like a chimney. There was a low hum of bees, but they didn't seem angry, just calm. She raked the bottom fire out of the hole, scraped some dirt over the hot ground, and crawled partway inside.

It was too dark to see anything. She could see a small bit of light that was admitted through the upper hole, but everything else was in shadow.

The brand she'd used to ignite the fire was still smoldering, so she swung it through the air until it burst into flame. Pushing the flaming torch in front of her, she re-entered the hole. Now she could see that the bees had lived in the tree for a long time. There was a massive honeycomb that descended in sheets along one side of the tree. A part of it came down almost within her reach. She stretched, but it was just a little too far.

She pulled an arrow from the quiver she'd laid outside the hole and poked with it. Still too far. Unstringing her bow made her feel exposed and helpless, but it was long enough to reach the honeycomb. Back inside, she poked and prodded until she'd loosened a large chunk of the waxy comb. It dropped, striking her cheek. The bees were still under the smoke's influence and made no protest.

She immediately restrung her bow and returned to the camp. By the fire, she cut off part of the comb and examined it. The honey tasted incredibly sweet. She hadn't eaten any sugar since she'd arrived in the past, and the contrast with her daily diet was shocking.

She crawled in by Cadeyrin, pulled his shirt up, and removed the poultice. The wound looked inflamed, but the flickering firelight wasn't the best light by which to examine a patient. He had wakened and was watching her through partially opened eyes.

Kathleen said, "I'm going to put some honey on the wound. It may hurt."

He murmured something indistinct and rolled his head. She cleaned the area around the wound as best she could and then, a little fearfully, smeared honey around it, forcing some into the opening. A little yellow fluid came out, followed by some blood. She pushed more of the honey into the wound with her finger. Cadeyrin's forehead was covered with sweat, and his face was pale, but he hadn't made any complaint.

When she stopped her ministrations, he drew a deep breath and then groaned a little. She made a fresh poultice with the yellow-root. It looked vaguely familiar. Then she paused, lifting her head in surprise as she said, "Oh!" She had suddenly remembered that she'd seen the plant he called 'yellow-root' on a website about herbs. It was called 'Golden Seal'. As she recalled, it did have some antibiotic properties. She hoped that it and the honey would have a positive effect.

She took the last of the daylight to bring water from a nearby spring to him. It wasn't very good since she had to use one of their leather pouches. The pouch leaked, and the water smelled a little from the leather, but he seemed grateful for the drink.

The darkness fell, and Kathleen took up the task of watching, something that Cadeyrin had always done. She kept her senses as alert as possible, despite feeling extremely sleepy. Ulfsa lay by her side, his eyes open and staring into the darkness. His presence was a great comfort to her.

Her mind drifted. *At a certain level, she was aware that she was no longer the same person that she'd been in the modern world. She was more trusting, and her entire attitude had changed from the self-pitying, hopeless girl to a more self-assured woman. She'd mostly stopped thinking of herself as undesirable at the same time that she became aware of the change. She now understood that she'd seen herself that way in a futile attempt to justify the circumstance of her birth.*

She had accepted herself as she really was, and that was mostly due to Cadeyrin. *She'd found love, something she'd never thought would be a part of her life. It was wonderful, but she also lived under the constant fear that it would end, somehow. She just had to keep him alive. He couldn't die from infection now that they had found each other. She'd be lost without him. She doubted that she'd live long, either.*

In the middle of the night, his fever broke. He stirred a little and asked for more water. He drank the small amount still in the pouch and then lay back, resting more easily. She sat by him, caressing his forehead until he fell asleep again. Then she bent and gently kissed his dry lips. He smiled a little in his sleep.

⚬

Kathleen had been asleep since early dawn. When it became light enough for her to see, she built the fire up and then allowed herself the luxury of closing her eyes.

There was a sound, and she started up, grabbing at her bow in alarm. Her eyes widened as she saw Cadeyrin sitting by the fire, eating some jerky. He smiled at her, swallowed, and said, "I feel much better. The hotness and chills are gone. What did you do to me to defeat them?"

"Honey. I used honey that I got from the bee tree," she said.

His forehead wrinkled, "Honey? Bee tree? I don't remember any bees."

She pointed in the general direction, "There's a hollow tree. I asked you how to get honey, and you said to use smoke. I lit a fire and put leaves on it, and the bees left me alone. I took a big piece of their honeycomb."

She showed him the chunk of wax. Honey was dripping off it in a sticky mess where the cells were broken.

He reached and broke off a small piece, sniffed at it, and then put it in his mouth.

"That's good, but how can it help a wound?" he asked.

Kathleen tried to explain, a difficult task when one is unsure about the exact mechanism. "I read somewhere that honey will kill germs, so I cleaned the wound and forced honey into it. Then I put the yellow-root poultice back. It looks like it worked since you feel better today."

Cadeyrin looked even more puzzled, "What is 'read' and what are 'germs?'"

She'd have to be more careful communicating with him on modern topics that she took for granted.

"Cadeyrin, I'm sorry. I used words that are common in my time, but they refer to things that aren't known here," she began.

He nodded.

"In my time, we put words on...on..." she dragged to a halt, then thought of a simple way to explain. "We put words on flat surfaces like leaves of trees. Then we bind all of the leaves together. When someone looks at the leaves, they can understand the words. That's what I mean by reading."

She saw that it was still unclear. Suddenly inspired, she took a partly burned stick from the fire and used the charcoal point to write the word 'wolf' on a convenient stone.

Pointing, she said, "That means 'wolf.'

His face cleared, "Oh, you mean signs. I know some. The Shaman of our tribe knew many. They were kept on a tanned hide to remember the tribe's past. He was teaching them to me before he died. They are like animal tracks. I see the tracks, and I know what animal made it and what it was doing. You use different marks for your signs, but I understand the idea."

His mind leaped to another question, "How do you get the signs on small leaves?"

She smiled. He was quick-witted. He might not have the knowledge base she had, but he was fast.

"The leaves are large, and the marks are very small," she explained. "We could use birch bark to make the marks on. That would be a large, flat surface."

"I begin to see, but the idea is difficult to understand. How many words would be on one of these leaves? A few or many?" he asked.

"Many," she answered.

He shook his head in amazement, then returned to the second part of his question, "And germs?"

She'd noticed that he already understood the basic concept of hygiene, so that made explaining easier. She answered, "They are the tiny creatures I mentioned before. They are too small to see but can get into wounds and make you sick as they eat the damaged flesh."

He nodded, "I remember you speaking of that. The Shaman said that small insects and other creatures should be kept out of wounds. I've always kept my injuries clean for that reason. It works. I don't often become ill. Perhaps the spearhead held some of these creatures on its surface, and they got in me when it struck."

He moved to lie down, resting his head on her lap. She kissed him, noticing that his temperature was almost normal. She placed her hand on his forehead and said, "You should rest and regain your strength, but first, I want to clean the wound and put more honey on it."

He nodded, silently watching her face as if it were the most important thing he would ever see.

He was strong enough to travel the next day. They made progress towards the cave, although it was not very fast. He stopped often to rest, apologizing to her because he wasn't as strong as normal. She used the rest periods to inspect his wound. It had sealed up and was no longer inflamed. The honey had worked, but then, his constitution was so strong that it had probably needed little assistance.

She knew that he was on the road to recovery when they camped that night. He could move his left arm, albeit gingerly. They located their camp in the middle of a large, flat area, well away from the undergrowth. It was sheltered by a single hickory tree with strings of bark that hung down as if it were tattered and torn by the weather and its age.

Kathleen was building the fire. She'd gotten proficient with her fire starting, but tonight she was having some trouble. She managed to get her tinder lit, but then it burned out. She was startled as Cadeyrin leaned over her, holding a hand of hickory bark.

"Here, try this. It should make a good fire," he said.

This time the fire took, and she quickly built it up. Then she turned to see what he was doing. He'd been watching her as she bent over the fire and was leaning against the tree trunk with a smile on his face.

He motioned for her to come closer and said, "I would be dead without you."

She paused and looked coyly at him.

He smiled and motioned again, "Come here."

She laughed breathlessly. The heat of his smile sent warmth deep into the pit of her stomach. The thought passed through her mind that *honey was really a miracle*. Her lips moved silently as she mouthed, "Thank you, bees." Then she lost herself in the fire of rising passion.

Chapter Twenty-Two

Security and Danger

They hadn't been traveling very quickly, and it took until the middle of the next day to reach their cave. Cadeyrin had been increasingly anxious to get there and had been upset that he wasn't strong enough yet to walk faster. He had become more worried about the Deer People finding the deceased hunter. He felt that they'd  need the security of the stone walls in the event of an attack.

They'd risen with the dawn and stretched out their kinks in the cold of the morning. Kathleen reflected on the fact that she'd adapted to the cold weather far better than she'd thought she would. She'd believed modern-day Minnesota was cold, but the glacial ice brought a whole new meaning to the concept of coldness. Now that she'd been living out-of-doors, she'd reached the point where anything above freezing felt warm.

They traveled a little faster today. Cadeyrin wasn't fully healed, but he'd regained much of his strength and was able to maintain a better pace. He continually flexed his arm as they walked, trying to regain his full range of motion.

They arrived back at the small lake a little before noon and paused for a break. Kathleen looked at the water and the rock formation on the other side that held their cave. There was a sudden doubling feeling as if she'd seen this view before under different circumstances. She drew a deep breath in alarm. It seemed that there was extreme danger hidden in the view, but she couldn't exactly decide what it was.

Cadeyrin had turned to her at her startled breath. Now he put his arm around her, and the sense of deja vu and danger faded. The day was clear, and the wind, though chill, promised the advent of a brief summer.

"What is it?" he asked.

"I don't know. It seemed that there was danger somewhere, but I can't really say what it was or where it was," she answered.

He glanced at Ulfsa, who'd come wandering up a minute before. The wolf was lying down, working on one of his back toes with his teeth. He gave no sign of danger or alarm.

Cadeyrin watched him for a moment and then bent over, taking the wolf's hind paw in his hand. He carefully felt around the pad of the offending toe and then used the edge of an arrowhead to scrape a small thorn out. Ulfsa had allowed the operation with no sign of distrust. When the thorn had been removed, he unconcernedly stood up, shook to arrange his fur, and then looked at the two humans as if to say, "I'm ready to go. Come on."

———◆◇◆———

When they neared the cave, Cadeyrin made her walk behind him as he scouted the general area. At a certain point, he motioned her forward and pointed out the large tracks of a heavy cat. At least she thought it was a cat since the claws were not showing.

She asked, "What is it?"

His reply was a little alarming. "It's a big piskat, a saber-tooth. It was curious about the cave, and it looks like it scouted the area to see if we were here. I do not think it would go in. The smell of smoke is strong, but we need to take care when we approach. It might be inside or waiting to attack somewhere in the rocks."

They took their time approaching the cave, bows ready, despite the unconcerned attitude displayed by Ulfsa. He'd hunted around and apparently thought there was no reason to be alarmed. When they got close to the cave, Cadeyrin pointed out more cat tracks in the dirt. There were at least three or four different animals, possibly of different species, that had snooped around. None of the tracks were closer than about ten meters. The smoke odor had been enough to discourage the beasts.

Now sure that there was nothing inside, the two entered and set to work building a fire and tidying up. They hadn't been gone long, but there was dust on the skins they'd left stacked against the cave wall. Once everything was arranged to Kathleen's satisfaction, Cadeyrin gathered up his weapons, flexed his left arm experimentally, and then snapped his fingers at Ulfsa.

"We need meat. The meat on the hooks is probably bad. We could eat it, but it might make us ill. I am going to get a deer. You stay here and keep the fire going. No beast will enter with the fire going," he said.

Kathleen patted her quiver of arrows meaningfully. "If anything tries to enter, it will regret it," she said, walking around the fire to where he stood. "In my time, it's customary for a man to kiss his mate goodbye before he leaves to go hunting."

He turned back with a grin and obliged her. It was harder to let go than she'd anticipated, but they finally pulled apart.

"If we continue this much longer, I am not going hunting. I will not be able to leave you, but I have to go. We need meat," he said.

She pushed him towards the entrance while he put on a show of resisting her. They were laughing like children. Then his eyes turned wide and dark as he looked at her face. He touched her cheek and traced along her scars slowly and lovingly, an act she would have resented a short time ago. Now she pressed her face into his hand.

He softly said, "I think the spirit world brought you to me. I was alone, but then you came. Now you are more important to me than anything. Stay in the cave, and stay alert. I could not live if anything happened to you."

He turned and went out, leaving Kathleen to wonder about herself. The old Kathleen would have broken down completely if anyone had touched her facial scars. Now the scars were just incidental. They were part of who she was, but they no longer seemed to define her.

True, she'd always be slightly limited in motion by the scars around her hips and legs, but they were much better. She could live with that. The marvelous thing was that the deformity no longer bothered her. She had a man who loved her as she was, and somehow that meant that it was permissible for her to love herself in a way that she'd never before understood.

— ◄O► —

Cadeyrin and Ulfsa trotted around the extended line of rocks to the south and circled around the lake, heading westward along the edge of the evergreen forest. Ulfsa glanced at the man and then ranged out ahead, searching for game.

The wolf pup was a pack animal and instinctively cooperated in the hunt. Grown now to nearly his full adult size, he had been with the humans long enough to accept them as his pack. He read the man's intentions and knew that they were hunting game.

Ulfsa's sense of smell was far superior to that of a human. He sorted through the scents borne on the breeze. There were deer somewhere ahead. He looked at the man, and Cadeyrin sped up, understanding the glance.

Ulfsa ran ahead until the scent heated up, then he slowed and waited for the man. When he caught up, Cadeyrin paused. He could barely scent a deer, but he knew it was there.

Looking ahead along the edge of the trees, he planned an ambush. When chased, most elfra would eventually circle back, not wanting to leave territory they knew. He could use that tendency to set a trap.

There was a small copse of deciduous trees and shrubs standing a little away from the evergreens. He circled out to come in from the farther side of the copse. Meanwhile, the wolf headed deeper into the spruce trees. If things went as planned, they'd catch the deer between them.

Cadeyrin took position in the shadow of the copse, making sure he was screened from view. As he watched, he heard a distant crashing noise as the deer started in alarm. Ulfsa hunted silently, so it was difficult to track the hunt, but it sounded like the deer had bounded through some thick brush and headed off farther to the west. There was nothing to do but wait.

As he waited, Cadeyrin's thoughts were predominantly of Kathleen. Now that they'd consummated their relationship, he was more determined than ever to take care of her and keep her from harm.

He'd lost one mate due to his own stupidity and inability to protect her from a saber-tooth. They'd been arguing, and she'd run into the edge of the forest to get away from his anger. It had been a stupid argument, but he'd compounded his stupidity by chasing her without stopping to pick up his weapons. When the predator attacked, there was nothing he could do.

Despite that, he still blamed himself. If he'd really wanted to save her, he could have... he didn't know what. Died, maybe. Thinking of that day always made him feel physically ill. Perhaps he was a coward. He could have attacked the tiger with his bare hands, but, rationally, he knew that would have led to two dead humans rather than one. He wasn't even sure if she had still been alive when he drew near. He had convinced himself that he didn't deserve the trust of another woman. As a result, he'd remained unmated.

Now, he had another chance with a woman who was as beautiful as the sunrise and sunset combined. The contrast of her scars seemed to make her more rather than less beautiful. She'd been afraid to fully accept him, but now that she had, she had transformed into the most loving person he could imagine. He'd do anything to protect her.

While he reflected, his eyes had remained alert. A brief flicker of movement drew his attention. There it was again, far away to the west. The deer was bounding close along the edge of the spruce trees, heading towards him. He couldn't see Ulfsa, but he knew the wolf was following along behind, keeping to the deer's trail.

The elfra rapidly drew closer. As it came within range, he pursed his mouth and made a snorting sound that sounded remarkably like that of a buck. The bounding doe stopped short and looked at the copse. It was a little farther away than he'd intended. He adjusted his aim slightly and released.

The arrow made a quick streak across the intervening space and struck the deer. It leaped up, bounded forward, and then turned into the dense trees. Cadeyrin took his time, readying another arrow, then started across towards the spot where the deer had been struck.

Ulfsa came past him at a dead run, stopped to sniff a spot of blood, and then ran into the trees in pursuit. If he'd been hunting alone, Cadeyrin would have followed up slowly. If the deer was wounded, giving it time to lie down and stiffen up was a good tactic. It would run farther if it were chased and not given the time for its fear to fade. The wolf's speed and incredible sense of smell changed his hunting pattern.

With the wolf in pursuit, he was confident that the deer wouldn't get far before Ulfsa caught up. It had been hard struck and wouldn't be able to run quickly. He followed the trail, noticing that there were drops of blood on the ground. He wound his way through the trees until he came on the wolf.

Ulfsa had stopped in the cover of a small tree and was standing there, his hackles up and head lowered with flattened ears. There was something dangerous ahead. Cadeyrin quietly approached, and Ulfsa looked at him for guidance. When he stepped forward, the wolf cautiously circled the tree and led him on through the taller evergreens, stopping as the sound of a warning snarl came from close ahead.

A cougar had ambushed the wounded deer, breaking its neck with a single bite. Now the cat was claiming the deer for its own. It stood with its front paws on the deer's chest, its face wrinkled in a tooth-baring threat. Ulfsa slanted off towards the left, and Cadeyrin came on directly at the cat.

The cat was a big male and weighed as much as Cadeyrin. It could put up a fierce fight. He was probably the only human it had ever seen, and it had no instinctive fear of him.

He stopped just at the critical distance. Any closer, and it would charge. It made a screaming yowl and prepared to leap. As it did, Ulfsa came at it from the side, and the cat turned swiftly to meet the wolf's rush, exposing its neck.

Before it could finish its turn, the arrow was on its way. Cadeyrin quickly drew a second. The puma had moved, and the first arrow grazed its side, cutting a strip in its fur. It screamed and spun around to slash with its claws at whatever attacker had struck it from its blind side.

The second arrow took it in the lungs, and it staggered and coughed. Deciding that the man was its main assailant, the cougar turned and charged. Cadeyrin was still trying to draw another arrow, but he didn't have time. He threw his bow in the cat's face, slowing it. His knife was instantly in his hand as he dodged to the side.

The cougar came on in a leap, its paws outstretched. It would have caught him with its left paw, but Ulfsa jumped in and caught the cat's leg just as it leaped. It crashed to the ground at Cadeyrin's feet, rolled over, and slashed at the wolf.

The hunter dropped to his knees, reached over the cougar's back, and drove the flint knife into its lower chest. It jerked and tried to turn towards him. He'd left the knife in place, and the cat bit at the handle, splintering it. That was its last act. Its head abruptly dropped, and the fight was over.

Ulfsa limped up and sniffed the cougar. His leg had been slashed in the final instant of the battle. Cadeyrin bent to inspect the wound. The wolf whined a little as he carefully touched the bloody leg. The wound was bad enough that Ulfsa wouldn't be able to hunt for a while, but it looked as if it would heal without crippling him.

Cadeyrin quickly skinned the cat and arranged a pack to carry as much venison as he could. He then took a small strip of deer hide and wrapped it around Ulfsa's wound. That was something the wolf wasn't going to tolerate. He had immediately chewed it off. Cadeyrin shook his head in understanding. Wolves were used to being injured. They lived a hard life, and Ulfsa would probably keep the wound cleaner by licking it than the bandage would.

The two set off towards the forest edge, heading home. They reached the edge of the trees and halted while Cadeyrin scanned for any danger. He was about to proceed when Ulfsa made a low growl, freezing him instantly.

There, far to the west, he could see some men coming over a low hill. As he watched, trying to make out any details, they disappeared into the shallow valley. As the last one descended out-of-sight, the sun glinted on what was undeniably light hair. They were members of his own race and not the enemy people.

If they were hunters from the Deer People, they weren't coming for a friendly visit. He could only assume that they'd found the hunter he'd killed and were coming for vengeance. He had no idea how they'd found his territory. It might have been by chance, but more likely, they'd traced every step he'd taken, following every tiny clue in their quest.

He retreated into the forest edge and began to move as quickly as his load and the limping wolf would allow. There was a chance the hunters were here for some other reason, but common caution insisted that when he came face-to-face with them, he should be in a position of strength. He couldn't think of a better spot than the cave. A single man could hold off many hunters there, where they couldn't get at his sides or back.

He wound through the trees in an elaborate fashion, occasionally back-tracking in an attempt to cloud his trail, should they pick it up from where he'd butchered the deer. They'd been heading along the forest edge as the most likely place to pick up sign of him. No human would spend the time winding through the dense and prickly trees when they could walk relatively unimpeded in the open, especially since walking in the open was safer. Predators would find it more difficult to ambush an exposed human who could see what was coming.

Eventually, he hit an outcropping of rocks, scarred by the slow movement of glacial ice. He stayed on the stones as far as possible, leaving no tracks. Ulfsa followed closely at his heels. Near the end of the rocks, there was a small stream, and he waded along in the icy water until it grew too deep. He climbed out on the far side of the water and began a large circling path that would end on the northwest side of their lake.

Once at the lake, he sped up, no longer trying to cover his tracks. He'd left so much sign in the area that it was a useless exercise. The hunters would easily locate the cave, should they get this far.

Along the way, there was a thicket with thin willow shoots. They were mostly straight and provided a good source for arrows. He paused to cut a small bundle of the shoots. It wouldn't do to run out.

He had several extra points that he'd knapped. The points were always breaking in use and required constant replacement, so he tried to keep extras. Even if they shot all of their pointed arrows, he could make do with sharpened sticks. They wouldn't be as accurate or fly as far, but they could still kill.

The major issue was water. That could be the flaw that did them in. The lake was close, but they wouldn't be able to leave the cave if they were besieged. That could be a problem, one for which he had no ready solution.

He'd seen more than a hand of men but possibly less than two hands. He couldn't be sure. There might be more. If it came to a fight, Cadeyrin thought that Kathleen and he could shoot enough arrows to hold off any but the most determined mass attack.

With a little luck, they could repel the attackers. That result would leave its own potential complication. There was a high chance the remaining hunters would then simply lie in ambush, waiting for their inevitable exit from the cave when they became too thirsty. Even a straight path to the lake was within atl-atl range of the rock walls that led to the cave. Water was going to be a serious problem.

The two of them trotted up to the cave entrance, where he paused and called to Kathleen, being careful to pitch his voice so that it wouldn't carry too far. They'd agreed that he'd always call her prior to coming in. The possibility of her launching an arrow at the entrance if she was surprised made it imperative for him to alert her.

She popped out of the entrance, all smiles, and good humor. "Cadeyrin, guess what I've found?" she began, but then she saw his face. "What happened?"

He answered, "Some of the Deer People are trailing me. I fear they come for vengeance for the man we killed. They will not know or care that he ambushed us. They also might have been angry by the way you left. They could have talked themselves into a killing anger."

She sensibly asked, "How close are they?"

"It may take them a while to get here. It is near dark now, and they are probably working out my trail through the trees. I made it hard to follow, so they will have to take their time picking it out. I think they will camp for the night. No one travels in the dark," he said as he unpacked the deer meat.

Kathleen had just noticed that Ulfsa was tending to a wound on his leg.

"What happened to him?" she asked.

She bent to inspect the wound, and the young wolf paused in his ministrations and greeted her with a cursory lick.

"Shouldn't we do something about his leg? It might get infected," she asked.

He stopped and looked at her, trying to recall the meaning of the word, "Infected?"

Once again, she'd used a word that he was a little vague on.

"I mean, the small creatures that are everywhere might get into the wound and make it rot," she explained.

He turned back to his work as he said, "Oh. You mean the germs. I remember now. I tried to tie it up, but he wouldn't let me. I'll make some yellow-root paste with honey and smear it on if we have time. That might help."

Kathleen had now realized what having a group of hunters attacking them might mean. She touched his shoulder and asked, "How will we defend ourselves? They can walk right up to the entrance and throw spears inside."

He'd been planning on the steps to take to defend the cave as he returned. "We must gather more wood and build a fire at the entrance as we did before. That will keep them from running straight in. If we make the fire closer to one side than the other, they'll have to edge past on one side only. It will be easy to defend that," he said, thinking aloud. "They can still throw spears into the cave. Perhaps I can build up some rocks or wood directly in front of the entrance. The spears will strike that. We should be safe if we stay out of the direct entranceway."

Kathleen eagerly added to the idea, "I can drag those rocks from the back up here. They can be stacked to give us some sort of cover."

Cadeyrin nodded, his eyes still showing his concern.

She seemed to notice and asked, "What else do we have to worry about? We have the deer meat you brought in, and I checked the remains of the meat hanging from the ledges. It's smoky tasting, but I think it's good. The smoke prevented it from spoiling."

He looked up at the smoke-hazed ceiling.

"That is good, but our main problem is water. We will need to drink. We should fill all of our skin pouches. Once we get too thirsty, we will have to come out, and it will be easy for them to kill us," he answered.

"Water!" she exclaimed, "That's what I was going to tell you when you first came in. I forgot. While you were gone, I went in the small back chamber and pried some of the rocks loose. You know the ones that filled the crack at the back wall? There is a pool of water behind them. I can't reach it, but maybe you can move the larger rocks."

Cadeyrin leaped to his feet, startling Ulfsa.

"That is what we need," he said. "Let me see if I can get the rocks out of the way."

He took a flaming brand and wormed through the small opening. The walls narrowed quickly, but Kathleen had, indeed, removed some of the rockfall that plugged the back. The moist draft was more noticeable.

Cadeyrin carefully wedged the torch in a cleft, high on one of the walls, and investigated. The rocks were wedged in tightly. Kathleen had pulled out two of the top ones, and she was right. When he looked through the opening, he could see a little gleam of light that was reflected from the surface of a small, dark pool.

If I can just wiggle this rock loose, the others will be easy to move, he thought.

It required throwing all of his weight back and forth to move the stone. It gradually moved forward as he pulled and rocked. After a few minutes, it dropped to the floor. He grunted as he lifted the thing and then backed up until he could turn around. The entrance was just wide enough at the bottom for the stone to fit, and he struggled to push it out.

After much heavy labor, the crack leading to the pool was clear. It grew too narrow for Cadeyrin to slide through unless he lay on one side. Kathleen could fit through and reach the pool, provided she wormed through the tight section on her stomach.

She slid through and then called back to him, "I think the water is good. At least, it doesn't smell bad. I don't know where it comes from. It might trickle in from up above when it rains. I can't see the back edge. It bends around the rocks, and the end is out of sight."

She reached deep into the icy water, then reported, "This pool is deeper than I can reach. There are a few leaves in the water, but I don't see anything else. I'm going to try a drink."

He stopped her, "Not yet. Bring a skin-full out to me and let me smell it. Sometimes water can seem clear but have something in it that can make you sick."

Once she'd brought out a skin filled with water and he'd smelled it, he said, "Let's let Ulfsa smell it. His nose is better than mine."

The wolf was thirsty and wasted no time drinking from the open pouch. They looked at each other, and Cadeyrin smiled.

"That is a good sign. He thinks it is good. I think we can drink it," he said. He lifted the mostly empty pouch and shook it. There was a little water left, and he poured that into his mouth.

Kathleen looked surprised. Cadeyrin grinned at her. Ulfsa was almost as close to them as they were to each other. If he could drink water that the wolf had been drinking, then she could, also.

She said, "I'll go and get some more. Then I can drink."

"Wait a little," he said, wiping his mouth with the back of his hand. "If it is not good, I will be the one to get ill."

Kathleen snorted, "That's not going to do me much good if those Deer People attack. I'll need you. I can't fight them off by myself."

He turned and slid out of the back chamber, then began to stack the loose rocks by the main entrance to form a shield that would block projectiles. When he was done, the stack covered most of the entrance.

He'd built the wall so that it butted against one side of the entrance. The only place a thrown object could enter was to the right. As he stacked, he had left the middle of the top of the pile a little lower. It would provide an opening over which he could shoot arrows.

While he was stacking the rocks, Kathleen had laid a fire in the entrance, a little back from the opening and just in front of the rock pile.

Cadeyrin said, "Let's not light that now. There will be time to start it in the morning. We should wait until they attack, so we do not run low on wood. I think we have time to gather some more before it gets too dark. Will you help?"

They brought in several loads of wood, some very dry and some that were unseasoned. The green would burn more slowly, and that meant it would last longer.

They finished and returned to sit by the back fire, which had died down to a bed of embers with a few flames shooting up now and then. Cadeyrin put some more wood on, and the flames lighted the cave.

Ulfsa stayed near the entrance, acting as a watchdog. He obviously felt the fire made the cave too hot for comfort and preferred to sit where he could sample the scents on the night air and remain cooler.

The two humans sat by the fire, Cadeyrin engrossed in converting several of the willow shoots into arrows and Kathleen watching him as she worked with an awl to stitch another pouch together. There was a spit with venison balanced over the flames. When it was done, they ate.

—◆—

Kathleen was getting sleepy, but there was something that she felt she had to do. They were possibly going into battle in the morning, and who knew what would happen? The thought made her nervous and fearful.

She slid over beside Cadeyrin and began nuzzling his neck. At first, he tried to ignore her. He was working on mounting flint points on the arrows that he'd prepared. His resolve didn't last long. He laid down the arrow on which he was working and took her in his arms.

They kissed, and then, as if they had no need for verbal communication, they moved as one onto the sleeping skins, shedding their buckskins as they did. They made long slow, passionate love, their shadows moving rhythmically on the cave wall in the flickering firelight. At a certain point, she gasped and cried out in time with his heavier breathing.

The sound caused the wolf to get up from his position by the door and stick his head around the pile of rocks so he could see what was happening. The fire flickered in the chill breeze that blew through the cave, but the two humans were snuggled together under a tanned hide, warm in each other's arms.

Chapter Twenty-Three

Attack

When the morning breeze came off the lake and blew into the cave's opening, the two were already up, had eaten breakfast, and were ready. They'd laid out their arrows in strategic locations and also piled up some fist-sized stones that could be thrown as a last-ditch weapon. The small fire burning in the entrance could be built up quickly from a nearby pile of wood.

They'd let the back fire die down. From outside, looking over the front fire into the dark cave, it was impossible to see anything inside. The pile of shielding stones reflected the fire's light, leaving the opening at the top in dark shadow. Only a little light came back to where the two were waiting.

Ulfsa was the first to detect the hunters. He stood up, listening, and then oriented towards the north arm of the rocks leading to the cave. The hunters were there, trying to determine the layout.

They'd followed Cadeyrin's trail until they saw the lake, then the smell of smoke had led them around to the rocks. Now they were planning their approach.

Cadeyrin was standing in the dark, just inside the opening. He could see their location but doubted they could see him. The sun was rising and just starting to shine over the rocks, casting its light in the attackers' faces while leaving the mouth of the cave in shadow.

The hunters conversed among themselves, apparently arguing about how to approach the opening. Finally, one came forward, his spears held in his hand, but none mounted on his atl-atl. He walked slowly into the center of the semi-circle of rocks and called out.

"We know you're in there. Come out and talk," he shouted.

Cadeyrin stepped forward until the man's eyes fixed on him.

"Welcome to our camp, People of the Deer," he replied formally. "What brings you so far to the east?"

The hunter had retreated a few steps as Cadeyrin moved forward. He answered, "We trailed the witch-woman seeking to right the wrong she did to our brother, Spotted Cheetah. Then we found where you had met her. She had accepted Spotted Cheetah's skin. You mated with her there, with another man's woman. That is unforgivable. We trailed you, and then we came upon the spot where you ambushed Spotted Cheetah. There was little remaining of him, but we knew our brother. His bones cry out for vengeance. We took up his cry and followed. You led us a long way, but we are here now and will have our vengeance."

His voice had grown higher and shriller as he spoke, reflecting his rising anger as he got caught up in his own words.

Cadeyrin calmly replied, "Spotted Cheetah made a mistake in your camp. He tried to take a woman of my tribe without my permission. When she rejected him, he followed and ambushed us. He attacked from behind a tree like a coward. He deserved what happened."

"Spotted Cheetah was never afraid. He was one of the foremost in the hunt! He would not have ambushed you. He would have met you in the open, and he would have killed you. He was a mighty fighter. It is you who lie. You ambushed him. Come out and let us have our revenge. It will be quick. If you stay in the cave like fearful rabbits, we will light the fire of pain, and you will die slowly, roasted on the flames."

The hunter started to mount a spear on his atl-atl for a cast.

Cadeyrin drew a deep breath, let it out, and drove an arrow into the man's chest, dropping him in his tracks. There was a series of shrieks, and the others ran out from the sheltering rocks and cast their spears at the cave. The shafts clattered on the rocks harmlessly. Cadeyrin had stepped inside and ducked around the corner. Only one spear made it into the entrance, bouncing off the rock pile, just as he'd planned.

He stooped and snatched it out of the fire before it could be damaged. The tip had shattered, but the shaft was still useful, so he propped the spear against the wall.

The hunters were encouraged. They couldn't see him and thought he might be injured, so they advanced. He moved into view and shot another arrow as they launched their spears at him. He ducked back before the spears arrived and did not see the effect of his shot.

This time, four of the spears entered the cave mouth. One flew over the top of the rock pile and clattered across the floor. He glanced back to make sure Kathleen was safe. She was standing to one side, out of the way, her bow at the ready. She gave him a crooked grin as he looked.

He jumped forward and fired a third arrow directly into the chest of one of the hunters who'd incautiously rushed the cave. The man screamed and pulled at the shaft, then staggered off to one side. Three of the hunters had been following hard on his footsteps, spears ready to throw.

They drew back their arms, but before they could cast their weapons, the middle one received Kathleen's arrow, striking in the depression at the base of his neck. He choked and collapsed, rolling in agony on the ground. The other two cast their spears, but their aim was disrupted, and both missed.

Cadeyrin shot one, and the other scuttled back quickly to the shelter of the rocks. That was four down. There were at least five more back there, waiting for them to make a mistake.

One of the hunters showed himself, and Cadeyrin loosed a shaft at him. The man leaped back behind the rocks just in time, and the arrow plowed into the ground. The same hunter jumped out again, this time drawing an arrow from Kathleen, who was shooting over the rock pile. It missed, also.

Cadeyrin held up his hand, motioning Kathleen to cease shooting. The hunters were trying to get them to exhaust their arrows by giving them a target. At the same time, they were trying to keep them occupied with the leaping hunter while the others were undoubtedly circling around, searching for a better spot from which to throw.

Having been all over the front of the rocks, Cadeyrin knew that there was an area to the right that provided shelter from below yet offered a good perch for throwing spears downwards. He kept an eye on that spot.

It wasn't long before he saw some motion there. He ducked back inside the cave as a spear flew downwards, striking where he'd been standing. It buried its head in the ground.

He cautiously peered around the edge of the opening, and another spear just missed his head. He decided that his position was becoming untenable and retreated backward farther into the cave. He kicked some more logs on the fire as he passed and waited for the men to try the entrance.

After a while, there was a shadow in the entrance. He drew his bow, preparing to shoot. The hunter was cautious and didn't expose himself. Instead, he threw a stone into the cave. It rattled off the wall, having passed the rock pile on the only side that was open.

Kathleen kept her hand on Ulfsa's head. He was quivering with the urge to attack the men, but he'd be killed quickly if he tried. She restrained him until he understood that he was to wait, then she readied her bow again.

The rattle of the stone made her jump and caused Ulfsa to snarl, but he didn't move. Instead, he had his eyes fixed on her face, waiting for her to give the signal to attack. Cadeyrin looked at the two of them and motioned her back farther. She moved back, following his instruction.

For a long time, nothing happened. Finally, Cadeyrin looked out. The hunters were down by the lake, in plain sight. Two of them watched the cave entrance while the others gathered wood. They were making a camp just out of arrow shot.

They'd figured out exactly what he'd feared. They knew the two inside the cave would eventually have to drink, and they were making sure they couldn't reach water. All they had to do was wait. When thirst drove the couple mad, they'd stagger out in no condition to fight, and the hunters would have them.

Cadeyrin unconsciously brushed back his hair. He usually kept it tied back, but the strip of leather had come off somehow. The three hunters watching the cave apparently saw the motion. They leaped to their feet and yelled, alerting the others.

The group grabbed their spears, ran forward, and stood in a cluster, watching the cave mouth. They were bunched closely together, and this looked like an opportunity to Cadeyrin. He nocked an arrow, drew it fully back, watching the leaves on a birch that was beside the lake.

The leaves were flashing in the wind. When the breeze paused, they stilled. Cadeyrin estimated the distance, elevated the bow, and released.

The arrow flew high. As he shot, he ran forward a few paces to keep the group's attention on him. Only one of them watched the arrow. The others focused on his actions.

The arrow arched through the clear air and then began its downward flight. Finally, the one man who had noticed it figured out that it had a chance of hitting them. He shouted and quickly backed up. It was an ineffectual warning. The arrow dropped squarely into the center of the group. Cadeyrin tensed in hope.

One of the group yelled in fear or anger. All of the hunters turned to look. When they spread out a little, Cadeyrin could see the arrow sticking in the ground. It had come down and nicked one of the men, causing only a shallow cut but frightening him.

The injured man shouted and jumped up and down in anger, shaking his spear at the cave. Cadeyrin withdrew back into the shadows. He'd only succeeded in demonstrating how far he could shoot. Now they'd take care to stay outside of his range.

Kathleen came up, her bow slung over her shoulder, tying a strip of leather around her forearm. She had a slight cut on her forehead that had released a drop of blood that ran down her temple.

"What happened?" he asked.

"The spear that struck the stones," she said. "The point broke, and a little piece struck my head. It doesn't hurt much. Is it a bad cut?"

He licked his finger and wiped the blood off of her head.

"No, it is just a scratch. I do not want you hurt. Stay out of the direct entrance. That way, they won't hit you," he said, bending a little to kiss the wound.

She moved closer to him and leaned against his shoulder for a moment, still keeping her eyes on the entrance.

"What are they doing now?" she asked.

He looked at the men. They were still agitated. As he watched, one snatched up the arrow and broke it, then hurled the pieces in the general direction of the cave.

"I think they are angry with us," he said. "It looks like they are going to camp by the lake and wait for us to come out. I think we showed them it is too dangerous to attack us head-on."

Kathleen returned her attention to the leather she was tying onto her left forearm. He watched curiously.

When she was done, there was a sort of sleeve that she'd arranged on the inside of her arm.

He asked, "What's that for?"

Kathleen flushed and looked embarrassed. She explained, "It's protection from the bowstring. It struck my arm when I shot this time." She hoped he wouldn't laugh.

Cadeyrin nodded his head in understanding. "That happens to me. It hurts and ruins the shot, too. I did not think of a leather wrap. That is a good idea. I will do it, too."

She smiled in relief and then looked at the men in the distance. "Won't they attack during the night when we can't see them coming?" she asked nervously.

He brushed at his hair again and said, "Maybe. If we have the front fire built up, they will find it hard to get in, but they could possibly overtake us."

"We still have some loose stones. Maybe if we stacked them against the wall so that they'd have to slide past the fire and then turn a little, rather than being able to move directly along the wall, that could slow them down," she said, thinking aloud.

He turned and quickly began to lug one of the heavy stones into position. When he had it against the wall near the opening, he asked, "Is that what you meant?"

"Yes. If we can stack the rest of them in that area, it will make it hard for them to throw a spear into the cave that way, and they'll have to turn before they can enter," she answered.

He nodded and went back to moving the rocks.

⸺◆⸺

By the time it was full dark, he'd constructed a short second wall that came out from the entrance wall at right angles. A fire, backed up by the original barricade extending to the right cave wall, now protected the entrance. On the left side, there was a narrow corridor that slid along between the cave wall and the fire until it was forced to turn at the new wall. No one could come directly in. They could possibly throw spears into the cave, but the opening over the barricade was high enough that they'd have to be close to the front, and they'd risk receiving an arrow in return.

Cadeyrin said, "I am hungry. We better eat, and then I want you to keep watch for a while. If they attack, it will probably be in the early morning, and I need to rest a little now. I will let you sleep later."

⸺◆⸺

The night darkened. Down by the lake, the fire of the remaining hunters flared high, reflecting along the small wavelets that the night breeze raised on the water.

Inside the cave, Cadeyrin slept as Kathleen kept watch. She fed the fire a few times when it burned low. Ulfsa was a good guard and good company. He lay beside her, his eyes shining a little in the reflected firelight. When she got up to feed the fire, he came along with her.

As the night drew on, a small pride of saber-tooths came to patrol the area between the opposing forces. The hunters' fire and the commotion had served to draw the attention of all of the predators in the area.

The big cats already had checked out the cave and knew there was fire within. They dared not enter, so they gave most of their attention to the hunters' camp, prowling around the circumference of the firelight.

The hunters were used to such tactics. They sat sullenly by the fire, a few chewing on jerky. They hadn't had an opportunity to hunt, but they carried some supplies. They'd have to get fresh game if their siege went on for more than a day. Meanwhile, they talked quietly among themselves, occasionally glancing vindictively at the cave.

The saber-tooths paused, coming to attention as one of the men walked to the lake to drink. The fire was close beside the water, and he remained within the light. The cats resumed their track, snarling a little with anger and frustration.

The pride eventually gave up and headed south towards the forest's edge in search of easier game. Then all was quiet as the stars marched in their rotation high above.

Chapter Twenty-Four

Death in the Mist

Kathleen was sleeping, and Cadeyrin was watching when the first hint of dawn showed. A heavy blanket of mist lay on the lake's surface, extending past the hunters' fire and making it hard for him to see them. He concentrated, trying to pierce the mist, but it swirled thicker, now coming nearly to the cave's entrance.

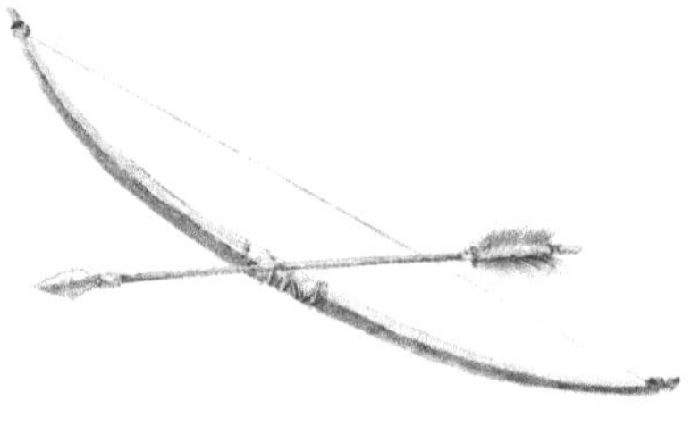

Behind him, Kathleen moaned and then sat bolt-upright.

"They're there! Watch out," she cried.

He jumped back around the corner and collided with her.

"Cadeyrin, there's something that's happened, or..." she paused, trying to focus on the rapidly receding vision. "There's something that's going to happen. It was foggy, and I couldn't see well, but there was a terrible threat hidden nearby. I'm frightened!"

She clung to him desperately for a moment, then, taking strength in his presence, she ran back for her weapons.

"We must be ready. It will happen soon. I'm sure of it," she said, panting from the adrenaline.

Her face was bloodless, and he was shaking as he turned back to the entrance, readying his bow.

There was a sudden chorus of wild shrieks from the hunter's camp, making them jump. There was something unexpected going on over there. The muffled sounds of battle filtered through the fog.

The mist was now thicker and blew in eddies and swirls, sometimes becoming almost translucent, then turning almost night-dark the next moment.

A figure burst into view. It was one of the besieging hunters running at full speed towards the cave. Before either of them could react, the man screamed, stumbled, and fell, skidding almost to the rocks, a long spear sticking out of his back.

Another man ran out of the mist, intent on the fallen hunter. The pursuer bent and grabbed the blond hair with one hand, then dragged a piece of sharp stone across. He yanked, ripping off most of the scalp. The new warrior straightened, whipped his long, black hair back over his shoulders, and then held the scalp high in triumph as he let out a bone-chilling cry. Others, muffled by the intervening mist, answered it.

Kathleen's heart almost leaped out of her chest with fright. Cadeyrin whispered to her, "The Enemy. We must fight now, harder than ever before. They will do the same to us."

Without thinking, she raised her bow and drove an arrow into the black-haired man's chest. He made a gurgling noise and staggered backward, disappearing into the swirling mist.

Cadeyrin started forward, motioning to her to follow, but a strong gust of wind came suddenly out of the north, lifting the mist and exposing a battlefield. All of the Deer People hunters were dead. They'd been ambushed by over a hundred of the enemy, who were now clustered in the area between the rocky arms leading to their cave.

Some of the warriors sighted the two, back-lit as they were by the glowing embers of the door fire. Instantly, a dozen voices screamed war cries as the black-haired men rushed to be the first to strike down the last two blond hairs.

A steady stream of arrows met them. Cadeyrin and Kathleen fired, one after the other, loading and releasing as quickly as they could. Their arrow supply dropped rapidly, and for a moment, Kathleen thought they'd run out before the charge was turned back.

Ten of the oncoming men went down before the charge broke, and the enemy warriors turned and ran for cover. The entire group paused by the lakefront, turned, and looked at the cave mouth as if they expected some kind of monster to come running out. The few that had actually seen Cadeyrin and Kathleen were lying on the ground with arrows buried in their bodies. The rest had no idea what had initiated the heavy rain of small, deadly spears. They'd charged forward, following the leaders. Now they were confounded. This was like nothing they'd ever faced. They bunched around their war chief to plan how best to dispose of this new threat.

The group stayed far enough away from the cave that Cadeyrin wasn't tempted to try a long shot. Instead, he and Kathleen gathered up their extra shafts, replacing the ones they'd expended.

While they reloaded their quivers, Kathleen worried, "What will we do? There are far too many of them. We don't have enough arrows."

Cadeyrin suddenly remembered the water source in the back room. He asked, "Do you remember the pool of water? Did you say it went around a corner or something?"

She answered, "Yes, I couldn't see the back of it."

He thought about that for a moment and then asked, "Was the pool a little wider than the entrance crack? Did it stay that wide all the way back?"

Kathleen tried to remember. She'd only gone back there a couple of times. There was still water left from her second trip. She tentatively answered, "I think it's wider the farther back it goes." Then, getting the idea, she asked, "Do you think we can get back there and hide?"

Before Cadeyrin could answer, there was a heavy thump from just outside the cave. Ulfsa jumped and snarled in response, but he didn't go near the entrance.

The two of them peered over the stacked rocks. There was a large piece of wood lying directly in front of the cave. As they watched, another piece fell, bouncing off the first. It was followed by a number of smaller pieces.

Cadeyrin grunted, "Ugh. They didn't waste any time. They know just how to get us. They're going to build a huge fire in front. The wind is blowing the smoke from the door fire back into the cave to exit the ceiling crack. It will blow the heat of their big fire back into the cave, also. They want to roast us inside."

"Like a giant oven," Kathleen whispered. Her hand covered her mouth.

The enemy warriors continued to heave branches from the rocks above the cave mouth. They'd come up with a plan quickly and were intent on executing it.

Cadeyrin looked out and then turned to the back of the cave.

"Come," he said. "We don't have much time to see if there is a way out there."

Ulfsa hesitated as the two crawled sideways through the open crack carrying flaming brands from the fire. When Cadeyrin clicked his fingers, the wolf moved forward and eased his way through. The crack was a little wider at wolf level, and he had no difficulty entering the back room.

They faced the smaller crack leading to the pool. Cadeyrin lowered himself to the floor, exhaled, and forced his heavy shoulders sideways through the gap. His legs kicked for a moment, trying for purchase, then disappeared.

Kathleen handed him their weapons and one torch. She started to lower herself to go through, then thought better of it. She turned and caught Ulfsa's furry ruff and pulled him to the crack. He resisted a moment, then crouched and worked his way through with a whine of discomfort. She followed close enough that his tail brushed her face repeatedly.

Once inside the narrow space, she was startled to see that Cadeyrin had lowered himself into the deep pool and moved to the back, where the water disappeared behind a corner of rock. He glanced back at her silently, eyes reflecting the torchlight. He motioned for her to follow and then disappeared around the intervening rocks.

Ulfsa looked at her and whined in unease. She pushed at him. He was blocking her access to the water. He hesitated and then plunged in, swimming strongly. In an instant, he was around the corner, and she was alone. The torch, which Cadeyrin had wedged in a narrow cleft between two of the rocks, started flickering, showing that it was on the verge of going out.

Kathleen drew a deep breath. This was something she had never dreamed she'd have to do. Suddenly the walls seemed to be pressing in on her. She'd never felt claustrophobic before, but now her breathing increased, and she felt the onset of panic.

If the torch went out, she'd be back here in the dark. The enemy warriors were behind, building a fire that would turn the cave into a deadly, high-temperature trap. The only exit, if exit there was, was ahead through the dark, icy water. It seemed like something out of a nightmare, something she'd seen or done before, but she couldn't remember how it turned out, only that there was terrible danger ahead and behind.

She felt like crying for Cadeyrin to come back, but then something that she hadn't known was part of her came to the fore. She shook her head as if to throw off the fear, drew a deep breath, and lowered herself into the pool.

It was so cold it was hard to breathe. Her diaphragm seemed paralyzed. Once in the pool, she found that her toes barely reached some rocks on the bottom. She waded towards the corner in the last light of the burning branch, trying to keep her nose and mouth above the surface.

As she reached the corner, the flame guttered out. It was startlingly dark. She gasped and inhaled a little water, then had a spasm of coughing while trying to hold her head above the surface. She stood still in the icy water, hoping her eyes would adapt. After what seemed like minutes, she could see a little light trickling around the corner.

"It must be from Cadeyrin's torch," she whispered to herself. The whisper sounded abnormally loud in the quiet cave.

She slid forward, feet seeking solid footing on the slippery rocks of the bottom. As she rounded the corner, she stepped into a hole and plunged completely under. She thrashed and came to the surface, gasping for breath.

A couple of strokes with her arms and her feet reached another rock. She stood on it, wiping the water from her face and pushing her hair back. The light ahead seemed to be stronger. She carefully crept forward, arms outstretched, feeling the dense rock walls on each side gradually narrow inward.

She stopped, feeling ahead. There was a giant rock that had fallen from the ceiling and wedged itself between the walls. The bottom of it cleared the water, but only by an inch or so. She had a momentary feeling of deja vu. Had she been here before? She shook her head in confusion.

Her breathing became more panicky as she contemplated the prospect. Then she told herself, *If Cadeyrin and Ulfsa made it through, I can do it.*

She ducked, keeping her face turned to the side so that her nose and mouth were clear. Carefully, she worked her way under the rock, keeping her nose barely above the surface. The passage was several feet long and seemed to take forever. The only thing that kept her going was the fact that the light seemed brighter ahead.

Suddenly, her head was clear, and she straightened. The light glowed brighter. She moved forward, finding that the pool grew rapidly shallower. It turned another corner, and then she was able to climb out onto a rock ledge.

Leaving the pool behind, she moved forward with more confidence. The light seemed blinding now; it was so bright. She found a narrow crack and wormed through it. She was through the cave and outside.

Drawing a deep breath of relief at her escape, she started to call for Cadeyrin. Instead, she let out a cry of alarm. Two sets of rough arms had grabbed her, wrestling her hands around behind her back.

Her vision adapted, and she saw her captors: two of the black-haired savage warriors. They tied her hands and spun her around.

The scene before her was heartbreaking. Cadeyrin was lying on the ground with blood covering the side of his head. A bloody, fist-sized stone lay nearby. She screamed his name, but he didn't move.

The two men laughed at her, and one yanked at her arm in a way designed to cause pain. When she gasped, they laughed again. Then Cadeyrin groaned, and his hand moved a little.

One of her captors jumped over him, raising a sharpened piece of deer antler that seemed to have bits of obsidian embedded in its sides, making an effective but crude knife. The other man said something in a guttural language, and the first grunted and shoved his knife in his belt.

He stooped and tied Cadeyrin's arms behind his back, then yanked at them, partly lifting the heavy hunter. Cadeyrin made an effort and staggered to his feet. The side of his face was covered with blood, and one of his eyes was squinted partly shut. The warrior dragged him forward through a screen of trees. Her captor pushed her ahead of him, following them.

Kathleen tried to figure out where they were. To the best of her knowledge, Cadeyrin had investigated the whole hill, but perhaps he'd missed the crack they had exited. The group moved along the side of a massive pile of glacier-worn rocks.

Her captor jerked at her arms at random intervals, laughing if she showed any reaction. They passed the rocks and wound through some trees, then came out on the lakeshore.

The man dragging Cadeyrin raised his head and let out a triumphant scream. A chorus of similar screams answered it from a short distance. She could hear the enemy warriors coming. They were making no effort to keep silent.

They burst out of the trees and surrounded them, laughing and poking at Cadeyrin with the butts of their spears. They quickly tied him to a slim birch tree and began to gather dry wood. It was obvious that they meant to burn him to death.

Kathleen despaired, wondering what they'd do to her. They were already clustered around her, their tan faces flushed with triumph. Two of them reached for her at the same time and then began arguing with each other over who got her first.

There was a loud shout, and a burly man shoved his way through the group. They showed him deference, and she understood that this was their leader. He stopped in front of her, inspecting her up and down. Then he lifted her face so that she looked directly at him. She resisted for a moment.

His face split in a grin as he backhanded her. It was a hard blow, and she dropped to the ground, trying to regain her senses. Her cheek felt like it had been ripped off.

Someone grabbed her arms and pulled her to her feet. The chief yelled at him. She was left to stagger, trying to regain her balance. The chief grabbed her arm, spinning her around. She felt the bindings strain, then release as he cut the bonds off.

Her arms swung limply as the chief spun her around to face him. He said something, licking his lips as he spoke.

She shook her head. He frowned, then grasped the front of her buckskin shirt and tugged. She suddenly understood he wanted her to undress. She tried to raise her arms in defense, but they were still weak from the rough handling.

He didn't wait. Drawing his antler knife, he pulled at her shirt and sliced it from neck to waist with a single motion. The stones that were embedded in the sides of the antler were as sharp as scalpels and cut the thin leather easily.

Her breasts swung free, and the chief stroked one, his tongue protruding a little from his lips. She tried to move away, but he grabbed her arm and then started tugging at the drawstring of her pants. She tried to resist again.

He made a spitting noise and slashed his knife across her chest above her breasts. It left a blinding flash of pain, and she cried out. The chief laughed, shoving her to the ground.

There was hot blood running over her breasts. Her hands now recovered, she reached for the wound and found that it was little more than a deep scratch. Then she looked at the man.

He was removing his heavy coat. Underneath, he wore a piece of leather that was drawn through a waistband. Below that were leggings that were attached to the waistband by strips of leather. He yanked at the leather covering, and it came free, uncovering him.

Kathleen froze as he dragged her pants off, the other warriors making sounds of approval as she was exposed. The burly man's eyes narrowed as he looked at her scars, giving her a moment of hope. Maybe he'd reject her the way the young hunter had. Then he moved forward, dropping to his knees, forcing her legs apart.

This wasn't happening. She was frantic, her eyes searching for a way out. She gagged in disgust and fear. This man was nothing compared to her lover. She looked to her side and saw Cadeyrin, bound to the tree, surrounded by branches piled up around his feet. His head was hanging down, his bloody hair obscuring his face.

She started to call to him, but then her mind stopped, flashing on her equation. She focused on her internal world, shutting out all physical sensations. The time-travel equation stood out in her mind, written in molten gold against a black background.

Now she grasped their entire relationship. The equation, which she had understood intellectually, was suddenly clear. She didn't just understand it; she felt it emotionally. In this extreme moment, she intuited the true meaning.

All she had to do was move into a deeper state, an altered consciousness state. She saw her room in the apartment house. There was a man with his back to her, bending over a woman. Her!

With a brief, fully conscious effort, she snatched the antler knife from the chief's loose waistband and descended into waves of blackness that enveloped her.

Possibility wave matched possibility wave from the past to the future. They combined to form a probability of +1 that her existence was present elsewhen. There was no transition period. She focused on being in her apartment, and – she was.

Chapter Twenty-Five

Revenge and Amnesia

There was a momentary flicker. She seemed to be standing behind Drew as he prepared to rape her in her apartment. She could see herself, bruised and bleeding, lying on her bed for just a moment. Then her past/future self snapped away as abruptly as the flicking of a light switch. At the same time, she felt a wave 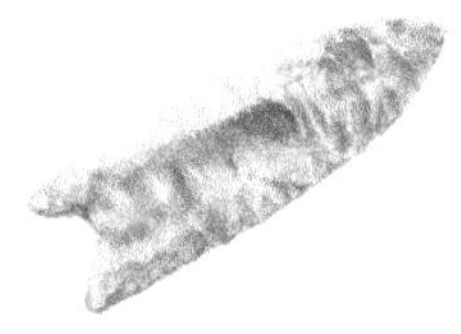 of confusion wash over her. She wasn't sure how or why she was standing where she was.

Drew fell forward onto the now vacant mattress, swearing. He scrambled to recover and pushed himself up with his hands, then stood up with a curse. Sensing something, he spun.

His eyes widened when he saw her. He stuttered, "H – how did you get there?"

He belatedly saw that she was nude, blood running between her breasts and trickling down her stomach to her lower belly.

"What the hell?" he exclaimed. "What's going on? How did you get your clothes off, and what's that blood?"

Then he changed in an instant from confused to aggressive. He snarled, "Come here, you witch! I don't care how you got there. Time's running out. I've got to get the hell out of the country, collect my money, and be rich." He made a nasty smile. "Right now, I'm going to have my fun with you and then beat the encryption key out of you. You'll enjoy the first part, but not the second."

A bolt of fear shot through her. This over-fed, flabby man meant to force her, to take her for his sadistic pleasure, and she was weak and without defense. She was naked, exposing her scars.

Her eyes teared up, but then she shook her head as if to clear her mind. No. That wasn't right. That wasn't her. It might have been once, but not now. Her memory was strangely fuzzy. She'd had a dream in which she was competent, bold, and loved. She was revolted at the thought of weakness. She wasn't a timid, reclusive physics student any longer. She had changed somehow.

She smiled at Drew and stepped closer, saying, "Here I am, but you won't enjoy the first part."

He reached for her with both arms. She lunged forward before he could grab her, shoving the antler knife deep into his gut and slashing it sideways.

His eyes widened in shock as the room filled with the acrid scent of blood and feces. He screamed and dropped to his knees, grabbing at his insides in a vain effort to close the gaping wound.

Kathleen, still smiling grimly, bent down and drew the razor-sharp, stone-edged knife across his throat, changing his scream into a bloody gurgle. He collapsed forward, convulsed, and was still. Blood flowed over the threadbare carpet, mingling with that of the dead policeman.

She looked at her hand, studying the antler knife incuriously. Then she dropped it into the pool of blood.

The next-door neighbor pounded on the wall and yelled, "Hey, quiet in there!"

She faced the wall and answered loudly, "Sorry."

Everything was still.

———— ◆◆◆ ————

She looked around her old room. It was as if she'd awakened from a bad dream to find that it had intruded on reality. Her possessions were thrown around, and there were two dead men – horribly dead – on the floor.

She drew a deep breath contemplating the justice of the situation. The murderer was dead. Professor M was avenged. She shuddered, then calmly turned to the bathroom and began to clean herself. She bandaged her wound and washed herself thoroughly.

After she had dressed, she used the old wall phone and dialed 911.

When the police arrived, she was sitting on the front steps to the apartment building, wearing a skirt and a tee shirt.

One of the officers said, "We got a call that there's been a murder here."

Kathleen looked up calmly and said, "There are two dead men in my apartment. One is a policeman. Andrew Smith killed him. The other dead man is Andrew Smith. He was going to rape and torture me. I killed him."

The cop's mouth dropped open. She seemed to be too calm.

Kathleen stood and opened the door.

"Here, let me show you."

They took her to the station to give a statement. Kathleen figured it was because they didn't believe her. They were polite the entire time, but she had to repeat her story to several different men.

She was a little blurry on the details. She could remember that Drew was leaning over her on the bed. She was dressed, but he was about to rip her clothes off. Then, somehow she was naked, standing behind him and holding a knife.

The knife was something they asked about. Where did she get it? Whose was it? It was a weapon having nothing in common with any they'd previously seen.

She couldn't remember. Maybe Drew had brought it for some reason or other. It wasn't hers. She'd never seen it before.

It was covered in blood, and any fingerprints that might have been present were unrecoverable. Eventually, they agreed that Drew must have brought it with him.

The other thing they wanted to know was how she'd managed to escape and where she got the slash across her upper chest.

She couldn't answer either of those queries. She wasn't sure how she'd escaped, and the slash? Well, it was fairly shallow, so she wasn't worried about it, although they insisted on dragging her to the emergency room, where it was cleaned and bandaged again.

In the hospital, her memory was still fuzzy. The attending physician checked her face since it was obvious that she'd been struck. He initially felt that she might be concussed but decided that she wasn't. Perhaps her memory was blanking out part of the experience in shock. He thought she might eventually remember what had happened.

When the physician was done with her, the cops were going to take her back to the station for another round of questioning, but there was a little argument with a man in a black suit. He'd just come in, pushing past the two policemen as if they weren't there.

When one of the cops grabbed his arm, he spun and flashed a badge. Kathleen wasn't curious enough to pay close attention, so she didn't hear what agency he was from. However, the cops backed off, and he introduced himself.

"Hello, I'm Agent Reed. Are you Kathleen Whitby?" he asked.

She nodded.

"My agency has been following your research. I'm taking custody of you now. The police will finish their investigation, and you'll be able to go about your life as before. I just need you to present your research to a group of qualified scientists tomorrow. That's all," he said.

He took her arm and began to lead her out towards the parking lot.

She pulled back, resisting, and asked, "What do you know about my research? I haven't published anything yet."

He didn't let go but continued to pull her towards the doors.

"Who do you think was providing funding for you?" he asked curtly. "We've been paying for your research all along and getting updates from Mackleroy. Did you think you could get the CERN data so easily? We greased the skids, so to speak. My agency thinks your ideas about time-travel are important."

Kathleen was stunned. "But the money was from some corporation. The professor said – "

He interrupted, "It was from us."

She asked, "But what about Drew? Was he working for you?"

He shook his head negatively. "We thought he was, but now we know he was a double-agent. He was a sleeper. His real name was Shashlov. We just found out. That's why I'm here. However, it looks like you took care of our problem for me."

She didn't say anything, so he added, "We need your discovery. We can use it to save lots of lives. Time-travel will be a great advantage for our country."

She didn't answer. She was thinking, Yes, you'll use it to spy on people, maybe even go back and kill people before they become a problem.

She said, "If you mess with the recent past, you might cause some unpredictable results. When I saw myself…" She trailed off.

That was it! That was why her memory was blurry. The energy systems of the past her and the present her were so similar that they had somehow blended. That must have overwritten parts of her memory. She'd felt strange when she'd seen herself on the bed, and it had been almost like the two of them, her past self and her present self, couldn't exist at the same time in the same location. The Kathleen on the bed had snapped out of existence instantly. That was when her uncertainty about what had happened started.

The equation implied that she couldn't be in the same place at the same time. She'd seen herself, and that had caused a sort of paradox. Her energy waves had blended to a certain extent.

He picked up on her statement, "When you saw yourself what?"

She dissembled, "Oh, I meant when I saw myself in trouble."

He ignored her answer and said, "Get in. You can ride in the back seat."

He took her to a hotel near the Mall of America. She'd never stayed in such a nice place before. Her room was spacious and was far nicer than her apartment had been.

The agent had room service bring up a meal for her. When she answered the door, there were two other men guarding it. They jumped up when they saw her, checked the room-service cart, and then wheeled it into the room themselves. Kathleen tried to engage them in talk, but they wouldn't say much, only that she should get some sleep.

Agent Reed showed up again after she'd eaten. He told her that they'd have the scientists there tomorrow. Some of them were flying in from each coast. She'd have to present her findings then.

"But, I don't have my computer, and all my calculations are on it," she objected.

He smiled and said, "We've got it. It was at Smith's house. Look, all you have to do is to explain your formula, show how it was derived from the data, and then let the scientists ask you some questions. They'll know what to do from there."

She protested, "I want to publish it. I need the data to remain unpublished until I've had a chance to fully verify my calculations. How will I know these guys, whoever they are, will keep it quiet for me?"

He shook his head. "No. You can get that out of your mind right now. That data and your formula are top secret. They'll never be published. We can't risk other nations finding out about it."

"What do you mean? Once science starts on something, science always wins, even if some people try to suppress it. It can't be top secret. Someone will figure it out eventually. I don't see why I can't get credit for it. It's my research," she complained.

"Not anymore. It now belongs to the government, and it's going to be held secret. I think you'll probably be invited to work for the agency on further research. You won't have to worry about your degree. You'll have a good job, and the degree isn't necessary. Besides, that way, we can keep an eye on you," he said, implying a threat that she tried to ignore.

She knew when she was beaten and didn't respond; instead, she bent her head over the food and ate. It was surprisingly tasteless, but then, she'd been eating fire-roasted venison – Where did that memory come from?

She jerked. Her memory had volunteered something that she could hardly believe. She wasn't the type to eat outside and kill deer. At least, she hadn't been. Her memory came in flashes. It was as if she'd forgotten days and days of events, but she'd only been out of it for a few seconds.

The agent eventually left her to sleep, explaining that he'd reserved one of the hotel's smaller meeting rooms for the conference in the morning. Just before he shut her door, he said, "We'll start at nine a.m. You'd better be ready to explain everything then. Good night."

As an afterthought, he added, "Don't try to leave your room. The guys outside won't like it."

Chapter Twenty-Six

Memory and Action

Kathleen listlessly turned on the TV but quickly turned it off again. She'd need to review her math, and the mindless TV wouldn't help.

It was hot in the room. She shut the heater off and opened the window. A chill breeze came in, and she sniffed it. It was full of automobile exhaust and other chemical scents. Not like the pure air she'd been recently breathing.

She jerked her head around and stared at the window. Where had that memory come from? She'd been thinking about washing her face, and the thought had come into her consciousness, but it hadn't seemed random. It was related to something, but what?

◆

The sun was down. Kathleen was trying to get to sleep. The bed seemed too soft, the room too hot, the traffic far too noisy. She had nearly managed to doze off when some vehicle downshifted and roared by.

She jumped out of bed, her heart beating rapidly. The noise had sounded like a threat. Like a – a piskat. She sat down abruptly, making the bed bounce. *Like a what? What did that mean?* She racked her brain, trying to think. Finally, she lay back in defeat. That action seemed to free the strands of memory, and she generated a mental picture of a lion-like cat with huge incisors. *A saber-tooth.* She remembered danger that involved a saber-tooth. *But, they'd been extinct for at least ten thousand years. How could she remember such an experience? What had she been doing to generate fragments of such a memory?*

She mulled the problem over in her mind. There were some pieces of memory that seemed linked, but they offered no real clue. She finally gave up and closed her eyes. Her breathing deepened and slowed. Her eyes moved under her eyelids.

She drifted, seemingly hovering just over her body. There was something she must do. She couldn't remember. Then she was floating along a high, cold wall. As she sensed that, she floated nearer. The wall was ice. A glacier. It faded into mist. Now there was a feeling of transition, a movement across miles of something green and irregularly shaped. She was flying across trees – a forest. There was a small lake in the trees with a large, rocky hill close by. The vision faded out, and she moaned, moving her arms slightly.

The traffic was still. Most of the activity outside had died down, and the ambient sounds were less. The wind picked up, blowing from the north, chilling the hotel room.

Kathleen was still floating. There was a sense of isolation. She couldn't see anything, however; she heard a sound as if someone was calling. Calling her.

She was moving down to the lake, gliding through the trees a slight distance above the ground. There was something ahead, something that she desired, something important and dear to her. She strained to see; it was like looking through a semi-opaque fog. The mist flowed around her, obscuring her vision. Then it cleared. There was a man's figure there.

A warm feeling of intense love overwhelmed her, and in her dream, she began to weep. She couldn't remember his face or even his name, but she wanted him...so badly. She tried to move closer, but then she was lifted up higher and higher by a cold wind. The mist swirled between them, and he was lost.

She sat up gasping for breath, her pulse pounding in her head. Raising her hand to her face, she felt tears on her cheeks. *What was the meaning of that dream?*

She got up, went to the bathroom, washed her face again, and went to sit in an armchair by the open window. The cold wind from the window failed to chill her. Somehow she seemed to be adapted to the cold.

Morning found her still curled in the armchair. She'd slept on and off but hadn't really gotten any true rest. At seven, one of the guards pounded on her door and called to her to get ready for the conference. She sleepily went through her morning ablutions, dressed, and then sat on the bed, waiting for the next event.

Agent Reed showed up shortly after room service had delivered breakfast. He helped himself to a bagel and paced back and forth, waiting for her to finish eating. Finally, he said, rather ungraciously, "That's enough. You're done now. Let's get going."

Kathleen raised her eyes to him in a way that part of her found far too bold.

"I'm not done yet. Unless you think you can carry me, you'll have to wait until I'm ready," she said in a matter-of-fact tone.

He spun and looked at her, then said, "I was under the impression from all of the reports I'd read that you were afraid of confrontation. I must have been misinformed."

Kathleen smiled and took another bite of fruit, then finished off her coffee. She made him wait while she brushed her teeth. When she indicated she was ready to go, he impatiently yanked the door open. The two guards outside jumped up, startled.

"C'mon, let's go," he said roughly.

She followed him downstairs to a second-floor conference room. There was a convention or meeting next door, the Loyal Order of Pipe-fitters or something. She didn't really look.

The people sitting in the small conference room drew her full attention. She recognized a few of them. She'd never seen them in person, only their picture on book jackets or in magazine articles. They were some of the top physicists in the country.

Agent Reed shut the door after stationing the two other agents outside as guards. Then he turned to the group and said, "Nothing that is said inside this room is to be repeated outside of this room. This topic and the information that Ms. Whitby is going to present to you has been classified top secret by the government. Your job here is to listen, ask questions, and then to prepare a report on the feasibility of time-travel. I ask that you suspend any skepticism for the moment. Ms. Whitby has apparently discovered some kind of relationship that she's formulated into what we think might be a usable tool."

He turned to Kathleen, nodded in an appearance of congeniality, and said, "Ms. Whitby, the meeting's all yours."

Kathleen stood in front of the audience. Behind her was her computer, resting on a table. It was attached to a projection display. She turned to it, adjusted the focus, and keyed in the encryption key. The machine cranked for a bit and then became ready for use.

The audience faded into the background as she concentrated. She opened a spreadsheet filled with data. Before she started to explain her ideas to these people, she wanted to refresh her thinking.

She scanned the columns, looking at the first numbers and subconsciously reading the column heading letters. A, B, C, D, E... *What? What had she just read?*

⸻ ◄O► ⸻

She paused, concentrating. *The letters moved into a different order in her mind: CADE –*

She jerked, looked over her shoulder at the audience, and drew a deep breath. Her memory of the man from her dream was back, and she knew his name – Cadeyrin. Now, she remembered the man she loved.

With that recollection, the remainder of her knowledge suddenly came to her. She understood why her memory had been clouded. The energy field of the prior her and the present her was similar enough that the new knowledge was obscured – stored in a different location, like a fold in her memory. The fold had now opened, revealing the hidden, and giving her complete access once again.

She stood frozen, thinking furiously.

⸻ ◄O► ⸻

Agent Reed cleared his throat, trying to prompt her, and said, "Ms. Whitby, anytime."

She typed something, turned, smiled at the scientists as she said, "Please excuse me, I've just recalled something that I need to attend to."

With that statement, she vanished.

The room exploded in an uproar. Agent Reed shouted for quiet, then jerked the doors open, shouting at the two agents, "Try and find that damned woman. She's escaped somehow. Check her room. Check downstairs. Stop anyone from leaving."

Behind him, the physicists were arguing. Two of them had approached her computer and were looking at the screen. A program was just finishing its task. One of the men looked more closely, then turned to the crowd and said, "It's a shredder program. She's wiped the disk."

There was a disappointed groan from the crowd.

Kathleen walked quietly out of the deserted conference room and down the empty hall. She'd jumped back five hours, and few people were up. There was no one in the hotel lobby, save for two of the night staff. She waved at the sleepy night manager and walked out into the cold.

A cab moved forward from its stand, and she got in.

"The University, please," she said and relaxed as the cab pulled out.

She had a few dollars she'd pocketed in her apartment after she dressed the day before. She paid the fare and walked quickly to her office. There was no one there. It was too early for the professors to show up and too late for the grad students to still be working.

She opened her desk drawer, removed a small notebook and a pen, picked up her cell phone which was still there, and then turned to Drew's computer. She started to sit in his chair but then drew up a different one. Touching any trace of him was repugnant.

The computer wasn't even asleep. He'd simply turned the monitor off. She started the browser and quickly did some research, visiting a prepping site where she printed out a list of survival supplies. Next, she checked the state lottery site and jotted some information in the notebook. She then cleared the browser history, turned the monitor off again, and left the building.

She walked into a dark alcove between two buildings. There was a brief pause, and then she was gone, moving backward in time.

Four days earlier, a student, heading to an early class on the far side of the campus, walked past the alcove. It was empty, but then it wasn't. He did a quick double-take. He must have missed the woman. She was standing in the shadows.

He said, "Good morning."

Kathleen smiled at him, waved, and quickly walked off. He shrugged and hurried on to his class.

The sun was starting to show some signs of life. There was a little dawn light in the sky as she walked off the campus to a nearby gas and convenience store.

The clerk looked up as she stopped in front of the counter.

"I'd like a lottery ticket, please. Here are the numbers," she said.

The clerk apparently viewed himself as a wit. Kathleen smiled a little as he tried a little humor, "Only one ticket? You must be really sure of the numbers."

She laughed and said, "One ticket is all I need."

Holding the ticket, she walked outside. A motorist was pulling in for a morning coffee. He honked and stopped abruptly, but no one was there. He looked in both directions, then shook his head, parked, and went in.

———◆———

She had jumped to ten o'clock the next day. She walked to the bus line and headed downtown. As she rode, she called Professor Mackleroy's attorney. She'd met him once at the professor's house. The professor had told her that he both swore by and swore at the man, but he was absolutely trustworthy in either case.

The receptionist didn't want to let her by but finally agreed to call Mr. Jarpe. He came down to rescue her from the reception area.

She followed him to a conference room, where he offered her some coffee and said, "What can I do for you. Ms. Whitby? Do you mind if I call you Kathleen? After all, we've met once. I'm not a stickler for formality. Why don't you call me Geoff?"

Kathleen sipped her coffee and said, "I need some legal advice. Professor Mackleroy always said you were dependable, and I don't know anyone else."

He smiled and said, "He's a great guy. How's he doing?"

Kathleen's memories betrayed her for a moment. She looked down, trying to suppress tears. It was easier than she thought it would be. Her experiences had changed her. She swallowed, then raised her gaze to him and said, "He's just the same as he always is today."

That's the truth, she thought.

Geoff looked closely at her in response. Before he could comment, she continued, "Now I need your help on another matter. You see, I'm about to come into a large sum of money, and I don't know quite how to handle it. I want to travel but still have access to the funds. In addition, I don't really know how to manage money, so I need someone to set something up that will handle it for me."

Geoff picked up a pen and began to write. He paused and asked, "How large a sum?"

She answered, "I think it will be about seventy-four million."

He dropped the pen and looked carefully at her again to see if she was joking.

She read his expression and explained, "I'm telling the truth."

She paused and pulled out the lottery ticket, handed it over to him, and said, "This is the winning ticket. The way I calculate, once the taxes are paid, the payout is about seventy-four million. I want to take it in a lump sum."

He picked up the ticket, looked at it, shook his head, wonderingly, and said, "This is a new one for me. Let's see. You'll want to set up a trust and appoint a manager, someone who can be relied upon to do a good job. If we set up a limited-liability corporation first, say in Nevada, where the privacy laws are good, then we can keep your name mostly out of it. The LLC can hold the trust. Between the two vehicles, it should offer you considerable privacy."

He looked at her to see what she thought.

Kathleen nodded her head in agreement, "Whatever you say. I don't understand any of this kind of stuff. I just want to have cash available when I need it, and I also want to have the bulk of the money invested wisely."

He smiled, handed her the ticket, and said, "Just for safety, sign the back of the ticket. Here..."

He handed her the pen.

"Our firm will hold the money in our escrow account until the documents are prepared. Then it can be transferred into the trust and invested. I'll need you to come back tomorrow to sign the paperwork. Do you have someone you want to appoint as the trustee for the trust?"

Kathleen shook her head, "No. I don't know anyone who could do that. Why don't you handle all of the details? I assume there will be enough money available to pay for your services."

He laughed, "There's plenty to pay for everything you want us to do. Can you be back tomorrow at, say, two p.m?"

She considered for a moment, reviewing her plans. She'd jumped back four days to purchase the ticket. Then she'd jumped forward one day so that the ticket number had already been drawn, entitling her to the money. She could sign the papers tomorrow. That would be the last day of the professor's life. Drew had killed him before midnight. She hadn't found out until the police came the next morning.

She quickly considered saving the professor. It was tempting, but she wouldn't do it. He'd lived to see her discovery. He'd been happy, and then he'd died suddenly and without lingering or agony. She was convinced that it was somehow meant to be. She was convinced that it was better if she didn't try to change his fate.

So, tomorrow she'd sign the papers and then complete her plan. The one thing she didn't want was to accidentally meet herself – any of her other-selves. She'd experienced being present in the same room as her previous self, and it had almost ruined her memory. She didn't want that to happen again – best to avoid all possible paradoxical complications.

Of course, right now, she was in the same city as her previous self, but since there was no chance of the two of them meeting, she had suffered no ill effects. That was right in line with her theory. Despite that assurance, she didn't want to chance being in the same time as two of her previous selves. The extra presence just might be too much for the time-stream to reconcile.

She looked up at Geoff and smiled, "Two will be perfect. I'll see you then."

He escorted her down to the entrance, and she left. She walked down the street, turned into an alley, and disappeared. No one saw her go, except a scruffy cat that was focused on raiding a dumpster behind a restaurant.

She exited the alley exactly twenty-four hours after she'd entered, although only a few seconds had passed for her. On the street, she paused and brushed off some imaginary dust on her sleeves, then walked back to the law firm. There was a different receptionist today who was far more polite than the previous one.

She signed the papers for Geoff, trying to pay attention as he explained each of them. When they were done, he said, "It will be a few days before the entities are formed. However, the money is already in our escrow account."

Kathleen smiled, "You move fast. I need some funds fairly quickly. Is there any way to release them to me?"

He laughed, "Young lady, when there's seventy-four million at stake, I move very fast. To answer your question, yes, we can release some to you. How much would you like?"

She'd thought it over as she walked back to the firm. "I will need maybe ten thousand now for miscellaneous expenses. Later today, I'm going to be purchasing a four-wheel-drive pickup and a small mobile home. I'll call from the dealerships and give you their wiring instructions. Can you have the funds wired to them? I'd like to take delivery of the two vehicles tomorrow."

"Got it all planned out, huh?" he smiled. "Are you going to hit the road for an extended vacation?"

She grinned conspiratorially. "Sort of. Let's just say that I'm going to take them back to prehistoric times and live there for a while."

Geoff broke out in amused laughter. When he got his breath, he said, "Alright, I stand reproved. I shouldn't have asked. Your business is exclusively yours. All you have to do is to call the firm any time you need money. We'll handle the trustee job. It won't cost you too much, and I'm confident that we can arrange for the investments to make enough money to grow the fund and pay for all expenses."

⸻◆⸻

Back on the street and holding a load of cash in an envelope, Kathleen took a cab to a truck dealership. There she worked through the purchase process for a large and exceedingly capable four-wheel-drive pickup. Driving it was a little intimidating, but she thought she could manage, especially if there was no traffic. That wouldn't be a problem where she was going.

The dealership had to wait until her wire cleared before she could take the vehicle. She arranged to pick it up tomorrow. The delay was a little bothersome. It meant that she'd have to get everything and leave before three. Drew had attacked her about then. Shortly after that, she'd arrived back from the past and killed him. There had been a tiny period of overlap when two of her were present in her apartment. She didn't want to be in the time when that happened. She wasn't sure what would happen to the time-stream, and she didn't want to find out.

A few hours later, she purchased a nice mobile home. She called Geoff to wire the funds for it, also.

The mobile home was well-designed with a compact kitchen, a neat bathroom, a living area, and two bedrooms. She finished signing the documents, told them she'd be back to pick it up tomorrow, then shook the salesman's hand and left.

He watched her walk off the lot and down the street.

That's funny, he thought. *Usually, customers drive here.*

She walked around a corner, paused, and disappeared into tomorrow.

———◆———

She took delivery of the pickup, drove to the RV dealership, and had them hook the trailer on the truck. The mechanic was very friendly and gave her a quick lesson on how to hook and unhook the trailer.

She left and drove to several stores, referring to her printed list of prepping supplies. She loaded up on unprocessed, organic food that she thought Cadeyrin could safely eat, clothes, and other items. She bought some cooking tools, two light but powerful semi-automatic rifles, a case of ammunition, a couple of deadly-looking hunting knives, two powerful compound bows with hunting arrows, and some over-the-counter medications. Stopping by a gas station, she picked up a couple of extra propane bottles for the camper's cook-stove.

She'd planned her timing carefully, but the three p.m. deadline was approaching. She drove down a quiet residential street and parked. She was a little worried. She'd demonstrated that she could move her body and clothing along with some small items through time. Her calculations told her that she could move the truck and trailer, but trying something for real was a little different from just calculating that it could be done.

She sat still for a few moments, reviewing her preparations, and considering if she had forgotten some critical element. There was nothing that she could think of that would prevent her from proceeding.

"Now, let's see if I can move this entire rig." She spoke aloud to encourage herself but still hesitated, feeling a little fear. The truck and trailer were heavy. It made no difference, she had to try.

She adjusted one of the variables in her equation, did some mental math, then shut her eyes.

The truck and trailer flickered, then disappeared from the street.

An older, retired woman had seen her park but had walked away from the window before Kathleen had translated in time. She was surprised to see the truck and trailer in the same spot early the next morning. The driver started the truck and left as she watched.

Kathleen arrived in the same day in which she was supposed to be giving the presentation at the hotel. She could imagine Agent Reed's reaction when she disappeared. Too bad. He would never get to hear her explain her research.

She had made sure that she had no chance of meeting herself. She had gone from the hotel to the campus and then to the convenience store, ending up downtown at the law firm. Now, she was in another part of town, driving her truck, towing the trailer, and completing the plan that she'd formulated while standing with her back to the scientists in the conference room.

As her last stop, she pulled into the parking lot of a pet store. Inside, she purchased a large quantity of fish antibiotics. Amoxicillin probably wasn't the most powerful antibiotic, especially in this modern time of antibiotic-resistant bacteria, but it would work like a miracle in the Pleistocene.

Some hours later, she was driving down a narrow, wooded road, miles west of Lake Minnetonka. There was a smaller lake nearby, one with a rocky hill.

Kathleen stopped the truck and reviewed her plan once again. To avoid a paradox and the potential mental confusion she'd previously encountered when she had seen herself in her apartment, she'd have to make sure her second arrival in the past was immediately after she had disappeared from under the enemy chief and was safely out of the Pleistocene and back in her current 'now,' the future.

The thing she was most worried about was Cadeyrin's safety. There would be a lapse of a few minutes when the enemy tribesmen might hurt him.

She couldn't plan for that yet. She had to go and see what had happened. If he wasn't safe, she'd have to think up a way to go to him before he was injured. That would be difficult since it potentially created another paradox. It was almost too complicated.

She stopped worrying about it and shut her eyes. Now it was time to take action.

***

One moment the truck and trailer were there, the next, they were far in the past.

Chapter Twenty-Seven

Somewhen Along the Time Line

Cadeyrin's head was pounding. His wrists were tied behind the trunk of a tree. He'd been trying to work loose from the bindings that held him fast, but all he'd accomplished was to tighten the strips of sinew. Now his hands were getting numb.

His head sagged, and he mentally drifted with his eyes closed. He somehow felt that the spirit world was close, and he tried to find Kathleen. There was a moment where he seemed to see her asleep. The vision was so real that he cried out, calling her. She seemed to reach out for him, but then mist drifted between them, and his vision faded. He shook his head a little. The pounding increased, and he opened one eye, remembering the last time he'd seen her.

He'd been watching when Kathleen disappeared from beneath the enemy tribe's chief. The whole group of the warriors had panicked and run screaming for the trees, some so frightened that they'd dropped their weapons. As far as he could tell, they were still running. He could hear no sound from them. He smiled wryly. If he hadn't been tied, he'd probably have run, too.

It was uncanny. One second she was there, the next she was gone. The chief had fallen flat on his face, making his nose bleed. He'd leaped to his feet, stared at the spot where she'd been, then screamed and taken off as if evil spirits were chasing him. His spear was still lying where he'd dropped it as he prepared to take Kathleen.

Now there was something coming through the bushes behind him. Cadeyrin sighed. His situation was hopeless. He couldn't get loose. He smelt of blood. Any predator would be moved to investigate the battle noise. There were dead enemy bodies in front of the cave that would draw scavengers, but a piskat or daoilfa wouldn't hesitate to take a helpless man.

The steps paused and then came on. He considered yelling in the animal's face. Maybe it would be intimidated and leave.

There was a 'whuffing' noise, and then a cold nose touched his arm. There was pressure on his leg, and he looked down. Ulfsa was leaning against his thigh, looking directly at his face with as much of a worried expression as a wolf could make.

"Good Ulfsa," he laughed in relief. The wolf snorted and then sat, watching him.

The problem was that Ulfsa couldn't be told to chew the sinew to release him. He went back to moving his arms, trying to loosen the binding.

He paused. He'd heard something else. It sounded like a human footstep. Someone had incautiously stepped on a dry branch, and it had broken. The sound meant that one of the warriors was returning. He wouldn't survive that.

There was a rush of feet and he dropped his gaze in despair. He didn't want to see the triumph in the warrior's eyes. He waited.

He heard a soft cry and jerked erect. Kathleen was standing in front of him. She was dressed in something that made her look like a part of the woods. There were leaves and branches on her clothes. She was carrying some sort of club that had odd, shiny things attached to it.

He didn't care. He whispered her name again and again, "Kathleen, Kathleen, Kathleen."

He wanted to continue saying her name, lest in ceasing he somehow allowed her to disappear. He started to say it again, but her lips were burning against his, and he lost himself in the kiss. When she paused for breath, he said, "I believed you'd gone back where you came from. I was afraid I'd never see you again."

She whispered, "Oh, Cadeyrin. I love you so much. I came back for you. Even time cannot separate us. I'm here with you now, and I'll never leave you alone. I'd die first."

She moved behind him, and suddenly his bindings went limp. She helped him out of the stacked branches.

"Can you walk?" she asked, inspecting the bleeding lump on his head where he'd been struck. "We need to get away from here. Those warriors might be back soon."

He nodded and followed her. The three of them passed the cave, moving along the lakeshore. Kathleen carried the odd club in both hands as if it were a deadly weapon.

He trusted her but had picked up some discarded spears so that he could fight, if necessary. Their bows were gone somewhere. He didn't worry about it. He could always make more.

At the southern verge of the lake, the prairie was close. They followed a game trail and then burst out of the trees. Before them was something odd and frightening.

He pushed his matted hair back and tried to understand what he was seeing. It looked like two attached objects, but they were so regular and smooth. He'd never seen anything like them. Not knowing if they were a threat, he glanced at her to see if they frightened her.

She pointed and said, "They're ours. I know you don't know what they are, but they're full of food, and they belong to us. We're going to go inside and take them back two hundred thousand years."

He looked puzzled and she explained, "We're going to go back before any humans come to this land. The weather will be warmer, and there will be no one else but you and I and the animals. We'll have all of the land to ourselves. We can live there, and if we need supplies, I can return to the future to get them. We'll be safe there."

Cadeyrin didn't quite understand, but he was sure of her love and trusted that she knew what she was saying, even if it made no sense to him. He pulled her close for a kiss. Time seemed to stop, and he almost forgot to breathe.

Kathleen pulled back from him, her eyes wide and her face flushed. She tugged at his arm and said, "Oh, I love you. I never believed I'd find someone who loved me, especially someone so wonderful."

He kissed her again, holding her close until she breathlessly said, "Let's go inside right now. I want to show you what a modern bed is like." She took his arm, pulling him after her.

He glanced at the strange double structure. It was hard for him to understand. Its shape was smooth, but there were regularities to it that suggested that it was man-made. He suddenly realized it was from the future and that made it somehow frightening.

He resisted her pull slightly, but then she turned and smiled at him. That was all he needed. The momentary fear disappeared instantly.

Arms about each other, the two entered the mobile home.

Ulfsa sniffed around the entire assembly, then crawled under the back and lay down. He came back out quickly, glancing over his shoulder, suspiciously, his ears lowered.

The structure had started rocking.

The End

About the Author

Eric S. Martell set out to become a scientist when he was five. He has a PhD. in experimental psychology. When personal computers came along (way back in prehistory), he became adept with them and spent years in software design, working on projects that ranged from early childhood learning software to military training. He has been trained in various types of energy healing, is an expert in real estate investing and sales, and holds a black belt in Tae-Kwon-Do. He is also a pilot, scuba diver, guitar player, outdoorsman and is addicted to both science and science fiction.

Eric's science fiction books offer both believable science and compelling characters set against realistic action. They are carefully researched, and while his fictional science sometimes strains against the bounds of current knowledge, it is always plausible. His stories cover alien invasion in an apocalyptic setting, political structure, space travel, advanced weapons, quantum physics, hunting, war, romance, time travel, and alien worlds.

He's been published in a series of anthologies and has published many full-length science fiction novels. His writing goal is to provide his readers with stories they cannot put down, and he takes readers' suggestions seriously.

Notices about new books, free short stories, opinion posts, and preview pages for many of his books can be found on his author blog at
EricMartellAuthor.com

A Request for You

Dear Reader,

I make every effort to ensure your reading experience is enjoyable. This involves multiple editing steps, interior book layout, design, and using a professional cover artist/designer. Even so, it is becoming more difficult to find readers. If you liked this book, please leave a review and tell your friends. Those small actions help a lot.

Reviews may be left on the platform of your choice or emailed directly to me through my blog.

Thank you,

Eric Martell

Venice, 2021

Also By Eric S. Martell

*Florida Authors and Publishers President's Award Winner

www.ingramcontent.com/pod-product-compliance
Lightning Source LLC
Chambersburg PA
CBHW070427120726
47910CB00003B/681